SUCH CHARMING LIARS

BOOKS BY KAREN M. McMANUS

One of Us Is Lying

One of Us Is Next

One of Us Is Back

Two Can Keep a Secret

The Cousins

You'll Be the Death of Me

Nothing More to Tell

Such Charming Liars

SUCH CHARMING LIARS

KAREN M. McMANUS

DELACORTE PRESS

Text copyright © 2024 by Karen M. McManus, LLC
Jacket photos: top necklace © Serge/GettyImages, bottom necklace © Ramzi/
stock.adobe.com, glass © by runrun2/stock.adobe.com & zenobillis/stock.adobe.com.
All other photographs used under license from Shutterstock.com. Polaroid and
velvet background © by Travis Commeau. Lettering by Kerri Resnick.

All rights reserved. Published in the United States by Delacorte Press,
an imprint of Random House Children's Books, a division of
Penguin Random House LLC, New York.

Delacorte Press is a registered trademark and the colophon is a trademark of
Penguin Random House LLC.

Visit us on the Web! GetUnderlined.com

Educators and librarians, for a variety of teaching tools, visit us at
RHTeachersLibrarians.com

Library of Congress Cataloging-in-Publication Data
Names: McManus, Karen M., author.
Title: Such charming liars / Karen M. McManus.
Description: New York : Delacorte Press, 2024. | Audience: Ages 14+ |
Summary: Sixteen-year-old Kat's con-artist mom takes on one last heist
before going straight for good, but the job takes a deadly turn.
Identifiers: LCCN 2023022326 (print) | LCCN 2023022327 (ebook) |
ISBN 978-0-593-48505-7 (hardcover) |
ISBN 978-0-593-48506-4 (library binding) | ISBN 978-0-593-48507-1 (ebook) |
ISBN 978-0-593-81521-2 (int'l ed.)
Subjects: CYAC: Mothers and daughters—Fiction. | Swindlers and swindling—
Fiction. | LCGFT: Novels.
Classification: LCC PZ7.1.M4637 Su 2024 (print) | LCC PZ7.1.M4637 (ebook) |
DDC [Fic]—dc23

The text of this book is set in 12-point Adobe Garamond Pro.
Interior design by Michelle Crowe

Printed in the United States of America
10 9 8 7 6 5 4 3 2 1
First Edition

For Jay, Julie, Luis Fernando, and April

CHAPTER ONE

Kat

"Would the young lady like to see something with a pearl?"

"I'd love to," I say.

The voice I use isn't mine. It's what Gem calls "vaguely posh"; meant to convey a childhood at British boarding schools interrupted by a transatlantic move to New England that almost, but not entirely, eliminated my accent. It's a lot to get across in three words and I don't think I nailed it, but the man behind the counter smiles kindly.

"Sixteen is an important birthday," he says.

I couldn't agree more, which is why I spent mine in my friend Hannah's hot tub with Nick Sheridan and a flask of tequila. But now is not the time to share that recollection, so I just smile demurely as Gem says, "A special day for my special girl."

Gem's accent is impeccable. She sounds like a BBC presenter and looks like a twenty-first-century version of the grandmother on *Downton Abbey*. I barely recognized her when she came to pick me up, and couldn't stop stealing glances at her transformation during the drive to the Prudential Center in Back Bay. Gem's coarse steel-gray hair is concealed beneath a silvery chignon. She's decked out in an elegant blue suit that would fit in at a royal wedding, and she's done some kind of makeup magic that's tamed her leathery skin into soft, powdery lines.

I don't recognize myself, either, when I glance into the mirror behind the counter. I'm a buttery blond, for one thing, and I'm wearing a blouse-and-skirt combo that looks expensive, even though I'm sure it's not. The nonprescription tortoiseshell glasses I have on are so cute that I might make them a permanent part of my wardrobe. Gem and I are cosplaying the kind of people who swan into Bennington & Main to celebrate birthdays with expensive jewelry, and we are *pulling it off.*

"Something like this?" the sales associate asks, holding up a delicate rose-gold ring with a single gray pearl. It's exactly the kind of ring a wealthy, indulgent grandmother would buy, and even though Gem is none of those things, she gives a regal nod of approval.

"Try it on, Sophie," she says.

I slip it onto my right index finger and hold out my hand, admiring the subtle shine. Not my style at all, but perfect for Sophie Hicks-Hartwell. That's my getting-into-character name, which I picked not only because it, too, sounds vaguely posh, but because it's the name of a girl whose Instagram identity was stolen in a twisted true crime story that I devoured recently on my favorite podcast. A little inside joke that even Gem didn't catch.

"It's so pretty," I say. "What do you think, Nana?"

"Very sweet," Gem says, peering over her bifocals. "But a bit on the small side."

That's the cue for the sales associate, whose name tag reads BERNARD, to show us bigger and better rings. Gem's eyes rove over them like dual cameras, capturing every detail of the luxe designs and storing them away for future reference. Gem might be pushing seventy, but her memory is a thousand times sharper than mine. *Photographic,* my mother always says.

"Should we look at something with a diamond?" she asks.

Hell yeah is on the tip of my tongue, but that's a Kat response. Sophie would never. "Really? Could we?" I simper as Bernard pulls out another tray.

"Looks like your grandmother is getting ready to spoil you," he says, eyes gleaming with the reflected glow of a bigger commission.

For the first time, my stomach swoops guiltily. When Gem proposed this little field trip, I was more than happy to come along, because Bennington & Main is a retail nightmare— a historic family-owned store that got snapped up by an obnoxious crypto billionaire and transformed into a Tiffany copycat. The new CEO hired an emerging designer to update what he called the company's "staid" style, then fired her once her designs took off.

In other words, Bennington & Main is the perfect target for Gem's latest business: selling near-perfect fakes of iconic jewelry designs. Customers get the look they want at sterling-and-cubic-zirconia prices, and a shady company loses value. Win-win, if by *win* you mean a crypto bro loses. Which I do.

But none of that is Bernard's fault. We're just wasting his

time while Gem studies the latest Bennington & Main designs, cataloging all the tiny details you can't see on a website. "Exquisite," she murmurs, holding up a diamond vine ring that's so perfectly constructed it looks like a wearable sculpture. I know from our online stalking that the ring Gem is holding costs more than $20,000, so it's out of even Sophie's league.

Still, I can't help but lean closer, imagining what it would be like to own something so beautiful. To wave at a friend or swipe at my phone while it casually sparkles on my hand. I've seen an unusual amount of fine jewelry in my lifetime for someone who's (a) sixteen and (b) flat broke, but this . . . this is something special.

"And not for you," Gem adds with an arch smile in my direction. And even though she's playing a role, the words still sting. *Not for you.* Sometimes it feels like that applies to almost everything a girl my age is supposed to have. "Maybe on your twenty-first birthday."

"We'll hold it for you till then," Bernard jokes, and it's official—I feel like a jerk. I want out of this store, and more important, out of Sophie's pampered little head. Surely Gem's had enough time by now? But when I try to catch her eye, she's still peering at the vine ring.

"Nana, I think . . . I didn't have lunch, and I'm a bit lightheaded. . . ." I back away from the counter, hand brushing my temple. "Could we get something to eat?"

"Let me get you some water," Bernard says solicitously. He makes a beckoning motion, and the next thing I know, a miniature bottle of Evian is being pressed into my hand by another black-clad associate. I twist off the cap and take a sip as Gem

4

finally turns my way, transforming instantly into the picture of grandmotherly concern.

"Sophie, dearest, of course we can," she says. "I should have suggested that first thing. I know you never eat enough for breakfast. Thank you so much," she adds to Bernard, handing him the vine ring. "You've been wonderfully helpful. We'll be back once we've had a bite."

"Of course. Anything you'd like me to set aside?" he asks.

I want to soften the blow of us evaporating from his life once we leave the store, so I say, "I really liked the first one I tried on. The pearl." The smallest, cheapest ring.

Bernard, champ that he is, smiles graciously. "A perfect choice," he says as I chug the rest of my water in a decidedly un-Sophie-like manner. "Enjoy your meal." His associate comes back to take my empty bottle, whisking it quickly out of sight.

Gem and I walk across the plush carpet to the gleaming silver doors, which the security guard opens with a nod and a smile. "Have a good afternoon, ladies," he says.

"You too," we say in unison as we step across the threshold.

Once the door closes and we're in the mall, I breathe a sigh of relief. Not because what we were doing was wrong—although, okay, technically it was, or would've been if we were doing it to a less sketchy company—but because this was the first time Gem has asked for my help. Gem Hayes might not be my actual grandmother, but she's as close as I'll ever get to one. I don't know what life would be like if my mother hadn't met Gem twelve years ago, but I do know this: it would've been grim.

So when I grab hold of Gem's arm to pull her close and say

"Love you, Nana" in Sophie's lilting voice, it sounds like a joke, but I actually mean it.

I can only say it like this, though. Gem is, as she puts it, a "flinty old broad," who'd either roll her eyes or cuss me out if I tried that under normal circumstances.

Gem responds with a light titter that's nothing like her usual guffaw. "And I you, Sophie dearest." She waits until we're down the escalator and away from the crowds before adding in her normal tone, "So, you really hungry or what? Wanna hit the food court?"

"No, that's okay," I say, swallowing a grin at the mental image of Gem, in her tasteful suit and pearls, chowing down at Panda Express. "I can wait till we get home."

Gem insists on buying me a coffee from a gourmet pop-up that specializes in caffè mocha, and I sip the velvety-smooth concoction as we make our way outside. It's a gloriously sunny late June day, and my spirits stay high even when my feet start to ache. Gem had to park six blocks away to find a metered spot, and Sophie's shoes weren't made for that kind of trek.

We're almost at Gem's car when it happens. One second we're walking, and the next I'm tumbling headfirst to the ground, my caffè mocha flying everywhere, because Gem pushed me unbelievably hard. No—Gem *was* pushed, by a guy who came out of nowhere to grab her purse. He tries to take off but can't, because Gem has one of the straps in a viselike grip.

I heave myself into a sitting position. My lungs can't catch air and my knees are on fire, scraped raw from the pavement. Gem and the would-be thief are still wrestling for the purse, in what looks to my dizzy brain like a slow-motion tug-of-war.

"Let go, you old bitch, or I'll fucking gut you," he grunts.

My heart jumps into my throat. Does he have a *knife?*

I've managed to get myself into a crouch when Gem lets go—only to lunge straight for his eyes, her nails extended like talons. He shrieks in surprise and pain as she gouges him, then staggers to his knees and drops the purse. I grab hold of it as I scramble to my feet, but seconds later it's yanked roughly from my grasp—by Gem, who uses it to clock the guy in the head, knocking him fully onto the ground.

Then she hands the purse back to me and pulls her keys out of her suit pocket. "Open the car, please, Kat," she says, tossing me the keys. I manage to not fumble the catch and shakily press the fob while she kicks, hard, at the prone man's head with her lethal heels. "Don't even think about getting up," she growls. Miraculously—or maybe not, because she's kind of terrifying right now—he obeys.

I dive into the passenger seat and slam the door behind me, my heart pounding so hard that it feels like it's skipping beats, then wait an endless minute for Gem to slide into the driver's side. As soon as she closes the door, I press the lock. "Holy shit," I say breathlessly, craning my neck to see if there's any sign of the guy behind us. "Was that . . . Did that really happen?"

"He picked the wrong old lady, didn't he?" she says, turning on the ignition and pulling into the street without bothering to look over her shoulder. A horn blares loudly as she adds, "You okay? Scraped up those knees pretty bad."

"I'm fine," I say, grabbing a couple of Kleenex from the glove compartment to dab at my bloody knees. The thin tissue sticks and pulls apart when I tug at it, creating an even bigger mess. There's still a lump of fear in my throat, but I swallow it down and try to mirror Gem's calm tone. "Just got the wind knocked out of me. What about you?"

Gem is the toughest woman I know, and she's been taking self-defense classes for decades, but *still*. If you'd asked me how long she'd need to take down a full-grown man, I would've said more than a minute.

"I'll feel it tomorrow," she says, rolling a shoulder. "But not as much as he will. Goddamn asshole. Spilled your drink, too."

I look down at my ruined blouse and swallow a laugh. I'd say *Good riddance,* but I'm not sure Gem thinks that Sophie's Pilgrim preppy look is as awful as I do. "That was a lot of fight over a worthless purse," I say instead.

"Worthless?" she says in mock indignation. "How dare you." Gem's purse is a running joke with everyone who knows her. No matter what type she's carrying—her usual tote, or this stodgy grandma handbag that I've never seen before—it's stuffed to the brim with so much junk that she couldn't fit a wallet even if she wanted to. Which she doesn't, because Gem always keeps anything important tucked in a pocket. "I need every last thing in there."

"If you say so." I offer a wan smile before slumping against my seat, giving in to exhaustion as the adrenaline starts draining out of me.

"Besides, I couldn't let your good work go to waste," she says.

"My what?" I ask.

Gem smirks. "Look in the side," she says.

"The side of . . ." I glance around the car, then realize I'm still holding her purse in my lap. When I rotate it, I notice an open pocket on the left. I reach inside and my fingertips brush against a small, hard object—something that's both textured and impossibly smooth. I have a feeling, suddenly, that I know exactly what it is even before I pull it out.

I'm right. It's the diamond vine ring from Bennington & Main, glittering in the afternoon sun like an entire galaxy of stars.

CHAPTER TWO

Kat

I've only seen my mother truly angry twice.

The first time was four years ago, when her ex—or, as she puts it, "that garbage excuse for a human Luke Rooney"—tried to friend her on Facebook after eight years of no contact. Luke was the first person my mother dated, if you could call it that, after leaving my nightmare of a father. He was also the last, because their short and spectacularly ill-fated romance convinced her that her taste in men was irredeemable.

And the second time is right now, at Gem.

"You brought Kat *where* to do *what*?"

"Relax, Jamie," Gem says. She's the picture of calm except for the hard set of her jaw, which makes it clear how little she likes being questioned. There aren't many people besides my mother who get away with it. "She did great."

I should've suppressed my grin at that, because Jamie gives me a death glare when she sees it. "Wipe that look off your face," she snaps before turning back to Gem. "Are you kidding me? She shouldn't be *doing great*. She shouldn't have a part in all this. In any of this!"

At "this," she waves her arms around Gem's business headquarters, which is split into a couple of areas. The front is a neat, compact office, with a sign reading SPOTLESS dominating one wood-paneled wall. Spotless is the cleaning business that Gem's run for a couple of decades, although the name—and the address—changes frequently. My mother started there as a cleaner when I was four, and gradually worked her way up to being Gem's bookkeeper. Jamie is in night school now, just a few credits shy of getting her associate's degree in accounting.

But that's the front room. "This" also refers to the back room, where the other half of the business lives. Long tables are crammed full of luxury goods like handbags, electronics, and designer clothes—but mostly jewelry. Some of it is made here, like Gem's fakes, but most of it isn't. Most of it's stolen, because Spotless and all its other iterations are a front for Gem's most profitable business: jewelry theft.

Her name isn't actually Gem, either; I don't know what it is. But Gem is one of those no-brainer nicknames she got way before I met her.

"Careful, Jamie," Gem says, voice sharp. "*This* pays for your life. And Kat's."

Jamie sucks in a breath. I've always called my mother by her first name; she's only eighteen years older than me, and for a lot of my childhood she seemed more like an overwhelmed older sister than a mom. Or a babysitter, maybe, who was doing her best but counting down every second until the parents got home.

"I know that, Gem," she says in a more controlled tone. Her nose scrunches, highlighting the spray of freckles we share. Her dark hair is in a messy topknot, almost exactly like mine now that I've shed the blond wig. We're mistaken for sisters a lot, especially when she wears clothes that she's had for more than a decade. If Jamie had known she was going to have to stand up to Gem today, she might've chosen something other than threadbare leggings and her ancient Perry the Platypus hoodie. "And I'm grateful. I know you look out for Kat. But I thought we were transitioning. The replicas are starting to take off, and—"

"And they make a fraction of what we need," Gem interrupts. "For Christ's sake, Jamie, you know this. You handle the books. We got material costs, we got overhead, and we got new girls coming in. Should I tell them there's no place for them? What if I'd said that to you twelve years ago in Vegas? Where would you be now?"

I grip the edge of the table I'm perched on as Jamie recoils like Gem just slapped her. Vegas. It's a tender, shameful spot for my mother, and Gem almost never pokes it. Usually, the word is enough to make Jamie retreat from any argument.

But not this time. She shakes off her wince and says, "Kat is *sixteen*."

"And right here," I say, waving. "Can I say something?"

Apparently not, because Jamie keeps going. "It's unacceptable. We've never talked about something like this, and if we had—"

"Okay, well, Jamie, here's the deal," Gem says. "I didn't go to Bennington and Main planning to take the ring. I just wanted another look at it, to compare it to the replica. Which, by the way, is flawless. I happened to have it with me, and Kat staged a perfectly timed distraction—I know you didn't mean to," she adds, holding up a hand to cut off any commentary from me. "But you did. So I did what any businessperson with half a brain would do in that situation, and took advantage."

Jamie is quiet for a few beats, her gaze flicking between Gem and me. Then she says, "Happened to have it with you?"

"Hmm?" Gem asks.

"The fake. That was a coincidence? Not a plan?"

Gem's voice drops a few degrees. "Isn't that what I said?"

Their eyes lock, and my pulse starts to skitter. These stand-offs between Jamie and Gem have been happening a lot lately, and they fill me with a nameless dread I can't fully explain. I understand where my mother is coming from; it's not like I don't have the occasional nightmare about Jamie being arrested, or stabs of guilt and shame about how she pays for our apartment, our clothes, and our food.

But I also don't know how we'd manage them otherwise.

And Gem is careful and calculated with her targets; it's a point of pride with her not to steal from anyone who'd genuinely miss it. Or, she says, who genuinely earned it. All she's doing is taking crumbs from the corporate raiders of the world.

"I didn't mind," I blurt out, sliding off the table. "Helping, I mean."

Gem's face softens, but before she can speak, Jamie grabs me by the arm and spins me toward the door. "Go wait in the front office," she says through gritted teeth. *"Now."*

"Seriously? This is a conversation about me, but I can't be here?" I protest as she pushes me forward.

"This is a conversation about a lot more than you," Jamie

says before shoving me through the door and shutting it behind me.

Well, that's ominous.

What does she mean? And what did *I* mean? It felt like the truth when I said I didn't mind helping, but then again . . . what about poor hapless Bernard? I don't want him to get in trouble. Not to mention, Gem and I weren't exactly subtle at Bennington & Main. We were memorable, almost to the point of being cartoonish. Disguised, sure, but will that matter if the fake comes to light and someone checks the security cameras?

If I'd known what we were doing, I would've tried a lot harder to avoid them.

"Those two going at it again, huh?"

I whip around at the voice, but relax when I see Gem's daughter, Morgan, seated at the desk behind a monitor. Morgan is about the same age as my mother, and since Gem's always treated Jamie like her own child, that makes her and Morgan practically twins. Sibling rivalry included, especially since Gem sometimes seems to favor Jamie.

"Yup," I say, sinking into the chair across from her and spinning in a half circle.

"Does it have anything to do with the fact that you're dressed like a . . ." Morgan cranes her neck for a better look at me. "How would one describe that ensemble?"

"Repressed boarding school transplant," I say.

"If that's what you're going for, then I'd say you nailed it, Kat."

"I'm not Kat. I'm Sophie Hicks-Hartwell."

Morgan smirks. "Of course you are."

It's strange. When Gem told me to pick a name—"Any

14

name," she said, waving her hand like a genie granting a wish—
I almost said *Kylie Burke*. I'm not sure what came over me; it's
a name I never say out loud. Part of me has always wondered if
Gem knows anything about that long-ago girl. Gem bringing
me on a job for the first time today felt like a sign, maybe, that
we could talk about things like that. But in the end, I didn't
dare. Even with Gem, who I trust more than anyone except
Jamie, it's safer to be Sophie.

Or Kat.

"And how did Sophie make out today?" Morgan asks.

When I tell her the rest, she starts to laugh.

"It's not funny," I mutter, still unnerved by the look in
Jamie's eye when she propelled me out the door. Jamie is a go-
with-the-flow kind of person; in our little household of two,
I'm usually the one who decides when to eat, what to watch,
and whether to feed the stray cats we tend to attract (always
yes). The glint of pure determination before she slammed the
door in my face was something new.

"It kind of is, though. You and Jamie are like the grifter
Gilmore girls."

A reluctant smile tugs at my lips as I say, "Pretty sure I'm
one and done."

"How bad was the argument?"

"Gem brought up Vegas."

"Oh hell." Morgan looks suitably impressed. "Shit's getting real." She squints at me over the monitor and adds, "How
come that doesn't freak you out like it does Jamie?"

"I was four," I remind her. "I barely remember it. And
what I do remember wasn't scary." Maybe because I wasn't
alone—my clearest memory of that weekend is gripping the

hand of Luke Rooney's five-year-old son, so tightly and for so long that it felt like an extension of my own. *Had to practically pry you two apart,* Gem's always said.

Morgan shrugs. It's exaggerated like all her movements, her shoulders practically touching her ears. She's a runner, tall and wiry, with short hair she cuts herself and a sleeve of intricate tattoos on one arm. "You can act as tough as you want, but being lost in Las Vegas for six hours must've been terrifying."

Sometimes I think I must be misremembering—that wandering around Las Vegas as a preschooler with zero adult supervision was a worse experience than I'm willing to admit. But no matter how often I poke at the memory, it doesn't poke back. Maybe because, even at four, I'd already been through much worse.

That memory I don't poke at. Ever.

"The hotel buffet kept me calm," I say with an airy wave of my hand. "I ate my weight in dessert that day." Then, before Morgan can keep asking questions, I lift my chin toward her computer and ask, "What are you working on?"

Her expression darkens, but all she says is "The usual. Tech support."

That's Morgan's official role at Spotless. Unofficially, she specializes in fleecing the ultrarich, and she's usually pretty good at it. But rumor has it she botched her last heist, badly enough that Gem's been in a foul mood with her ever since. Even Jamie doesn't know the details, though, and Morgan's certainly not going to share them with me.

I take the hint that she's done talking and pull out my phone to scroll through messages. I have a few; Boston's been one of the better cities I've lived in for making friends. Whatever Morgan did, I hope she didn't screw up badly enough that Spotless has to move again.

I'm about to answer a text from my friend Hannah when Jamie finally enters the office. Alone, and looking thoroughly exhausted.

Morgan leans back in her chair and asks, "How'd it go in there?"

"I'm done," Jamie says simply.

Morgan and I exchange confused glances. "Done talking?" I ask.

"Yes. But also *done* done. With everything," Jamie says. Which is still clearly not enough information for Morgan and me, so she makes a sweeping gesture around the office with her arm and says, "With Spotless, and whatever it's going to be next. With working here, with doing jobs for Gem. Just . . . all of it."

"Wait," I say, alarm stirring my stomach as Morgan's jaw drops. "You quit your job? Because I helped Gem *one* time?"

"Yes and no," Jamie says, tugging hard at the hem of her hoodie. "I quit, but not because of you. The backroom business—it's not for me anymore. It hasn't been for a while. This isn't a new discussion. It was just . . . accelerated."

Because of me. She just doesn't want to say it. My heart is racing, my chest squeezing with something that feels a lot like panic. *And now what are we supposed to do?*

Morgan's thoughts seem to be cruising along a similar, though less anxious, wavelength. She points her pen at Jamie and asks, "So if you're done with the business . . . what, exactly, are you planning to do for money?"

"Gem's going to help me out with that," Jamie says. "She

knows someone at a real estate firm in Cambridge—*legit* real estate—who's looking for an accounting assistant. She said she'd put in a good word for me."

I just stare. Objectively, sure—this is the kind of job Jamie has wanted for years. It's why she's been wearing herself out with night school. And it's a relief that Jamie didn't storm out of her argument with Gem without a plan.

But working for Gem means that someone is always looking out for us. It means we get to live in the kind of neighborhood where, frankly, *we're* the worst thing that ever happens to people. Someplace safe and secure, where you can leave the past behind because it wouldn't even think of looking for you there.

"Really? As simple as that?" Morgan sounds almost jealous. "You say you're done, and suddenly you've got a nine-to-five with, what? A 401(k) and shit?"

"It's not as simple as that," Jamie says.

Something in her tone pricks my nerves. Morgan sits up straighter and says, "Ah, so we're talking a little quid pro quo here, huh? What do you have to do?"

"It's not a big deal," Jamie says, in the kind of faux-casual tone that screams *This is a very, very big deal.* "Just one more job."

Morgan taps her pen against the desk and asks, "Which one?"

"The Sutherland compound," Jamie says. "In August."

The name means nothing to me, but Morgan frowns and says, "Wait, seriously? Sutherland is *my* contact. Last I heard it was a no-go."

"What was?" I ask.

Jamie ignores me, keeping her gaze on Morgan. "Not according to Gem," she says.

Morgan snorts. "Would've been nice if she'd told me."

Neither of them are looking at me, and my patience wears thin enough that I snap my fingers in both their directions. "Hello? Remember me? Still in the room. Still clueless. What's the Sutherland compound?"

Morgan points her finger like a gun, then cocks it as though she just pulled the trigger. "The Sutherland compound," she says, "is your mother going out with a bang."

CHAPTER THREE

Liam

As soon as I step into the restaurant, I realize I've made a mistake.

I don't know much about the dining scene in Portland, partly because I've only lived in Maine for six months, but mostly because Five Guys is my go-to. Online, Leonardo's looked reassuringly basic. A no-frills old-school place—the kind of restaurant that says *Don't expect much from this date.* And cheap enough that somebody ordering, say, a single glass of wine while waiting on said date wouldn't be stuck with a giant bill.

But the reality is different. It's all dark wood, white flowers, and twinkling lights. The air-conditioning is precisely the right temperature for a warm early July night. Soft classical music plays quietly in the background, and a small bronze plaque on the wall reads BEST OF PORTLAND: MOST ROMANTIC RESTAURANTS.

As if on cue, a smiling, hand-holding couple walks past me, both guys wearing sharp blazers and well-tailored shirts. Along with the sinking feeling in my stomach, I'm hit with a pang of nostalgia. It's not like I miss my ex-boyfriend Ben anymore, but life in general was a lot simpler when we were together.

"Welcome to Leonardo's," the host at the podium calls out. "Can I help you?"

She's young and pretty, with a high ponytail and a bright smile that somehow makes everything worse. This seemed like a good idea from behind my father's laptop, but now I'm deeply regretting all the choices that brought me here tonight.

Not as much as I regret everything that wasn't a choice, and there's nothing I can do about that, but this—this felt like *something*, at least.

"Are you lost?" the host asks kindly.

You have no idea.

I push down the honest response, along with the urge to flee, and say, "No, this place just looks different from what I expected."

She smiles. "Amazing, right? The new owners totally transformed it."

They should transform the website while they're at it, I think, but all I say is "Yeah, it's great. I have a reservation for Luke?"

It's not my name, and saying it feels like sucking on a lemon, but she either doesn't notice or is too polite to react. "Oh, sure, I seated the other member of your party a few minutes ago. Right this way." She grabs a couple of menus and heads for the dining room, calling over her shoulder, "Having dinner with your mom tonight?"

Kill me. Just kill me now and get it over with.

21

"Mmmff," I mumble, which I hope is neutral enough to not make it weird when we get to the table. Who am I kidding, though? Of course it's going to be weird.

The host winds her way through the dining room until she reaches someone sitting alone at a table beside the window: an attractive dark-haired woman in her late thirties, wearing a neat navy dress and lots of silver bracelets. Her name is Rebecca Kent, and according to her profile on First Comes Love, she's "giving online dating one last try."

Big mistake, Rebecca. Gigantic.

My stomach twists as we halt beside her table and she looks up with a polite but quizzical expression. "Luke is here!" the host says cheerfully, with a ta-da flourish that I really, really could've done without.

Rebecca blinks in startled confusion. I'm obviously not who she came here to meet, and yet—I look uncannily like him. As though he got shoved into a time machine and went back twenty-five years. "I, uh . . . sorry?" she says. "I think I misheard you. What was that?"

"Luke is here?" the host repeats with less certainty.

Rebecca's brow furrows. "There must be some kind of—"

"We're gonna need a few minutes with the menu," I break in before she can finish that sentence with "mistake." I grab both menus from the host's hand and drop into the chair across from Rebecca with an apologetic grimace. "Hi," I add limply. "How's it going?"

Rebecca just stares.

I can't even look at the host as she backs away with a muted "Enjoy your meal." I set the menus on the table, careful not to knock over the flickering votive candle between us. Then I reach for the full glass of water to my right and guzzle half of it while Rebecca, still staring, clutches the stem of her wineglass.

"Who are you?" she asks.

"Liam Rooney. Luke's son," I say.

"Luke's son?" she repeats. "But you're not—"

"Five years old? No, not for a while now." I take another sip of water, but it doesn't do any good. My throat is impossibly dry.

"Do you have a little brother, or—"

"No. Only child."

Rebecca cocks her head, and I can almost see the wheels of her brain turning as she compares the seventeen-year-old sitting across from her to the kindergarten picture Luke shared while they were chatting on First Comes Love.

And to Luke himself. The resemblance is striking; I have Luke's floppy auburn hair and bright-blue eyes, and a dimpled smile that looks like I'm about to let you in on a really great secret. My father and I both have the kind of face that draws people in, and he uses that to full advantage. "And what about . . ." Rebecca trails off, her eyes wary.

"The cancer? Don't have it. Never did. I'm not being treated at Children's Hospital in Boston. There's no experimental operation that might save my life, if only it were covered by insurance." I finish the rest of my water before adding what I came here to say. "So there's no reason for you to give my father money for that."

"He hasn't asked—" Rebecca starts, and then presses her lips together for a few seconds. "I see. You're telling me that he will."

"It's what he does," I say.

While I was growing up, I'd occasionally wonder how my

father managed to support himself without ever appearing to have an actual job. But back then, it wasn't my problem. Mom divorced Luke when I was a toddler, and refused to allow visitation after he took me to Vegas during one of his weekends, married a woman he'd just met, and lost track of me and the woman's four-year-old daughter for six hours.

He didn't fight to keep seeing me, so Mom and I lived a blissfully Luke-free existence for more than a decade in Maryland. He'd occasionally hit her up for money, but she'd always delete those emails with a breezy "Absolutely not." Luke was like a cartoon character to me—the bad-apple father who gave me his looks and nothing else.

Then, six months ago, Mom died in a car accident and my whole world collapsed.

I didn't know what grief was before that. I'd never lost someone so essential, and couldn't imagine a future without my favorite person. It broke me for a while, and I was so miserable that I barely cared when a judge granted Luke custody.

I never asked why he agreed to take me, and it's only recently that I've wondered whether he thought refusing might have required too much time in a courtroom.

"How long have I been corresponding with you?" Rebecca asks dryly.

"Just since the dinner invite," I say.

I stumbled across Luke's profile on First Comes Love by accident, when my phone ran out of power and I went to his laptop to check the weather. He hadn't logged out, and a chat window was still open. When I realized it was a dating site, I almost bailed, because the last thing I wanted was a glimpse into my father's love life. But then I saw it—my kindergarten picture in all its gap-toothed glory. *I don't know what I'll do if I lose him,* Luke wrote to some other woman—this was pre-Rebecca—and I had to read their entire conversation a few times before I fully absorbed that he was using me as catfish bait.

It took a minute for my reaction to kick in. Two months after I moved in with Luke, grief gave way to numbness. I'd gotten used to sleepwalking through life. Everything had felt so flat for so long that I didn't recognize the hot spike of emotion running through me.

And then it hit me: I was *furious.*

It felt good to care about something again, even if what I cared about was the fact that my father was an asshole and a fraud. So I decided to do something about it.

I might, however, have underestimated the awkwardness factor.

"Well, I feel like an utter fool," Rebecca says, releasing her wineglass. "I like to think I wouldn't have given him money, but . . . I don't know. He's very convincing." I just nod, and she adds, "I take it he's done this before."

"A few times." That I know of.

"He should be in jail," Rebecca says bitterly.

You could press charges. I came here partly to say those words, to suggest that she pretend tonight never happened and keep corresponding with Luke. Give him enough rope to hang himself. I'm no expert, but all of this is wildly illegal, right? Let him rot in jail while I convince Mom's brother, my uncle Jack, to end his Doctors Without Borders assignment early and move home.

Now that I'm here, though, the words stick in my throat.

It's not loyalty to my father, but it's . . . something. *He gave me the best part of himself,* Mom used to say whenever her friends would bad-mouth Luke. *He gave me Liam, so I'll cut him some slack.* I don't know what she'd want me to do right now, and before I can figure it out, Rebecca starts gathering her things.

"I guess I should thank you," she says. She doesn't sound grateful, and I can't blame her. She's probably thinking, *Like father, like son.* But then her expression thaws a little, and she adds, "I'm going to head home, but can I buy you some take-out first?"

God, no. I can't let her spend money on me, and I'm desperate to get out of here. "I'm good, thanks. And . . . I'm sorry."

"You have nothing to be sorry for," Rebecca says, getting to her feet. "Other than the unfortunate accident of birth that saddled you with Luke Rooney as a father." She pauses before adding, "What did you say your name was again? Is it actually Liam?"

"Yeah," I say.

"Well, Liam, best of luck to you," Rebecca says. She pulls a wallet out of her purse and extracts a twenty-dollar bill, setting it on the table beside her wineglass. "I have the feeling you're going to need it."

CHAPTER FOUR

Liam

I remember a lot about Vegas.

I was five years old, and I remember being intimidated by the noise and the bright lights. I remember liking Jamie Quinn, the woman we met by the pool. I remember her and Luke getting married by an Elvis impersonator, and the bored photographer who handed Jamie a couple of "family photo" Polaroids after. She tucked one into her purse and gave the other one to me. I still have it; it's the only picture of me and Luke that didn't get tossed at some point.

I remember the hotel room, and how Jamie's daughter, Kat, and I were given a bunch of pillows and blankets and told to make a fort in the bathroom. I think we probably slept there.

I don't remember why Jamie left us alone with Luke the next day, but I do remember the moment when Luke decided that he'd leave, too. "Look out for your sister," he said before grabbing his sunglasses and placing them over red-rimmed eyes. "I'll be right back."

I remember saying *She's not my sister,* but I said it to a closed door.

Time doesn't mean much when you're five, but Luke definitely wasn't "right back." I got bored, so I turned on the television and we watched cartoons for a while. Then some show I'd never seen before, called *The Haunted Sandbox,* came on, and Kat backed away from the television like it was on fire. "I *hate* this show," she said, and the next thing I knew, she'd walked straight out the door. I didn't know what to do except follow her. And once we were in the hallway, we just . . . kept going.

I still can't believe that we wandered around alone for as long as we did. I guess people either assumed our parents were right behind us or they didn't much care. I remember it being fun at first, especially because there was so much free food sitting around. But once we left the familiarity of our own hotel and got hopelessly lost, I started feeling scared. I grabbed Kat's hand and kept holding it even when my own went numb.

At one point, exhausted, we curled up behind an empty desk in a shabby hotel lobby and fell asleep. When I woke up, completely disoriented, a gray-haired woman was on her knees beside me and Kat—whose hand I was still clutching in a death grip. The woman was wearing some kind of apron over her clothes, and her face looked a little rough but not mean.

"Well, hello," she said. "What brings you two here?"

Once everyone was reunited, Jamie told Luke that she was

filing for divorce. She grabbed Kat and took off with the gray-haired woman, and I never saw any of them again.

My steps slow as I near our loft-style apartment building and see the lights burning bright in the kitchen. I turned them off before leaving, which means Luke is back early from wherever he was. Usually, I can count on not seeing him if I go to bed before midnight.

Does he know? Maybe he saw Rebecca's confirmation message in the trash folder on First Comes Love and realized that I posed as him. What could he say, though? *Quit messing with my con, you little shit. How do you think we afford this apartment?*

It is, without question, a much nicer apartment than we deserve. High ceilings and big windows, accented by a brick wall and industrial pipes. It's strewn with half-finished impressionist-style paintings that Luke claims are his, although I have my doubts. I've never seen him working on anything, and I wouldn't put it past him to buy them for peanuts from a starving artist and pass them off as his own.

Halfway up I hear a woman laughing and stop in my tracks. Is he . . . Oh God, he's on a *date,* isn't he? That's a first; Luke never brings anyone home. My robustly healthy teenage self would be a dead giveaway.

A grim smile tugs at my lips as I pick up the pace down the hallway. It would've been nice if the first spark of energy I felt in months had come from something I used to enjoy—playing lacrosse, maybe, or having friends—instead of spoiling my father's dating con. But beggars can't be choosers, so I might as well ruin his game twice in one night.

I pull open our front door to see Luke—I can't bring myself to call him Dad—leaning against the kitchen counter with a glass in one hand. His auburn hair is casually rumpled, and he's wearing his usual uniform of a fitted oxford shirt and jeans. He's talking to a black-clad blond woman whose back is turned to me, and when he meets my eyes I expect him to freeze in dismay. Instead, he grins with such unexpected delight that I find myself looking over my shoulder for whoever he's so happy to see.

"Liam! Buddy!" he calls out. "Perfect timing."

Buddy? I don't even know what to do with that.

"Oh, hello!" The woman turns, beaming. At first, all I can see is her necklace—blinding diamonds so huge that they have to be fake. Then I realize that I'm technically staring at her chest, and I snap my eyes to hers. They're light brown, like my mother's, and I almost yell *Run away!* as she clasps my hand in her own. "We were just talking about you."

"Oh yeah?" I ask. "Am I . . . what you expected?"

"Just as Luke described," she says warmly, and now I'm really confused. She didn't think I was five? Or dying? "I'm Annalise. Sorry to barge into your home like this, but I've been so eager to see the studio."

The *studio?* I gaze around the open-concept apartment and note that there are a lot more half-finished paintings now than there were when I left. Is Luke going to try to sell one to her? What could that possibly be worth? Surely not as much as experimental cancer treatment, unless he's a better fake painter than I thought.

"Poor Liam gets tired of living with his old man's mess,"

Luke says, and truer words have never been spoken. But he ducks his head modestly, like what he really means is *Can't expect kids to recognize genius, can you?*

"It's wonderful to meet you, Liam," Annalise says. "But I wish it could've been under better circumstances." I'm not sure what she means until her voice softens and she adds, "I was so sorry to hear about your mother. I lost mine in an accident a few years ago, and I know how incredibly difficult it is. There's nobody in the world I loved more, and I still miss her every single day. You must miss your mom, too."

Jesus. I wasn't ready for my father's date to rip open the heart I haven't used in months, and all of a sudden I can't breathe. I want to go back to being numb—or angry. Angry was good. It felt *purposeful.*

"He sure does," Luke says in a hushed tone, which helps restore my equilibrium since it makes me want to punch him. He doesn't know the first thing about how I feel, because we never talk about Mom. I don't talk about her with anyone except Uncle Jack, and that's usually over text. He'll send me pictures from when he and my mother were little, and I'll send some back from when I was—me and Mom at my lacrosse games, dressed up for Halloween, pulling goofy faces for no reason. A digital trail of memories that's somehow less painful than trying to put into words the gaping hole her death has left in both our lives.

Annalise squeezes my arm, then asks, "Could I give you a hug?"

She doesn't wait for my response before folding me into a floral-scented embrace. It's a little bit suffocating and a lot uncomfortable; I haven't hugged anyone since Mom's funeral, and it feels as though I've forgotten how. Where do my arms go? Why do I feel like there's a steel rod in my spine keeping me painfully upright? It's made worse by the sight of Luke over Annalise's shoulder, smiling a Cheshire cat grin. For some reason, this is exactly what he wants.

"Thanks," I say, disentangling myself. "That means a lot."

Annalise pats my cheek. "I hope you're settling into Maine as well as can be expected. Winters are brutal, as I'm sure you learned, but our summers are lovely."

"Yeah. Really, um . . . nice so far."

I'm tongue-tied, but it doesn't matter, because Annalise is one of those effortless conversationalists who carries you gracefully from one topic to the next. We talk about what it was like going to a new school for the second semester of my junior year, the kind of basic question that Luke has never bothered to ask. She asks me about lacrosse, which she's clearly taken the time to learn about, and urges me to try out for my new school's team senior year. Then she asks if I've met any nice guys, which is a short conversation, since I haven't been interested in anyone since Ben dumped me almost a year ago.

The whole time, Luke smiles proudly and occasionally injects meaningless yet affable dad talk, like, "That's what I always say!" or "This kid! What am I supposed to do with him, huh?" It's all so disorienting that my head starts to pound.

Finally, Annalise glances at the clock on our microwave. "Goodness, it's much later than I realized," she says with a light laugh. "I'd better get on the road. But it was so nice chatting with you, Liam. I hope we'll see one another again soon."

"Hope so," I manage.

"What a fun night, huh?" Affable Dad Luke says, rubbing his hands together.

"And I'll let you know about my father's birthday next month," Annalise says to him. "You'd love the compound. So pretty in summertime, absolutely full of inspiration."

He beams. "Perfect. Let me walk you to your car."

They leave, and I spend the next five minutes pacing the apartment, massaging my aching temples while trying not to think about what harm I might've done to Annalise by playing along with Luke. Although . . . I wasn't really playing, was I? I was honest throughout the entire conversation, because nothing Luke told her about me was a lie.

He used my real name. My real age. What does that mean?

Then I hear Luke bounding up the steps, whistling. When he opens the door, he's still grinning as widely as he did when Annalise was here. "Isn't she terrific?" he asks.

Is he . . . Wait. Does my father actually *like* Annalise? For real? "Yeah," I say cautiously. "Where'd you meet her?"

"Gallery opening downtown," Luke says, grabbing a bottle of bourbon from the counter and topping off his glass. "You know how I like to stay on top of the art scene around here." I don't know that, but he clearly doesn't need a response from me because he keeps right on going. "I walked in, and bam—there she was. Took my breath away."

"Okay," I say. There has to be more to the story, because Annalise isn't my father's usual type. She's older, for one thing, and a lot more momlike.

"Annalise is a big patron of the arts, obviously," Luke says. "All the Sutherlands are." I must look as confused as I feel,

33

because he adds, "Come on, you've been to the Sutherland Wing in the Portland Museum of Art, right?"

"No." I almost remind him that he's not an actual artist, but the name Sutherland catches my attention. I don't know the museum, but I do know the real estate company. You can't miss them in downtown Portland. "Wait, like Sutherland Towers? And Sutherland Plaza, and—"

"That's the one," Luke says, taking a long sip of bourbon. He smacks his lips in a highly disconcerting way and adds, "Let me tell you, Liam, Annalise is one extraordinary woman. *Extraordinary.*"

Extraordinarily rich, he means. "What are you going to do to her?" I blurt out before I can collect my thoughts enough to ask a question he might actually answer.

He's still in Affable Dad mode, though, because he doesn't notice the accusatory tone in my voice. Or doesn't care. He just smiles dreamily and says, "I'm going to marry her."

CHAPTER FIVE

Kat

Pre-nostalgia is a strange thing.

I was just in Gem's back room yesterday, talking reality TV with some of the regulars like always—a normal weekday afternoon in early August, no different from countless others. But today, right before Jamie is planning to drop me off at my friend Hannah's for the weekend and then head to the Sutherland compound in Maine, it feels like I'm gazing around the familiar space through a sepia-toned lens.

It doesn't help that it's barely six-thirty a.m. and the room is empty. Jamie's in the front office with Gem, getting everything she needs for the weekend, and Morgan is double-checking fluids in our ancient Honda SUV, so I'm alone here for the first time ever. Without people filling the chairs around the long tables, the back office looks dusty, abandoned, and, to my overtired brain, a little ominous.

I've had more than a month to get used to the fact that the

only life I can remember is about to change, but it's not nearly enough time.

"Memory, all alone in the moonlight," an off-key voice warbles behind me.

It's so unexpected in the morning silence that I let out an involuntary gasp. When I whip around, my pulse spiking, I see Gem holding an extra-large stainless-steel thermos, her gray hair scraped into a low bun. The expression on her face is as close as she gets to smiling. "You look like a glum extra from *Cats,*" she says.

I let my heartbeat settle back down before asking, "From what?"

"*Cats.* The musical? Come on, my voice can't be bad enough that you didn't recognize 'Memory.' It's only one of the most iconic theater songs ever." She rolls her eyes at my blank expression. "Good Lord, your generation is culturally illiterate. Try getting off TikTok every once in a while." She doesn't wait for me to answer before adding, with a shade less sarcasm, "It's not like you'll never be back here, you know."

"I know," I mutter, rubbing my bare arms.

Nothing escapes Gem's eagle eye, including the fact that it's much too hot back here for goose bumps. "What's got you spooked, then?" she asks. When I don't reply right away, she cocks her head and adds, "Jamie will be fine, you know. This one's easy."

I nod. "That's what she says."

Tomorrow real estate magnate Ross Sutherland is turning eighty and celebrating with a three-day extravaganza in Bixby, Maine. Nearly a hundred people are working the event, and they're all staying at an apartment complex across the street from the family's gated compound. Thanks to a disgruntled member of the Sutherland household staff who Morgan has been cultivating for a while, Jamie has the credentials to join them.

Gem smiles wryly. "But you don't believe it?"

I can't let her think that, or my plan for this weekend won't work. "No, of course I do," I say. "It's too early, is all. I'm still half asleep."

"I figured. Which is why I made you this." Gem holds out the thermos. "Extra-strong black coffee with a disgusting amount of sugar. Just the way you like it."

"Thanks." There's a weird little lump in my throat as I take it, and a moment where I think, *Do we hug now? We've never hugged. Should we start?*

Then Gem makes a shooing motion and says, "Go on, get in the car. Jamie's just finishing up in the office. She'll be right behind you. Have fun at Hannah's."

No hugging, then. Probably just as well. "All right," I say, and head for the door.

"Kat! One more thing." I pause and look over my shoulder at Gem, who's kind of . . . fidgeting in place? It's a strange look for her. "Jamie was right, you know. About the ring. I overstepped, bringing you along for that."

"It's fine—" I start, but Gem holds up a hand.

"Let me finish. I overstepped, so . . . when that ring gets sold, the money will go into your college fund. Okay?"

I blink, too startled to say anything except "I don't have a college fund."

"Well, now you do," Gem says gruffly. Then she turns away and stalks toward the front office, firmly shutting the door behind her as if to say *Still no hugs*.

I walk out into the back alley behind Spotless in a daze. The ring will probably sell for two-thirds of its retail worth, which means . . . thirteen thousand dollars. Does Jamie know about this? She can't possibly, right? The whole point of this final job is for the two of us to become, as Jamie puts it, "pillars of respectability." My mother has been spending less and less time at Spotless over the past few weeks, and encouraging me to do the same. Even though Gem said, *It's not like you'll never be back here*, I'm starting to think that's what Jamie wants. As though she can flip a switch, and more than a decade of working for a jewel thief never happened.

I'm so lost in thought that I almost walk right past the car. I barely manage to stop short before colliding with Morgan, who's standing at the open hatchback, holding Jamie's backpack. Startled at the sight of me, she drops it.

"Jesus, you're a stealthy little thing, aren't you?" she says, hauling the backpack off the ground by a strap.

The side pocket is unzipped, and I reach over to close it. God forbid we lose one of Jamie's snacks before we even get on the road. "What are you doing?" I ask.

"Making sure your spare tire is still underneath all your crap," Morgan says, tossing Jamie's backpack into the trunk. "It's a long drive to Bixby, especially in this death trap."

Fair enough. Jamie's Honda is nearly as old as I am, and our constant moving from one state to the next means it goes through a lot of tires. I've been changing them since I was twelve.

My mother appears in the alley then, holding a slim leather box in one hand. She joins us at the trunk and tucks it into the main compartment of her backpack before asking me, "Ready to go?"

"Ready," I say cheerfully, which should really be her first hint that something's up. Normally, I'd be pestering her for a look inside that box—at the fake ruby necklace Gem created that's the centerpiece of this entire weekend.

"Let's hit the road, then," Jamie says. "I'll text you when I get there, Morgan."

"Good luck," Morgan says. She slouches inside, and Jamie and I climb into the car and buckle up. Jamie shifts into reverse and backs slowly out of the alley while I fiddle with the radio until I land on Jamie's favorite news station. It's not until we're a few roads away from Spotless, stopped at a red light, that I speak up. "Okay, slight change of plans," I say.

"Hmm?" Jamie asks distractedly, adjusting the sun visor.

"Hannah and I decided to go to Splash Country today, but she has to work until eleven," I tell her. "Can you just drop me off there, instead of her house? I don't want to have to hang around for hours with her creepy brother."

Jamie blinks. "Since when is Josh creepy?"

"Since forever," I say, sending a silent apology to noncreepy Josh.

"Okay, well, that's news to me. And drop you off where? At Splash Country?" Jamie asks. It's a water park in Portland, Maine, an hour and a half from here. "By yourself? What are you going to do until Hannah gets there?"

"Ride the slides," I say. "Obviously."

"You could have told me this earlier," Jamie says, biting her lip. "I'm on a schedule, you know. I have my first staff meeting at eleven."

"It's right off the highway," I say as the light turns green. "Barely a fifteen-minute detour."

"Ugh, okay," she sighs. "Fine."

Just like I knew she would.

CHAPTER SIX

Kat

"Twizzler?" I ask Jamie, waving one at her.

"You know I can't," she says, her eyes trained on the road.

"You could. You just choose not to."

Jamie is going through a sugar-free kick, which, when added to the fact that she can't eat gluten for health reasons, means we enjoy precisely none of the same snacks. "Can you get me a packet of crunchy chickpeas instead?" she asks.

"Gross," I say unhelpfully. But I turn and stretch behind me to grab one of the grocery bags in the back seat, pawing through it in search of my mother's favorite snack. I dig for a good two minutes without any luck and give up. I unbuckle, stretch a little farther, and haul her backpack from the trunk. I open the side pocket and pull out a Tupperware container, giving it an experimental shake. "Want a handful of granola?" I offer.

"No. I already had some for breakfast."

"It's still morning."

"I don't want to run out."

There's no point in arguing; my mother is nothing if not a creature of habit. She's been eating homemade granola for breakfast for years, and consistency must be maintained. Jamie craves control over the small things in life, and even though I tease her about it, I understand where it comes from.

I stuff the Tupperware back into her backpack and dig further, pulling out the first packaged snack I can find. "How about some tofu crumbles?" I ask.

"That works."

I rip the package open and hand them to her. "Enjoy. If that's even possible."

She finishes half the bag before leaning forward for a better look at her phone, which is displaying Google Maps from a dashboard mount. "Next exit is Splash Country," she says.

Here we go.

"Yeah, about that," I say. "I'm not actually hanging out with Hannah there today."

"What?" Jamie takes her foot off the gas, and a car behind us changes lanes so it can zip past us. "What do you mean? Kat, I do *not* have time to take you back—"

"I know. You can't anyway, because Hannah's not home. Her family went to Nantucket for the weekend."

"Katrina Quinn," Jamie says in her most ominous voice. "What. Are. You. Doing?"

"Coming with you," I say.

"Oh, you little . . ." Jamie exhales a growl. "Nooooo. What are you *thinking*? You can't be anywhere near that place!"

"Why?" I ask. "Because it's not safe?"

"Of course it's safe! But I'm not supposed to be *me* this weekend. I'm working! I can't just show up with a kid—"

"It's not like I'm going to crash some old guy's birthday party," I say. "I'll stay in the staff quarters all weekend. You said they're totally separate from the compound, right? And everybody gets their own little apartment? Nobody will even know I'm there."

"But *why*?" Jamie asks, her voice tight.

"Because we stick together," I say. "Always."

Well, not always. But that's the whole point; bad things happen when we don't. Not just Vegas, but more important . . . pre-Vegas. When she was Ashley Burke, and I was Kylie.

My mother didn't have an easy start in life. Both her parents died from drug overdoses before she turned eight, leaving her with a great-aunt who had no idea what to do with a little kid. The aunt tried her best for almost ten years, until she died a month before Jamie turned seventeen. Instead of going into foster care for a year, Jamie took off. Then, before she'd ever really figured out how to be an adult, she had to be a mom. Alongside someone who decidedly didn't want to be a father.

I have very few memories of my first few years, and the ones I do have live in the deepest, darkest corner of my mind. Any time they threaten to surface, I push them down.

Like now. It's almost a physical thing—a hard, hasty shove. *There. Gone.*

Jamie leans back in her seat with a frustrated huff. "Of course we do. But not for something like *this*. It's an important weekend, and I don't need any distractions."

"I won't be a distraction," I say as we sail past the Splash Country exit. "Maybe I can even help. Somebody to run through your checklist with, make sure you've got all the details straight. Why don't you start by telling me about these Sutherlands?"

A couple of hours later, I know all about Ross Sutherland. Who, Jamie says, is now only a half billionaire due to some unfortunate business decisions. "Poor guy," I say, fishing through my bag in the hopes of finding a stray Twizzler. "Can he even afford this party?"

"Barely," Jamie says dryly. She seems to have forgiven me, for now. "I'm sure it's just paper losses that'll bounce back with the stock market, or the real estate market, or whatever market the Ross Sutherlands of the world use. I doubt his standard of living has changed."

"Must be nice," I say, thinking about the smooth weight of the diamond vine ring in my hand. For the Sutherlands, buying something like that is probably the equivalent of me buying a pack of Twizzlers: barely a blip on their financial radar. "Are his kids filthy rich, too?"

"Well, they're his kids, so yeah," Jamie says. "But none of them have struck out on their own, professionally speaking. They don't really work, except at the kind of vanity jobs that only rich people can afford to have. Seems like they've floundered on the personal side, as well. Two of them are divorced, and two have never married."

"Nothing wrong with being single," I say. Jamie, of all people, should know that.

"Of course not," Jamie says. "It's just interesting, because Ross Sutherland stayed married to his childhood sweetheart until she died a few years ago. That hit everyone very hard, and this is the first family party at the compound in a while."

We pass a sign saying BIXBY, 5 MILES, which means we're getting close to our destination: a small town nestled in the foothills overlooking a national forest. "Why do they call it a compound?" I ask. "Because there's a gate around it?"

"That's one reason," Jamie says. "But also because it's huge—more than two hundred acres, although not all of that is gated. Ross Sutherland's mansion is the centerpiece, of course, but all four of his children have homes there, too. They call them 'cottages,' even though they're massive. Plus there's an office and an entertaining space, a golf course and tennis courts, two barns that hold Ross's car collection, and a bunch of other stuff I can't remember right now. Oh, a vineyard, I think. But not a working one."

"Sounds like the Sutherland kids," I say, which earns a chuckle from Jamie. "Do they all live there all the time? Just one big happy family?"

"No," Jamie says. "Most of the Sutherlands are based in New York, and only visit the compound during the summer. Except Ross's youngest daughter, who splits her time pretty evenly between Bixby and Portland. Annalise."

Her tone drops a half octave on the name, a telltale sign that she's nervous. "Annalise," I repeat. "Is that the one whose necklace we're taking?"

"There's no *we* about it, Kat."

"Okay. Is that the one whose necklace *you're* taking?"

"Yes," Jamie says. Her cheeks redden as she adds, "It's odd, because although it's a lovely necklace, it's not all that expensive—at least, not compared to other pieces the family

45

owns. Ross is something of a collector, and he's been criticized for owning artifacts that ought to be in museums. I suppose that sort of thing is under lock and key, though, and this . . . this is more of an everyday necklace. But one of Gem's private clients got outbid by Ross Sutherland at an auction for it, and he's desperate to have it."

I turn that over in my mind for a minute. Tomorrow night is supposed to be simple. According to Morgan's contact, all the family homes have doors that lock automatically, but Annalise leaves her windows open in the summer, and there's a trellis beneath one of them. Apparently, the Sutherlands don't bother with safes for personal items in the compound, so the necklace will be easy to find in her dressing room. All Jamie needs to do is sneak away from the party, climb through the window, make the switch, and then go back to passing plates of hors d'oeuvres. But nobody's mentioned, at least to me, what seems to be a glaringly obvious flaw in the plan.

"What if she's wearing it?" I ask.

"Hmm?"

"Annalise," I say. "What if she wears the ruby necklace to the party, and you can't swap Gem's fake for it? Or what if she doesn't have it with her? She has a whole other house, right?"

"You really think Gem would leave that to chance?" Jamie asks. "Morgan's contact gave us an inventory of everything Annalise Sutherland is wearing this weekend. She's bringing the necklace, but not planning to wear it Saturday night."

"What if she changes her mind?"

"She won't."

"How do you know?"

"Because," Jamie says, a note of impatience creeping into

her tone, "it would clash with the coral gown she special-ordered for her father's party."

"Is that on the inventory, too? Is this stuff actually written down, or—"

"Kat, enough!" Jamie snaps. "You don't need to know all this. You're not some kind of . . . *apprentice,* here. This isn't your future."

"I know!" I say, stung. "I didn't say it was."

I might've *thought* it once or twice, but I could never figure out how that made me feel. And now I guess I never will.

"Sorry," Jamie sighs, putting her blinker on for the Bixby exit. "I'm just a little on edge. To be honest, I don't like thinking about how we've managed to keep such close tabs on a woman who's done nothing wrong."

Neither do I. "Her father sounds shady, though," I say. "Owning things he doesn't have a right to. And he's the one who bought the necklace, so . . . it's fine." I'm not sure whether I'm parroting Gem's Robin Hood logic to make Jamie feel better or myself.

Jamie doesn't answer right away, and when she does, her tone is guarded. "It's not *fine.* You get that, right? I wish . . . Look, I owe Gem so much, and I'm grateful, but I've done things I'm not proud of, and I'm really trying—"

"I know," I say, staring out the window so I don't have to see Jamie's pained expression. The town of Bixby is gorgeous, surrounded by mountains and towering trees. Every stretch of winding road looks straight out of a postcard, framed by stone walls and wildflower fields that are more vibrant and well tended than most people's gardens. The sky is bright blue, dotted with puffy white clouds, and even though our windows are closed, it feels as though the air surrounding us is already cleaner and fresher than anything I've breathed before.

This is what money can buy, I think.

Then there's a loud pop, and the car lurches wildly. I let out an involuntary yelp as we careen out of our lane—which could've been dangerous if the road weren't completely deserted—before Jamie gets control of the steering wheel and pulls off to one side. "What was that?" she asks breathlessly, gazing wildly around us. But from the way the back of the car is tilting slightly, I already know.

One of our tires has blown out. Again.

CHAPTER SEVEN

Liam

I'm starting to think like Luke, which is *incredibly* depressing.

I get why he was truthful about me to Annalise now. It's as calculated as everything my father does. She lost her mother a few years ago in a boating accident, and that made her instantly empathetic toward the idea of me, even before she met me. Not to mention impressed by the kind of stand-up guy who'd dedicate his life to supporting his grieving son.

Which isn't who Luke really is, but whatever. Once again, I was a way in. He just didn't count on me figuring it out.

I give him more credit than he gives me, because I can tell he's started to figure *me* out. I'm pretty sure he knows I've been messing with his First Comes Love contacts; even though I haven't met with anyone except Rebecca, I've been quietly rejecting all his ongoing chats. *It's been great talking with you, but I've decided to become exclusive with someone else,* I tell everyone who's gotten my kindergarten picture. Then I try to cover my tracks by deleting those outgoing messages and any responses, but I doubt I've caught them all. Plus, it can't have escaped Luke's notice that his inbox is suddenly, unusually empty.

Now we're in an unspoken standoff. He doesn't trust me, and he definitely doesn't want me tagging along on his "meet the family weekend" with Annalise at the Sutherland compound. They dated through all of July, with Luke on his best behavior, and now Annalise is bringing him to her father's eightieth birthday party. Since my sole source of satisfaction lately is foiling whatever Luke wants, that means I need to go, too.

Last week I wormed my way into one of their dinner dates—at Leonardo's, of all the ironic destinations—and put on a full-court press about how much I wanted to see the Sutherland family compound. "It sounds amazing," I told Annalise.

"It really is," she said. Warmly, but not in a *Join us* kind of way.

So I laid it on thicker. "A once-in-a-lifetime kind of spot, like the gardens at Giverny," I said, hoping the five-minute YouTube video I'd watched on Claude Monet got that pronunciation right. "I paint too, you know."

"Do you?" she asked delightedly as Luke's eyes narrowed.

Spoiler alert: I do not.

"I mean, I'm still a beginner," I said modestly. "Not nearly good enough to show anyone, but my dream is to become a working artist someday."

"That's news to me," Luke said through gritted teeth.

"Just like you," I said, with my best effort at a guileless grin. It was good enough for Annalise, who clasped her hands together and said, "Oh, how wonderful! That's it, Liam, you *have* to join us next weekend."

"You sure you want to give up a weekend home alone, buddy?" Luke asked. "I thought you already had plans with the gang."

The gang. Like I've made any actual friends since I moved to Maine. "Not really," I said, putting on a wistful tone. "Everyone's on vacation."

"He's a little young to stay all by himself for three days, isn't he?" Annalise asked, a hint of reproach in her voice.

"He's very responsible, and he'll be eighteen . . . soon," Luke said, after making a brief and unsuccessful attempt to remember my birthday. "Plus, you asked for this, didn't you, Liam? Some time on your own?"

I did not. Normally, I'd be thrilled about it, but the fact that Luke is trying to keep me away from Bixby makes me want to go even more.

"Yeah, it's just . . . it gets so lonely in the apartment sometimes," I said, letting my eyes drop to the ground. "I try to stay busy, but . . ."

That did it for Annalise. "You're coming with us," she said firmly. "You'll love the compound, and you can keep my nephew Augustus company. He's seventeen too, and the only teenager in the family. He gets terribly bored at these things."

"Sounds great," I said, even though I doubted that anybody named Augustus Sutherland would want to hang out with me. I felt a quick, vicious stab of satisfaction that I'd gotten the upper hand over Luke . . . until it occurred to me that I'd done it by acting just like him.

Now we've been alone in the car for nearly three hours, on our way from Portland to Bixby, and I keep fixating on a single unwelcome thought: *Is this who I am now?*

Lately I can't feel anything but contempt, and my only hobby is alternately messing with and mimicking my father. Putting on a show for Annalise felt like second nature, and I did it because I'd decided to crash a weekend I would've run screaming from a year ago. Because a year ago, I would've had a dozen better things to do.

My mother would hate this. She was a sunny-side-up kind of person, and she'd always encourage me to stay positive when I was having a hard time with something. *Find one thing to feel good about, and focus on that. There's always at least one good thing.*

I study Luke's profile as he drives—so like my own that it's unnerving. It would be nice if we had something in common beyond cheekbones.

"So you really like Annalise, huh?" I have to practically yell over the music, which Luke has kept blasting the entire drive.

"She's a great woman," Luke says shortly.

"What do you like most about her?"

He gives me a sideways look beneath his sunglasses—like, *Since when do you care?*—but says, "Her generosity."

I shouldn't ask, but: "Is that what you liked about . . ."

Nope. I was going to say *Mom,* but I can't do it. I can't bring her into this, and I don't really want to hear his answer. My mother was generous, too, but Luke isn't talking about the kind of person who'd give you the shirt off their back. He means the kind of person who can pay your bills at Gucci, or whatever designer store sold him those too-tight pants.

"Your last girlfriend?" I finish.

Luke lets out a light snort. "Annalise is entirely unique."

"Are you excited about meeting her family?" I'm genuinely curious about that one. From what I've read about Annalise's father over the past couple of weeks, he's the kind of savvy self-made guy who's probably met a hundred Lukes in his lifetime.

"It's pretty around here, isn't it?" Luke asks, craning his neck as he turns down the music. It's a blatant attempt at changing the conversation, and I guess I don't mind. Peering into my father's brain isn't my favorite pastime.

"Yeah, it's great," I say as he takes a sharp turn along a curving road.

"What do we have here?" Luke asks when we've rounded the corner and a car comes into view. It's parked on the side of the road, and a woman is crouching beside the rear tire. He slows to a crawl and says, "A damsel in distress. Lucky for her that we came along."

Maybe *this* is a positive? That he wants to help someone, even if it's in a cringey knight-in-shining-armor kind of way? Or be seen as helpful. Either way, at least he stopped.

Then the woman hauls the tire off its rim with practiced ease. "I don't think she's in distress," I say as she glances our way.

She's perfectly visible in the bright sunshine, and I can feel my jaw unhinge as I take in the familiar lines of her face. Holy shit, I *know* this person. I know her from a Polaroid where she's standing between Luke and an Elvis impersonator, wearing a blue sundress and holding a skimpy bouquet of wilted flowers that look like they were plucked from a half dozen vases in a cheap restaurant. Because they were, by Luke.

It's Jamie Quinn. My forty-eight-hour Las Vegas step-mother, changing a tire on the side of a deserted road in Bixby, Maine. I blink a few times, just in case she's a mirage, but nothing changes. It's really her. What the hell are the chances?

"You're right," Luke says with a hard edge to his voice that makes it clear he's recognized her, too. "She doesn't need our help."

He taps the gas pedal and speeds up, preparing to pass. As Jamie stands and heads for her trunk, I can hear my mother's voice as clear as a bell in my head.

Yes, she does.

Before I even realize I'm doing it, I grab the hand brake and yank it as hard as I can, bringing the car to a screeching halt.

"What the *hell*?" Luke yells as we both rattle in our seats. "Jesus, Liam, are you out of your mind? Why did you do that?"

"To double-check," I say, unclipping my seat belt and opening the door before he can release the brake and drive away. "Just in case."

"She's fine. Get back in the car," Luke hisses as I exit. "Liam! I'm not kidding. Get. Back. In. The. *Car.*"

I ignore him and step onto the road's shoulder. I'm a lot closer to Jamie now as she watches my approach, her expression quizzical. Close enough to realize that there's no way this is Jamie; she's much too young. Around my age, which means it has to be her daughter, Kat. Who either hasn't seen the Elvis photo or doesn't think I look as much like Luke as everyone else does, because there's not a hint of recognition on her face.

"Thanks for stopping, but I don't need help," she says, pushing back a wisp of dark hair that's fallen out of her pony-tail. Her hazel eyes are as clear and bright—and as wary—as

54

I remember from twelve years ago. Even at four, she always looked like she was waiting for something bad to happen.

"Yeah, I noticed," I say.

Then I pause, because . . . what else is there to say? This is beyond surreal. Luke honks loudly, and I can see a woman turn around in the driver's seat of Kat's car. Is that Jamie? Are we seriously having a roadside Vegas reunion that nobody except me asked for? And the ghost of my mom's voice, but . . . God. This is ridiculous. I couldn't help Kat even if she needed it; I have no clue how to change a tire.

"I'll be done in a sec. You don't have to keep your ride waiting," Kat says, shading her eyes with her hands. She's wearing a black tank top and well-worn jeans, the knees dusty from where she was just kneeling on the ground. Luke honks again, and she shoots me a wry grin. "Seems like he wants to get a move on."

"Right. It's just . . ."

She cocks her head, waiting, until I shrug. It's just *nothing*. I should go. I'm nobody to Kat, or to Jamie, and probably the worst thing I could do for either of them is drag Luke Rooney back into their lives. Even briefly, in an awkward *Lol, what are the odds?* kind of way.

I lift one hand in a half-hearted wave, and then . . . a lot of things happen at once. There's the squeal of brakes as a truck rounds the bend behind us—a truck that clearly wasn't expecting anyone to be stopped in the road, because it's moving fast and has to veer sharply to avoid hitting Luke's car. Kat turns at the commotion as something flies off the back of the truck, heading straight for her.

All of a sudden, it's like I'm back in that Las Vegas hotel

room from twelve years ago, getting an order that I feel compelled to follow even when I know it's impossible.

Look out for your sister.

"Duck!" I yell, sprinting toward Kat.

She drops to the ground with impressive speed before I can reach her. And then, something slams into my forehead and explodes, covering my face in a wet, slimy mess. Even though I shut my eyes instinctively before contact, whatever hit me seeps into them enough to sting. My heart is racing, my temple feels like one giant bruise, and I can't catch my breath.

God, this crap in my eyes is making them hurt like hell. Is it acid? It must be acid. That was an acid-wielding truck that just flung its toxic cargo directly into my pupils.

This is your own fault, Liam, I think as I sink to my knees. *You're about to go blind because you couldn't mind your damn business.*

"Oh no!" Kat cries out. A hand grasps my arm. "Shit, you're bleeding. We have to get you to a hospital. You're covered in blood—"

"No, he isn't." A calm voice speaks over Kat's, and the next thing I know some kind of cloth is gently wiping at my forehead and cheeks, then around my still-closed eyes. "That's not blood," the woman tending to me says. She pours something cool over my face before adding, "This brave young man just saved you from a flying tomato, Kat."

CHAPTER EIGHT

Kat

Oh, thank God. This nice, awkward boy probably won't die.

"Open your eyes, okay? Let's rinse them out," Jamie says gently. The boy squints up at her, his face contorted and spattered with what I now realize is tomato pulp. Jamie carefully pours small amounts of water over him, mopping up each application with a towel from our trunk, until his terrified expression relaxes. Jamie is in her element now; caretaking comes easily to her. In a different life, she would've made a great nurse.

"Thanks," he croaks, blinking furiously. Then he opens his eyes fully, lets them roll around for a few seconds, and sighs, "Everything is beautiful, and I can see all of it."

"Do you think he has a concussion?" I ask Jamie as she screws the cap back on her water.

Now that the sun is out of my eyes and the tomato is off his face, I can see that the boy lying beside me is really cute—

auburn-haired and blue-eyed, with the kind of dimples you can see even when he's not fully smiling. Like me, he's wearing jeans even though it's a little too hot for them, along with a faded green T-shirt that reads TOWSON LACROSSE.

Jamie's lips quirk. "I think he's just—"

And then, as she turns back to the boy, she goes suddenly and utterly rigid. "Oh my God," she whispers, sitting back on her heels. I've never seen my mother look this stunned; every bit of color drains from her cheeks, and her eyes are huge as they move across the boy's now-clean face. "You're . . . You look just like . . . But you can't possibly be . . ."

The boy clears his throat and says, "No, yeah, sorry. I am."

"You're what?" I demand, gazing between them. When neither answers, I twist around to peer at the man driving the other car. He still hasn't gotten out, and all I can see of him are oversized sunglasses. "Do we know you? Both of you? Either of you?"

Jamie acts like she didn't hear me, staring intently at the boy as he hauls himself into a sitting position. "Liam?" she says softly, clutching the damp, stained towel that she used to wipe his face tightly between both hands. "Is that really you?"

My heart drops straight into my stomach and executes a slow flip. *Liam?* I know that name. We don't speak that name, though, and we especially don't speak that *other* name—

"What am I even saying? Of course it's you," Jamie says before the boy can answer. "You look exactly like him."

"Like who?" I ask. Even though I already know.

As though we're on some sort of timer, we all swivel our heads toward the parked car. Then we scramble to our feet, one after the other, as the driver's-side door finally opens. "Speak of the devil," Liam says weakly.

I've never known what Luke Rooney looks like. Jamie didn't keep any photos from that Vegas weekend, and out of solidarity, I haven't Googled him. Not even once. Which now seems like a massive oversight as the man himself steps out of the car and pulls off his sunglasses, looking like a decades-older mirror image of the boy beside me.

Luke Fucking Rooney. Twelve years ago, after Jamie left my father and started a new life for us in Nevada, she won five thousand dollars on a scratch ticket. She thought it was a sign that her luck had changed, and went to Vegas in the hopes of turning it into a down payment on a home. Instead, she lost everything, overindulged in free cocktails, and married the first guy she met by the pool. The next day, when she was hungover and went to buy Tylenol, Luke took off and left Liam and me alone.

That disaster of a weekend is Jamie's most shameful moment, especially because she thinks she should've known better. Should've used the small windfall more wisely, should've stayed focused on me, and should've recognized relationship red flags after living with my father. Luke, however, was a different kind of asshole.

"Weird, huh?" Liam says, turning toward me. "You and I are both exact replicas of our parents. I recognized you right away, except I thought you were Jamie." There's an ease to the way he says her name, like he doesn't harbor any of the utter disdain I feel for Luke.

"You were five," I say. "How do you remember?"

It's hardly the most important question to ask right now, but I can't think of any others while Luke Rooney—*Luke Fucking Rooney*—is walking toward us in what feels like endless slow motion. Suit jacket flapping in the light breeze, shiny shoes crunching on the gravel-strewn road, every step slightly hobbled by the fact that his pants are ridiculously tight.

Seriously, what grown man wears pants that tight?

"The wedding picture. With Elvis?"

I just blink at him, and Liam mumbles, "Yeah, you two probably didn't hang on to a copy. That's fair. That totally tracks."

"Jamie. Hello," Luke says when he's a few feet away. The road is back to being deserted now that the produce truck has disappeared. Jamie swallows but doesn't say a word; she's staring at Luke like he's a dangerous predator that might slink away if she stays quiet enough. "What an odd coincidence. How've you been?"

Not *How's my son?* Not *Hey, Liam, you okay after that tomato attack? Looked brutal from the car where I was sitting and not helping at all.* "Liam is fine. Nice of you to ask," I snap before Jamie can answer.

"And hello to you too, Kat," Luke says. He's annoyingly handsome, with the kind of bone structure you'd see in the *after* photos lining a plastic surgeon's office. But somehow, the features that look open and honest on Liam come off as smarmy on Luke. "I can see you haven't changed a bit."

"You can fuck right off, Luke Rooney," I say with relish. I didn't fully realize it until this very second, but I've been waiting *years* to say that.

"Katrina," Jamie sighs, but not with the warning tone that

she usually applies to my full name. Meanwhile, Luke polishes his sunglasses on the hem of his jacket while murmuring "Not one little bit," seemingly to himself.

Jamie presses both hands to her still-pale cheeks. "This is unreal," she says, her gaze darting between Liam and Luke. "I can't . . . You're not . . . What are you *doing* here?"

"Just a little family vacation," Luke says, hiding his eyes once again behind sunglasses. His voice is rich and smooth, but I don't miss the strain beneath it. He's as rattled as Jamie, but better at hiding it. "We saw you were having car trouble and wanted to help, but you clearly have everything in hand, so . . . Let's get back on the road, shall we, Liam?"

"Family vacation in *Bixby*?" I ask skeptically. "Really? There's nothing here except woods and a billionaire's compound."

"That's where we're going," Liam says, right as Luke practically yells "Time to go!" and starts speed-walking backward toward his car.

"Wait, for real? You know the Sutherlands?" I turn to Liam as Jamie puts a hand to her temple and mumbles, "This isn't happening. This *cannot* be happening."

Liam's eyes meet mine. "Yeah, Luke is, uh, kinda seeing—"

"Liam, there's no need to discuss personal business with old acquaintances who we'll never see again," Luke says, still backpedaling.

"You *will* see her," I say. "Jamie is working there this weekend."

"*Shut it,*" Jamie hisses as Luke stops in his tracks.

"Oh," he says. Both his expression and tone are unreadable; he might as well be a mannequin standing by the side of the road. "Well."

Then nobody says anything for what feels like a very long time, until Liam starts making an odd strangled noise. It takes a few seconds for me to realize that he's trying not to laugh, but once I do, it's contagious. I have to choke my own laughter back, which makes Liam's spill out, until we're both clutching our sides and trying not to fall over.

"This isn't funny," Luke snaps. And I know he's right—honestly, it's probably disastrous, given what Jamie is here to do—but somehow, the peeved expression on his face only makes me laugh harder. It's a stress response, and I have *no* control.

"Listen, Luke. You and I don't know one another, okay?" Jamie says in a low, urgent voice as Liam and I both continue to wheeze. "Let's just do our own thing this weekend and keep our distance, as if we've never met."

"Absolutely," Luke says quickly. "I couldn't agree more."

"Good," Jamie says. I finally get control of myself as she turns to me and adds, "I'm going to finish changing the tire, Kat, and then we'll be on our way."

"Okay." I wipe my eyes as she stalks off, hoping she knows my quick agreement means I'm sorry about the laughing-so-hard-I'm-crying portion of the day.

Luke spins on his shiny heel and starts walking toward his car, calling, "Let's go, Liam!" over his shoulder.

Liam rubs the back of his neck and says, "I guess I better get moving."

"Yeah, me too," I say. "Good luck with, uh . . ." I wave a hand in Luke's direction. "You know. All that."

"I'll need it," he says grimly.

I turn to follow Jamie, but before I've gone more than a step, Liam says in a loud whisper, "Kat. One more thing."

"Yeah?"

His blue eyes are a lot kinder than Luke's when he leans forward and says, "I'm 'Liam Rooney' with five *y*'s on Instagram, if you ever wanna say hi."

CHAPTER NINE

Kat

"Damn," I say, dropping my bag on the floor as we step inside the apartment where we'll be staying for the weekend. "All this for a bunch of temp workers? It's so nice!"

I spin in a circle, arms wide, but Jamie doesn't even crack a smile. "It's fine," she says tersely, shutting the door before whipping out her phone.

The Sutherland "staff quarters" are in a neat multistory brownstone across the street from the compound's main entrance. Jamie says it was an actual apartment building once, before Ross Sutherland bought it for his personal use. I'm sure he didn't like the idea of a bunch of middle-class renters living a stone's throw from his estate.

Still, I have to hand it to him: he keeps the place up. The lobby downstairs looked freshly painted, and so does every inch of this space. The ceilings are high, the arched windows are accented with gauzy white curtains, and the floors are gleaming hardwood. Everything is clean and modern, from the blond wood furniture to the sculptural-looking light fixtures. There's a kitchenette to the right of the door and a sitting area to the left, framed by a balcony that overlooks the woods behind us. The small hallway directly in front of me leads to a bedroom—with a single twin bed, so it looks like I'll be sleeping on the couch—and a bathroom with an oversized shower that's fully stocked with shampoo, conditioner, and bodywash.

I pick up the shampoo and inhale a heavenly citrus scent. "Jamie, what's Molton Brown?" I call. "Is it fancy?"

When she doesn't answer, I reluctantly replace the bottle and return to the living area. Jamie is pacing up a storm, her phone pressed to one ear. "Come on, Gem, pick up," she says urgently. "Pick up!"

"It'll be fine," I say, lining her snacks up beside the kitchenette sink. Maybe the familiarity will be comforting. "Luke will keep his distance."

"It doesn't matter. He knows who I am. I can't *believe* this," Jamie fumes, her voice rising as her strides lengthen. "What are the chances? Why do I have the worst luck in the entire universe? This was supposed to be *it*. Everything was set, and now—" She lowers her phone and glares at the screen. "No, I don't want to leave a message!" Then she drops into one of the kitchen chairs and buries her face in her hands.

"What are you going to do?" I ask tentatively. The leather case holding Gem's fake necklace is sitting on the table, and I undo the clasp with a backward glance toward Jamie. She's paying no attention to me, so I open it fully and look inside. Rubies and gold gleam against a black velvet background, so lustrous that it's hard to believe they aren't real.

"I'm supposed to be in a staff meeting at the compound in half an hour," Jamie says, her voice muffled. "But now . . . I don't know. I'll try to reach Morgan, and then wait for Gem to call me back, I guess."

"Are you going to tell her *I'm* here?"

"Oh God, right. *That.*" Jamie's shoulders slump even lower. "I just . . . I don't even know. Maybe not. She's going to be mad enough as it is." She raises her head and adds, "I need a few minutes to decompress before talking to her. Why don't you take a walk?"

I hesitate. The woods behind us look pretty, and I wouldn't mind stretching my legs. That's not exactly sticking together, though, and Jamie isn't thinking clearly if she's already violating her own *No one can see you* rule. But I know my mother well enough to realize she's desperate for some alone time. "Okay," I say. "I won't be gone long."

"Take your time," Jamie says wearily.

I grab my sunglasses and my phone, and slip out the door. I've barely gone two steps when I hear another door opening, and I quickly duck into the shadows of a nearby alcove. A man with slicked-back red hair emerges from the apartment across from ours, holding what looks like a whiskey bottle in one hand and a stack of Solo cups in the other. Then he crosses to our door and knocks. "Hello!" he calls. "Is anyone there?"

Jamie, not surprisingly, doesn't respond. My pulse picks up as I watch him knock again. Who is this guy? Did he hear us? Is he a friend of Luke's, or—

"I'm busy!" Jamie yells after the third knock.

"My apologies!" the man says theatrically before pivoting to the door next to us and knocking on it. "Hello! Is anyone—"

The door swings open before he can finish, framing a small short-haired woman. She peers suspiciously at the red-haired man as he says, "Hi there. I'm Jermaine, from across the hall. Unofficial welcoming committee."

"Vicky," she says. But it sounds like what she's really saying is *Go away*.

Undaunted, Jermaine holds up the whiskey bottle like a toast. "Can I offer you a drink?"

Vicky frowns. "It's ten-thirty in the morning."

"Time is just a social construct," Jermaine says smoothly.

I slip farther down the hallway and into the stairwell, taking care to keep my footsteps silent. Once I'm outside, I follow a well-worn path into the woods behind the building, my thoughts churning. Jamie's freaked, and for good reason. Luke Rooney's presence at the Sutherland compound this weekend could blow up everything. And if Jamie backs out, then what? Will Gem give her another chance, or will she be angry that the job she spent so much time and effort setting up came to nothing?

The key question is: What will Luke do? Why is he here? If I could get to the bottom of that, then maybe I could give Jamie the reassurance she needs to keep going. There's no doubt in my mind that Luke is shady as hell; chances are, he doesn't want to reveal his connection with Jamie any more than she does. Maybe the weekend can be salvaged after all, but there's no way to be sure without knowing more about what Luke's up to.

I pull out my phone, open Instagram, and type *Liam Rooneyyyyy* into the search bar. His profile pops up instantly; it's public, and filled with a handful of photos. Most are of

Liam with what looks like friends his age, and a few are with a smiling middle-aged woman. They're all old, though—the last one was posted eight months ago. Still, if he gave me the name, he must at least check notifications, right?

I tap the message button and type, *Hi.*

CHAPTER TEN

Liam

"You're a really good listener," I tell Kat as we walk past the wildflower fields that line the outer limits of the Sutherland estate.

Traipsing through a billionaire's compound with my Vegas stepsister wasn't on my bingo card for the weekend, but it's strangely comfortable. Maybe because I've been desperate to unburden myself about what living with Luke is like, and Kat Quinn—despite the fact that we barely know one another—might be the only person in the world who could understand.

"I'm so sorry about your mom," she says, shoving her hands into the pockets of her jeans. "She sounds great."

"She was," I say.

"What would you be doing now if you were at home?" Kat asks. "How would you and your mom spend a beautiful weekend like this?"

I like the way she asks that—calm and straightforward.

Somehow, it makes it easier to talk about how life used to be. "Probably having a crab feast," I say. Kat raises her eyebrows in an unspoken question, and I add, "It's a Maryland summer thing. You get a bunch of crabs, put them on a picnic table, cover them with Old Bay seasoning, and smash them open with mallets. Well, that last part is optional. You could also just use your hands."

Kat grins. "If you ever invite me to one, I'll insist on a mallet."

"Someday, I will." I kick at a clump of grass, wondering if I'll make it back to Maryland anytime soon, before adding, "I'd probably be getting ready for lacrosse camp, too."

"Aha," Kat says, gesturing to my T-shirt. "So that's not just a fashion statement. You're an actual lacrosse bro?"

I roll my eyes. "I *play* lacrosse. Do I strike you as the bro type?"

"Not really," she admits.

"What about you? Do you play any sports?"

"Sort of," Kat says.

"How do you *sort of* play a sport?"

"Well, I like running," Kat says. "So sometimes I join the track team at school, but . . . Jamie and I move around a lot. You know, for work and stuff. So it's not always worth the trouble to get involved in anything official."

"Is that hard?" I ask. "Moving a lot?"

"No," Kat says breezily. "I'm used to it." She gazes around us and adds, "It's really pretty here. What's the rest of the compound like?"

"A prison. But a nice one," I say, only half joking.

When we arrived, Luke had to give his name and license to a security guard in order to get through the gates that surround the main area—the family's homes, offices, and what Luke called the "entertainment complex." I immediately pictured an arcade with video games and bowling, but the reality is more ballrooms and gardens. I'd planned to leave the same way when I told Luke that I was going for a run. But Annalise produced a slim key card, and told me I could take a much prettier path through an unmanned gate that led to the wildflower fields.

"This will get you in and out," she said, adding to Luke, "I'll have to get an extra for you to use while you're here."

I almost yelled *Don't do it,* because Luke was practically salivating at the idea. But it felt like a different kind of eagerness for him, like he was more excited about becoming a Sutherland insider than anything else.

"They can lock me up anytime," Kat says. Then she stops abruptly and holds out her arm, adding "I don't think we want to go any farther."

I'm briefly confused, until I realize that I haven't been paying attention to the fact that the trees in front of us look different. It's because we can only see the tops; we're at the edge of a plunging ravine. I take a few more steps forward to glance into it, and immediately get dizzy. "Good call," I say as we start to backtrack.

Kat's quiet for a few beats, until she tentatively asks, "So, does Annalise know that Luke and Jamie used to be married?"

"God, no," I say. "He'd never tell her something like that."

Kat adjusts her oversized sunglasses, which make it hard to read her expression. "Are you sure?" she says. "Because Jamie really needs this job, and she needs her boss to know that she's a steady, reliable kind of person. If things get messy with Luke—"

"They won't," I say. "He started lecturing me about keeping my mouth shut as soon as I got back in the car. Trust me, getting married and divorced within forty-eight hours and losing a couple of kids in the process doesn't fit the image he's trying to project. He'd kill me if he knew I was talking to you now. He thinks I went for a run."

Kat exhales and says, "Okay. That's a relief."

It's nice, the way she's trying to look out for her mom. "Luke didn't even want to help you guys with the tire," I say. "Not that you needed it."

"Why'd you stop, then?" Kat asks.

I hesitate, not sure if I'm comfortable enough with her to tell the truth. But then again, this is the first conversation I've had in months where I wasn't just going through the motions. It's such a relief to feel normal that I find myself saying, "It's going to sound weird."

"Excellent," Kat says brightly. "I love weird."

"I thought it was what my mom would want," I say. "I could actually hear her voice in my head, saying that you needed help, so . . . I pulled the hand brake."

"I don't think that's weird at all," Kat says. "I think people stay with us after they're gone in lots of different ways. It's what she would've done, right? Even though I never got the chance to meet her, I can already tell you two were a lot alike."

"I hope so," I say. It's a little hard to talk around the sudden lump in my throat. "She used to worry about you, you know. If you were okay after what happened in Vegas. Being lost for so long . . . it messed me up for a while." I'm too embarrassed

72

to give more detail than that, but I was twelve before I could set foot inside a hotel without breaking into a cold sweat. "We used to wonder if it was the same for you."

"No," Kat says. I huff in disbelief, and she adds, "I know it sounds strange, but it felt kind of like an adventure. I never felt . . . unsafe."

"Well, that's good," I say. "Luke told me . . ." I squint as the sun pops out from behind a cloud. "Before he took off that day in Vegas, he said, 'Look out for your sister.' And obviously you're not my actual sister, and as a general rule I don't listen to anything Luke says, but . . . in a weird way, that stayed with me."

"Is that why you took a tomato in the face for me?" Kat asks, her voice amused.

I rub my still-tender forehead. "Maybe."

"Much appreciated, by the way."

"Anytime."

"You know, it's interesting," she says thoughtfully, pushing her sunglasses into her hair as she glances my way. "Objectively, you're very good-looking. But I'm not the slightest bit attracted to you."

"All right," I mutter, feeling mildly insulted even though I'm glad to hear it. "Thank you for sharing that unsolicited feedback."

"Are you attracted to me?"

Wow, she's disconcertingly blunt. Not to mention off base. "No," I say. "Not at all."

"Are you just saying that because I said it first?" she asks, giving my arm a consoling pat. "It's okay if you are."

She's not getting it, so . . . "I like guys, Kat," I say, shrugging.

"Ah," she says. "Okay, well, my point stands for me, anyway. Even though I thought you were cute right away, I also thought there was something almost *brotherly* about you. So I get what you're saying. In a deeply nonfunctional way, we're the closest thing to siblings that either one of us is ever going to have, right?" She bumps my shoulder with hers. "Unless Jamie stops being a nun, or Luke manages to con Annalise into having kids with him."

"God forbid," I say with a shudder.

"There's a certain kind of bond that got imprinted on us at a young age in an extreme situation, and . . . maybe it stuck," Kat says. "You're right—it's weird. But it could be worse."

We share a grin, but it's interrupted by someone shouting my name. "Shit," Kat says, looking around wildly for the source. "Is that Luke?"

I catch sight of a figure moving toward us, close enough for me to tell that it's not my father. "No," I say. "I have no idea who that is."

"Liam!" the guy calls again. He stops and waves, then cups his hands over his mouth and shouts, "Annalise sent me."

"Ohhh. Right." I lift a hand, and he starts walking toward us again. "That must be Annalise's nephew, Augustus," I say. "She's got this idea that—"

"Augustus *Sutherland*?" Kat asks, lowering her sunglasses back onto her face. "I need to go. I'm not supposed to be here, so . . . you don't know me, all right? If he asks, I'm just some random jogger you bumped into."

I give her a once-over as she starts backing away. "You expect him to believe you went jogging in jeans?" I ask.

"Well, come up with something better, then," Kat hisses.

74

"But do *not* give my name. Or Jamie's, or . . . anything, okay? Promise me."

"I promise," I say. "Relax. I'm not—"

Before I can finish, though, she's sprinting for the edge of the woods. And she's fast; within a few seconds, she's disappeared behind a rolling hill. "Nice talking to you, too," I murmur to myself.

I'm not even being sarcastic, though. It *was* nice talking to her. I feel lighter, like some of the gloom that's been weighing me down for months just slipped off my shoulders. Maybe this weekend doesn't have to be a soulless exercise in thwarting my father; maybe I can actually figure out a way to enjoy myself. And Kat and I have exchanged numbers, so . . . who knows. Boston isn't all that far from Portland, and I've never been there. If she's willing to show me around, that could be something to look forward to.

I turn back toward Augustus, who's taking his time strolling across the meadow. He's tall and lean, his hair a golden tangle of half curls, and he's wearing a white-shirt, white-pant combo that makes him look like a guest at a beach wedding. When he reaches me, he grimaces and says, "That was entirely more exercise than anyone should have in a single day. Can't imagine why you'd do it by choice. I'm Augustus, by the way."

He licks his lips, and . . . Huh. I'm shaking off my apathy in all kinds of ways today, because I track the motion with a little too much interest. Even though he's not my usual type, there's something compelling about his sharp cheekbones and piercing blue-gray eyes. "Aunt Annalise asked me to make sure you hadn't gotten lost running around here," he adds. "Where'd your friend go?"

"My what?" I ask, glancing over my shoulder to where Kat disappeared. "Oh, you mean that girl? She was just, um, going for a walk and we ran into one another."

Come up with something better, Kat said. Mission not accomplished.

Augustus raises his eyebrows. "One doesn't simply 'go for a walk' on the Sutherland compound," he says in an affronted tone. "Is she aware that this is private property?"

"Guess not," I say. That little flicker of attraction vanishes, and my good mood, already fragile, plummets at the thought of being stuck with this guy all weekend. Of course I'm not going to get along with someone who looks like the Google search result for *rich boy.*

Then Augustus bursts into laughter. "Jesus, your *face.* Kidding. I couldn't care less." He flops onto the ground, which is probably a death sentence by grass stain for his all-white ensemble, and adds, "Welcome to Bixby. You meet the old man yet?"

I assume he means Ross Sutherland. "I haven't met anyone except Annalise," I say.

"My favorite aunt by a wide margin," Augustus says. I'm not sure, but I think he might mean it.

"She's great," I agree.

Augustus plucks a handful of grass. "Unfortunately, it's all downhill from there," he says wryly, sifting the blades through his fingers. "My aunt Larissa is the biggest snob in our family, which is really saying something. She'll talk your ear off if you let her, which you shouldn't—unless you enjoy discussing how impossible it is to get good help nowadays?" He drops the last blade of grass with an inquiring look.

"Uh, no," I say.

"Uncle Parker is easier to deal with. If you're not a venture capitalist with pockets deep enough to fund one of his terrible business ideas, he'll generally leave you alone."

Augustus has an interesting not-quite accent; he's definitely American, but he doesn't sound like anyone I know. Maybe this is how prep school kids talk, or maybe he's just more formal than I'm used to. Either way it's kind of distracting, although not in a bad way.

He's waiting for a response, but I can't think of anything to say except, "Huh."

"Whatever you do, don't play poker with him."

That feels like the kind of statement with a story behind it, so I wait for more context. When none comes, I say, "Wasn't planning on it."

"Good. You might survive the weekend yet."

So far, Augustus has only mentioned his aunts and uncle. When Annalise first told me about him, she said that his parents are divorced and his mom is spending the summer in Italy with a new boyfriend. *Augustus will probably drive up from New York with his dad, unless . . .* She flushed a little before adding *Unless Griffin's not feeling well.*

Later, when Luke and I were home alone, he told me that Augustus's father, Griffin, the oldest Sutherland sibling, has been in and out of rehab since his mother died. *Not feeling well* is Sutherland family code for a relapse.

I'm not sure if it's bad form to ask Augustus if his father is here, and before I can decide, he skips right over him. "My grandfather is a whole other deal," he says, stretching his legs out. "I can't stand the old crank, but I have to admit—he's sharp. He'll x-ray your entire goddamn brain as soon as he meets you, and if he finds something he doesn't like, he'll use it against you in ways mere mortals can't imagine." He shades his eyes as he looks up at me and asks, "Is that going to be a problem for you, Liam?"

"No," I say, barely avoiding a nervous swallow.

"How about your father?"

I hesitate. Should I be honest here? Maybe this is my chance to look out for Annalise, but . . . all of a sudden, there's Kat and Jamie to think about, too. What if exposing Luke sends Ross Sutherland on a deep dive into his past? Annalise's father must have endless resources at his fingertips, and I have no idea what kind of records might still exist, and . . .

And I'm taking much too long to answer. "No," I blurt out.

Augustus's lip curls, and I'm pretty sure he can tell I'm lying. But all he says is "Well, I guess neither of you have anything to worry about, then."

CHAPTER ELEVEN

Kat

It always starts with sand.

Sparkling in the sunlight, beckoning me to play. Forming a soft, welcoming bed for brightly colored toys. But before I can grab a shovel or a pail, it starts to shift. There's something hidden underneath, working its way to the surface. Making hissing, mournful, haunted noises. *This sandbox is haunted,* I think, and start to back away.

But then the screaming starts. And the shouting. And the thudding. I want to leave, but I can't. I'm trapped. It's dark, and I start to whimper, and then—

"Oh my God," someone croaks before violently retching.

I bolt upright on the couch, sweat-drenched and hopelessly tangled in a thin, scratchy blanket. It takes a few seconds to get oriented, and to reassure myself that I'm okay. I'm in Bixby, Maine, and nobody is screaming. That sound was . . .

My mother, vomiting her guts out in the bathroom.

"Jamie?" I push the blanket aside and get unsteadily to my feet. I'm always lightheaded after one of these nightmares. I haven't had one in a while, and I'd almost let myself hope that I was done with them. "Are you okay?"

Her only response is another retch.

"I'll get you some water," I say, running for the kitchenette. The clock on the microwave reads eleven in the morning—much later than I meant to sleep. There's an untouched pot of coffee on the counter—brewed for me, since Jamie doesn't drink it—and a cereal bowl resting on the drying rack beside the sink. I don't know how long Jamie's been up, but it looks as though she managed to start her usual routine.

When I bring a full glass into the bathroom, I find her still dressed in the clothes she slept in: sweatpants, a T-shirt, and her Perry the Platypus hoodie. Her dark hair is loose and lank around her face, and I grab an elastic off the side of the sink to pull it back.

"What time are you supposed to be at work?" I ask.

"Noon," she whimpers.

An hour. We can work with that, right? Maybe she just needs some hydration. "Here," I say, holding the glass to her lips. "Have a drink."

"I can't," she moans.

"Just take a tiny sip," I coax.

She finally does, and manages a couple more before shaking her head when I urge her to keep going. "Let's get you into bed," I say, crouching beside her so I can sling one of her arms over my shoulders and help her to her feet. "Do you think it was something you ate?"

"All I've had is granola."

"Do you feel like you have a fever?"

"No. I'm not sure if it's such a good idea to lie down," she says, head drooping. "I might need to throw up again."

"Oh, it's *definitely* a good idea to lie down," I say, staggering a little beneath her weight. With every step we take, she's doing less of the work. "I'll find you a bucket."

I shuffle her into the bedroom and help her crawl beneath the covers before placing an empty wastebasket by her side. Then I return to the vomit-spattered bathroom, rummage beneath the sink for cleaning supplies, and scrub the entire room until it sparkles. After that I feel gross, so I take a long shower that almost manages to be relaxing thanks to substantial overuse of Molton Brown products.

By the time I go back in the bedroom, wrapped in a thick white towel with my teeth freshly brushed, it's eleven-thirty. "Jamie?" I ask tentatively.

No response. She's asleep.

I stand with my hands on my hips, staring at the clock on the dresser and willing it to move backward. Last night, I thought we were on track. Jamie had gotten newly freaked-out when I told her that Luke is dating the woman whose necklace she's supposed to steal, but then Gem called and talked her down.

Jamie had her on speaker, so I could listen silently beside her. "Don't worry. I put the team on Luke as soon as I got your message," Gem said. *The team* is shorthand for Gem's intelligence team; if there's a speck of dirt to be found in an otherwise pristine existence, they'll dig it up. "Let's just say your ex has had an interesting life since the two of you parted ways. He wouldn't dare rock the boat. If he tries, we'll bury him."

"Okay," Jamie said uncertainly, her eyes flicking toward me. It was clear she wanted to tell Gem about Luke dating Annalise, but then she'd have to explain how she knows that, which would require explaining that I was here, and so far, she'd managed to keep that out of the conversation. "But what about, um . . . should we be concerned with whatever connection he might have to the Sutherland family—"

"The more invested he is in the Sutherlands, the less he's going to want his past to come out," Gem said. I nodded, since that tracked perfectly with what Liam had told me.

Eventually, Jamie calmed down. She was so relieved that I almost stopped feeling bad about extracting information from Liam. Not that he needed much encouragement; he couldn't wait to vent. It still pricks my conscience, though. Sweet Liam, the polar opposite of Luke Rooney, talking about me as his *sister*. I don't think of myself as a softhearted person, but that got to me. Someday I'll make it up to him, because I wasn't lying about everything I told him. I do genuinely feel a connection, and I wish we could've met under better circumstances.

There's no way Jamie is going to make her shift. It's not *the* shift—that's at tonight's party—but if she doesn't show up for lunch, she'll be fired before dinner. I don't know exactly how these things work, but I can't imagine whoever's in charge would just shrug off an absence during such an important weekend. They could even decide to send her home. Either way, all Gem's carefully laid plans would be for nothing.

I almost pull out my phone to call Gem and confess everything—that I'm here, that Luke is dating the person who owns the necklace, and that Jamie is sick—but I can hear her voice in my head as clearly as if she were standing in the room.

You always need a Plan B. What's your Plan B?

Maybe I can fix this. People still mistake Jamie for a teenager—even Liam said how much we look alike—and we're exactly the same size. I can put on her uniform, pull back my hair just like hers was yesterday, and . . .

A miniburst of inspiration hits and I pull my bag off the floor. I dig out Sophie's glasses, still here from my trip to Bennington & Main with Gem. They're the perfect final touch. If anyone thinks I look different, they'll blame it on the glasses.

It'll be a breeze. I know how to wait tables; I did it all last summer. I just need to figure out where to check in, and I should be able to follow the crowd heading over from the staff quarters for that.

If I think about it too long, I'll talk myself out of it, so . . . "Right," I say to a sleeping Jamie, setting Sophie's glasses on top of the dresser. "I can do this. Simple. You just rest, and then you'll take over tonight."

I go into the bathroom and pluck Jamie's makeup bag from the edge of the sink, then head back into the bedroom and position myself in front of the dresser. I pull out everything Jamie uses when she's trying to look professional—ultrafine liquid eyeliner, nude lipstick, and a little too much foundation. Then I pull my hair into her signature messy bun and put on the catering uniform they gave her yesterday. I smooth the collar and look into the mirror with a satisfied nod.

"Perfect," I tell Jamie. "If I didn't know better, I'd think I was you."

Jamie stirs but doesn't wake. My heart squeezes as I put on the Sophie glasses, and uncertainty washes over me again. This shift is only a couple of hours long, so I'm hoping she'll sleep through it, but what if she wakes up feeling just as bad? The least I can do is leave her water and some Tylenol.

I return to the kitchen, fill a glass of water, and place it on the bedside table. Then I dump the rest of Jamie's makeup bag onto the dresser. There's nothing even vaguely medicinal there, so I haul her suitcase out of the bedroom closet and unzip it. As usual, my mother has overpacked, preparing for every conceivable wardrobe requirement even though she's supposed to wear a catering uniform for the entire weekend.

And yet, she forgot Tylenol. Unless she's stuffed it into her backpack. Which is . . . where, exactly?

Despite how compact the apartment is, my search takes a surprisingly long time. It's not until I'm on my hands and knees in the living room that I spot Jamie's backpack hidden underneath the couch. "Right," I mutter, hauling it out. "Protocol." The fake ruby necklace is inside, and Gem's rule number one is *Protect the product.*

I bring the backpack into a spot of sunshine in the middle of the room and start going through the pockets. My heart sinks when I get to the last one; it's too small for a bottle. I poke a couple of fingers inside anyway, hoping to find a travel packet, but all I can feel is something hard and smooth and oddly familiar.

It can't be. Can it?

I suck in a breath as I pull out the Bennington & Main diamond vine ring. The light streaming through the windows makes the diamonds catch fire, and somehow, it feels like being greeted by an old friend. I can't help myself; I slip the ring onto my finger.

"Why are you here?" I murmur, holding out my hand to

admire the sparkle. Is there another part to this weekend that Jamie and Gem didn't tell me about? A buyer for the ring, maybe? If Jamie is fencing this, does that mean she knows the proceeds are supposed to go to my college fund? Is she okay with that?

All valid questions that I don't have time for. If I stay here any longer, I'll be late, and all of this will have been for nothing. I take hold of the ring to twist it off my finger, but it doesn't budge. I tug harder, and . . .

Oh God. Oh no. No no no no no.

The ring won't come off. *It won't come off.*

It's as though my knuckle has suddenly grown to twice its normal size; no matter what I do, I can't move the ring past it. I stick my finger in my mouth, hoping my saliva will act like a lubricant, but if anything, the ring feels even tighter.

"Fuckity fuck!" I groan, trying to push down the panic that's rising in my chest. A desperate glance at the clock over the microwave confirms what I already knew: I have *zero* time. I'm just going to have to wear the damn thing and hope no one notices.

I grab Jamie's badge and key off the table and lunge for the front door, barreling through it so fast that I nearly knock over the woman standing outside in the corridor. It's our neighbor Vicky, wearing a uniform identical to mine and a sour expression.

"Oh, hi," I say breathlessly, shutting the door behind me. "Sorry about that."

"Where's the fire," she says in the kind of monotone people use when they neither expect nor want an answer.

It's too bad Jermaine's not here, because Vicky looks as

though she could use that welcoming committee drink. Or three. What would a normal caterer say in this situation? "Are you working lunch, too?" I ask, locking the door and stuffing the key into my pocket.

"Kitchen prep. Just got back," she says. Then her voice goes up a half octave as she adds, "Holy hell. That's quite the rock you got there."

Her beady eyes are fastened on my right index finger. *Shit.* So much for hoping nobody would notice the ring. It managed to shake Vicky out of her utter disdain for life in less than thirty seconds, and even though I've just met her, I have to believe that's a record.

"Yeah, I, um . . . Listen, I'd love to chat longer, but I'm running late," I say, darting for the staircase. "See you around!"

I hurry down the stairs, twisting the ring on my finger until the gems face my palm and only the platinum vine pattern is visible. Then I force myself to take deep breaths as I pull out my phone. 11:55. This is fine. I'm going to make it to the compound on time, and everything will be fine.

After all, what else could go wrong?

CHAPTER TWELVE

Liam

Annalise looks different in Bixby. Younger, happier, and a lot more casual as she leads Luke and me down a small path surrounded by dense lilac bushes. It's the first time I've ever seen her in pants and sneakers, although something tells me I wouldn't be able to find those mother-of-pearl Nikes at Foot Locker. Annalise is a big jewelry person, I've come to realize, but all she's wearing right now is a simple gold charm bracelet that jangles as she gestures us forward.

"Come on, come on," she says, clasping her hands together as she stops beside a small stone building. "I can't wait for you to see!"

"See what?" Luke asks.

I'm not sure my father has fully settled into Bixby. He can't seem to figure out his wardrobe; all of his designer stuff has been flung onto an armchair, and he changed four times before Annalise knocked on our door this morning. He's finally settled on his tried-and-true oxford shirt and jeans, but he still doesn't seem comfortable.

I'm not either, but I don't mind. There's something almost refreshing about feeling unsettled—like I care enough about what's going to happen next to worry about it.

Annalise beams. "Well, I know this is an incredibly hectic weekend. You boys are out of your element, and you have lots of people to meet still. And I'm sorry, *so* sorry, that you haven't yet had the opportunity to speak with my father. I was hoping to bring him by last night, but then one of his partners showed up early, and there's a potential merger on the line, and—"

"It's fine," Luke breaks in with a strained smile, like he wasn't pacing our suite muttering about that for half of last night. "He's a busy man."

"He is, of course. We all are, but we still have to make time for beauty and reflection, and most important, for *art*. Don't you agree, Liam?"

"Absolutely," I say. It's a relief to be with only her now; last night, we had dinner at her house with her sister, Larissa, who's just as awful as Augustus said. She kept up a running stream of complaints that were so out of touch I would've thought she was trying her hand at satire if Annalise hadn't kept desperately changing the subject.

Augustus was supposed to join us, but he never showed up. "Augustus and Larissa don't always get along," Annalise murmured to me, like she was worried I'd take it personally. I didn't, though. Much.

Annalise takes a deep breath as she grasps the doorknob. "Okay. *Well*," she says, her face bright with anticipation. "You're both artists, and you have such a wonderfully close relationship that I couldn't think of a better way to welcome you to Bixby than . . . this!"

She flings the door open and ushers us inside. We're in a small light-filled room that's nothing but windows on one side, overlooking a lushly flowering garden. The floor is bluestone, and a long table lines one wall, holding dozens of steel canisters filled with tubes and paintbrushes. Two easels are set up side by side facing the windows, and—

Oh. *Oh no.*

"It's a studio!" Annalise says gleefully, grasping my arm in a hug as she pulls me farther into the room. "So that the two of you can create together. Lunch isn't for an hour, so I thought now might be the perfect time for an impromptu father-son artistic session. Luke was awfully coy about what medium you work in, Liam, so I hope it's okay that I got a little of everything?" Her eyes fix anxiously on my face as I stare in frozen horror around the room. "We have acrylic paint, of course, and oil and watercolor to get you started. Just let me know if you'd like something different. The surface on your easel is canvas, but I've got paper in the back room, or composite panels, or . . ."

I don't know half of what those words mean.

"No, it's great," I manage. I can't even look at Luke, who's probably as horrified as I am. The two of us are *fake painters.* I've never used any of this crap, and yet . . . I'm going to have to stand here for the next hour, apparently, and paint with my dad.

Or do we sit? I have no idea.

"Is this okay?" Annalise asks anxiously, releasing my arm. "I know I sprang it on you when you've barely settled in, but—"

"Annalise. This is *wonderful*. I can't imagine anything better," Luke says with so much sincerity that I almost believe him. He cups her face in his hands and pulls her close for a lingering kiss, which gives me the opportunity to wander over to the table and survey the paintbrush selection. It's extensive, and overwhelming, so I just grab a few of the closest ones and hope for the best.

"So thoughtful," I say, filling my free hand with paint tubes. "Thank you, Annalise. I can't wait to get started."

"Should I leave you to it?" she asks when she finally separates from Luke. "I know inspiration doesn't come on command, of course, but I have to admit—I'm curious to see what the two of you create in this space. If you don't mind sharing, of course."

I grab the out like it's a life preserver. "I'm a little protective of my work—"

"I understand," Annalise says in a hushed tone. "Don't you dare feel pressured, Liam. Just have fun with it, okay?"

"Okay," I say, feeling like a heel as I attempt to pop the top off a tube of paint. Which doesn't work, because it's a screw cap.

This hour will never, ever end.

"I'll have coffee sent over in a little while in case you want a break," Annalise says as she exits the room. "Have fun, you two!"

"Oh, we will," Luke says, adjusting his easel.

After that . . . what is there to say? Neither of us wants to be here, and neither of us has an ounce of talent, but we're going to have to fill our—what did Annalise call them? Canvas? Canvases?—anyway. Maybe it'll be fine. Art is subjective, right? I've seen stuff at the Portland Museum of Art that looks like a fifth grader made it.

"This must be a dream come true for you, Liam," Luke murmurs as he gathers supplies.

"Yup," I say succinctly, squirting out a large dollop of paint. It's red and oozes like a wound, which seems fitting for the occasion.

And that's all we say for a while. Luke's sketching instead of painting, and he slashes at his easel like he actually knows what he's doing while I dab uncertainly at my red circle. Once I've spread the paint as far as it will go, I squirt another color beside it. I thought I'd grabbed black, but it's green. I swirl my brush in the center and briefly enjoy the vibrant color, until it smears into the red and everything turns brown. *More green*, I think, aiming the tube again. But now it's unbalanced, so I add another healthy burst of red.

It's almost fun, actually. Kind of a stress reliever. I use alternating brushes to feather out little lines from the giant red and green dots, then step back to survey my work. Should the lines be thinner, maybe? No, thicker. More paint is needed.

I'm so absorbed that I wouldn't have noticed someone knocking on the door without Luke muttering, "Come in." I glance up, and nearly drop my paint-laden brush.

"Coffee service," Augustus Sutherland calls, stepping through the entrance with a silver tray balanced on one hand. He drops it smoothly onto the table beneath the windows, adding, "I hijacked the server so I could apologize for missing dinner last night. The drive from New York wore me out." He lifts his chin toward Luke and adds, "I'm Annalise's nephew,

Augustus, in case that wasn't clear. You must be the infamous Luke."

"I am," Luke says, holding out his hand. There's something reserved about the motion, as though he's not sure his Affable Dad persona will work on Augustus. Or maybe he didn't like the word *infamous*. "Nice to meet you, Augustus. Annalise speaks very highly of you."

"She's too kind," Augustus says, briefly clasping Luke's hand. "And she has terrible judgment." Before I can figure out whether that was a self-burn or a Luke burn—or both—Augustus rubs his palms together and adds, "So, what have the Rooney men created in this hallowed space? I'm dying to see."

Nerves twist my stomach. *He knows.* Augustus knows we're frauds, and unlike Annalise, he won't let us get away with it.

"We've barely gotten started," Luke says, but Augustus waves him off.

"I'm the easiest critic you'll ever meet. Honestly, it all looks the same to me, but let's have a look." And then, before Luke can say another word, Augustus is peering over his shoulder. I keep my eyes on my green circle for what feels like a very long time, wondering if anyone's ever been kicked out of the Sutherland compound for forging their own art.

And then Augustus says, very quietly, "That's lovely."

My head snaps up. *It is?* Before I realize what I'm doing, I've put down my brush and sidled over to Luke's easel. And . . .

Holy shit. Luke's the real deal.

It's a charcoal sketch of Annalise, and it looks incredibly like her. The real magic is in the eyes; somehow, Luke has captured her zest for life with just a few strokes. She looks like she's about to share a wonderful secret; in fact, she looks like she just led two people she cares about into what she hopes will be the studio of their dreams.

Luke's an artist. Up is down, left is right, and I no longer know anything.

"Needs work," Luke mutters, picking up his charcoal.

"Don't let me get in your way," Augustus says in the most respectful tone I've heard him use during our short acquaintance. It's kind of a nice moment, until he adds, "Let's see what you've done, Liam."

My defenses are down; I'm too busy staring at Luke's sketch to realize that Augustus has already made his way to my easel. Luke glances up with a malicious gleam in his eye, and there's nothing I can do but wait for the inevitable train wreck.

"Well," Augustus says, staring at my canvas. "Well, well, well. Look at that. Kind of like Christmas, isn't it?" He squints and adds, "Are those meant to be . . . suns? Or flowers?"

I refuse to look at Luke, but I know he's smirking up a storm and loving my discomfort. Screw him and his actual talent. "They're open to interpretation," I say through gritted teeth as I return to my easel.

"I'm going to go with suns, then," Augustus says. "Christmas suns."

I can't think of anything else to say except, "Needs work."

"Really?" Augustus asks. "I think it's perfect."

"No," I say stubbornly, lunging for my paintbrush. I'm going to ride this train until I die, apparently. "It needs . . ." And then I paint another ray on what I guess is a red sun, except I accidentally grabbed the green paintbrush, so . . . there's that.

"You're right," Augustus says with a sage nod. "*Now* it's perfect. Can I have this?"

I drop my paintbrush like a soldier surrendering his weapon and say, "Sure."

"Fantastic. It's going straight into my room," Augustus says, hoisting the painting carefully in both hands. "Also, I'm supposed to remind you—fifteen minutes till lunch." He lowers his voice to a conspiratorial whisper and adds, "By the way, Liam . . . I passed our table on my way here, and guess what?"

"What?" I ask tiredly. It can't be any worse than what just transpired.

"Your friend from the fields is there," he says. "She's our server."

Okay, maybe it can.

CHAPTER THIRTEEN

Liam

Lunch is in the estate's arboretum, where white-draped tables are set on a wide expanse of manicured lawn that's so green and even that it looks fake. Flowering plants and trees line either side of us, and a cobblestone path leads to a quietly bubbling marble fountain. The silverware gleams, and the crystal glasses sparkle. The entire setup makes Leonardo's look like a shack.

Annalise called this a "small" gathering, but I think our definitions of the word differ. There are hundreds of people milling about, almost all of them casually dressed. The notable exception is an elegant silver-haired man wearing a sharp charcoal suit, who raises his hand as Annalise, Luke, Augustus, and I approach the tables.

"Annalise!" he calls. "Slight change of plans."

"Who's that?" Luke asks, pausing midstep.

"The man behind the curtain," Augustus murmurs, too quietly for anyone but me to hear.

"Oh, that's Clive," Annalise says. "Dad's right-hand man. He's something of a family manager for this kind of event." As he approaches, she adds more loudly, "Hi, Clive. These are the guests I told you about. Luke and Liam, meet Clive Clayborne."

"It's an absolute pleasure," Clive says, flashing his teeth as he grasps Luke's hand and mine in turn. Up close, he has the smoothest skin I've ever seen on someone with so much gray hair. "Welcome to the compound, gentlemen. I hope you're enjoying your stay so far?"

"Very much, thank you," Luke says. "Couldn't be better." That seems like response enough for both of us, so I just nod.

"What's the change in plans?" Annalise asks.

"Shuffling the seating a bit," Clive says. "I just spoke with your father, and he'd like you and Luke to join him at the head table. You'll be on his left, Annalise."

Luke's chest puffs out as Annalise asks, "I thought Griffin was sitting there?"

Clive's smile gets a little tight. "Not anymore."

Annalise's brow furrows. "Well, of course Luke and I would be delighted to join Dad, but Liam barely knows anyone here, so—"

"It's fine. I'm totally fine," I break in before she suggests that I join them. I don't think I'm ready to meet Ross Sutherland yet.

"He knows me," Augustus says with a shrug.

"Marvelous. Liam, I'm going to leave you in Augustus's very capable hands," Clive says before steering Luke and Annalise away.

"Lucky you," Augustus drawls.

My cheeks get warm. Is he flirting or making fun of me? I can't tell, and I shouldn't care, because he's not my type. I'm probably not his, either, in multiple ways.

He's just . . . unsettling, is all.

And he's right; Kat is here. She's standing beside our table dressed in a tailored black shirt and pants, wearing oversized tortoiseshell glasses and holding a pitcher of water. No one else is paying attention to her as they settle into their chairs, so I take the opportunity to stare openly, with my eyebrows raised in a question: *What are you doing here?*

Kat glances around the table before approaching with her pitcher. She leans over my shoulder to fill my glass and whispers, "Jamie's sick. Just go with it."

I nod and watch her move along to Augustus, who leans back in his chair and says, "Hello again. Nice walk yesterday?"

Kat eyes him for a split second before making the correct calculation: if she tries to argue with Augustus that she wasn't there, he'll drag it out endlessly. "Yes. Gorgeous grounds," she says smoothly, reaching for his glass.

He plucks it off the table and hands it to her. "The glasses suit you, by the way," he says, mouth curving in a half smile.

Right. Of course. *That's* his type.

"Thanks," Kat says, pouring the last of her pitcher into his glass. "Be right back."

She leaves, and Larissa Sutherland takes a seat across from me with a bored "Hello again." She's the only nonblond Sutherland I've met so far, with graying brown hair that she wears pulled back into a severe bun. Her pale eyes, overly large in her thin face, flick toward Augustus as she asks, "I thought you were going to join us for dinner last night?"

"I fell asleep," Augustus says, spreading his napkin over his lap.

I was already 90 percent sure that was a lie when he told it to Luke and me in the studio, but now he's not even trying to sound convincing. Larissa doesn't seem to care, though. "And how was Brightwood this year?" she asks.

"Couldn't begin to tell you," Augustus says with the air of someone who's had this conversation many times in the past and has resigned himself to having it many more times in the foreseeable future. "Since I go to Stuyvesant."

I glance at Augustus in surprise. I've heard of Stuyvesant; one of my former classmates used to go there, before her family relocated from New York City to Maryland. It's a public school—in other words, free—which I wouldn't have expected for a Sutherland.

"Still?" Larissa asks. "I thought you were transferring."

"You *suggested* I transfer," he corrects.

Larissa purses her lips. "Always have to buck tradition, don't you?" She focuses on me again and adds, almost accusingly, "Brightwood Prep has been our family's high school alma mater for generations. Every Sutherland has gone there. Until now."

Augustus stirs restlessly beside me as I say, "Stuyvesant is a fantastic school. I know about it, and I've never even been to New York." I almost add that I've never heard of her alma mater, but I've already forgotten the name.

"It's public," she sniffs.

"It's really hard to get into," I say. "One of the most competitive high schools in the country." I'm not sure why I'm

98

defending Augustus's school so hard when I barely know him—except, maybe, that it's the kind of thing I'd do for my friends back home.

"Thanks, but you're wasting your breath," Augustus murmurs. His lips twitch briefly downward, then back up into the smirk I'm starting to get used to. "Aunt Larissa doesn't value anything she can't overpay for."

"What did you say?" she snaps.

"Nothing," Augustus says blandly.

Larissa narrows her eyes at him. "Where is your father?"

Augustus's mouth tightens, but before he can speak, two men settle into the empty chairs beside Larissa. One of them is dark-haired and built like a former football player, and the other is tall, blond, and striking. He looks so much like Augustus that it's no surprise when he unfolds his napkin with a flourish and says, "And how is my least favorite nephew?"

"*Only* nephew would suffice, Uncle Parker. No reason to choose violence every time you see me. Have you met Liam Rooney?"

"I have not," Parker says, extending a hand. "But I've heard great things from Larissa. You and your father are making quite the impression." He smiles as he says it, but it's a cold kind of smile that makes me feel distinctly unwelcome. Parker glances over his shoulder and adds, "Looks like he's in the process of charming the old man as we speak."

I follow his gaze. Luke is seated between Annalise and a wizened old man with sparse white hair and thick-framed black glasses. As I watch, the old man tips his head back and roars with laughter at whatever Luke just said.

So much for Ross Sutherland's amazing powers of perception.

"Maybe Luke will soften him up for you, Uncle Parker," Augustus says.

Parker's nostrils flare. "I don't know what you're talking about. You remember Barrett, don't you?" he says, jerking his head toward the dark-haired man. "My roommate at Princeton," he adds for my benefit.

"Pleasure," Barrett says, barely glancing at me before flashing Larissa a toothy smile. "Larissa, it's been far too long. How's summer treating you?"

"Dreadfully," she sighs. "You wouldn't believe the mess the contractors have made of my place in Gull Cove. It's positively unlivable."

She launches into a litany of complaints about her summer home on some Massachusetts island I've never heard of. Barrett listens attentively and makes sympathetic noises, while Parker yawns and checks his phone. For the first time since he sat down, I find him semirelatable.

I catch Augustus's eye and incline my head toward his uncle. "Why am I not supposed to play poker with him?" I whisper.

"Because he'll cheat," Augustus whispers back. "He gambled away a fortune, and he's constantly trying to get it back."

"He must know I don't have any money, though, right?"

"Doesn't matter. Neither does he."

Well, *that's* interesting. But before I can ask more, Kat returns with a fresh pitcher of water and heads for Parker. She's reaching for his glass when Larissa's hand shoots out and clamps firmly around Kat's wrist.

Oh shit, I think as Kat's eyes go wide. *Does she know Kat's not supposed to be here? Should I say something? What should I say?* "Hey, you're not . . . You can't just grab somebody like that!" I sputter.

"I'm trying to help," Larissa says, twisting a ring on Kat's finger. "Didn't anyone ever tell you, dear? The diamonds face *out.*"

Kat flushes a deep red as Barrett cranes his neck to get a look at her ring. He lets out a low whistle and says, "Damn. Who knew waiting tables was so lucrative?"

"It's fake," Kat says, quickly moving back to our side of the table. "I bought it off a street vendor."

Parker gives her an appraising look. "Best fake I've ever seen," he says.

Kat looks like she wants to crawl beneath the table. I can't blame her; she was probably hoping to stay under the radar while subbing for Jamie, and now everyone is staring at her. And her ring. Which, yeah—wow—it's a stunner.

"Parker! There y'are." A new voice, loud and slurring, rises above the chattering crowd. I turn to see a big man with silvery-blond hair staggering toward our table. His face shows a trace of the Sutherland sharp features, but on him they look soft and bloated. "Been looking for you," the man calls. He stumbles, and has to grab the back of a chair to keep from falling.

Augustus goes rigid beside me as Larissa lets out a light snort. "Really?" she asks, her voice dripping with disdain. "On Dad's birthday? He couldn't control himself for *one* day?"

"Shut up," Augustus says in a low, angry tone.

"Parker!" The man cups his hands around his mouth to amplify his voice, even though he's practically on top of us.

"Hey, Griffin." Parker drops his napkin onto the table and stands. "I'm right here."

So is his son, I think, but Griffin doesn't look at Augustus. His bleary eyes are focused on his brother as he slings an arm around Parker's shoulder. "Parker, let's go," Griffin says. "Get outta here, jus' you an' me. Whaddya say? Like old times."

"Maybe later," Parker says, trying to duck away. "Once you've had a chance to rest. Why don't you head back to your place, and we'll talk after lunch."

"No, *now,*" Griffin says, holding tight. "Got a car waiting an' everything."

The entire arboretum has gone silent, conversation grinding to a halt as guests stare openly at Griffin and Parker. My stomach twists, and I wish I were anywhere but here, watching what should be a private family drama play out in public. I steal a glance at Augustus, who's glaring stone-faced at his plate. Secondhand mortification warms my cheeks; after six months of living with Luke, I know what it's like to be humiliated by a parent. But I also know that when you're in that situation, the last thing you want is attention. Or pity.

"Please, Parker," Griffin says.

I look away from Augustus, shifting my focus to Ross Sutherland's table. Ross is the only person in the arboretum who's not staring; in fact, he's calmly eating a roll as though nothing out of the ordinary is going on. Then he lifts one hand, and all of a sudden, Clive Clayborne is standing next to him. I don't know where he came from; it's like Ross conjured him out of thin air.

Ross doesn't bother looking at him, but when he makes a shooing gesture Clive nods and heads our way. Seconds later, a

102

burly gray-suited guy who looks like he's part of a security team starts trailing behind Clive.

"I'm not leaving, Griffin," Parker says. Despite his pasted-on smile, the tension in his voice is unmistakable. He's as angry as Larissa, just better at hiding it. "I'm going to celebrate Dad's birthday, and *you* are going to sleep this off."

"Parker, no, you gotta lissen—"

Clive reaches them then, smoothly stepping in between Parker and Griffin. "We'll take it from here," Clive says as the gray-suited guy grabs hold of Griffin's arm. Clive moves to Griffin's other side, murmuring in his ear as Griffin continues to protest. But quietly, like he realizes he's already lost whatever argument he's trying to make.

Parker sits back down and carefully replaces his napkin on his lap. There's a moment of strained silence, until Barrett loudly clears his throat and says, "Parker tells me you were in the Maldives recently, Larissa. How was it?"

"Scorching," she replies.

"You picked the wrong time of year for it," Parker says. And they're off, chatting about vacation spots as if Griffin Sutherland was never here.

I turn toward Augustus, who's still glaring at his plate. "Hey, are you—"

"Don't," he says quietly.

"Okay," I say.

Just a single word, but maybe there's something in my tone that lets him know I get it, because he looks up and manages a wry smile.

"Not now, anyway," he says. "We have more important things to discuss."

103

"Like what?" I ask. Whatever it is, I'm going to discuss the hell out of it, because Augustus clearly needs the distraction.

Augustus leans closer to me, his breath tickling my ear as he lowers his voice to a near whisper. "Like why your friend is wearing a ring that costs at least ten grand to serve lunch," he says.

CHAPTER FOURTEEN

Kat

Nothing, and I mean *nothing*, is going as planned.

It's less than two hours until Ross Sutherland's birthday party, and Jamie is still out of commission. She has a raging headache and stomach cramps, and she'll throw up anything that's not water. "I think I have the flu," she whimpers as I lean over the bed to mop her clammy brow with a cool towel.

"Maybe," I say. I'd told her earlier that I'd subbed for her at lunch, but it barely seemed to register. Which is just as well, since I was dreading the inevitable follow-up conversation: *Oh, and by the way, I found the Bennington & Main ring in your backpack, tried it on, couldn't get it off, and wound up getting interrogated by half the Sutherland clan. Some good news, though—they forgot all about me once their older brother made a drunken scene.*

I never should've left the apartment wearing that ring. Once I got back, I managed to loosen it up with dish soap, and now it's safely tucked away in one of my socks. It would have been better, probably, to show up late and bare-handed, but what's done is done. It looks like it was all for nothing anyway, since Jamie is running out of time to recover.

I finish wiping her forehead, and she turns to one side with a deep, pained sigh. "I can't remember how it feels to feel normal," she croaks.

"Maybe you should see someone," I say. "I could find a doctor, or a hospital—"

"God, no," Jamie moans. "No hospitals. You know I hate those."

I do know. The only time Jamie was ever in the hospital, except for my birth, was after the worst day in both our lives. "Yeah, but if you're really sick—"

"It's just the flu, Kat. I'll live. Call Gem and let her know what's going on, okay?" Jamie whispers before closing her eyes. "Tell her I'm sorry. And that I'll make it up to her."

"Are you sure?" I ask. Her only response is a faint nod.

I quietly shut the bedroom door as I leave, and head to the kitchenette to grab my phone. I can't bring myself to call Gem, though. What am I supposed to tell her when she doesn't even know that I'm here?

The apartment feels stifling and oppressive, even though the AC is on. I can't concentrate when it's like this; I need fresh air. *I'll take a walk,* I think. *I'll clear my head, and then I can talk to Gem.* I know it's nothing more than a stalling tactic, but I'm out the door and in the hallway before I can second-guess myself.

Only to run into Vicky, returning to her room. She's holding a Snickers bar in one hand and a Diet Coke in the other, like she just made a snack run from the vending machine downstairs. "Well, if it isn't the bling queen," she drawls, and I suppress a groan.

"Hi again." I wave limply and try to edge past her.

She doesn't move. "You worked lunch, right?" she asks.

I pause, a little surprised that she's bothering to make conversation. "Yeah," I say.

Her eyes glint maliciously. "Was Griffin Sutherland as wasted as everyone says?"

I enjoy a good gossip session as much as the next person, but (a) not with Vicky and (b) not now. "I don't know," I lie. "I was in the kitchen most of the time."

"Well, apparently he was a mess. Got his ass thrown out and everything. Guess money really doesn't buy happiness." Vicky's eyes take on a faraway look as she gazes over my shoulder. "I'd like to give it a try, though."

"Yeah, me too," I say, moving closer to the stairs.

"Where you headed?" she asks.

"Just meeting a friend," I say, pulling out my phone with a dismayed look at a nonexistent text. "And I'm late, so I'd better hurry."

"See ya," Vicky says, before she finally, mercifully, lets me pass.

I make my way down the stairs and outside, to the same wooded path I walked yesterday. I take deep breaths of pine-scented air and let my mind go blank, until I've gotten far enough into the woods that, when I turn around, I can't see the staff quarters anymore.

Now what? Do I have any alternative to calling Gem and coming clean about everything that's gone wrong? Or can I somehow salvage this weekend?

Yesterday, I was still ambivalent about Jamie's new direction in life. I didn't like feeling like a stranger in Spotless before we'd even left it behind for good. But now, with twenty-four hours of lying and scheming under my belt, all I can think is what a relief it would be if I could just, for once, be *normal*. To have re-met Liam as myself, and not the girl I have to be in order to keep my secrets. To be able to laugh at the Sutherlands—because Larissa, at least, is genuinely ridiculous—instead of fearing them. To find a pretty ring in my mother's backpack and imagine that she'd treated herself, instead of wondering when she's going to fence it.

Jamie was right. We need to get out. And we're so, so close.

I hop onto the trunk of a fallen tree and walk it like a balance beam, arms stretched wide as my thoughts swirl. What if . . . What if *I* made the necklace swap? None of the staff noticed that I wasn't Jamie when I subbed for her today. I could do it tonight, too. I know the plan. I know how to find Annalise's house, and I know how to get in. If I can pull it off, Gem would never need to know what happened. Jamie would be angry, sure, but she'd forgive me.

I reach the end of the tree trunk and spin to walk back. It's not the worst plan in the world—except for the part where I accidentally raised my profile ultrahigh at lunch today. I can't rely on being an anonymous background figure anymore; if the Sutherlands see me, they're going to remember me. Still, they'll be busy with their father's birthday party, and there will be hundreds of people to distract them. If nothing else, I could bring the necklace with me and see if the right opportunity presents itself.

It could work. I'll *make* it work.

Instantly, I feel better. Gem was right; you always need a Plan B. Or a Plan C, I guess, since my original Plan B didn't go far enough.

I hop off the log and hurry down the path to the parking lot. The sun is getting low in the sky, and I don't want to have to rush around like I did before lunch. I pick up my pace, practically jogging down the path, and I'm a little out of breath by the time I reach the front entrance. A few people I worked with at lunch are standing beside the door, smoking, and I give them a cheery wave as I pass.

My good mood lasts until I get back to the apartment and step inside. It's like I've walked into an invisible wall—I stop short, nerves tingling as my eyes dart around the room. *Something's different.* I know it instantly, even though I don't know how.

I run for the bedroom and open the door, breathing a sigh of relief when I see Jamie sleeping peacefully. Her suitcase is where I left it, half-open on the floor, and the contents of her makeup bag are still strewn across the dresser top.

I backtrack into the main room and gaze around. All the furniture looks exactly the same. The sliding door onto the balcony is closed and locked. Jamie's food is lined up neatly on the kitchen counter. Her backpack is on the floor where I left it—

The floor. Not returned to its hiding spot under the couch, where I should've put it before I left. It's just sitting there with the front compartment . . .

Unzipped. I didn't leave it that way. I'm sure of it.

I kneel beside the backpack, my heartbeat roaring in my

ears, and look inside. I nearly collapse with relief when I see the leather jewelry case. But when I pull it out, it feels much too light. I fumble with the clasp and lift it open, my hands shaking.

It's empty. The fake necklace is gone.

CHAPTER FIFTEEN

Kat

My stomach drops. For a few seconds, I'm positive that I'm going to be even sicker than Jamie was. Then the nausea passes and I scramble to my feet, racing back to my mother's bedroom. "Jamie!" I hiss, grabbing her shoulder.

"Mmmph," she mutters, pulling the covers over her head.

"Do you have the necklace? Did you put it somewhere?"

My voice trembles like I'm a scared little kid, which is exactly how I feel. And how I'm acting. Even as I repeat the question, I know I'm being ridiculous. Jamie is out cold; there's no way she woke up, noticed that I left her backpack sitting out, and decided to hide the necklace somewhere different. But I search the bed anyway, then her suitcase. I dump out my overnight bag, too, relieved to feel the diamond vine ring still tucked safely into my sock. No necklace, though.

Then I stagger back into the living area, and I see it.

The front door key, hanging on a hook beside the door.

Where I left it when I took off in such a hurry that I forgot to lock up.

"Nooooo," I moan, sinking to my knees. My stomach rolls again, and this time I double over, gagging on nothing. Then I flop onto my side in utter despair.

This is bad. This is very, very bad. I forced my way to Bixby despite Jamie's protests, so smug in my certainty that we needed to *stick together,* when she clearly would have been much, much better on her own. If I hadn't started interfering once Jamie got sick, the door would've stayed locked the entire weekend. Jamie's backpack would still be safely stowed under the couch. There wouldn't have been any chance for someone—

Wait.

I sit up and push a chunk of hair away from my face. Vicky's eyes practically popped out of her head when she saw the diamond ring earlier. She called me "bling queen," and watched me leave the staff quarters to "meet a friend." She probably even noticed I wasn't wearing the ring anymore. She has no idea I'm not here alone. Her words echo in my mind: *Guess money really doesn't buy happiness. I'd like to give it a try, though.*

When I left, Vicky must've tried our door, found it unlocked, and gone inside to look for the ring. Instead, she saw Jamie's backpack sitting on the floor like an invitation. All she had to do was pull a zipper to find what must've looked like an even bigger prize.

A burst of adrenaline propels me to my feet, and within seconds, I'm standing in front of Vicky's door. If she thinks I'll sit back and let her steal from me, she has no idea who she's dealing with. I manage a restrained knock at first, but when there's no response, I start to bang.

"Hey!" I yell. "Open up!" I pause to press my ear to the door, and when I don't hear anything, I bang so hard that the door shakes on its hinges. "Vicky, open up! Now!"

"Relax, babe. If you break that door, you pay for it."

I turn to see Welcoming Committee Jermaine leaning against his doorframe, dressed in his black catering uniform. "Sorry," I say. I'm panting a little, both from panic and exertion, and it's a struggle to sound even halfway normal. "I just really need to talk to her."

"I can see that, but she left for her shift." He steps into the hallway and closes his door, locking it before facing me again. "Which is where I'm headed, and—assuming you're a fellow caterer and not Vicky's heartbroken ex begging for a second chance—you should be, too. All hands on deck for the big event, right?"

To hell with the big event. I couldn't possibly care less at this point. But Jermaine keeps smiling indulgently, waiting for a response, and all I can think to say is "I'm not an ex."

Jermaine smirks. "Then you'd better get your ass in gear, girl, because it's ten minutes till showtime," he says. Then he stuffs his key in his pocket and adds, "Don't be late. A guy who's worked these things for years was three minutes behind schedule for lunch and got canned on the spot."

As he heads for the stairs, I sag against the wall. There's no way I can pull myself together in time, so now I'm going to get fired, too. Which doesn't even matter, because there's no point in posing as Jamie without the necklace. I should have cut my losses and called Gem when I had the chance, because at least then, I had the fake in my possession. At least then, Jamie could've tried another time.

Now we're doomed. Unless . . .

I push away from the wall and place my hand on Vicky's doorknob, giving it an experimental twist. Locked—she's smarter than me. But not, I hope, sneakier than me.

I go back into the apartment, sort through the mess from Jamie's makeup bag until I find a couple of bobby pins, and return to the hallway. I wish Gem were here to guide me, but since she's not, one of her lessons will have to do.

I strip the rubber knobs off one bobby pin with my fingernail, then bend the other at a right angle. I use the two pins as a pick and a lever, carefully moving the pick up and down against the front pin of the lock. And to my surprise, there's a near-instant click. When I try the knob again, the door swings open.

"Thank you, Ross Sutherland," I murmur as I step into Vicky's darkened apartment. "If you had to cheap out on one thing, I'm glad it was the locks."

Vicky's apartment is a mirror image of ours. I search every inch of space from top to bottom: opening cabinets and drawers, sifting through Vicky's suitcase, running my hands between cushions. It takes almost an hour to inspect the entire apartment, and when I'm finally done, there's no doubt.

The necklace isn't here.

Vicky must have learned her lesson from my stupidity and taken it with her to the Sutherland compound. And I can't follow her there, because I'm an hour late for Jamie's shift. If I try, I'll be turned away at the gate.

Credentials revoked. Game over. Jamie—and Gem—will never forgive me.

My nerves are at such a fever pitch that when my phone

buzzes in my pocket, I almost shriek. But it's just Liam, sounding unreasonably normal like always.

Augustus thinks your ring is real. Crazy, right?

Is Jamie okay?

Are you?

He's so bizarrely nice. How are he and Luke even related?

And then one last message: *Do you need anything?*

I stare at my screen, mind churning. I need . . . so many things. I need to find Vicky so I can take back the necklace, but more immediately than that, I need access to the Sutherland compound. I need someone who can get me through the gate without catering credentials, and I *have* that someone.

Plan B didn't work, and neither did Plan C or Plan D. So far, I'm oh for three. But I have a whole alphabet to go through before giving up.

I reread Liam's last message over and over, tapping my phone against my palm until Plan E starts to take shape.

Do you need anything?

Actually . . . , I text back.

CHAPTER SIXTEEN

Kat

Here's the thing, I type to Liam. *The ring I was wearing today? Was real.*

He sends back a bunch of exclamation marks.

Jamie was holding on to it for a friend who's proposing next week, I continue. *While she was sick I tried it on, and like an idiot didn't take it off. While I was working today, I lost it.*

More exclamation marks.

I don't know Liam well enough to tell whether that means he's empathizing or thinks I'm full of crap, but I plow ahead anyway. *Yeah, and Jamie's supervisor took her badge because she's too sick to work, so I can't sub for her and find it.*

That's the foundation of Plan E: a compelling excuse for sneaking into the compound that also covers for the fact that pretty much everyone at lunch, except Liam, knew perfectly well that the diamond ring was real. I think Gem would be proud—if I dared tell her.

A text comes in from Liam: *Do you want me to look for you?*

Finally, actual words. But not the right ones. Of course Liam Rooney would try to kill my plan with kindness.

I reply in a rush: *I don't want to ruin your night! Plus I think it would be too hard to retrace my steps via text. I need to be there. Is there any way you could let me in?*

My phone goes quiet, and I imagine Liam thinking through all the reasons why this is a terrible idea. I've thought of a few on my own, including the fact that tonight's event is ultra-fancy; after all, Annalise Sutherland special-ordered a ball gown for the occasion. If I show up like I'm dressed now, in sneakers and jeans, I'll stick out like a sore thumb. But maybe, if I take advantage of Jamie's chronic overpacking, I can pass for a guest.

I'll dress nicely so I don't raise any eyebrows, I text. *I wouldn't want to get you into trouble. I'll be in and out, I promise.*

Then I force myself to stop and give Liam time to respond. One of the many lessons I've learned from observing Gem over the years is this: If you want somebody to do something that they know deep down they shouldn't, you can't act desperate. You might think you're convincing them, but what you're actually doing is putting them on guard.

So I wait, like my entire future isn't hanging in the balance, until Liam finally responds.

Let me see what I can do.

Half an hour later, I'm waiting at the far gate of the Sutherland compound, near the wildflower field that Liam and I walked through yesterday.

I've transformed myself as best I could. I coaxed my hair

into loose curls that obscure my face, thanks to hot rollers and a few strategically placed bobby pins. My eyes are lined with dark kohl pencil, and my lips are ruby red. I'm wearing Jamie's little black dress, along with a pair of strappy heels and a cute beaded bag that, if everything goes well, will be perfect for stuffing a necklace into. It's not exactly ball-gown attire, but it's the best I can do.

I should be feeling triumphant—*Almost in!*—but mostly, I'm anxious. The only way Liam could get access to a key card, as it turns out, was by telling Augustus my engagement ring story. *It was either him or Luke,* he texted, and I had to admit that he'd picked the better option. Still, I'd been hoping for a Sutherland-free night, especially since Augustus doesn't strike me as the gullible type. My nerves have me pacing, until I spot two shadowy figures approaching the gate, and force myself to stand calmly in place.

"Hey," Liam calls in an entirely unnecessary stage whisper. "Kat! It's us!"

Some people are simply not meant for a life of subterfuge.

"Hi," I say as Augustus pulls a slim card from his suit pocket and holds it up to a panel mounted on the gate.

"We meet again," he says.

"Thanks for doing this," I say.

"Not a problem," Augustus says as the gate buzzes and starts to swing open. He steps back and adds, "Look at you. I barely recognize you. You've really pulled out all the stops, haven't you?"

"Just trying to blend," I say, keeping my voice light as I walk through the gate.

Both of the boys look handsome, although Liam's slightly

rumpled navy suit doesn't fit him as well as it could. Like he's grown an inch since his mom bought it for him, but he wears it so infrequently that he couldn't be bothered to replace it. Augustus's sharp black suit, on the other hand, looks like it was tailor-made for him last week.

"I didn't want to embarrass myself any more than I already have," I add as Augustus pulls the gate closed behind me. "I feel like such an idiot."

"Happens to all of us," he says, repocketing the key. "Well, not really. Chaos tends to follow you around, doesn't it?"

That hits entirely too close to home. I was right about Augustus: he's perceptive enough that I wish he weren't here. "I'll be in and out, I promise. I'm pretty sure I know where I dropped it," I say as we start down a winding cobblestone path. Faint lights glow in the distance, but I can't hear any noise except for the chirping of crickets. "Where are we headed? Is the party starting now, or—"

"Not yet," Liam says. "We're going to, um, my studio."

I blink at him, curious enough that I'm briefly distracted. "You just got here yesterday. You already have a *studio*?"

Augustus flicks a curling strand of blond hair out of one eye and says, "Talent like Liam's requires proper housing."

"Oh my God, stop it," Liam mutters, shoving his hands into his pockets. "We both know I'm trash."

Augustus snorts. "My Christmas suns beg to differ."

Before I can ask what that means, he makes a quick left turn that leads us to a small stone building. "Here we go," Augustus says. "Studio Rooney."

He pushes open the door, and we walk into total darkness. "The light is somewhere," Augustus says, fumbling against the wall until he finds the switch. "We can hang here until the party starts. Otherwise, you'll be the only guest roaming the grounds, and security *will* notice. I assume you'd rather not attract their attention?"

He gives me such a pointed look that my heart sinks into my already-hurting feet. Augustus clearly knows something is up; he just doesn't know what it is. "Right," I say absently, gazing around us as though I'm too intrigued by the space to focus on my so-called mission. "This is cute. So it's a studio, huh?"

"It is now," Augustus says. "My aunt transformed it for Luke and Liam."

That seems like a lot for a couple of weekend guests, but I suppose when you have as much money as Annalise Sutherland, you might as well throw it around to dazzle your new boyfriend and his kid. "I didn't know you were an artist, Liam," I say.

"I'm, um . . . still learning," he mutters, tugging at his collar.

"Augustus seemed impressed," I point out.

Augustus smirks and says, "That's putting it mildly."

He has an interesting accent. Or not an accent, exactly— more like a cadence that's both unusual and familiar. "Are you British?" I ask, even though I know that's not it. Anything to keep him talking about things that aren't me.

"No. But my mother is," he says. "She grew up in London." His lips quirk. "I've been asked that question before. I guess her speech patterns rubbed off on me."

That's it—he sounds vaguely posh. The vocal style I tried and failed to pull off at Bennington & Main. Gem would love him.

"So that's what it is," Liam says.

Augustus raises his eyebrows. "What *what* is?" he asks.

Liam fidgets with his cuff. "I thought it sounded like you come from someplace else. But also from here. I couldn't figure out why."

"You could've asked," Augustus says with an arch smile. Which Liam misses, since he's still focused on his cuff. Augustus gazes around the room, hands on his hips, and adds, "You know what? Something's not right. I'll be right back."

He takes off without another word, and I watch the door anxiously as it closes behind him. "Do you think . . . Is he going to tell someone that I'm here?"

Liam looks up. "Augustus?" he asks. Like there's anyone else we could be talking about. "No. Why would he? He likes you."

Then his cheeks turn rosy, which makes me smile despite all the tension pressing down on my shoulders. No wonder Liam has been overly fixated on his sleeve length; Augustus Sutherland makes him nervous. "I think he likes *you,* actually," I say.

"No," Liam says quickly, turning redder. "I don't get that vibe at all."

"Then you suck at reading vibes, my Vegas brother."

His lips twist. "I don't think so. Pretty sure you're his type."

"There's only one way to find out," I say cheerfully as the door opens and Augustus reappears with a bottle of champagne and three cups.

"Whatever you're thinking," Liam says quietly, "don't."

"*Now* it's a party," Augustus says, setting the cups on the table before popping the champagne. The move is expert and graceful, as though he's done it a hundred times before. He lets the foaming liquid overflow on the stone floor before pouring some into all three cups. "Or a pre-party, anyway."

"Augustus. Question for you," I say.

I can feel Liam grow rigid beside me as he whispers, "Do not."

"Ask away," Augustus says, handing us both a drink.

Sorry, Liam. But this is a much safer topic than just about anything else. Besides, I think it'll work out for him. "Which of us is your type?" I ask, gesturing between me and Liam, who briefly squeezes his eyes shut like that might make him disappear.

"Sorry," Liam mutters. "She's—like this."

Augustus is entirely unfazed, though. He takes a sip of champagne and cocks his head to one side, considering. "Technically, both of you," he says.

Even though I'm not looking at Liam, I'm pretty sure he just turned beet red.

"But *you*," Augustus adds, lifting his cup in my direction, "seem like the kind of chaos I don't have enough energy for. No offense."

"None taken," I say, because: fair.

"And Liam," Augustus says, giving Liam a much more lingering look, "is entirely too wholesome for someone like me."

Points to Augustus for nailing us both. "Isn't he, though?" I say affectionately. Liam, meanwhile, looks as though he can't decide whether he's relieved or disappointed by Augustus's analysis. "A treasure among men."

I'm teasing, but I'm also serious. The more Liam and I hang out, the better I like him. Being able to call on him for help, even though I couldn't be fully honest about why I needed it, made me feel a lot less scared and alone.

"Too pure for this cruel world," Augustus says, taking a slow sip of champagne. He's definitely attractive, with his wolf eyes and wicked smile, but I've already mentally written him off. Even if he wasn't a threat to Plan E, it'd be bad form to flirt when (a) my mother came here to rob his aunt and (b) Liam met him first and is clearly crushing. "We must protect him," Augustus adds.

"Cheers to that," I say, clinking cups with him.

"I'm right here, you know," Liam grumbles. "In the room."

"Being wholesome," I say, patting his arm. "Like milk."

"I hate you," he sighs, and for a moment, we really do feel like brother and sister.

CHAPTER SEVENTEEN

Kat

By the time Liam, Augustus, and I make our way to the massive sculpture garden behind the arboretum, the party is in full swing. It's a good location for what I came to do; there's a mazelike quality to the garden that will make it easy for me to disappear around corners while looking for Vicky.

I've never been surrounded by this many wealthy people. Everyone who's milling around has perfect hair, perfect smiles, and clothes that fit them like a dream. They all seem ageless— I can't tell who's twenty-five and who's fifty-five—and look as though they hit the gym at least five times a week. And the amount of jewelry on display would keep Spotless running for years. I keep my head down as we walk, nervous about running into Parker or Larissa—or, God forbid, Luke. But I don't recognize anyone in the crowd.

A jazz band plays softly on one side of the garden, across from a table holding the biggest, most extravagant cake I've ever seen. It's like a wedding cake on steroids—I count a total of nine tiers, ranging from the massive bottom layer to a top that looks like it's made entirely of delicate sugar petals. The rest of the tiers are alternating silver and white, with one notable exception—the middle is covered with big golden *R*'s and *S*'s, intertwined with gold-tipped white roses.

Augustus taps his chin and asks, "Do you think we have enough cake?"

He grabs two champagne glasses off the tray of a passing server and holds them out to Liam and me, but I make a shooing motion with my hand.

"You keep it," I say. "I should go."

"Sure you don't want help looking?" Liam asks.

"Positive," I say. I'm practically vibrating with anxiety, and if I stay here much longer, I won't be able to hide it. "You guys have fun."

"And *you* stay out of trouble, Chaos," Augustus says, his eyes glinting.

"Always," I lie before melting into the crowd.

I scan every face I pass, looking for Vicky. It's especially packed in the middle of the garden as people linger near the more interesting-looking sculptures. "Imagine that," a woman murmurs as I pass a giant stone head with a long, skinny nose. "Having a Modigliani just sitting in your backyard."

"It has to be a reproduction," the man beside her says.

I pause for a better look, and a black-clad server immediately descends on me. "Champagne?" she asks.

I don't recognize her, thank God, but I duck my head anyway. "No thank you," I murmur, and keep moving forward until I reach a part of the garden where the trees aren't lit by strings of Edison bulbs. It's much darker and quieter here, and the handful of guests chatting in groups of twos and threes pay me no attention. I've almost reached the last sculpture—a towering metal piece that looks like an abstract horse—when the sound of voices makes me freeze.

"He's always like this," a man says, clearly angry. "All I'm asking for is a little help. He'll do anything for you. But me? I can go fuck myself, I guess."

My pulse picks up as I duck behind the horse. I know that voice; it's Parker Sutherland, the last person I want to run into. Well, second-last, after Luke. Maybe I should backtrack, and get lost in the crowd for a little while.

Before I can move, though, a woman's voice replies. "He wants to see you standing on your own two feet, Parker. Is that really so much to ask?"

"Like you do?" Parker asks bitterly. "Did *you* pay for that dress, Annalise? That jewelry? Literally anything you own?"

Annalise. I can't help myself; I peer around the edge of the sculpture for a glimpse of the woman at the center of all this. Her blond hair is piled high, and she's wearing a gorgeous coral ball gown—just like Jamie said she would be—accented by a glittering diamond necklace and matching bracelets on both wrists. Luke, thankfully, is nowhere in sight.

"This isn't about me," Annalise says. "I'm sure if Dad could see you making a good-faith effort to pay down some of your debts—"

"With what money?" Parker whines.

"Money you *earn*," Annalise says. "From a job you get on your own, without asking him for help." At Parker's incredulous snort, she adds, "You have to prove that you're sincere."

"Sincere, huh? Like that new boyfriend of yours?" Parker asks.

"We're not talking about Luke—"

"*I* am," Parker says. "Someone has to, because you clearly haven't done your due diligence. You're going soft, Annalise. You're nothing but a mark to this guy. That kid of his is probably doing the exact same thing with Augustus. Like father, like—"

"Stop it," Annalise says sharply. "I know you're frustrated, but you don't have to take it out on a harmless boy."

"He's not your kid, Annalise," Parker snaps. "You can't have those, remember?"

Wow. The cruel words are like a slap, hitting me so hard that I can only imagine what they do to Annalise. She doesn't respond for a long moment, and when she does, her voice is flat and quiet. "Why, Parker? Why is it that every time you have a choice between being decent or being awful, you choose to be awful?"

He shrugs. "I'm just speaking the truth."

"That's one way of putting it. Goodbye, Parker."

As she walks away, I feel a prickle of shame. Before the fake necklace went missing, I was planning to finish Jamie's job for her, and I didn't give Annalise Sutherland a second thought. Why should I worry about taking something from her, when she has so much? It never occurred to me she might have problems that even endless money can't fix.

"Spoiled bitch," Parker mutters to himself.

Then he strides off, and I give myself a mental slap. I can't let myself get distracted like this again. I need to find Vicky, grab the necklace, and get out.

I start to move around the grounds more freely, less worried about being seen than about missing Vicky. I gaze full-on at every member of the catering staff I pass, only to be disappointed time and time again. After nearly an hour of searching, I've come full circle, back to the horse statue, and there's still no sign of Vicky.

I bite my lip, frustrated. Is she working someplace I can't see her, or is she not even here? Maybe one of these rich people was rude to her while she was serving them and she decided, *I don't need this. I have fuck-you money now.* But if that's true—if I wasted time drinking champagne with Liam and Augustus while Vicky snuck back to her apartment, packed up, and left town—then this whole night will have been for nothing.

So now what?

As I hesitate, I notice that all the other guests are starting to head in one direction—toward the dining area where I left Liam and Augustus. "Time to cut the cake," a woman says in a singsong voice as she passes me.

"With what?" someone else asks. "An ax?"

Cake-cutting time. That's when Jamie was supposed to swap the necklace, while everyone was distracted. What if I climb through Annalise's window and snap a few pictures of her jewelry collection? Maybe then Gem could at least create some new fakes, and the night wouldn't be a total loss.

Would Gem consider that taking initiative or taking a foolish risk? I'm not sure, but there's one thing I know—if I'm going to do anything, it has to be now. Once everyone's had their cake, people will go back to moving around more freely.

I'll go as far as Annalise's house, I tell myself. *And then I'll decide whether or not to go any farther.*

Within seconds of stepping into the trees, I'm swallowed in darkness; this is more than the simple pine grove it looked like from a distance. It's actual woods, and I start to worry that they're big enough to get lost in. I risk turning on my phone flashlight, shining it in a semicircle until I spot a wide path. It looks as though it's been painstakingly cleared, lined on either side with branches and small rocks. I breathe a sigh of relief as I start to follow it, keeping the light on low so I don't trip. Crickets chirp loudly as the party sounds grow increasingly distant. I didn't realize that Jamie's "slipping away" was going to involve a hike.

It can't be more than ten minutes, though, before I see a faint light shining through the trees, which means I must be getting close to the family cottages. I pause to shut the flashlight app off, confident that I can manage the rest of the way without it. But before I can take another step, a familiar voice cuts through the night air like a knife.

"What the hell are you doing here?" Parker Sutherland snaps.

I freeze, my heart jackhammering in my chest. Of all the goddamn people. He's supposed to be eating birthday cake! What can I say? Will he believe me if I try to explain that I got lost, or should I just take off? Will he come after me, or—

The low growl of a second voice pierces my panicked thoughts, and Parker lets out an irritated snort in response.

He's not talking to me, I realize, nearly melting into the ground with relief. And he's farther away than I thought. He's lowered his voice to a hiss, and even though my heartbeat starts to recede from my ears, I can't make out specifics of the argument. As long as I keep out of sight, there's a good chance they'll never know I was here. I slip behind a tree, prepared to wait out whatever fight Parker's gotten himself into.

The voices give way to grunting and scuffling. It sounds like they're getting physical, which is my cue to sneak away. But before I can move, a thunderous crack makes me jump.

All the breath leaves my lungs. I've never heard a gunshot before, but from the way it reverberates through my ringing ears, I'm almost positive that's what it was.

A gunshot.

Before I can even make a conscious choice about what to do, I'm stumbling toward the noise. *He needs help,* I think, even though I don't know which *he* I'm talking about—Parker, or the man he was arguing with. And then, when I've gone only a few steps, a shadowy figure takes shape in the path ahead of me.

I can't make out anything except for the fact that whoever it is, he's much bigger than Parker. Which means the huddled mound at his feet is . . .

Parker Sutherland. And he's utterly still.

The other man kicks at the body and curses. He leans down, as though he's feeling for a pulse, and then his angry whisper carries clearly.

"Serves you right, you goddamn idiot."

Panic floods through me and roots me in place, even as my inner voice screams at me to run. *Get away, get away, get away get away get away—*

But I can't move. I might never move again. My body stays rigid, even as the broad-shouldered man straightens and seems to look straight at me.

You can't see me, I think desperately. *You can't possibly see me. It's too dark.*

But that's wishful thinking, isn't it? Because I can see him.

He takes a step toward me, and that does it. The fear that's kept me frozen explodes like a bomb, spinning me around and propelling me into blur of frenzied motion.

I sprint through the woods, running for my life.

CHAPTER EIGHTEEN

Liam

At first, I think it's fireworks.

There's a loud crack just as Ross Sutherland is being served a slice of cake, which seems like the right time for another showy display. But there's only one explosive pop, followed by a deafening echo. As soon as it fades, a murmur starts running through the crowd. "Sounded like a car backfiring," someone says.

"Or a gunshot," another person says with a nervous laugh.

Augustus and I are seated at the same table as Ross Sutherland, across from Luke and Annalise. She cranes her neck, frowning, and says, "Where did that come from? Was it . . . It sounded like the woods, didn't it?"

"I'm not sure," Luke says.

"I think you're right, Aunt Annalise," Augustus says, dropping his napkin on the table as he gets to his feet. I stand too, earning a glare from Luke.

"Sit down," he hisses. His eyes cut toward Ross Sutherland

as he adds, "Let's not overreact while Mr. Sutherland is about to—"

"Who the hell is shooting on my property?" Ross Sutherland roars.

And then it's . . . well, not pandemonium, exactly, because everyone here is much too well behaved for that. But nobody's interested in cake anymore, either. The jazz band, which had been dutifully playing "Happy Birthday" as though nothing was wrong, goes silent. A lot of people start moving toward the main gate, like they don't want to stick around for the answer to Ross's question. Annalise, on the other hand, heads straight for the woods. Augustus and I follow, and after a moment's hesitation, so does Luke. We haven't gotten far, though, before a bunch of guys wearing gray suits and earpieces materialize in front of us.

"Ms. Sutherland," one of them says. "This way."

The next thing I know, the four of us are surrounded, being herded down a path I've never seen before. There's an intensity to the guards that makes me think of the Secret Service in movies—like we're politicians who've just survived an assassination attempt and need to be whisked away to a safe house. Their urgency has a domino effect; all of a sudden, the guests I glimpse through the wall of gray suits are moving a lot faster. "Hey!" someone calls as we push past them. "What's going on? Are we in danger?"

I pause on instinct, expecting the guards to answer, but the one closest to me grabs hold of my arm to propel me forward. "Keep moving," he says tersely.

We're ushered through the door of a squat building into a cramped, windowless room. Once we're all inside and the door is shut behind us, one of the guards crosses to the far side of the room and presses his hand against the wall. To my astonishment, the wall slides away to reveal a much bigger room behind it. It's like an upscale hotel bar with polished floors, recessed lighting, and plush seating scattered around the room. Built-in marble shelves hold a neat array of bottles and glasses, and I catch a glimpse of what looks like a restroom around one corner.

"Just until we know what's going on," the guard says, pressing a spot on the interior wall as soon as Luke, who's bringing up the rear, steps inside. The door closes seamlessly.

Holy shit, this *is* a safe house.

Ironically, that sparks the first tremor of fear I've felt all night. The firework noise and the rush through the crowd felt almost like a game, but this sleek, hidden space makes me shudder. And I don't think I'm the only one; when I look around at the other people scattered throughout the room, I don't see the untouchable Sutherlands. Annalise is deathly pale, and Ross—who's seated in a leather armchair beside an anxiously blinking Larissa—doesn't seem to realize or care that his usually neat white hair is sticking straight up. When a guard tries to offer him a glass of amber-colored liquid, Ross peevishly swats his hand away.

"I don't want a drink," he snaps. "I want to know what the hell just happened."

"We're working on that, sir," the guard says.

I need to shake off my nerves by focusing on something else. There's a single framed photograph on one wall, and when I approach it for a better look, I see a slightly younger Ross Sutherland—five years ago, maybe—and a woman around the same age. She has Annalise's bright smile, and she's holding tight to Ross's arm. They're on an elegant white boat, framed by a cloudless blue sky.

This must be Annalise's mom, I realize, and my throat tightens. *I still miss her every single day,* Annalise said. Even though I've been doing better this weekend, I know the feeling. And I'll know it for the rest of my life. Annalise is proof of that.

I wish my mother could've met Kat. I think they would've liked one another, and I think Mom would've especially liked the way Kat casually asked Augustus a question that I couldn't. Even if I don't know what to do with the answer yet.

She probably would've liked Augustus, too. Although I'm pretty sure she'd have said, *Be careful with that one.*

"Lovely picture, isn't it?"

The voice beside me makes me jump. It's Larissa Sutherland, the last person in this room I want to talk to. But she probably needs a distraction, too—and when you come right down to it, she's another person who lost her mom.

"Yeah," I say. "Really lovely."

"My parents on their fiftieth wedding anniversary," she offers.

"That's a nice boat," I say.

Larissa's jaw tightens. "It was my mother's pride and joy," she says.

"I can see why," I say. "I've never been on a boat, but—"

There's a sudden tug on my arm, and when I turn, Luke is there with a fixed grin. "How you doing, buddy?" he says. "Let's check in."

Buddy, I've come to realize, is Luke code for *Something's up.* He steers me a few feet away, and then the smile drops. "Could you not?" he hisses.

"Not what?" I ask, bewildered. I'm hardly trying to score points with Luke, but if I were, I would've thought making nice with prickly Larissa would do it.

"This is a stressful enough situation without talking about the *boat*."

I blink in confusion. "The what?"

"Nobody needs the reminder," Luke says.

I'm out of patience with him. "*What* reminder?"

His lips thin. "I told you this."

"I promise, you did not. I have no idea what you're talking about."

He grits his teeth. "I did, but . . . I guess I have to tell you again, since you have selective hearing. Annalise's mother died on that boat."

Ohhh. He actually did tell me that, but I didn't put two and two together when I complimented the picture. "Okay, yeah. Sorry," I say, fully meaning it.

"You should be," Luke snaps. Then his face transforms so quickly into concerned-dad mode that I look over my shoulder to see who's behind us. It's Augustus, approaching with two water bottles. "Stick to neutral topics," Luke whispers before slipping away.

As if I know what those are.

"Was it something I said?" Augustus asks, handing me a bottle.

Unlike the rest of his family, he seems calm and unbothered, and I don't know him well enough to tell whether he's putting on a front. "No, he just . . . We've never been through something like this before," I say. "Does it happen often?"

"Last time was my eleventh birthday, when somebody misfired a rocket launcher," Augustus says, twisting the cap off his bottle. "Loud noises tend to set my grandfather's security detail on edge. We might be here for a while."

"Do you think that's all it was?" I ask. "A loud noise?"

"Probably," Augustus says. But there it is: a too-visible swallow. He licks his lips and adds, "My dad's not here. I haven't seen him since lunch, and I . . . I don't know where he is."

Crap. That's not good. But before I can full-on panic, Annalise, who'd been passing behind us, stops short. "Oh, darling, I'm sorry," she says, touching Augustus on the shoulder. "I thought you'd been told. Your father decided to head back to the Cape after lunch."

An odd expression crosses Augustus's face—part relieved, part miserable.

Larissa comes up beside us then, mouth pursed. "Griffin never should have *left* the Cape," she sniffs.

Augustus walks away without a word, moving to the opposite side of the room. I look after him, confused—why is everyone talking about the Cape all of a sudden, and why does that clearly bother Augustus?—and catch Luke's eye. He tips his hand to mimic taking a drink and mouths, *Rehab.*

Oh. I guess I should be grateful that Luke has decided to act as my Sutherland safe-house guide, because otherwise, I'd have stumbled onto yet another conversational land mine.

Larissa Sutherland is glaring around the room, oblivious to the fact that she drove Augustus off. "But what about Parker?" she asks. "He's not here, either. Do you suppose he's holed up somewhere with Barrett?"

"I haven't seen Barrett all night," Annalise says.

"This is unacceptable," Larissa says tightly. "Everyone needs to be accounted for."

"Folks, your attention please!" I turn to see Clive Clayborne standing beside the door with a security guard. The guard is frowning, one hand pressed to his earpiece. "Can I ask that you cease your conversation for a moment?" Clive says. He tilts his head toward the guard and adds, "Dan has information coming through that may be critical."

Instantly, the room falls silent. Dan clears his throat and says, "Go ahead." He listens for a few beats, and his impassive face doesn't change when he asks, "And where was this?"

It's interesting; I thought we'd all been standing still before, but now we're *truly* still. As if everyone in the room is collectively holding their breath while Dan continues to listen intently. "I see," he says. "Is medical attention required, or . . ." A red flush starts creeping up his neck. "I see." Dan drops the hand that had been pressed to his earpiece and whispers something to Clive. Clive goes rigid, shock flashing across his face.

"That's impossible," he says.

Annalise moves closer. "What happened?" she asks. "Is someone hurt?"

"Clive," Ross Sutherland calls from his armchair, making that subtle hand gesture that means Clive is supposed to magically appear beside him. But Clive doesn't move, and Ross's pinched features settle into a surprised frown. *"Clive,"* he repeats.

"Just a moment, Mr. Sutherland." Clive tugs at his collar, then turns to Dan and says, "Can you please escort anyone who's not part of the family outside?"

CHAPTER NINETEEN

Kat

When I burst out of the woods behind the sculpture garden, my heart pounding and my lungs burning, I head straight for the abstract horse. Somehow, its familiar solid form feels like a safe harbor as I struggle to catch my breath and organize my racing thoughts.

I made it out of the woods. I'm alive. Now what?

This is a different party from the one I left; the sound of the gunshot that killed Parker Sutherland clearly carried. Raised voices float through the night and vibrate with a range of emotions: fear, confusion, anger, and, yeah, excitement. Even some high-pitched laughter. An old man's party just got a little more interesting: *Did I ever tell you about the time I was at Ross Sutherland's eightieth birthday and a shot rang out?*

No one understands yet that this is a different kind of story. That a billionaire's son was just killed on the family compound, by a man he fought with for reasons I couldn't hear.

I'm not even sure if they knew one another; the only thing I heard Parker say clearly was *What the hell are you doing here?* At the time, I was so sure he was talking to me that it didn't occur to me to try and parse his tone. Did he emphasize the *you* as though it was someone he knew but didn't expect, or was it a more general question?

Serves you right, you goddamn idiot.

That doesn't sound like something you'd say after shooting a stranger, does it? Did the man follow Parker to get him alone?

Except Parker wasn't alone. I was there, bumbling my way into yet another disaster.

A full-body tremor runs through me. I need to get out of here, fast, before fear takes over and freezes me again. Dozens of well-dressed guests are hurrying away from the party, toward the compound's main gate. Exactly where I need to be.

I race through the rest of the garden until I reach the lawn where the dinner tables are arranged, and slip into the stream of people leaving. Guests are talking loudly among themselves, pausing occasionally to demand answers from the men in gray suits who are suddenly everywhere.

Didn't Morgan say security was going to be *minimal* for this event?

"We believe this area is secure, ladies," one of the guards says blandly to two gray-haired women who've stopped a few feet in front of me. "But since we're still investigating the source of the noise, we encourage all guests to vacate the premises if they feel safer doing so."

"How helpful," one of the women snorts, adjusting the train of her dress before she starts moving again. "I notice Ross

Sutherland is nowhere to be found. If *he* doesn't feel safe, then I suppose we shouldn't, either."

I try to lose myself in the chattering crowd, stealing furtive glances at every man I pass. The guy I saw in the woods could be almost any one of them. All I could see was his shadowy form, but how good of a look did he get at *me*? Enough to tell that I'm a girl with long hair and a short dress, when almost everyone else is wearing ball gowns or a catering uniform? Could he hear my heels clattering against roots as I ran away?

It's silly, I know, but the thought makes me pause to slip off my shoes. My feet are killing me anyway, and I need to move faster.

The compound gates finally loom in front of me, wide open. But once I reach them, I hesitate. Everyone around me is a guest, headed for the parking area. There's not a single uniformed caterer in the crowd. I can barely see the turnoff for the path that leads to the staff quarters; unlike the rest of the well-lit compound, it's utterly dark. And if none of the workers are leaving yet, I'll have to walk it alone.

The thought is unbearable. I suck on my lower lip, pull my phone from my bag, and dial my mother. "Come on, Mom," I whisper. I only use that name when I desperately need her, and right now, what I desperately need is for her to pick me up and take me home. *Home* home, all the way back to Boston.

"Hi, this is Jamie. Leave a message!" My mother's voice fills my ear all too briefly, and then her voice mail beeps, and I disconnect with a sinking heart. I should've known better; Jamie sleeps like the dead even when she's not sick.

I'm on my own. I glance toward the path that leads to the

staff quarters again; if anything, it looks even darker and more foreboding.

It'll be okay, I tell myself. *It's barely a quarter mile. Just get through the gates and worry about the rest later.*

But before I can make myself move, someone grabs my arm.

I turn in what feels like slow motion, noticing with almost clinical detachment how tight a grip whoever is holding me has. My vision narrows to a pinprick, and all I can see is my shoe, dangling carelessly from a man's fingers. When I look up, though, I see a familiar face.

"You dropped this, Cinderella," he says.

It's the man who was sitting next to Parker Sutherland at lunch—Barrett, he called him. Somehow, despite keeping a careful eye out all night for Parker, Larissa, and Luke, I'd forgotten about this guy. I wasn't making any effort to avoid him, and I have no idea if I accidentally crossed his path while trying to find Vicky.

Under normal circumstances, I'd spin a quick lie, grab my shoe, and be done with him. But I've hit my limit, and all I can manage is a mute stare.

"I wasn't expecting to see you at this ball," Barrett says, looking me up and down. "Not dressed like that, anyway."

Is he just being an asshole, or is there something more going on here? *Not dressed like that, anyway.* Like what? Like a noncaterer, or like a silhouette that just ran away from him in the woods? Was he . . .

Oh my God. *Was he?*

"Sweetheart!" A woman's voice is suddenly beside me, and someone wrenches me firmly out of Barrett's grasp. When I turn, I see the same gray-haired lady who was talking to the security guard earlier. She circles my arm protectively with her own and adds, "There you are. Did you lose a shoe?"

"I . . ."

It's the only syllable I can push out, but this woman doesn't require an answer. She tut-tuts and says, "I know they're uncomfortable, but you should really wait until we get to the car." Then she plucks my shoe from Barrett's grasp and adds "Thank you for helping my granddaughter" in the kind of chilly tone that means *You're dismissed.*

What is *happening*?

Even if I could find the words to ask, I wouldn't have had the time, because she's already spinning me around and marching me away. We walk in silence for a few confusing seconds, until the woman says, "Put your shoes on, dear. There are rocks everywhere."

I obey without question. I don't know who this woman is, but right now she could tell me to stand on my head and I'd gladly do it. As I'm fastening a strap around my ankle, her friend appears on my other side and murmurs, "What was that about, Jean?"

Or maybe it's her sister. They have similar curly gray hair, wide-set brown eyes, and even features dominated by a strong jawline. They're both dressed too warmly for a summertime party in long-sleeved full-length velvet dresses.

Jean—my unlikely savior—snorts and says, "Did you *see* that man, Catherine? Forty if he's a day, and hitting on this literal child! I can't stand that sort of thing. Some people have no shame. Are you all right, dear? You looked terrified back there."

"I, um . . . I'm okay," I manage. "Thank you."

We start walking again. Jean pats my arm and says, "If you see something, *do* something. That's what I always say. Women need to look out for other women. Especially at a party like this. Some of these men have an obscene sense of entitlement."

"Isn't that the truth," Catherine sighs.

"Are you here with your parents?" Jean asks me.

"I . . . yes," I say automatically, my eyes darting once again toward the path that leads to the staff quarters. If it was intimidating before, it's a thousand times worse with Barrett lurking somewhere behind me. What's to stop him from following me once I'm alone? He's tall and broad enough to be the man I saw in the woods, and if he recognized me . . .

I need to get as far away as possible. From Barrett, from the Sutherland compound, from Bixby, from—everything.

"Do you want to call them?" Jean asks. "We'll wait with you until they come."

God, I wish. "They, um . . . had to leave early."

"Well, then, how are you supposed to get back to wherever you're staying?" Jean asks in exasperation. "Do you *live* in this godforsaken town?" I shake my head, and she sighs. "I don't understand parents today. I really don't. Too much freedom."

"I was supposed to get a ride with a friend, but I . . . I can't reach him."

Pressure builds behind my eyes, and cold prickles of anxiety crawl across my skin. I'm seconds away from dissolving into a sobbing, shivering mess. *I can't do this,* I think helplessly. I don't have enough mental or physical energy left to tell the right lies, in the right order, to keep myself safe. All I want is to throw my arms around Jean's lavender-scented shoulders and beg, *Get me out of here.*

"Are you staying at the Marlow?" Jean asks.

I don't know what that is, but . . . "Yes," I say.

"Well, that's fine, then. So are we. We'll take you."

Salvation. I don't care where the Marlow is, as long as it's not here. If we end up crossing state lines tonight, so be it. That's a problem for Future Kat.

"What's your name, dear?" Jean asks, tucking my arm more firmly under hers.

"Sophie," I say as I let her lead me away.

CHAPTER TWENTY

Kat

The Marlow, I realize on the drive away from the compound, is a hotel in the neighboring town of Randall, where most out-of-town guests are staying. It's maybe five miles from Bixby, so getting back should be walkable.

Not tonight, though. Not in the dark.

Which means I'm stuck at this hotel, where I most definitely am *not* a guest, until morning. Now that I'm out of panic mode, the reality of my situation is starting to sink in. I don't have a cent on me, and the debit card on my phone—which is running on battery fumes—is only good for the twenty dollars I have in my bank account. I don't know what a room here costs, but I have to think at least ten times that. Besides, they probably wouldn't let a sixteen-year-old book her own room even if I waved a gold card at them.

"I wonder if brunch tomorrow is still on?" Catherine asks as we pull into a circular drive in front of the hotel. It's a small but elegant brownstone, a surprisingly charming boutique in this sleepy town. A valet instantly springs from behind a podium as Jean shifts into park.

"Not for me," she sniffs. "I think we should sleep in, and then head straight home. This is no way to treat guests."

The valet opens her door and says, "Welcome back, Ms. Martin. How was your night?"

"Eventful," Jean snorts, handing him the car keys.

He flashes me a friendly smile as I accompany the ladies inside, and so does the clerk behind the reception desk. Jean and Catherine are the best kind of armor—so perfectly respectable that nobody even thinks to question my presence.

I follow them numbly, trying to kick my sluggish brain into gear. I need to find a place to hide out until morning, but I can't think of a good enough excuse to break away before we reach the elevators. Jean taps her room key on the UP button, and it flashes green as she says, "You look exhausted, Sophie. I hope you're going right to sleep."

"I am," I say. "I can barely keep my eyes open." It's the truth; I've never wished so desperately that I was headed for the comfort of my own bed.

The elevator doors open, and we step inside. Catherine presses the button marked with a 3 and asks, "What floor are you on?"

"Eight," I say. The top floor. Maybe I'll figure out a plan by the time I get there.

She presses 8 for me as Jean asks, "You have your room key?"

"Right here," I say, patting my bag.

"All right, then." There's a soft chime as we reach the third floor, and the door springs open. "This is where we leave you. Enjoy the rest of your weekend, Sophie."

"You too," I say. "And thank you so much."

"Of course," Jean says.

They step into the hallway, and when the door closes behind them I feel a sharp stab of loneliness. *Now what?*

The elevator keeps going, not stopping again until I reach the eighth floor. I step into the quiet, carpeted hallway and gaze around. There's a sign in front of me directing guests which way to turn for their room; 801 through 815 are to the right, and 816 through 830 are to the left.

The guest rooms aren't going to help me. I need someplace quiet and deserted, where there's little to no chance of anyone showing up in the middle of the night.

I turn right until I reach another fork; guest rooms continue right, and vending services are on the left. I choose vending, and when I turn down a small corridor, I find what I've been hoping for. A door without a number.

Please be open, I think, and grasp the knob.

It doesn't turn. That would've been much too easy.

I pull out two bobby pins from my hair and strip the ends with a sense of déjà vu. Maybe my subconscious was looking out for me while I got ready for the party, making me choose a hairstyle that could double as a key. It's been that kind of weekend, after all.

This lock gives me a lot more trouble than the one on Vicky's door, and for a long time all I feel is resistance. My throat gets thick with frustration, and I'm about to give up and look for a new hiding spot when I hear a beautiful click. I keep going with renewed determination until I've painstakingly lifted every pin. When I take hold of the knob once again, it twists freely and the door swings open.

Thank you, Gem.

It's a utility closet that's piled high with cleaning supplies and towels, along with a couple of massive laundry carts. I grab a stack of towels, tuck myself between one of the carts and the wall, and prepare a makeshift bed.

Then I pull my phone out of my bag. I'm down to 1 percent battery, and don't dare waste it checking notifications. I pull up my message string with Jamie—there's nothing new from her, so she must still be asleep—and type *I'm spending the night with Liam* so she won't worry if she wakes up and I'm not there.

I'll figure out everything else I need to tell her tomorrow.

I roll a towel into a pillow and put it beneath my head as I lie down. There's no way I should be able to sleep under these circumstances, with every horrible thing that just happened running through my mind in a vicious loop. But then again, it's not the first time I've tucked myself away in a strange hotel and collapsed with exhaustion.

I curl into a fetal position, close my eyes, and instantly drift off.

CHAPTER TWENTY-ONE

Liam

Parker Sutherland is dead.

Parker Sutherland is dead.

"This is unbelievable," Luke mutters, pacing the sitting room in the random building where security dumped all the non-Sutherland VIP guests once we left the safe house. "How does something like that even *happen*? It's impossible!"

For once, he and I are in full agreement.

No matter how many times I remind myself that Parker's death definitely happened—a white-faced Annalise updated us half an hour ago before leaving to join the rest of her family at Ross's house—it doesn't seem real. People like Parker Sutherland aren't supposed to die, and especially not the way he did: shot in the woods of his family compound, at almost the exact moment his father was being served a giant slice of birthday cake.

"I shouldn't be here. I should be with Annalise," Luke says, stopping to grab a crystal decanter filled with amber liquid from a side table. "She's devastated. She and Parker argued about something right before he died—"

"That's not new." Parker's college friend Barrett, who showed up twenty minutes after everyone else, looks up from his phone. "Parker got into it with everyone."

Got into it. I blanch at the use of past tense; it feels too soon. Half the time, I still forget to use it when I talk about Mom. People shouldn't fade from the world that easily.

Luke sips his drink, eyeing Barrett over the rim. "You're awfully calm for somebody who's been friends with Parker for, what—twenty years?" he says.

"Don't presume you know my state of mind," Barrett says coldly, turning back to his phone. "Or the Sutherland family. If you'd spent more than a weekend with them, you'd realize that the last thing they want is someone making a scene while they deal with a horrific tragedy."

Luke puts his glass down with a clatter. "Are you implying that I'm making a scene?" he asks, scowling.

"Not implying," Barrett says. "Stating."

"I'm going to find a bathroom," I say loudly, sidling toward the door. This room already feels oppressively small; a Luke–Barrett cage match will only make it worse.

I don't really need to use the bathroom, so I just wander down the hallway, peering into empty rooms that look as though they've never been used. Maybe I shouldn't be walking around alone after a night like this, but it doesn't feel unsafe. Guards are posted at the building's entrance, and they're probably combing the compound for Parker's killer. I haven't heard anybody speculate about who it might be yet; even Luke hasn't shared any theories.

I'd only just met Parker, but I'd already started to dislike him. He was arrogant and dismissive, and I wouldn't be surprised to learn that he had plenty of enemies. But it's either unbelievably ballsy or unbelievably desperate to kill a Sutherland in the middle of their father's birthday party.

Who could've wanted Parker gone that badly?

I reach the end of the corridor, where there's nothing except an oversized urn and the double doorway that leads outside. I turn to head back to the room where Luke and Barrett are, and stop at the only door in the hall that's closed. I put my hand on the knob, curious as to whether it's locked, when a familiar voice comes from inside the room.

"Oh, you can fuck *right off*," the voice says.

I freeze in place. That was Augustus, which means . . . the Sutherlands are *here*? I thought they'd gone to Ross's house. I hear a light thwack followed by a clatter, and then Augustus says, "Fuck you, too, you worthless piece of shit."

No one answers. Augustus's mourning style is kind of aggressive, but who am I to judge? I shouldn't be here, and I don't want to get accused of eavesdropping. I retreat farther down the hallway, and nearly bump into Luke as he hurries out of the sitting room.

"I'm heading to Ross's," he says. "I want to be nearby when the family meeting ends."

"The family meeting," I repeat, blinking at him. I turn toward the room where I just heard Augustus and add, "But that's . . . It's *here*, isn't it?"

Luke makes a disparaging noise as he brushes past me. "Of course not."

I watch him disappear through the exit at the end of the

152

hall, then make my way back toward the closed door. Am I so rattled that I'm hearing things, or . . .

Thwack. "You continue to suck beyond belief," Augustus says from behind the door.

Nope. Not hearing things.

I wait a beat, ears straining for the sound of another voice, but no one replies. Maybe I should leave well enough alone, but . . . his uncle just died, he's clearly upset, and whoever he's talking to can't be bothered to answer. "Augustus?" I call, rapping lightly on the door. "It's Liam. Are you . . ." How am I supposed to end that sentence? *Are you okay?* Of course he isn't. "Do you need anything?"

There's silence for a few seconds, and then Augustus says, "I need better—" But whatever else he says is lost in the rattle of the door as he opens it and leans against the frame. His suit coat and tie are gone, his shirt is untucked with the sleeves rolled up, and the circles below his slate-blue eyes are as dark as bruises. "Do you have any?" he says.

"Any what?" I ask as he steps back to let me inside. I peer around, looking for more Sutherlands, or at least a security guard or two. But Augustus is on his own.

"Darts," he says, holding one up. "These suck. They're too dull."

Before I can reply, he whips around and hurls the dart all the way across the room at a wall-mounted dartboard. It hits the bull's-eye center nearly dead-on, hangs there for an instant, and then drops to the hardwood floor with a clatter.

"Go fuck yourself," Augustus says to the dart, almost conversationally.

The room we're in looks as though it's meant to be an office, or maybe a library. Two of the walls have built-in bookshelves, and another is lined with file cabinets. There's a massive desk in the corner that has a spinning globe on one side and stacked marble trays on the other. No computer, though, so it doesn't seem like anyone actually works here. Two armchairs frame a stone fireplace that has wood piled to one side, ready for the first cold snap in case a Sutherland ever decides to wander in here and . . . play darts, I guess.

The floor beneath the dartboard is scattered with red and black darts. I want to ask Augustus why he's all by himself, but that feels too intrusive at such a raw moment. "You have good aim," I say instead as Augustus crosses the room and gathers up the fallen darts.

It's a pointless observation right now, but maybe that's okay. After my mom died, some of my friends and teammates avoided me because they were afraid of saying the wrong thing. It made me appreciate the ones who showed up, no matter how awkward they were.

"Yeah, and these darts are wasting it," Augustus mutters. "Here." He hands me three of the black darts. "Give it a go. Misery loves company."

In more ways than one.

I take aim and throw, but barely hit the outer ring of the board before my dart drops to the floor. "See?" Augustus says. "It's not just me."

"No, it's not just you." I step back and watch him throw another couple of bull's-eyes, swearing at the dart each time it drops to the ground, before I finally get up the nerve to say, "Tonight was awful. I'm really sorry about your uncle."

"He's an asshole," Augustus says roughly, gathering up his

darts. Present tense, which he quickly corrects as he adds, "But he was *our* asshole."

"I'm sorry," I say again, tossing another dart. This one gets a lot closer to the bull's-eye before dropping to the ground and, yeah—despite the fact that we have much bigger problems, it's weirdly frustrating.

Augustus doesn't say anything while I make my last throw. As I gather my darts from the floor, wondering what to say next, he drops heavily into one of the armchairs beside the fireplace. He twirls a dart in one hand and says, "They've shut me out."

"Huh?" I ask. "Who?"

"My family," Augustus says, pressing his thumb onto the tip of a dart. Not surprisingly, it doesn't draw blood. "After you left the safe room, Clive told us what happened. I went kind of numb, and my first thought was *I have to tell my dad.* So I went to the restroom to call him, but he didn't pick up. When I got back, all the security guards were gone, and Granddad and my aunts were in this little huddle in the middle of the room with Clive. Then I heard Clive say, 'It's the *way* he died, though. People are going to ask—' And Granddad said, 'They won't ask if they don't know. We need to contain this.'"

"Contain what?" I ask.

"Exactly my question," Augustus says. "But everyone clammed up when I tried to join the conversation. Granddad changed the subject, and said we'd go back to his house as soon as the guards checked it. I asked Aunt Annalise what was going on, and she told me not to worry. That it was nothing. But not like she really believed it."

" 'The *way* he died,' " I say, trying to make sense of Clive's words. "I mean, that's pretty straightforward, isn't it? He was shot. We all heard it. Is there something more?"

"Your guess is as good as mine," Augustus says. "Because once we got to Granddad's house, he took a call and ducked into his office with Clive. Then he yelled for my aunts. When I tried to follow, Clive literally slammed the door in my face."

"Seriously?" I ask. "Did he say anything?"

"Yes. He said, 'Wait in the sitting room, please.' "

"Jesus," I say. I can't imagine what could be so important that four adults would leave a grieving kid on his own. "I'm sorry, Augustus. That sucks."

"I shouldn't be surprised," he says bitterly, getting to his feet. "They never tell me anything. I didn't know my own father had gone to rehab until we were in the safe room. I mean, I'm not surprised, considering . . . lunch. But I didn't *know.*"

He hands me a dart, and I throw it without bothering to aim. It's my best shot yet. "I'm glad your dad is getting help," I say. "Can you visit him?"

"It's not encouraged," Augustus says, spinning the globe on the desk. "I tried to reach him again while everyone was holed up in Granddad's office, but no luck. I got sick of waiting around getting stared at by security, so I made them bring me here. And then I made them leave, because fuck them, too. Thanks for knocking, by the way," he adds, picking up a new dart. "You're the only person not paid to keep me alive who's bothered to check on me."

"I'm really sorry." It seems like I'm saying that a lot, but this night keeps finding new levels of bad. I wonder if Luke has managed to make contact with Annalise yet, or if she's still with her father and sister. Would she tell him whatever she's not telling Augustus? "Your family must not be thinking straight," I add.

Augustus squints at the dartboard, then lifts his hand to take aim. "That's a generous interpretation," he says.

"What's yours?" I ask.

He lets the dart fly. It's another perfect shot that lands straight in the center—and this time it stays there, quivering.

"That they care more about keeping up appearances than about Uncle Parker," he says.

CHAPTER TWENTY-TWO

Kat

I wake up to the loud scrape of a laundry cart being pulled backward, followed by a piercing shriek.

"Jaysus!" a woman yelps as I sit up, groggy and confused. For a few seconds my mind is completely blank, until I remember that I'm in a supply closet at the Marlow Hotel in Randall, Maine. Where I fled with a couple of kindhearted elderly women after . . .

After . . .

The memory of everything that happened hits me with such force that the cleaner standing in front of me barely registers. When I was at the Sutherland compound gates last night, all I could think about was escape. But now I have to deal with the mess I left behind.

Plan E was an epic failure. I didn't find Vicky or the fake ruby necklace; all I managed to do was become a sort-of witness to Parker Sutherland's murder. I should tell someone, probably, but . . . how can I? I wasn't supposed to be there, and the lies I used to gain access to the compound would never stand up against a murder investigation. I didn't even get a good look at the guy, and I'd be jeopardizing both Jamie and Gem.

Who are a whole *other* problem. Neither of them know that anything is wrong, but Gem is going to be expecting an update from my mother. What if she already checked in with Jamie? Or what if Parker's death made the news, or—

I need to get out of here.

I refocus on the woman in front of me. "What are you doing there?" she demands in a thick Irish accent, placing her hands on her hips. She's around Gem's age, wearing a crisp blue uniform and an expression that's beginning to look more angry than afraid.

That's my cue to talk my way out of this. What had Augustus said to me last night? *You seem like the kind of chaos I don't have enough energy for.* I can work with that.

"Oh my God, I am, like, *so* hungover," I say in my best spoiled party-girl voice, rooting around for my shoes and my bag with an exaggerated yawn. I'm sure I look the part; Jamie's cute black dress is a wrinkled mess, and a quick tug on my hair confirms that last night's curls have turned into tangles. The towel I used as a pillow is streaked with makeup stains, so I can only imagine what my face looks like. The bobby-pin lock picks I made are lying on the floor, and I quickly stuff them into my bag before adding, "I thought this was my room."

"How did you get in here?" the cleaner asks, narrowing her eyes as I put my shoes on. "These doors are always locked."

"I have no idea," I say, staggering to my feet. "I was soooo drunk."

"What's your room number?" she asks.

I give her a vacant smile. "It's, like, eight-something? I need to call my boyfriend and check. Have you seen him? He's supercute, really tall—"

"Just get out of here," the cleaner sighs, stepping aside.

"Thanks so much. Have a nice day," I coo. As I pass, she grumbles something under her breath that I'm sure I deserve.

Now what?

It's too overwhelming to think about this entire mess at once, so: baby steps. The first thing I need to do, I decide, is find a restroom. Partly because my bladder is about to burst, and partly because I need to make myself look like less of a disaster.

I head for the ground floor of the hotel, taking the stairs instead of the elevator, because the last thing I need is to run into Jean and Catherine while wearing last night's clothes. Or anyone, really; the cocktail dress that blended reasonably well into the Marlow Hotel on a Saturday night is going to look completely out of place on a Sunday morning. Or afternoon. I fish my phone out of my purse to check the time, but it's dead.

Now that I've walked down multiple flights of stairs in these heels, it's glaringly obvious that I'm never going to be able to trudge five miles in them to Bixby. But with a dead phone, how am I supposed to call for a ride? Also, *who* am I supposed to call for a ride? And what do I tell them?

Panic starts rising in my chest, and I push it down. *Baby steps,* I remind myself as I exit the ground floor stairwell. *All you have to do right now is find a bathroom.*

Once I spot a RESTROOMS sign, I move toward it like an

automaton and change the mantra running through my head, bit by bit:

All you have to do is get inside without anyone seeing you.

All you have to do is pee.

All you have to do is wash your hands.

All you have to do is scrub your face.

All you have to do is untangle your hair.

All you have to do is rinse out your mouth.

All you have to do is—

I've just about run out of instructions for myself when the bathroom door opens and a girl who looks a little older than me steps inside. She's dressed casually, in cargo pants and sneakers that I instantly envy, and gives me a brief smile in the mirror before heading for one of the stalls and shutting the door behind her.

All you have to do is steal that girl's shoes.

No, that's a terrible idea. But maybe . . .

All you have to do is get that girl to let you use her phone, I think, pinching my cheeks in the mirror to try and make myself look a little less grim.

I rewash my hands, taking my time until I hear a toilet flushing and see the girl emerging from her stall. When she heads for the sink, I grab a paper towel and wait until she catches my eye in the mirror again.

"Hey," I say with what I hope is a friendly yet apologetic smile. "This is going to sound weird, I know, but . . . is there any chance I could use your phone for a sec? Mine's dead, and I need to call my . . ."

My what? There are only two options: Jamie or Liam. Neither are great; Jamie might still be sick, and Liam would probably need to borrow a car from Luke. Not to mention the fact that Liam was hanging out with Augustus last night, whose uncle was *murdered* . . .

I'm taking too long to make this request. "Boyfriend," I say hastily. "We had a huge fight at a party last night, and I . . ." The girl cocks her head, taking in my rumpled dress, and I search my exhausted brain for a good story. "I got really upset and fell asleep in a closet."

It's honestly the best I can do right now.

"A closet?" the girl asks dubiously. "Really?"

My throat thickens. I don't know what directions to give myself anymore, and without them, the horror of last night is starting to crowd in. I take a deep breath, trying to calm myself, but when I exhale, it comes out as a shuddering sigh.

Instantly, the girl's hand is on my arm. "Oh no. I'm sorry! It's okay!"

"I just . . ." It takes another couple of breaths to get myself under control. "I just really love him," I finish, because how else can I explain myself right now?

"You poor thing. Here," the girl says, fishing her phone out of her pocket. She unlocks it and hands it to me, presenting me with my next obstacle: without being able to check the contacts stored in my own phone, I have no idea what Liam's phone number is.

"You know what? I don't know his number offhand," I say, cringing a little. That's normal, right? I've never had a serious boyfriend—Jamie and I move around too much for that—but I'm pretty sure that if I did, I wouldn't memorize his phone number. "Would it be ridiculously weird if I sent him a message through your Instagram?"

It would, obviously, but she's kind of invested now. "Not at all," she says, taking the phone from me to open the app. "What's his username?"

"'Liam Rooney' with five *y*'s," I say.

"Why five?" she asks.

I have no idea. "It's his lucky number," I say.

"Is this him?" she asks when his profile comes up. "Oh, he is *cute*," she says approvingly. "Good for you."

"Thanks," I say, taking the phone back before she can notice that none of his pictures include me. "You're so nice to let me do this."

"No problem."

Her phone says it's nearly eleven o'clock, which is much later than I thought. But at least it probably means that Liam is awake, and from our limited messaging interactions, I know he tends to be a lightning-quick responder.

Hey Liam, it's Kat, I type, then pause. Would I call him Liam if he were my boyfriend? Wouldn't we have some kind of nickname for one another? But then again, if I call him *babe* or similar, he's going to find that even stranger. I backspace and write, *Hey, this is Kat.*

I'm borrowing someone's phone because mine is dead, I continue. *I really need to talk to you. Is there any chance you could pick me up? I'm at the Marlow Hotel in Randall.* Poor Liam is going to be deeply confused, but it's all I can say while staying consistent with my cover story. This girl is obviously going to read the message when I'm done. I can't blame her; I'd do exactly the same thing in her shoes.

"Is he answering?" she asks, peering over my shoulder.

"Not yet."

"Tell him you love him," she urges. And, despite everything, I have to swallow a laugh at the idea of Liam getting *that* message.

"He's not the most demonstrative guy," I start, but then Liam's avatar pops up in the chat window, and I can see that he's typing.

I sag with relief as the girl smiles. "Ooh, he's quick. He misses you," she says, nudging my shoulder with hers. Most of the world's problems could be solved if everyone was as consistently kind and supportive to one another as girls are in the ladies' room.

Please, Liam, don't ask too many questions in this nice girl's Instagram, I silently pray as I wait for his message to come through. *Just go with it.*

Be there asap, he writes.

Ten minutes later, I'm sitting on the curb of the parking lot in the back of the Marlow Hotel. It's not really meant to be a waiting area, but the bench beside the front door felt way too visible. My new friend and I parted ways outside the ladies' room, so I'm once again alone.

With my thoughts. Not a good place to be.

The sun is shining so brightly that I wish I'd stashed a pair of sunglasses in my beaded bag. I shade my eyes with both hands and stare at the parking lot entrance, my head pounding as I try to come up with a plausible story to tell Liam when he gets here.

I ran into a friend from home . . .

One of the other caterers had an extra hotel room . . .

There was this really fun party bus . . .

I'm so tired of lying, though, that a radical idea keeps in-truding on every story I try to spin: What if I told Liam the truth? Not just about how I ended up at the Marlow Hotel, but also about what happened last night, and what Jamie and I came here to do. What we've spent most of my life doing. What happened to us. Who we really are.

It would be such a relief to get it all out.

Could Liam handle that much honesty, though? He'd been so horrified about Luke catfishing those women. I was, too, and I told myself that Luke is much worse than Gem and Jamie because he manipulates emotions and victimizes people who can't easily replace what he takes. But the whole Robin Hood argument had already started falling apart when I overheard Annalise last night. I can only imagine how it would sound to Liam's ears.

I've been keeping an eye out for the red Buick that Luke was driving when Liam forced him to stop for our flat tire, so when a shiny gray BMW pulls into the parking lot and moves slowly in my direction, I barely give it a passing glance. Until it stops directly in front of me. The driver's-side window slowly rolls down, and my heart drops when I see a familiar face.

Liam, come on. You had one *job.*

Augustus Sutherland pulls off his sunglasses, like he needs a closer look to make sure the bedraggled heap on the curb is the same girl he served champagne to last night. Then he heaves an exhausted sigh and says, "Somehow, this is not the least bit surprising. Get in."

CHAPTER TWENTY-THREE

Liam

"Party bus?" I ask doubtfully, twisting in my seat to look at Kat.

"It seemed like a good idea at the time," she says in a monotone.

She looks rough. I don't think she's happy about Augustus picking her up, but what did she expect after a summons like that? Luke was nowhere to be found when I got her confusing Instagram notification, and Augustus was. I think he was glad to have something to do. Plus, he did Kat a huge favor last night, so it never occurred to me that she'd mind.

"Did you find the ring?" I ask.

Kat blinks like she has no clue what I'm talking about, but then her face clears and she pats the beaded purse beside her. "I did, yeah. Safe and sound. Thanks again."

"Where was it?" Augustus asks with a trace of animation in his voice. If there was a thought bubble over his head, it would probably read *Finally, some good news.*

"Exactly where I thought it would be," Kat says. Before either Augustus or I can ask any follow-up questions, she bursts out with, "Also, I just wanted to say . . . I'm really sorry about your uncle, Augustus."

I blink in surprise as he grips the steering wheel more tightly. "You heard?" he asks.

Kat bites her thumbnail. "People were, um, talking. At the hotel."

"Already?" Augustus huffs a bitter laugh. "So much for keeping things *contained.*"

He and I played darts until nearly three o'clock this morning, when Augustus abruptly announced that he was tired and took off. I'd gotten a terse text from Luke telling me that Annalise couldn't bear to be alone after what happened, so she was moving into the top floor of our guest cottage. *Don't bother us,* he wrote, and I didn't.

I thought it would be impossible to sleep once I got to bed, but I shut my eyes anyway and managed to pass out for a few restless hours. When I woke up and went into the kitchen, Luke was preparing a thermos of coffee. He told me that nearly all the guests were gone or in the process of leaving—except us. "Annalise needs me," he added. "She's at her father's house now with the chief of police. I'm going to bring her this."

"Is there any news?" I asked. "About what happened to Parker?"

"You know what happened," Luke said.

"Sure, but I mean, like, *how* it happened. Or why."

"No," Luke said, twisting the cover onto the thermos. "And don't go pestering any of the Sutherlands about it, please. They've been through enough."

I couldn't have pestered them if I wanted to; I didn't see any of them this morning except Augustus, and I already know he's out of the loop. The compound staff, who'd been so noiselessly efficient my first day, were clustered in whispering knots every time I saw them, not even pretending to work.

Parker's death is clearly weighing heavy on Kat's mind, too. She looks sad and exhausted as she stares out the window, tapping her fist on her knee. "Do they know anything?" she asks. "About who did it?"

Augustus's voice is like lead when he replies, "If they do, they're not telling me."

It's the way *he died,* Clive had said.

One of the first things Augustus ever told me about his uncle was *Don't play poker with him.* When I asked why, he said, *Because he'll cheat. He gambled away a fortune, and he's constantly trying to get it back.* Is that what happened? Did Parker run up some kind of massive gambling debt he couldn't pay? Maybe killing him on the Sutherland compound was meant to send a message; that even privilege won't save you if you cross the wrong people.

I can't bring myself to ask, though. If Augustus wants to trade theories about his uncle's death, he should be the one to bring it up. He doesn't, and silence stretches until it's clear that none of us feel like talking anymore.

It's a beautiful summer morning, the bright sunshine giving the rolling green hills that we pass a golden glow. I sneak glances at Augustus as he drives, one hand on the wheel, his arm dangling out the open window. He's wearing another crisp white button-down, and his eyes are hidden behind aviator-style sunglasses. If I didn't know better, I never would've guessed that he'd just pulled an almost all-nighter.

I wonder how much longer he's going to hang out in Bixby now that the birthday celebration has been cut short and his father's gone to rehab. Annalise said his mother is traveling, so maybe he'll join her. Or maybe this weekend is just a short detour to summer plans with his friends, none of whom he's mentioned by name. Despite the intense bonding experience we've just been through, I barely know anything about Augustus Sutherland.

And after today, I might never see him again.

The thought makes me feel lonely. Not because I've been hoping he didn't really mean his *Liam is entirely too wholesome* speech—although, yeah, until everything imploded last night, I have to admit that I was. But it's more than that. In the six months since my mom died, he's one of only two people I've met who feels even remotely like a friend.

And the other one is about to go home to Boston. Once Kat and Augustus are gone, what happens to me? I don't want to sink back into a life of dull resentment with Luke, but I let my world shrink to almost nothing after I left Maryland. I'm not sure I can build it back up on my own.

"Turn left at the light," Kat says, just as Augustus puts his blinker on.

"I know," he says.

"Oh, right," Kat says as he turns into a parking lot. "I guess this is technically your property, isn't it?"

"No," Augustus says. "It's my grandfather's. But it's hard to miss."

"It's like a ghost town," Kat says as Augustus drives slowly through the near-empty lot.

"Everyone's left, I suppose," Augustus says. "The festivities were canceled."

"Don't the police want to talk to people who were there last night?" I ask.

"You'd think, wouldn't you?" Augustus says. "But a thorough investigation doesn't seem to be a priority at the moment." He pulls into a parking space close to the staff quarters entrance, shifts into park, and turns in his seat so he's facing Kat. "Last chance, Chaos," he says.

"For what?" she asks, unbuckling her seat belt.

"To tell a better story than 'party bus,'" he says.

I expect a laugh in return. But instead, Kat flushes and drops her eyes.

"Thanks for the ride. Sorry about—everything," she says, then launches herself out of the car so quickly that there's no time to say goodbye. Or anything else.

"What the . . ." I stare through the windshield at Kat scurrying toward the door. "That was weird. Do you think there's something going on with her?"

"Nah," Augustus says. "She seems fine to me."

"Really?" I ask.

"No, not *really*," he sighs, drumming his fingers on the steering wheel. Then he moves his hand over my forearm and taps it with one finger at a time until all four of them are resting on my skin. It's unsettling, how much that makes my nerve endings buzz. "One of these days, Liam Rooney, you're going to learn how to recognize sarcasm, and then your powers of observation will be truly unmatched."

My cheeks warm as Kat disappears into the building. So much for almost-brotherly intuition. "We should go after her, right?"

"I mean, I *would*," Augustus says, lifting his hand from my arm with the air of somebody who's running dangerously low on patience, "if it weren't obvious that she wants to talk to you alone."

"Right," I say, feeling even more foolish. *Way to prove that you're just as hopelessly naïve as they think, Liam.* "Be right back."

I exit the car and head up the path to the arched entryway. When I push through the revolving door, I find myself in a small, brightly lit foyer. There's no one in sight, and it's silent except for the light tread of footsteps above me. Mailboxes are on my left, framed by two huge potted plants, and a wide set of wooden stairs in front of me curve out of sight. I don't see anything that looks like an elevator, so it seems as though the only way to reach the apartments is up the stairs. I start climbing and call, "Kat!"

Her voice floats from what sounds like a couple of floors up. "What?"

"Do you want to talk?"

"I . . . Um, yeah. But . . ." A phone rings then, loud and insistent. "Hang on," Kat says. "I'll be down in a sec."

I stay where I am until the ringing stops. At first, I think Kat must have rejected the call, since I don't hear her speaking— just the tap of her heels and the click of a door closing. But then she appears at the top of the staircase with a phone in one hand. Her face is locked into a resolute grimace as she comes downstairs, like someone who's about to swallow a bitter but lifesaving dose of medicine.

"I have to make a call," she says before slipping past me.

171

CHAPTER TWENTY-FOUR

Kat

As soon as I saw Gem's name on Jamie's phone, I knew I couldn't avoid her any longer.

I wasn't able to answer her call before it went to voice mail, and I couldn't exactly talk to her with Liam downstairs, anyway. So now, I'm heading into the woods to call Gem back—on Jamie's phone, since mine is still dead. Once she hears my voice, Gem will know that this weekend hasn't, to put it mildly, been going to plan.

If she doesn't already.

"Jamie?" Gem picks up on the first ring. Her voice has a near-hysterical tone that I've never heard before, and it makes my heart sink. "Where the hell—"

"It's Kat," I interrupt.

Gem inhales sharply, then goes silent for a few long beats before asking, "Kat? Why—*how*—are you using Jamie's phone from Hannah's house?"

I take a deep breath before admitting, "I'm not there. I'm in Bixby. I came with Jamie for the weekend."

"You did *what?*" Gem asks, voice rising. "Why would you—for crying out loud, Jamie is on *assignment,* Kat. It's not a vacation for you. How on earth could she allow that?"

"I didn't really give her a choice," I say.

It seems like Gem and Jamie haven't talked at all since Jamie got sick, which means . . . Oh God. I'm going to have to explain everything, aren't I? There's no keeping this from Gem, and I don't want to anymore. Not after what happened last night. But how do I even start?

"Put her on, please," Gem says, sounding as though she's working very hard to keep her tone even.

"I can't," I say, pinching the space between my eyes with my thumb and forefinger. "I'm by myself in the woods at the moment."

"You're . . ." I can almost see Gem massaging one temple as she reaches for a shred of patience. "Kat, I don't know if you realize this, but we're in some potentially deep shit. Ross Sutherland's son Parker was *killed* last night. Scrutiny at the compound is going to be sky-high, and—"

"Oh, I realize," I say, sitting down heavily on the nearest rock.

Then I take a deep breath and tell her everything.

How Jamie got sick. How while I was trying to find some Tylenol for her, I came across the Bennington & Main diamond vine ring and got it stuck on my finger. How I took over for Jamie at lunch, only to catch the attention of half the Sutherland family. How Jamie didn't get better, and told me to call Gem and cancel the job. How I didn't listen.

I tell Gem about Vicky stealing the fake necklace, and how I dressed up and snuck into Ross Sutherland's birthday party hoping to find her. How I had no luck and decided to head for Annalise's house. How I overheard Parker in the woods.

And then I tell Gem how he died, how I fled from the compound to the Marlow Hotel, and how I got back right as she was calling Jamie.

Gem lets me get it all out without interrupting once. When I finally finish, she sighs heavily and says, "Jesus Christ, Kat. Are you kidding me?"

I'm not sure if that's an actual question, but I answer it anyway. "Unfortunately, no."

"Why is now the first time I'm hearing about any of this?"

"I . . . I thought I could handle it," I say. Even as the words leave my lips, I know how ridiculous they sound, and I brace myself for Gem's bitter laugh.

Instead, she sighs again and asks, "Are you all right?"

I squeeze my suddenly stinging eyes closed. I didn't realize, until just now, how much I needed someone to ask me that.

No, I think, but I can't give that answer to Gem. She values toughness, and I've always prided myself on meeting her standards. I haven't cried once this weekend, and I'm not about to start now. "I'm okay. I feel horrible that I couldn't help Parker, though, and—"

"You can't think that way," Gem says. "It's a miracle you weren't hurt."

"Yeah," I say, swallowing hard. *Definitely can't think that way.* Any time the image of that shadowy form tries to take over my brain, I shove it down. "I'm really sorry about the necklace. I know how much time it takes to make those, and I should have been more careful."

"Yes, you should have," Gem says gruffly. "It's rule number one, Kat. Protect the product. You sure this Vicky person took it? Could it have been anyone else?"

"I don't see how," I say. "Do you think you could find her and get it back?"

"Possibly. It's not a top priority right now, though." Gem clicks her tongue. "Maybe it's a blessing in disguise that Jamie couldn't make the swap. You said you didn't use her staff credentials to get into the compound last night, right?"

I nod before remembering she can't see me. "Right."

"So there's no record of her—or her alter ego, anyway—working the party. That's good news now that we're dealing with a dead Sutherland. Best to lie as low as possible."

Even as I wince at the callous referral to Parker, the knots in my stomach start to loosen. It doesn't sound as if Gem hates me, so maybe she'll give Jamie another chance. Which reminds me . . .

"Gem, do you have a buyer for the diamond vine ring?" I ask. "Is that why Jamie had it?"

"I have no idea why Jamie had it," Gem says, her voice cooling. "I certainly didn't give it to her."

"Really?" That possibility had never even occurred to me, and I wonder if I should've kept my mouth shut about the ring. Could Jamie have . . . But no. There's no way my mother would've decided to go rogue with such a valuable piece of jewelry when she was *thisclose* to a new life. "Do you think Morgan might have, and forgot to tell you?"

175

"That would be a major oversight," Gem says with a snort. "I'll ask her once she bothers returning my calls."

"She's not returning your calls?" Gem and Morgan aren't exactly the closest mother-daughter duo I've ever met, but they work together and live two blocks from one another. For as long as I've known them, they've spoken pretty much every day.

"Nope," Gem says flatly. "Shitty timing with this job falling apart."

"That's not like her," I say. "Maybe she's sick, too?"

"Could be," Gem says. "Listen, can Jamie drive home?"

I hesitate. "Umm . . ."

"If she can't, I'll send someone to get you."

I close my eyes and listen to the cheerful chirp of birds overhead. That would take at least three and a half hours, and there's no way I can bear to stay in Bixby that long. All I want is to get home as quickly as possible, collapse onto my bed, and sleep for days. Even though it felt great to unburden myself to Gem just now, one more white lie couldn't hurt.

I cross my fingers and say, "She's looking better. Once she's had a shower and something to eat, I think she'll be good to go. Probably in an hour or so."

Actually, from what little I saw of Jamie when I grabbed her phone, she looks the same. But if she doesn't recover soon, I'll load her into the car and take the wheel myself. I don't have my license—I haven't even gotten around to getting my permit yet—but I used to drive back roads all the time when we lived in Arkansas a few years ago.

"Good," Gem says. "Is there somewhere you can go until then?"

"Go?" I ask, confused. "What do you mean? Why would I leave?"

"Because if somebody knocks on the door wanting to ask Jamie about last night, you shouldn't be there," Gem says. "We've only got credentials for one, remember? And it'll get messy if anyone realizes you subbed for Jamie at lunch."

"Oh. Right," I say. I'm not sure where to go, though; I have a feeling I've already overstayed my welcome with Liam and Augustus. Maybe I can break into Vicky's apartment again. "Okay, I'll find someplace. Should I—"

"No," Gem says.

"You don't know what I was going to say," I protest. Neither did I, though; my exhausted brain is running on empty. As much as I'd like to make up for all my mistakes, I don't have a clue where to start.

"Whatever it is, don't do it," Gem says. "Do nothing. About anything. The grown-ups are in charge now, all right?"

"All right," I say, and I have to admit—that's a relief.

CHAPTER TWENTY-FIVE

Liam

When I hear the revolving door of the staff quarters building turn, I look up, assuming Kat's finally come back. Only it's Augustus instead.

He's getting impatient, I think. Of course he is; his uncle died less than twelve hours ago. He should be with his family, not playing chauffer to me and a frustratingly elusive Kat. "Sorry," I say sheepishly. "I haven't gotten the chance to talk with Kat yet. She—"

"I saw," Augustus says, pulling his sunglasses off and tucking them into the neck of his shirt. "She ran off behind the building. Then I thought I'd stretch my legs, so . . . I took a walk in the same direction."

I arch my brows. "Were you following her?"

"Maybe a little," Augustus says.

"You can't really follow someone *a little*," I say. "It's kind of an all-or-nothing proposition."

"Semantics," Augustus says, waving a hand. "Anyway, I lost her, because she's fast and I'm lazy. But that's not even the point. The point is—I saw something."

"Saw what?" I ask, just as the door turns again.

Kat appears, stopping short when she sees Augustus. "Oh, hey," she says warily. "What's up?"

I glance between them, feeling responsible for this hallway meeting that Kat clearly doesn't want and Augustus doesn't need. I should've gone back to the car to wait with him, and given him the option to leave. Before I can figure out how to smooth things over, though, Augustus says, "Someone just climbed onto the balcony and into a second-floor window."

"What?" I whip my head toward him. "Who?"

"I couldn't see him well," Augustus says. "Big guy, though."

Kat gasps, her eyes round and horrified. "Oh my God," she says. "That . . . That sounds like—" Suddenly she's a blur of frenzied motion, flying up the stairs so fast that she's out of sight before her words have a chance to sink in.

And then they do. "Shit," I say, starting after her.

"Is this a good idea?" Augustus asks. "Maybe we should call—"

Kat screams.

The piercing cry freezes me halfway up the stairs. Then, with a new burst of energy, I race for the top and barrel into the hallway. "Kat!" I shout, heart pounding as I lunge toward the half-open door. There's a crash from inside, followed by a muffled cry that, if I had time to think, would probably scare the life out of me. But I don't.

I burst into the apartment and follow the noise into a small bedroom. For a few seconds, I'm frozen in the doorway, trying to make sense of the scene in front of me. Jamie's lying on a bed by the window, unconscious, a pillow half covering her face. Kat's on the floor, one side of her head bleeding. And a third person—big, male, face distorted by something I don't have time to figure out—is heading straight toward me, fist raised.

I dodge the punch just in time, stumbling backward into the living room. I gaze around wildly for help—for *anything*— but before I can make another move, a massive arm loops around my neck and pulls tight. *Really* tight.

I can't breathe.

I claw desperately at the guy's arm, trying to loosen his hold, but it's like a vise. Black spots dance at the edges of my vision as I struggle to take in air. *This can't be the way I die,* I think as a grim kind of fuzziness seeps into my brain.

Then there's another loud crash and a grunt of pain, and all of a sudden, I can breathe again. I stumble forward, gasping, and turn to see Kat holding the base of a shattered lamp. She swings again, but the guy—*What the* hell *is covering his face?*— dodges and catches her by the arm, twisting so hard that she drops the lamp with an agonized yelp.

Everything's such a blur of pain and confusing movement that I barely register that Augustus is in the apartment until he manages to pull the intruder off Kat. But the guy turns around swinging, and Augustus can't get out of his way. There's a sickening crack as Augustus drops heavily to the floor, and the guy lifts a foot like he's about to deliver a swift kick to his ribs. Or his head.

Chair. That's the only possible weapon I see, so I grab it and swing as hard as I can at the guy's back. He staggers away from Augustus, and Kat lunges for him. *A stocking,* I think as her fingernails connect with his eyes and he howls. *That's what's on his face.*

Then I hit him with the chair again. And again. It feels good when he stumbles, even better when he falls. I've never thought of myself as a violent person—all my fights growing up were shoving matches that ended as quickly as they started—but right now, the only thing I want out of life is to beat this guy senseless.

And then I want to beat him some more.

Before I can, though, his legs flail out. He kicks me and I go flying, hitting the ground so hard that the breath leaves my lungs. Then he rolls away from me and springs into a crouch, and my body tenses as I scramble back. *Where the hell is my chair?*

Kat's on him in a flash, though, tugging at the stocking that covers his head. I freeze in place, waiting for a face to be revealed, but I barely see the beginnings of a chin before he shoves her to the ground and twists away. Then he spins and runs out the door, footfalls echoing in the hallway and down the stairs.

For a few endless seconds, Kat and I just stare at one another, breathing heavily. My heart is pounding, my throat is aching, and somehow, I got a long scratch down my left arm. One side of Kat's face is dripping with blood. She brushes at it and smears red into her hairline.

Did that really happen?

I thought I'd asked it out loud, but I must not have, because Kat doesn't react. Then she cries "Mom!" and runs into the bedroom.

I've never heard Kat use that word with Jamie before.

With a muted grunt of pain, Augustus slowly hauls himself onto his knees. I drop to the floor beside him as he cradles his jaw—already blooming with an impressive bruise. "Are you okay?" I ask.

"No. That fucking *sucked*," he rasps. But he lets me pull his hand away, and I'm relieved that I don't see anything worse than the bruise.

"Mom, wake up." Kat's voice is small and tearful. "Please wake up."

Wake up? Instantly I'm back on my feet, hurrying into the bedroom and toward a still, silent Jamie. With a growing feeling of dread, I shove away the pillow half covering her face. Was that guy *smothering* her when Kat burst in?

I grab Jamie's wrist, going limp with relief when I feel a steady pulse. Jamie's eyelids flutter as I say, "It's okay, Kat. She's okay."

"Mom?" Kat says again, as though I hadn't spoken. She backs away from the bed and takes hold of her face in both hands, digging her fingernails into her cheeks hard enough to leave marks. I gently take her wrists, and she lets me pull them back, but doesn't look at me. "I'm sorry," she says haltingly. "It's my fault, it's my fault, it's my fault—"

Kat is spiraling, and I'm not sure how to stop her. "It's okay, we'll take her to a hospital to get checked out," I say. "And then we'll call the police—"

"No!" Kat nearly shrieks the word. "No hospital! No police!"

"Why the hell not?" Augustus is beside me now, his fingers tentatively prodding his bruised jaw as his eyes flick between Jamie and Kat.

"We have to get out of here. We have to get out of here *now*," Kat says insistently. Her eyes have taken on a glassy sheen, and when she looks at me, I get the feeling that she's seeing something—or someone—entirely different.

"And go where, exactly?" Augustus asks.

"Someplace safe. Please," Kat says, her voice rising to a fever pitch. "It's not safe here! We're not safe! We need to leave! It's not safe, it's not safe, it's not safe—"

"Okay. Okay!" I say, scooping Jamie off the bed. She murmurs but doesn't wake, and she's as light as a feather in my arms. "We're going." I have no idea where, but we clearly can't stay here while Kat breaks down in front of us. "Augustus, is there anywhere—"

"Yeah," he says, taking a still-babbling Kat by the arm. "Follow me."

CHAPTER TWENTY-SIX

Kat

Something bad happened.

Something bad happened, and it's all my fault. I told Jamie that we needed to stick together—I *told* her—and then I left her alone and she almost died.

I never, ever should have left her alone. *My fault, my fault, my fault . . .*

The words vibrate through my brain, taking over until there's no room for anything else. I'm dimly aware that I'm moving, but I don't know where I am. Wherever it is, it's too hot and too bright. My eyes hurt, and my breath is coming much too fast.

My fault, my fault, my fault . . .

"Kat." It sounds like the voice is a football field away. "Get in the car."

I don't move. Something taps my cheek—not hard enough

to hurt, but hard enough to stop the voice in my head. I blink, and a face swims into view.

"You have to get into the car," Liam says.

"Mom," I say, pushing the word past the lump in my throat. "Where's my mom?"

"In the car. You can sit next to her."

My hands are numb. My heart is beating so hard that it hurts. When I burst through the door of Jamie's apartment in the Sutherland staff quarters, the scene in front of me was straight out of my nightmares. Unconsciously, I'd been waiting for something like that to happen. *Again.* And now memories are crowding my brain, refusing to be shoved down.

"Kat, please." Liam's voice takes on a near-pleading tone. "We need to go."

Somehow, I manage to slide into a seat—Augustus's back seat, I realize hazily—and stay upright while Liam buckles me in like a child. Jamie is beside me, slumped against the window as though she's sleeping.

"Can you tell me what's going on?" Liam asks.

My fault, my fault, my fault . . .

I need to stop the voice in my head.

"Yes," I say to Liam. We're all in the car now, and Augustus shifts into reverse. My voice is too small and too thin, like it belongs to someone much younger. "I can tell you."

"Great," Liam says. "I'm all ears."

He twists in his seat to face me, but I can't look at him. The only way I can tell this story is to stare straight out the window while I talk. "I guess the best place to start," I say, "is that my name used to be Kylie Burke."

Kylie Burke lived in a trailer park in South Carolina for just over four years. I liked it there; our home was small but neat, and our neighbors were friendly. Jamie—who was Ashley Burke back then—was always around. The only thing I didn't like was my father.

Cormac Whittaker. It's a surprisingly nice name for such an awful human. Jamie says he started hitting her once she became pregnant, and it got worse after I was born. But she was afraid she couldn't take care of me on her own, so she stayed.

He never touched me, but he terrified me. All I remember of him is that he was big, loud, and usually angry. It was impossible to please him, so I didn't try. I made myself into his opposite—as small and as quiet as I could get. But it was never enough.

The day everything fell apart, I was watching my favorite cartoon, *The Haunted Sandbox,* which Cormac hated because the ghosts' voices were so high-pitched. But he wasn't there, so I could watch it in peace. For a while.

I'm not sure if what happened next is an actual memory, or just what Jamie told me. It *feels* like a memory; that crystal-clear image of Cormac bursting through the door and yelling "Why is that fucking cartoon *always on*?" I tried to turn it off but accidentally turned it up. I burst into nervous laughter, and his face went purple with rage.

"You think you're funny, don't you, little girl?" he asked.

The cold glint in his eyes *has* to be a true memory. It was the first time he'd ever looked at me the way he looked at my mother.

Jamie scooped me up and ran with me into the bedroom, shoving me into the closet and doing something to the door so I couldn't open it. All I could do was listen while my father beat my mother nearly to death. I whimpered the entire time, repeating the same two words over and over again: *my fault, my fault, my fault.*

He probably would've killed Jamie and come for me next if one of our neighbors hadn't heard and called the cops. Cormac was arrested, and Jamie was hospitalized. The next and last time I saw that neighbor was after Jamie got out of the hospital—another memory that feels like mine, but probably belongs to Jamie.

"Men like that don't let go," our neighbor said. "You should disappear."

So we did.

Once Jamie had fully recovered, she changed both our names and moved us to Nevada to live with her friend Marianne from high school. Then Vegas happened, and Jamie agreed to work for Spotless. Becoming a thief probably felt like a surprisingly safe choice, because it meant being surrounded by people who knew how to take care of themselves.

Jamie and my father had never married, and she hadn't named him on my birth certificate. Most of the time it feels like he never existed, and like Ashley and Kylie Burke never did, either. I only Googled "Cormac Whittaker" once, when I was thirteen—enough to confirm that he was still in the middle of a twenty-year prison sentence, and that I look nothing like his dead-eyed mug shot. I'm Jamie's daughter, through and through. Still, those brief years with him seared my psyche in ways that keep rippling through my life.

Even now, in a car that's deathly quiet except for the sound of my voice.

"It's not just the fact that I'm afraid to leave Jamie by herself, although I am," I say as trees flash past me through the car window. I feel almost as though I'm in a fugue state—like mousy little Kylie suddenly grew a spine and clawed past all my defenses to tell her story. The words are tumbling out of me like water rushing through a broken dam, and there's no way to stop them. "It's everything. If Cormac hadn't nearly killed my mother after yelling at me for watching my favorite cartoon, that cartoon wouldn't have traumatized me. If that cartoon hadn't traumatized me, I wouldn't have left the hotel room in Vegas when it came on. If I hadn't left the hotel room in Vegas, we never would have met Gem. If we hadn't met Gem, we wouldn't be here this weekend. And if we weren't here this weekend, somebody wouldn't have just tried to kill my mother."

And if someone hadn't just tried to kill my mother, I wouldn't be saying any of this. I *shouldn't* be saying any of this. But the truth keeps coming. Not just about Ashley and Kylie and Gem, but about everything I've seen and done since arriving in Bixby—including running for my life after seeing Parker die.

Because the thing about breaking points is, you don't realize you've hit yours until you're already well past it.

CHAPTER TWENTY-SEVEN

Liam

The year before she died, my mother was flipping through channels in our living room when a 1990s movie called *Honeymoon in Vegas* came on. "Oh no," she groaned as dozens of Elvis impersonators flitted across the screen. "Anything but this."

She tried to change the channel, but nothing happened. The remote control's batteries had been low for a while, and we hadn't gotten around to replacing them. Mom started rising from the couch like she was going to hunt down a package of AAAs, until I put out my arm to stop her. "I'm sixteen, Mom," I said. "Elvis impersonators no longer traumatize me."

"They traumatize *me,*" she said, but smiled as she sank back into the cushions.

"Our Elvis was less glittery," I said, watching a bunch of bedazzled impersonators fill the pews of a chapel. Then an actress marched down the aisle in full jewels and a ball gown, her hair piled high. "And so was Jamie."

"That poor girl," Mom sighed. "She was just a kid."

"She was twenty-two."

But even as I said it, I remembered how I'd found that old Vegas wedding photo last year, shoved into the back of a drawer I was cleaning out. As I held it up, I was struck by how *young* Jamie looked. I'd always remembered her like a five-year-old would—as a towering adult, similar to Luke. In the photo, though, she could've passed for my age.

"To your father's thirty-four," Mom said grimly, like her mind was running along a parallel track. She pressed the remote once more before she gave up and tossed it onto the coffee table. "I know it's hard to grasp at your age, but that kind of gap matters. He was old enough to know better. *More* than old enough. But twenty-two, with a four-year-old? Jamie had all that adult responsibility before she'd even had a chance to figure out what being an adult means. If you ask me, latching on to Luke was a cry for help."

"She picked the wrong guy for that," I muttered.

"That she did," Mom sighed.

That conversation with my mom cycles through my brain for at least the tenth time since Kat's confession as Augustus snaps, "Did you know about this? That Kat's mother is a *thief*?"

"No," I say truthfully.

It's the first time we've spoken one-on-one since a nearly catatonic Kat spilled her guts. Not just about her life before Vegas, but about everything that came after—the job that Jamie has had for twelve years, and the job she came to Bixby to do. I don't think Kat fully grasped that she was sharing all of this with Augustus Sutherland. He didn't say a word the entire time.

Not that I said much, either, other than "Holy shit."

Kat finished talking right as Augustus pulled into a narrow gravel road, lined on either side with trees so towering that they formed a canopy above us. It felt as though we were driving straight through the woods for miles, until a tiny gray-shingled cabin appeared before us.

"The first place Granddad ever bought in Bixby," Augustus said tersely as he shifted into park. "Let's hope the spare key is still under the flowerpot."

It was. We managed to get a still-unconscious Jamie inside and into a first-floor bedroom, where Kat curled up beside her without another word. Then, in strained silence, Augustus and I brought all the bags we'd managed to grab from their apartment in the staff quarters into the bedroom. Once we'd piled everything in a corner, Augustus stalked outside, going far enough into the woods that the cabin was barely visible.

And I followed.

Now, Augustus's silver-blue eyes glint as he says, "You knew they used to be married. Your father and Jamie." Kat made that clear in her rambling confession, and at first, I thought that was the worst thing that Augustus was going to hear—that I hadn't been honest with him about the kind of person Luke is. And I was sorry about that, but I was also very wrong. There was much more to come. "But my aunt doesn't know, does she?"

"No," I admit. "I thought about telling her. Or telling you. But Kat made it sound like Jamie could lose her job—"

"Oh yeah, we wouldn't want her to *lose her job,*" Augustus

says sarcastically. "Heaven fucking forbid. Not till she got what she came for."

"I swear to God, Augustus, I didn't know about that," I say. "I hadn't seen or spoken to either Kat or Jamie in twelve years before this weekend."

I run both hands through my hair, tugging hard like that'll somehow help me think through this mess. I should probably be angry with Kat—not as furious as Augustus is, but close. She's been playing me all weekend. Tapping into my semibrotherly concern whenever she needed it, and practically turning me into her accessory. I got her into the compound last night, after all.

But mostly, when I think about Kat, I just feel sad.

I'd been relieved on Friday, when Kat and I walked the edges of the Sutherland compound and she seemed perfectly . . . normal. Fine. Well-adjusted and close to her mom, just like I used to be with mine. It's what I'd always hoped for when I thought about her and Jamie, and I was happy to buy the image that Kat laid out for me. I still haven't fully absorbed the reality—the multiple ways that my Vegas stepsister is not, in fact, *fine.*

I went home from that long-ago fucked-up weekend to my mother, the most stable, nurturing person I've ever known. And I was *still* messed up for years. Meanwhile, a traumatized Kat went home with a jewel thief. Who she and Jamie trusted, because a jewel thief is a hell of a lot better than an abusive parent who tries to kill you.

"I never knew about Kat's father," I say.

A flash of sympathy crosses Augustus's face. "Yeah, that's messed up," he says heavily. "Poor Chaos. Can't believe she had a whole other life."

"Kylie," I say, shaking my head.

Augustus scoffs. "Doesn't fit her."

"And I had no clue what Jamie was really here for," I say. "I just thought she needed the catering job, and that Luke could ruin things for her."

I shouldn't have mentioned Luke, because now Augustus is glaring at me again. "And vice versa, right?" he asks. "Jamie could ruin things for Luke. With my aunt."

Shame keeps me quiet, and he adds, "You know what the worst thing is? I *knew* something was off. With Luke, and even with Kat." He jerks his head in the direction of the cabin before returning his eyes to me. "But you? I didn't see that coming."

Jesus, I feel like shit. I thought I was telling a short-term lie of omission, something I could quickly and easily correct when it was more convenient. But now . . .

I don't know how Luke lives with himself on a daily basis. This is *torture.* Still, I force myself to hold Augustus's gaze, instead of staring at the ground like I want to, as he adds, "What else don't I know?"

"About Kat? There's nothing—"

"About Luke."

No more lies, I think. I owe Augustus that much.

"He's a con man," I say. "He catfishes women for money."

Augustus's lip curls. "Of course he does."

"I was going to—"

"Tell me?" he scoffs. "Add that to the list, huh? So many things you were going to tell me, if only we'd spent more time together this weekend."

"I'm sorry. I've been trying to stop him—I started posing as him to break it off with women he's met online, and I even

193

talked to one of them in person." It's pathetic how desperately I search Augustus's face to see if it softens at all with that revelation. "I came here partly to keep an eye on Luke, but then . . . I didn't know how to protect Kat and Annalise at the same time, and I thought . . . I thought Kat needed it more."

Nope. No softening.

"It's my own fault, really," he says coldly. "When I met you in the field that day, I fully planned to grill you about Luke. But then I saw those pretty, pretty blue eyes of yours, and I let you lie to my face."

I swallow hard and will myself not to blush, because now is definitely not the time to get butterflies over the fact that Augustus likes my eyes.

"I've let you lie to my face for, what? Almost forty-eight hours? About as long as Jamie and Luke were married. What symmetry, huh? I'm such an idiot." He kicks savagely at the ground. "My uncle is *dead,* and here I am taking a punch to the jaw for some random girl who tried to rob my aunt. Except she's not really all that random, is she? She heard Uncle Parker get shot, and said fuck-all about it."

Regret slams into me. This morning, I'd thought I was providing Augustus with a welcome distraction from his family tragedy. Instead, I've made it a hundred times worse. "I'm sorry," I say again. "I shouldn't have let Luke come. I should've told Annalise the truth as soon as I met her. I liked her right away. I really did. And Kat . . ."

I trail off because I know I shouldn't try to defend Kat to Augustus. I can understand her thought process, I guess, and the twisted loyalty she has to Gem and Jamie that made her feel like she couldn't tell anyone what she saw and heard in the woods. But I can't excuse it.

"And Kat's a target now," Augustus says.

I recoil at the words. "What are you talking about?" I say, taking a step back as my eyes search his. "Is . . . is your family going to *do something* to her?"

"Oh my God," Augustus mutters, scraping his palms across his face. "Did you seriously just say that? Who do you think you're dealing with here? The Mafia?"

"Well, you said she's a target, and—"

"Not my *family's*," Augustus says. I must look as confused as I feel, because he snaps his fingers in my face and says, "I know there's a lot going on here, Liam, but you need to keep up. Who did Kat just tell us she saw in the woods? And don't say *Parker*."

"I wasn't going to," I say, although I was. He's right; my thought process is lagging way behind his. "She saw . . . Parker's killer. But she didn't get a good look at him, and—"

"And he doesn't know that," Augustus says. "Does he?"

CHAPTER TWENTY-EIGHT

Kat

It's a cuckoo clock that brings me back.

A noisy clanging makes me shoot up from the strange bed where Jamie and I are lying, my heartbeat instantly going into overdrive. My bare feet hit a ropy rug as I stand up, and I smooth the skirt that's ridden up on my thighs and *Why am I still wearing this miserable dress?*

Also: *Where am I?*

The continued clanging propels me into another room, one that's sparsely decorated with a small love seat, two faded floral armchairs, and a few dark wood accent tables. There are two windows on one wall, both covered with thick plaid curtains that don't let in much light. And between them, there's the wall-mounted cuckoo clock. Its wooden front is carved like a chalet, with a little white fence and what looks like pine cones hanging from the bottom. As I stare, the doors of the chalet open and two tiny figures dressed in lederhosen emerge, spin in a circle, and retreat back into the interior of the clock.

"Good choice," I tell the closed door as the clanging finally stops. "Hide."

That's what I'm doing; I'm hiding. Because I panicked at our apartment in the staff quarters after the attack on Jamie, retreated into the darkest corners of my brain, and forced Liam and Augustus to bring me . . . wherever this is.

It's a modest little one-level cabin, nothing like the mansions I glimpsed on the Sutherland compound. Although it's perfectly neat, with whitewashed walls and no clutter in sight, the floors look like they haven't been swept in months. When I run a finger across the nearest table, I leave a shiny trail in the dust.

The first place Granddad ever bought in Bixby.

Augustus had said that, right before he and Liam hustled us inside.

After I told them . . . everything.

And now, the boys are nowhere in sight. I exhale noisily and wait for the panic to return, because, wow, I just royally screwed Jamie and Gem, didn't I? I might've been able to convince Liam to keep quiet, but Augustus? Augustus Sutherland, whose aunt we were supposed to rob?

The odds aren't good. And yet it's hard to care when somebody almost killed my mother. Tried to suffocate her with a pillow, because . . .

Because *why?*

The answer makes my knees go weak. *Because of me. Because I saw him kill Parker.*

That has to be it. Otherwise, there's no good reason why

after I ran into a big lumbering murderer in the woods, a big lumbering murderer climbed into our apartment and tried to kill . . . not me, obviously, but the person he thought was me. He got a good enough look in the woods to recognize me from . . . where? The staff quarters? That disastrous lunch? The party?

And then, somehow, he knew where to find me. He must have realized I was part of the catering staff, which would explain why he made his way to the apartment building. But how did he know the exact room? Does that mean Parker's killer was a caterer? Or someone on the planning committee, with access to details and a grudge against Parker?

Yeah, Kat, you've cracked the case, I think wearily. *Hell hath no fury like a party planner scorned.*

None of this makes sense, but I've already spent too much time pacing. I need to check on my mother—my poor, sick, clueless mother, who took the brunt of an attack meant for me. When I return to the bedroom, her lashes are fluttering, and I take that as a hopeful sign. "Jamie," I say, giving her arm a gentle squeeze. "Wake up."

She groans softly but opens her eyes. "Kat, what . . . What's going on?" she asks woozily.

Where do I even start? "Are you . . . How are you feeling?" I ask.

"Like I was hit by a truck," Jamie murmurs. "And yet, *starving.*" She manages to sit up a little with my help, and blinks around in confusion. "Where are we?"

"A friend's house," I say, noticing for the first time that our bags are piled up in one corner of the bedroom. Most of the zippers are half-undone, and clothes are spilling everywhere; it looks like Liam and Augustus hastily grabbed all of our stuff and brought it along with us. But after that . . . where did they go? Straight to the police?

No. I have to believe Liam wouldn't do that without at least giving me a heads-up.

"What friend?" Jamie asks. Her voice is sluggish and her expression vacant, but she doesn't look any worse than she did when she first got sick. The smothering attack, which she clearly doesn't remember, doesn't seem to have had lasting effects. *We stopped him in time,* I think, drinking in the comfortingly familiar lines of her face.

Jamie looks pale and tired, but not afraid. Not panicked, like she will be once I explain everything. What does Gem say about avoiding questions you don't want to answer?

Answer a different question.

"We brought you here to recover," I say.

I know I'm being cowardly, because I'm afraid to have this conversation until I know what Liam and Augustus are thinking. But also, Jamie nearly died today. Was nearly *murdered* today. How am I supposed to tell her that, and then tell her that she's probably going to jail?

Before Jamie can ask another question, I scramble to my feet. "I need to check in with them, but first . . . you should eat something. Here." I cross over to her backpack and haul out the ultimate comfort food: homemade granola. "No milk, but I can get you some water to wash it down," I say, popping open the container and handing it to her.

I expect her to protest, but I guess she wasn't kidding about being starving, because within seconds her mouth is too full to talk. Relieved, I hurry into the kitchen and start opening cabinets. There's not much, but I find a small stack of paper cups and fill one of them to the brim with water. I bring it into the bedroom and place it on the side table, then root around in Jamie's backpack until I find a phone charger. "I'll be right back," I say, before scurrying out of the room and closing the door behind me.

I find an outlet behind a small table, plug in the charger, and connect it to my phone. Once the battery has enough juice to light my screen, I open my messages and send one to Liam: *Are you still speaking to me?*

When there's not an instant response, I add, *I'm sorry.*

Now what? I'm desperate to call Gem. To explain that someone tried to kill Jamie—tried to kill *me*—so she can help. But the last time Gem and I spoke outside the staff quarters, she told me, very emphatically, to do nothing. Instead, I did a whole lot of somethings, including revealing her entire operation to her mark's nephew.

I can't sit still; I'm humming with too much anxiety. I leave my phone on the table and cross to the front door. As soon as I open it and step outside, I see Augustus's gray BMW still parked directly in front. *That's a good sign,* I tell myself, breathing a little more freely. *Maybe the boys never left.*

But if not, where are they?

"Liam?" I call softly. "Augustus?"

There's no response. I swat at a hovering bug before heading for the back of the cabin, hoping to find a deck, or a gazebo, or anyplace that people might go to get some distance from the criminals in their midst. But there's nothing except more trees. I walk farther into the woods, stepping softly through the crunch of leaves, and then I hear it—the low murmur of voices.

I pause and duck behind a tree. Even though I'm 99 percent sure that it's Liam and Augustus, I'd like to be at 100 percent before revealing myself. I wait for a few long heartbeats, until I hear Liam's voice say, "Yes, Kat."

I slip out from behind the tree—which, I now realize, was doing absolutely nothing to hide me—and say, "Yes what?"

"I'm still speaking to you," Liam says. He's not smiling, but he doesn't look as angry as I'd feared he would.

I exhale in relief, until I notice Augustus standing beside him with a deep purple bruise on his jaw. "You're hurt," I say, my stomach twisting with guilt. *My fault.*

"I've been told it looks worse than it feels," Augustus says. He touches it gingerly with his fingertips before adding, "Nice to see that you've rejoined the land of the living."

I managed to avoid a hard conversation with Jamie earlier, but I can't avoid this one. I knot my fingers together as the words come rushing out. "I don't even know what to say except that I'm sorry. To both of you for lying, but to you especially, Augustus, for what Jamie and I did to your family. We never should have tried to steal from your aunt. If we hadn't—"

"Why are you saying *we*?" Liam interrupts. "You didn't do anything."

I blink at him. "Huh? I did . . . many things."

"Well, yeah. You lied to me and manipulated me, and I'm not happy about any of it. But you're not a thief," Liam says. "Jamie is. And, look, I know her life's been rough—going from your father to Luke is a shitty hand. But it's *her* hand. *She's* the parent."

"But . . ." He doesn't get it. Doesn't understand that Jamie and I are a *team*. If I'd truly wanted to stop her, I could have.

Right? She would have listened to me. And she did listen to her own conscience, eventually. "She was trying to change. This was supposed to be the last job."

I force myself to meet Augustus's eyes. I don't know if it's possible to convince him to keep quiet about Jamie. But from the little I've gotten to know about him, my strongest impression is this: he hates bullshit. So I might as well be brutally honest.

"That's how I thought of it—a job," I continue. "I didn't spend nearly enough time thinking about how your aunt would feel to have something that she cared about taken away from her. And then, when Parker died"—I swallow past the lump in my throat—"I couldn't figure out how to tell anyone what I saw without blowing up my whole life."

"So you said nothing," Augustus says.

I hold his cool gaze. "I said nothing," I say. "I'm sorry."

"You do realize that *saying nothing* almost got your mother killed, right?" he asks. "And you. And me. And Liam."

I have to give it to him; he's right. "Yeah," I say. "Parker's killer must have gotten a better look at me than I got of him. And listen—I know this is late in the game and I should've said something before, but . . . your uncle's friend, that guy Barrett, acted weird when I ran into him after Parker died. And he's a big, strong guy, and he—"

"*Barrett?*" Augustus says incredulously. "You think Barrett Covington killed my uncle. Barrett Covington of the Scarsdale Covingtons, the family that built the biggest cancer research center on the East Coast and funds it almost entirely with their own money?"

"Well, I didn't know his whole résumé, but . . . yeah," I say.

"Hang on," Augustus mutters, pulling out his phone. "Let me check in with someone." I wouldn't have thought we'd get reception in the middle of the woods, but then again, this is Ross Sutherland's property. Even if he barely uses it, he probably still turned half the surrounding trees into cell towers.

Liam looks cautiously between us as Augustus taps at his screen. "It did sound as though the killer might've known Parker," he says. "What did you hear him say, Kat? 'You got what you deserve'?"

" 'Serves you right, you goddamn idiot,' " I say. The words are burned into my brain.

"Well, Barrett left for New York this morning," Augustus reports, looking up from his phone. "So he couldn't have crawled through your window."

"Says who?" I ask.

"Says our head of security, who made arrangements to get him to the airport."

"Did he actually see him get on the plane?"

"Oh, for— Listen, it's not *Barrett*," Augustus says with an exasperated groan. "Trust me on this. There's no reason. He and Uncle Parker have been friends for years."

"You never know what people are capable of," I say.

Augustus raises his eyebrows. "Touché, Kylie," he says.

Ouch. Maybe I deserve that, but the name still makes me hunch into myself with the instinctive urge to hide. "I never refer to myself as . . . her," I say.

To my surprise, Augustus actually looks regretful. "Okay," he says. "Sorry. You're just a lot to absorb at once, you know? Con artists and heists and—how does that even work, by the way? Did your boss honestly believe a jewelry nut like my aunt

203

wouldn't notice that her favorite necklace was suddenly full of glass?"

"She wouldn't," I say, and I can't help the note of pride that creeps into my voice.

"Impossible," Augustus says.

"It's true. Gem's fakes are so good that even people who've worked with her for years get mixed-up sometimes. Whenever there's a job like—" I was about to say "a job like this," before remembering that we're talking about Augustus's aunt. "Whenever there's a swap, Gem has to make a little scratch on the fake's clasp so nobody gets confused."

Augustus rubs his forehead. "This is a whole new world," he mutters.

"Look, Augustus . . ." I can't hold the question back any longer. "What are you going to do?" He cocks his head, and I clarify, "About me and my mother."

Augustus doesn't speak for a few agonizing seconds, and I listen to the rustling forest sounds that surround us, imagining them being replaced by sirens. "I'm not sure," he finally says.

"Jamie and I . . . we can leave," I say. "We won't bother your family again—"

"Kat, someone tried to kill her," Liam breaks in. "You can't just *leave*."

"We can, though," I say. "Jamie's staff credentials were fake, remember? Nobody knows her real name, or mine. Whoever this guy was . . . he won't be able to find us once we're gone. And you know everything I know, now," I say, turning back to Augustus. "You can give the police a description of the man who killed Parker and tell them what I heard. Maybe that'll help them find him. You can tell them . . . tell them it was an anonymous tip."

"You've really thought this through, haven't you?" Augustus says dryly.

Before I can keep begging, his phone buzzes. I step forward to peer at his screen, curious despite myself. "Is that security again?" I ask. "Did they realize Barrett Whatshisname isn't in New York after all? Did he—"

"Oh my God, will you get *off* the Barrett train," Augustus mutters. "And no." He pockets his phone, then turns to Liam and says, "It's Clive. We're being summoned."

CHAPTER TWENTY-NINE

Liam

"Two o'clock?" I say when Augustus turns his key in the BMW's ignition and the dashboard lights up. "That's impossible. Your clock must've stopped at some point."

"Precision German engineering does not simply *stop*," Augustus says, executing a three-point turn so we can drive out the way we came.

I'm pretty sure he's joking, just like he was the first time we met, when he acted like Kat wandering the Sutherland fields was a firing-squad offense. But I'm too stressed to laugh. "I know, but it was just a little after eleven when we went to get Kat. And since then . . ." I pull my phone from my pocket to compare clocks. 2:01.

"Since then," Augustus says, "we foiled an attempted murder and harbored a jewel thief, and I learned that Luke is a con man, Kat used to be your stepsister, and Jamie changed both their names more than a decade ago." He lost his sunglasses at some point, and squints as the afternoon sun slants through a break in the trees. "It's been a hectic three hours, hasn't it?"

"That it has."

We left Kat in the woods with a lot undecided. All Augustus said, once he pocketed his phone, was that she should check on Jamie and we'd come back as soon as possible. Kat just nodded, eyes huge, and I could almost see the wheels spinning in her head: *No car. Middle of nowhere. Jamie's weak. I'm stuck.*

I can't read Augustus well enough to know what he's thinking. I know what he *should* do, because it's what I should do, too: tell Ross Sutherland everything. But I also know that will land Jamie in jail.

And maybe she deserves it, but I still have a soft spot for Jamie. I haven't forgotten her kindness in Vegas, and it was awful to hear what her life was like before that. I think she's genuine about wanting to make a change, even if you could argue that she should've made a much cleaner break than she did. Plus, if Jamie gets arrested, what happens to Kat? As far as I can tell, there's not a single person in the world she can rely on except her mother.

The whole situation is impossible.

I'm relieved when, instead of continuing that conversation, Augustus reaches for the radio and snaps it on. Like he's saying, *Let's take a break.*

I could really, really use a break.

Music fills the car—a mellow but catchy song with '70s vibes that's immediately recognizable. But even as I tap my fingers on my knee along with the familiar tune, I know I'll never be able to name it. "What is this?" I ask as we make our way down the narrow gravel road through the woods.

" 'Right Down the Line,' " Augustus says. "This used to be my mother's car, and Sirius is very loyal to her. It's not interested in playing anything recorded after the eighties. Occasionally some grunge sneaks in, but very reluctantly."

"I like it," I say. Augustus turns the volume up to that perfect level where the song fills the car but we're still able to hear one another talk. "So your mom . . . I know she's out of the country, but if she weren't, would she have come to the party? Or is that not something she'd do?" It's ridiculous, considering everything we've been through this weekend, how little I still know about Augustus Sutherland.

"It's not something she'd do," he says. "Even when she and my father were married, she wasn't big on Sutherland family events. Not a fan of my grandfather."

"Do you live with her sometimes?" I ask. "Or just with your dad?"

"Both," Augustus says. "Usually I'm in New York with Dad during the school year, and I spend summers with my mother. But this year, she's traveling with her new boyfriend, so my father's stuck with me." He turns onto Bixby's main road and adds, "As you know, it's driven him to drink."

"That doesn't have anything to do with you," I say. I don't know much about addiction, but I do know that.

"Don't be so sure," he says. "You've only seen me at parties, or assisting secret stepsisters, or heroically taking a punch to the jaw. That's my entire upside."

I doubt that, I think, but the words get stuck in my throat.

I look at him sideways, taking in the bruise he keeps unconsciously touching, and have a sudden urge to trace the path of his fingertips with my own. To feel the sharp plane of his jaw beneath my thumb, before moving up to his full bottom lip. The timing couldn't be worse for that, though, so I clench my hands in my lap and ask, "Why do you go to Stuyvesant? Instead of . . . whatever fancy prep school the rest of your family went to?"

"Because my parents can't pay for it without my grandfather's help," Augustus says. "And I'd rather not be dependent on his whims. That hasn't worked out well for my father. Or anyone in my family, really."

"I think that's . . ." *Remarkable. Impressive. More than a little hot, if I'm being perfectly honest.* ". . . pretty cool," I finish limply. Then I'm too embarrassed to wait for his response, so I quickly ask, "So you're not seeing your mom at all this summer?"

"No," Augustus says with a shrug. "But it's all right. We're not close. She loves me, but she doesn't particularly like me."

This time I manage to say it: "I doubt that. Why would you think so?"

"Because before she left for Italy last month, she told me, 'Augustus, you know that I love you. But I don't particularly like you,'" he says, deadpan.

I'm not sure how to answer him, so I just go with the truth. "I can never tell when you're kidding," I admit.

"When in doubt," he says, "assume that I am."

His usual offhand tone sounds a little strained, though. I glance at his profile, all tousled golden hair and perfectly angular cheekbones, and wonder how much energy it takes to make the world believe that nothing ever bothers you. A lot, probably.

"I don't like Luke. At all," I say. "But a part of me is always going to wish that he liked me. And he never has. One of the things I remember most about Vegas is how after Jamie and Luke arrived at the hotel where we'd been found, Jamie fell to her knees, crying her eyes out, and yanked Kat into this bone-crushing hug, while Luke just stood there. I sat on the floor next to them and looked up at him, and he said, 'Why the hell did you leave the room?' "

A flush rises in Augustus's cheeks. That's a first; I'm usually the one who goes red when we talk. "And you were what, five?" he asks.

"Five," I confirm.

"Wow," he says. "You know, I complain about my parents a lot, and God knows they deserve it, but that . . . that's a whole other level. Not Chaos level, but still pretty bad."

"So there you go," I say, making my own attempt at lightness. "Kat takes the gold, obviously, but I get the silver medal in the Bad Parent Olympics."

"I guess you do," Augustus says.

James Taylor's "Fire and Rain" comes on then. One of my mom's favorites, and such a melancholy song that I have to turn the volume down before my already-fragile mood goes straight to miserable. "What's happening back at the compound?" I ask.

"Not sure," Augustus says. "Clive just said he needed us."

"Both of us?" I'm suddenly nervous. "Why would he need me?"

"He didn't say. Sorry," he says. "I should have asked, but I just assumed he wouldn't tell me anyway."

"Do you think it has to do with Parker?"

"Maybe," Augustus says, turning onto a road that I recognize as leading to the Sutherland compound. It's a little unnerving how close we are to the cabin we just left. "Maybe whatever happened can't be 'contained' any longer."

The words hang between us as we approach the gate, which is a lot more heavily guarded than it was when Luke and I first arrived. Augustus rolls down his window, and one of the guards waves him through. We cruise down a series of winding roads until we reach the biggest mansion I've seen yet. I don't need Augustus to tell me that it belongs to his grandfather; compared to this, the term *cottages* finally makes sense.

Augustus shifts into park, then glances at me and says, "Ready?"

"I guess," I say.

We both get out of the car, but once I shut the door, my feet feel like they've taken root in the driveway. "Augustus," I say, hanging back as he heads toward the front door. "Wait a sec."

He turns, brows lifted. "What?"

I glance at the windows in Ross's house; every curtain is drawn. Still, that doesn't mean we're not being watched. Or listened to. I move closer so I can lower my voice. "Look, I know you need to tell your family what Kat saw and heard in the woods," I say. "As for everything else, well . . . you can say it any time. But you can't *unsay* it."

"So you're recommending the anonymous tip approach?" he says, brushing his fingertips against his bruised jaw. "And how should I explain this? Sunday morning bar fight?"

"I don't know," I say, tired. He's right; I'm being ridiculous. "I'm sorry if that was out of line. It's just . . . Kat doesn't have anyone except her mom."

"I get it," Augustus says. "But that's not entirely true. She has you."

He starts moving again, and I have no choice but to follow. Before we reach the front door, though, it swings open. The security guard from the safe room, Dan, pokes his head outside and says, "Hey, Augustus. They're not quite—" He stares at Augustus's jaw. "What the hell happened to you?"

"It's nothing," Augustus says. "They're not quite *what*?"

"Ready for you," Dan says. "But seriously, kid, your face—"

"Clive said it was urgent," Augustus says. "That I had to come back right away."

"Well, we do need you here," Dan says. "Your grandfather wants to have an early dinner. Four o'clock, I think."

"Four o'clock?" Augustus says. He pulls out his phone, checks the time, and arches his eyebrows. "So . . . ninety minutes from now?"

"Don't shoot the messenger, okay?" Dan says with a sheepish grin. "I think Clive's planning on some prep work before dinner. Police will be back tomorrow afternoon for another round of interviews, and they're going to want to talk to you and Liam."

"What?" I practically squeak the word, and Dan focuses on me for the first time. I can feel my face growing hot as I add, "Why me?"

"Because you were here when Parker died," Dan says. "Don't worry. Just standard procedure."

Oh God. This morning, I would've been more than happy to help. But now, all I can think about is Kat's bombshell confession. I'd asked Augustus to cover for her, but somehow, it didn't occur to me that I might need to do the same. That I'd have to sit across from a police officer and pretend I don't have any new information about this weekend. What if I let something slip? Or if I tell a lie? Is that perjury? No, I wouldn't be under oath, but I—

"Relax, Liam," Augustus says. From the sharp tone of his voice, I can tell he knows exactly where my thoughts are headed. "All they'll want to know is what you heard and what you saw before we got into the safe room. That's it."

I swallow a few times, trying to open up my throat so I won't squeak again. "Sure. It's just . . . I've never talked to the police before," I say.

"That's where Clive comes in," Dan says. "He'll make sure you're ready."

Ready for what? For Ross Sutherland's version of events? *It's the* way *he died,* Clive had said in the safe room. *People are going to ask—*

Ross didn't let him finish the sentence. Ask what? Are we finally going to find out?

Augustus looks like he's wondering the same thing. "All right, we might as well get started," he says, trying to move past Dan to enter the house. Dan blocks him, and Augustus huffs out a laugh. "You're hilarious. Let me in."

"Sorry," Dan says. "Not yet."

Augustus's jaw drops. "Are you kidding me?" he sputters.

"Sorry," Dan repeats. "They're having a family meeting."

"I'm family!" Augustus protests.

"I know you are," Dan says. "But it's adults only for now. They're all shut up in your grandfather's office. Why don't you guys go play some darts? I'll come get you when they're ready." And then, without another word, he gently closes the door in our faces.

After a moment of stunned silence, Augustus smacks his

palm against the door in frustration. "This is unbelievable," he hisses. "They expect me to be at their beck and call, and now they want me to *play darts*? To hell with all of them. Let's get out of here."

He turns and strides toward the car, but before he's gotten far, I manage to catch up and grab hold of his arm. "What?" he asks, tugging free. "Do you honestly think I'm going to wait around for these assholes?"

"No," I say. "But that's not your only option."

Augustus snorts. "Do you think I should barrel into Granddad's office? Insist they include me? I already tried that."

"No," I say. "I think you should *listen* in."

Some of the frustration drains from his face, replaced by amusement. "Pretty twisted thinking for such a wholesome young man," he says, lips almost quirking into a smile.

"Does that mean you agree?" I ask.

His expression clears, as though he's suddenly realized exactly what to do next. "Obviously," he says. "Come on."

CHAPTER THIRTY

Liam

A few minutes later, after Augustus wormed his way past Dan the security guard by telling him we wanted to get a couple of books, we're on the second floor of Ross's house. I crane my neck to take in my surroundings, because even though it's just a hallway, it's the fanciest one I've ever seen. The ceiling is elaborately carved wood, the walls are filled with art, and lights flickering every few feet are encased in what look like solid gold sconces.

When we reach a closed door at the end of the hall, Augustus grasps the doorknob. "Granddad keeps a room full of kids' books, like a family library," he says. "I hung out here all the time when I was younger, but I haven't been in ages. I should've remembered before now—this would've come in handy when they were all holed up after Uncle Parker died."

"Remember what?" I ask.

"You'll see," he says, slipping off his shoes. He gestures for me to do the same, then puts his fingers to his lips. "Be quiet."

215

The room inside is a lot simpler than the hallway. It's small, with a sloped ceiling and waist-high built-in shelves, all of which are crammed with children's books. "Is Dan aware that all of these are picture books?" I ask, pulling out a copy of *Goodnight Moon.*

"No," Augustus says. "Only family ever comes in here." He pads silently across a striped rug and kneels on the floor at the far side of the room. I put the book down to follow, and it's not until I'm almost directly on top of him that I see the metal air grate.

"Granddad's study is directly below. If he talks loudly enough, I can hear him," Augustus whispers as I lower myself beside him. "I used to eavesdrop every December to try and figure out what he was getting me for Christmas." Then he presses his ear to the grate.

I do the same. Cool air brushes my skin, and I hear . . . something. The low murmur of voices, a mix of male and female. But they're being relatively quiet; all I can make out are a few scattered words. *Party. Impossible. Bixby. Parker.*

"Would we have better luck outside his door?" I whisper.

"No," Augustus whispers back. "It's too solid. Besides, his staff is constantly coming and going down that hall. This is better."

"If you say so."

Questions. Parker. Debts.

Debts. That was my very first theory—that Parker died because of gambling debts. Is it actually true? I inch closer to the grate, ears straining. There's a low, soothing murmur that I'm almost sure is Annalise, and then—as clearly as if he were in the room with us—Ross Sutherland snaps, "Because I don't want the entire world to know what my son was capable of!"

My gaze slides toward Augustus as Annalise says something unintelligible back. Then Larissa lets out a bitter laugh. "Do you honestly think they don't already?" she asks. "It's not just this weekend. It's—"

"This weekend is contained," Ross says.

"Like Mother's accident was contained?" Larissa says sharply.

Augustus and I both lift our heads, and I can see my confusion mirrored in his expression. *Mother's accident?* What does that have to do with . . .

Ross's tone is so weary that I have to scrunch back down to hear him. "What does it matter, Larissa? He's gone. Just like she is."

"It matters because she shouldn't *be* gone!" Larissa says. "And wouldn't be gone, if Parker hadn't gotten wasted and driven that goddamn boat into—"

"Enough!" Ross roars. Augustus inhales sharply as my heart stutters.

Annalise finally speaks loudly enough for me to hear. "Why do we always protect him, no matter what he does?" she asks.

"Because it's what your mother would have wanted," Ross says. "And that's that."

Their voices drop again. Augustus scrambles backward until he's seated in the middle of the room, his face deathly pale. "Holy shit," he says in a hoarse whisper. "Did you hear that?"

"Yeah," I say. "Your uncle . . ."

I don't want to be the one to say it. Augustus picks up

where I left off, his voice barely audible. "My uncle caused the accident that killed my grandmother," he says.

I sit beside him. "You didn't know," I say. It's not a question; it's obvious that Augustus had no clue what had really happened until just now.

He shakes his head. "God, no. They said she was alone when she collided with the shore. That *she* was driving the boat. I remember being surprised that Gran would have an accident like that when she'd spent half her life on boats, but . . . I never questioned it." He passes a hand over his mouth, then rises to his feet. "Come on. Sounds like they're done with the crap I'm not supposed to hear, so they'll probably head for the sitting room soon."

I follow him into the corridor and down the stairs, my mind racing. Is this what the Sutherlands don't want coming out—that Parker was responsible, even accidentally, for his mother's death? But that doesn't make sense; if nobody knew for years, there's no reason to think that they'd learn about it now. Besides, that doesn't seem to have anything to do with what Clive said in the safe room. *It's the* way *he died.*

Gambling debts? Or something else?

"This way," Augustus says breathlessly when we reach the bottom of the stairs. He pulls me into a room that's all windows on one end, with an enormous fireplace on the other. It crackles with roaring, dancing flames, even though—or maybe because—the air-conditioning is turned up high. The wallpaper is busy enough to hurt my eyes—huge flowers and twisting branches that hold bright-eyed, neat-feathered birds. We've barely settled ourselves onto a rock-hard couch before I hear voices coming down the hall.

"Dinner's at four sharp," Ross Sutherland says. "Dress appropriately."

"We always do," Annalise says, right before the three of them turn the corner and enter the sitting room. Then Annalise lets out a loud gasp, hurrying toward Augustus with one hand outstretched. "Darling, your face!" she cries out. She brushes her fingers against his bruise and asks, "What happened?"

A muscle jumps in Augustus's cheek. His eyes cut from his aunt to his grandfather, and then to me. I can feel myself tensing, waiting for the kind of revelation that'll send all the dominos in Kat's life tumbling down.

"Well?" Ross says, coming closer for a better look. "What have you gotten into?"

Augustus keeps his eyes on mine as he says, "Bar fight."

CHAPTER THIRTY-ONE

Kat

As soon as Augustus's taillights disappeared through the woods, I exhaled a deep breath and let my shoulders slump. That could've gone worse, but it also could've gone a *lot* better.

And now I'm essentially trapped here. There's nothing I can do except what I told Augustus I would: check on Jamie. She's probably eaten enough to get some energy back, and she must be incredibly confused. She'll have a lot of questions, and I have to start giving her answers. Maybe together, we can figure out a plan that actually works.

But as soon as I walk inside, I hear an all-too-familiar noise—loud, painful-sounding retching coming from the bathroom. "Jamie?" I call, sprinting to her.

She's huddled over the toilet, shaking. "It's back," she whimpers.

Guilt snakes through my stomach as I drop to my knees beside her. "I'm sorry," I say, smoothing her hair. She's all clammy again, her skin a grayer shade of pale. "I shouldn't have made you eat."

Why did I make her eat? Never mind, I know—because I'd wanted to distract her. Because I'd convinced myself that she couldn't possibly have the *Someone tried to kill you* conversation on an empty stomach.

I stay with her until even her dry heaves finally peter out. "Let's get you back to bed," I say, slinging an arm around her shoulder to lift her to her feet. It's tough going, though; she's deadweight, and I have to practically carry her into the bedroom.

Once she's on the bed, she curls into a fetal position.

"I'm sorry," I say again, putting the top back on the granola container that she left on the bedside table. "I thought food would help."

Then I pause, container in hand. Food *should've* helped, if she really was recovering from the flu or another virus. There's no reason the same homemade granola Jamie eats every day would make her sick again, unless there's something wrong with it.

I reopen the container and peer inside. The granola is brown and crunchy and, to me, entirely unappetizing. Just like always. I dump it onto the floor, leaving the container empty except for a grainy tan residue. I run my finger across the bottom, then tentatively lick the powder from my skin. It tastes like cardboard.

A memory hits me then: of me and Jamie making smoothies years ago, when she'd just started to eat healthier. We'd perfected a strawberry-banana recipe we both liked, but this time, after she'd poured almond milk into the blender, she showed me a bottle filled with tan powder. "We're going to add wheat germ," she said.

"Let me try." I took the bottle from her and shook some wheat germ right into my mouth. Then I immediately spit it out. "Gross! It might as well be cardboard," I complained, grabbing a can of soda so I could wash the taste out of my mouth.

"It's good for you," Jamie said. "And you won't even notice it once it's mixed in with everything else."

But after she drank the smoothie, she got violently ill. That's why she went gluten-free back then—because a tablespoon of wheat germ had knocked her out for days. She hadn't been that sick again until . . . *now.*

I pick up a handful of granola from the floor and stare at it. It wasn't obvious before, but now that I'm looking for wheat germ, I can't *not* see it. Tiny tan grains everywhere.

I drop the granola and sit back on my haunches with a loud exhale. In some ways, it's a relief to finally understand what's going on with Jamie, especially because I know she'll be fine once the gluten is out of her system. But now I have an entirely new problem, because there's no way my mother would make that kind of mistake. She hasn't touched wheat germ in years.

Which means someone else must have put it there.

But why? And *who*? Jamie had made this batch the morning we left for Bixby. She'd eaten a bowlful, packed up the rest in her backpack, placed the backpack in our trunk, and then—

I let out a gasp so loud that Jamie stirs on the bed.

Then I'd seen *Morgan*, who'd said she was checking the spare tire, holding Jamie's backpack. And it was unzipped.

"Oh my God," I say, scrambling to my feet. "It was Morgan."

No wonder she'd looked rattled when I'd appeared. She

knows about Jamie's allergies, and she essentially *poisoned* her. It's the only thing that makes sense, and yet . . . it makes no sense. Morgan has no reason to hurt Jamie like this, unless . . .

Unless she wanted Jamie out of the way.

"Maybe she's jealous of you," I say to Jamie's huddled form.

I always thought Morgan and Jamie had a friendly type of rivalry, but then again, how would *I* feel if my mother seemed to prefer one of my friends to me? Jamie has always been Gem's golden girl, so much so that Gem was once again helping her start a new life. What had Morgan said when Jamie told her? *You say you're done, and suddenly you've got a nine-to-five with, what? A 401(k) and shit?*

Meanwhile, Morgan had messed up so badly that Gem had cut her out of the Sutherland job. Maybe Morgan wanted to ruin Jamie's chance to go straight—or ruin her entire relationship with Gem. Morgan could've planted the diamond ring, too, to make Gem think Jamie stole it.

If Morgan was willing to do that, what *else* could she have done?

All of a sudden, half my theories about this weekend fly out the window. What if I've been looking at the missing necklace all wrong? I'd been so quick to assume Vicky took it, and at the time, that had made sense—she was right there, and I was desperate for answers. Vicky seemed like a problem I could solve.

But *Morgan*—what if she decided to not only take Jamie out of commission, but to take the necklace as well? Morgan knew exactly where to find it. All she'd have to do—even if she realized I was here in Bixby, frantically impersonating my mother—was wait for the right moment to make her move.

Then what? Would Morgan heroically "find" the necklace

that my mother was careless enough to let out of her sight? Or was she planning to double-cross Gem, swap the necklace herself, and sell it to her own buyer? That might've seemed like a win-win scenario, right up until the point that Parker Sutherland was killed.

And now Morgan has gone dark. Was she able to switch the necklace before everything went to hell? Does she know what happened to Parker? Is she afraid of getting blamed for his death? Or is she just afraid of Gem's wrath? It's too many questions for my brain to process at once—especially when that last one hits so close to home.

"I know the feeling," I mutter, rubbing my arms against goose bumps. Morgan isn't the only one who needs to worry about Gem. I'm not sure how much time has passed since the attack on Jamie, but as far as Gem knows, we're on our way back to Boston. I can't explain why we're not, without also explaining how I accidentally outed Spotless.

I need to fix this mess, and fast, before Gem starts wondering where we are. When Augustus comes back, I'll convince him to keep quiet. Somehow. And then I'll figure out what Morgan is up to . . . also somehow.

That one feels like the bigger challenge, because at least Augustus is *here*. Morgan could be anywhere, and she has zero incentive to talk to me. Unless . . .

I tap my knuckles against my palm as I think. Gem is already annoyed with Morgan—even without knowing everything that Morgan did, and might have done, this weekend. Maybe the incentive I should offer is this: *I can keep that hole you've dug from getting deeper.*

Or I can bury you.

I pick up my phone and open my contacts, searching for Morgan's name. I've lost track of what letter I'm on at this point, but I might as well call this Plan H, for *Hail Mary*. There's very little strategy involved here; all I'm doing, really, is throwing a metaphorical ball into the void and hoping that Morgan will lunge for it.

I'm in Bixby with Jamie, I type to Morgan. *She was really sick yesterday. I know why, and so do you. I was going to tell Gem, but I thought I'd give you a chance to explain yourself first. Meet me at the Marlow Hotel in Randall tomorrow at 9am.*

Then I take a deep breath and hit SEND.

CHAPTER THIRTY-TWO

Liam

I hear the faint sound of music when I step inside the guest cottage. Before I can creep upstairs, Luke calls out, "Is that you, my love?"

Definitely not. "It's Liam," I call back.

Luke emerges from the kitchen, holding a glass of bourbon even though it's barely three o'clock. "Don't give me that look," he says when my eyes linger on the glass. "It's been a long weekend." He frowns as I close the door behind me. "Annalise isn't with you? I thought she was meeting you and Augustus at Ross's house."

"She did, but then she ended up going with Augustus to Griffin's cottage," I say. "Augustus, um, got punched in the jaw. Bar fight," I add as Luke's eyebrows raise.

I hope he won't ask too many follow-up questions, because Augustus and I haven't had time to get our story straight, but Luke just rolls his eyes. "Fucking rich kids," he says.

I know better than to expect much from Luke in terms of support or sympathy, but he's the only person here and I'm still freaked out by everything I've learned since returning to the compound. "You know Dan, the security guard?" I say. "He told me I'm supposed to talk to the police tomorrow."

Luke's jaw twitches. "I heard that," he says. "Not sure why it's necessary, when you were with me the whole time and I already talked to them. But I suppose they have to dot their *i*'s and cross their *t*'s." He takes a sip of bourbon and adds, "Don't worry about it. You're meeting with Clive soon, right? He'll prep you."

"Yeah, but . . . why do I need to be prepped?" I ask. I might be filled to the brim with secrets about this weekend, but Clive doesn't know that.

"Because it's the Sutherlands," Luke says. "They have their own way of doing things, and it's important that we're all on message."

"On message?" I repeat.

"Image is everything for a family with this much influence," Luke says. "If tragedies get exploited for gossip, millions of dollars are at stake."

"Gossip? Like what? About how Parker died? Or about how . . . someone else might have died?" I search Luke's face for any hint that he knows what the Sutherlands are hiding about Parker or Augustus's grandmother, but he just scoffs.

"Nobody else died," he says. "Stop being dramatic. Just do what Clive tells you and you'll be fine. I already talked to the police, and it was very routine. They didn't go deep."

That's actually comforting. If the police didn't "go deep" with Luke—the guy whose first meet-the-family event with his heiress girlfriend ended in murder—they probably won't bother with his seventeen-year-old son. "Okay," I say. "Good to know. Thanks."

"You're welcome." He looks me up and down and adds, "You're a mess, by the way. Take a shower and put on something decent. Ross will expect a suit at dinner."

It's as close as I'm going to get to fatherly advice, so I take it.

Half an hour later, I'm looping my tie in the mirror of my suite when my phone vibrates in my pocket. I dig it out to a text from Augustus: *Coming by.*

I finish the knot and type back, *When?*

"Now," says a voice behind me.

I turn to see Augustus leaning against the doorframe, dressed in the same black suit he wore to Ross's birthday party. His blond hair looks damp, and it's pushed carelessly off his forehead. "Hey," I say. My collar feels too tight all of a sudden, and I reach up to loosen it. "How's your jaw?"

"Aunt Annalise thinks it'll be fine. She also thinks I should stop dragging you to dive bars to play pool," he says with a wry twist of his lips. "In case anyone asks." Then he tilts his head to one side, frowning, and adds, "Who taught you how to tie a tie?"

"YouTube," I admit.

It's one of those things I haven't thought of in years: my first middle school dance, when I'd ordered a tie off our Amazon account and then realized I had no clue what to do with it. I'd come into the living room where my mother was watching television, in a hastily ironed dress shirt with the tie dangling around my neck. "Mom," I said, waving one end of the tie. "Can you show me how to do this?"

I'd become used to my mother's easy competence—the casual way she took on dual parenting roles without ever seeming flustered. So I wasn't prepared for the uncertainty on her face, the regretful expression she couldn't hide as she said, "I don't know how."

Then she recovered almost instantly, saying, "But I can learn!" with a determined, cheerful smile as she half rose from the couch. I backed out of the room, though, and told her I'd figure it out myself. Which I did, eventually.

I don't want to think about that now, though, while Augustus is crossing the room with determined strides. "I think we're far along enough in our acquaintance for me to let you know that my grandfather will judge you harshly for that knot," he says, lifting the too-long bottom of my tie with a sly half smile. "Not to mention the unconventional length you've got going on here. May I?"

He's so close that I can smell his citrusy soap and see the silver flecks in his eyes. "Knock yourself out," I say. I was aiming for a casual tone, but that's not exactly what came out. Augustus's smile curves higher as he tugs at my tie to undo it.

I swallow hard and ask, "Heard anything new about your uncle?"

"I was just talking to Dan," Augustus says, draping the now-loose tie around my neck and carefully arranging the ends. "Trying to figure out what's happening with the investigation. You'll be shocked, I'm sure, to hear that it's confidential."

"Yeah," I say. "Shocked." It's not much of a response, but it's a little hard to think with Augustus's face inches from mine, scrunched in concentration, as he quickly and confidently reknots my tie. I blink and try again. "I wondered . . . I wanted to ask . . ."

"Spit it out, Liam," Augustus murmurs, his eyes locking with mine as his fingertips graze my neck and linger above my collar. It's the lightest possible touch, but it still makes me dizzy. "What did you want to ask about?"

"Kat," I blurt out, and Augustus's face goes blank.

God, my timing *sucks*.

He takes a step back, swiftly pulls the knot tight, and lets go. "Done," he says.

I glance in the mirror; it's a perfect Windsor. "Thanks," I say, smoothing a nonexistent wrinkle. "And sorry if that was . . . abrupt. It's just, we never really got a chance to circle back on the fact that, um . . . you didn't turn her and Jamie in."

I texted Kat an update before my shower. I thought she'd be thrilled, maybe ask a few follow-up questions, but instead she sent a barrage of *JAMIE'S BEEN POISONED* texts—which, once I'd calmed down enough to realize Jamie wasn't dead, struck me as the sort of message that Former Liam, living a comfortable and quiet life in Maryland, could never have expected to receive. Oh, how things have changed.

"Yeah, well," Augustus says. "It's not as though my family has the moral high ground after covering up manslaughter."

I blink, startled. "It was an accident."

"Not when there's alcohol involved."

I hadn't even thought about that. It's ironic, I guess, that *Griffin* is supposedly the Sutherland family member with a drinking problem. He might be struggling, but at least he didn't kill anyone. "Do you think your dad knows the truth?" I ask.

Augustus sighs. "I haven't had the chance to ask him, but I have a horrible feeling that he does. His drinking got a lot worse after Gran died. I thought he was grieving, which he obviously was, but he's always had a soft spot for Uncle Parker, too. Total big-brother complex, always sticking up for him even when he didn't deserve it. It must've eaten him alive."

I think about yesterday—how Griffin tried to convince his brother to leave with him. If he'd succeeded, Parker would still be here. Augustus stares moodily at the floor, then forces a smile and says, "This is all very dreary, isn't it? And not what I came here for."

"What *did* you come here for?" I ask. A little too hopefully.

"Never mind. Tie looks good, by the way. You're welcome." He gives my shoulder a pat that's almost like a dismissal, and I wish that I could have a do-over of the past five minutes. This whole interaction might've gone a *lot* differently if I'd managed to keep my mouth shut. "Have you heard from our little con artist friend?" Augustus adds.

I fill him in on Jamie, Morgan, and the wheat germ, and his eyes get wider with every revelation. "A mother-daughter double cross?" he asks when I finish.

"That's what Kat thinks."

"Fascinating. Someone should make a movie about these people. I still can't believe, though, that Aunt Annalise would've been fooled by their so-called brilliant fake. You should see this necklace of hers. It looks like it belongs in a museum."

"Can I?" I ask.

"Huh?"

"Can I see it? The necklace," I say. I've been curious ever since Kat told us about it. What piece of jewelry could possibly be worth this much effort?

"What, like, *now*?" Augustus asks.

I glance at the clock on the dresser. "We've got some

time before I'm supposed to meet Clive. But if it's too much trouble . . ."

"It's not," Augustus says. "Aunt Annalise moved all her stuff upstairs, right? It's probably in the dressing room." He stands and strides into the hallway, putting one hand on the stairway leading to the top-floor suite as he calls, "Aunt Annalise!"

She doesn't reply. "Was my father downstairs?" I ask. "Maybe they're together."

"He let me in, and then he left," Augustus says with a shrug. "We can still go up, though. She won't care."

"Are you sure?" I ask. But he's already halfway up the stairs, so I follow.

We enter a set of French doors at the top, which lead to an expansive sitting area. Everything in the room looks designed for comfort: velvet sofas, plush area rugs, and a window seat piled high with oversized pillows. There's another set of double doors across from the window seat, half-open, leading to a second room. I can see the edge of a four-poster bed from where I'm standing.

"It'll probably be in here," Augustus says, sidestepping the bedroom entrance and pulling open another door.

I follow him inside and gaze around what must be the dressing room. I've never seen so many racks of clothing outside of a department store. The wall nearest me is all evening gowns, arranged by color. There are shelves for sweaters, for hats, and for boots. A bronze-and-crystal light fixture hangs over a freestanding cabinet that reminds me of a kitchen island, except every single inch is covered with handbags.

"Looks like she moved everything in with her," Augustus says.

"It must've taken her ages," I say.

I realize how ridiculous that comment is a nanosecond before Augustus smirks. "Aw, Liam," he says, patting my shoulder. "It's cute that you think she did it herself."

He crosses to a built-in cabinet beside a huge mirror and pushes on the door. It swings open to reveal a dozen neatly stacked black velvet boxes. "Should be in one of these," he says, reaching for the top one. He opens the box, then holds it up to display a sparkling diamond necklace. "Not this," he says, tossing it aside and opening the next box. "Or these," he adds, waving two gold bracelets.

After eleven fruitless box openings, I can't help but feel that maybe Jamie's boss has the right idea after all—no one person needs this much jewelry. Then Augustus pops open the final box in the cabinet and says, "Here we go. Last, but definitely not least." He extracts a gleaming necklace and says, "What do you think?"

I don't know anything about jewelry, but . . . "Pretty amazing. Can I?" I ask, holding out my palm. Augustus hands me the necklace, and I stare at the deep-red glow of rubies against rich gold. The design is like nothing I've seen before, elegant and intricate and imposing. I don't know how you could ever copy it without having it right beside you the entire time.

Then I grasp the links beside the clasp, hold it up to the light, and freeze.

"Augustus," I say. "There's a scratch."

CHAPTER THIRTY-THREE

Liam

"What?" Augustus says.

"On the clasp," I say. "You know how Kat told us that all the fakes have scratches? Well, there is one. It's faint, but clear."

"Let me see," he says. I hand it over, and he squints at the clasp, frowning. "Okay, yeah, but . . . that might've been there already," he says.

"That would be a pretty big coincidence," I say.

"I know, but . . ." He inspects one of the larger stones. "It looks so real. Do you think . . . Shit." His eyes meet mine. "Did that Morgan person pull off the switch?"

"Maybe," I say.

We just stare at one another for a few seconds, until a distant voice makes us both jump. "I think that's my aunt," Augustus says. Then he swallows a laugh and adds, "Oh my God, you look guilty as hell and you didn't even do anything. She's going to know something's up. Tell you what, I'll head her off and keep her downstairs for a bit. You go back to your room and . . . do something with your face."

"Like what?" I hiss. But he's already halfway out the door. It's not until I hear his footsteps thudding down the stairs that I realize he left me with a pile of discarded jewelry boxes.

And one possibly—probably?—fake necklace.

I put the necklace carefully into its box, shut the cover, and put it on the top of the jewelry cabinet. Then I reach for the boxes Augustus set aside, lifting them all at once so I can quickly put them back, and—

My hand slips, and the boxes teeter. "Noooooooo!" I moan in horror, and reach out to grab them. But it's too late. All eleven boxes tumble to the floor, several of them opening and spilling their contents into a glittering heap at my feet.

I crouch down and start shoveling jewelry into whatever box is closest. They're all the same, right? They better be, because I can't tell what goes where. I work as quickly as I can, filling a box and then stacking it neatly atop the last one. Eventually there's only one box left, and one gold bracelet.

Wait. No. There's supposed to be *two* gold bracelets.

"Goddamn it," I whisper, gazing around me. It must've rolled out of sight somewhere. I start crawling around the glossy floor, hands outstretched. My phone vibrates in my pocket, probably with a text from Augustus wondering where I am.

Sorry, can't talk, I think, suppressing a frantic laugh. *On bracelet patrol.*

Finally, in the evening gown section, I feel cool metal brush my fingertips. I grab the bracelet, stuff it into the box with its twin, put it at the top of the stack in the cabinet, and close the door. Except . . . the box with the bracelets wasn't the first one

Augustus pulled out, was it? No, it was the second, and that seems like the kind of thing Annalise would notice. I'm about to reopen the cabinet when the sound of approaching voices freezes me in my tracks.

"I just feel a little underdressed," Annalise says.

My heart stalls. Who is she talking to? Please don't let it be—

"You look perfect," Luke replies.

Footsteps are coming my way. There's nothing I can do except lunge behind the evening gowns, flattening myself against the wall and letting the fabric conceal me. Sweat beads my forehead as my phone vibrates nonstop. Augustus has to know I've blown it, right? He'll create another distraction to get them out of here, and then I can put the boxes in the proper order and leave.

"Maybe some bracelets," Annalise says. "The gold ones."

Oh no.

Heels click on the polished floor, just a few feet away from me, and then abruptly stop. "Annalise, hold on," Luke says smoothly. "You don't need bracelets. There's only one piece of jewelry you're missing."

The real necklace, I think, squeezing my eyes shut. Have they already figured it out and Augustus, as usual, is the last to know?

Then there's a scuffling noise, and Annalise lets out a little gasp. "What are you doing?" she asks, suddenly breathless.

"Annalise, this isn't nearly the ring you deserve," Luke says. "And I know your family has just been through a terrible tragedy and needs time and space to honor Parker. But I've been carrying this around for over a week now, trying to work up the courage to give it to you. This weekend has made me real-ize how short life is, and how precious. I don't want to spend another second of mine without you by my side."

My eyes widen in silent horror. *Oh my God.*

"Oh my God," Annalise says, her voice hitching.

"If you'd put this ring on even for a moment to let me know you're mine, you'd make me the happiest man on Earth," Luke says. "Annalise, my love, will you marry me?"

No, I think, holding my breath. *Say no, say no, say—*

"Yes!" cries Annalise.

CHAPTER THIRTY-FOUR

Liam

"Thanks for making the time, Liam," Clive says, sitting across from me at the guest cottage's kitchen table. "I appreciate it."

It's not like I had a choice, but . . . "No problem," I say, shifting in my seat. These kitchen chairs aren't like any kitchen chair I've ever seen before; not only are they as soft as a cloud, but they swivel so you can turn and gaze out the window into the flowering gardens, or at the giant wall-mounted television.

When I first got here two days ago, I spent half an hour just spinning around. Now they seem normal. It's weird how fast you can get used to small luxuries. Still, I can't help swiveling a little as Clive says, "I know what a difficult weekend this has been."

You don't know the half of it, I think, pausing my chair so I can take in Clive's tanned, unlined face. After this weekend, I think I'll have more wrinkles than he does. He showed up so promptly that I didn't even have a chance to tell Augustus about

Luke proposing to Annalise. And that was only the fourth- or fifth-most traumatic thing that's happened today.

"I don't want you to be concerned or intimidated about speaking with the police tomorrow," Clive says. "It'll be a very short interview, and your father will be with you the entire time." He smiles, as though he genuinely thinks that's comforting. "And don't worry—you're not being singled out. All guests will be asked for their perspective."

"I didn't really see anything—"

"Of course you didn't," Clive says, nodding sympathetically. "How could you? You were seated at the head table during the cake cutting when you heard a gunshot. You didn't know what it was, but you thought that it came from the woods, so you and several family members headed in that direction. At that point, you were intercepted by Sutherland security, who brought you to the safe house. You remained there until you were asked to leave, while I broke the news about Parker's death to the family."

I blink at him, confused about why I'm here when he already knows all that. "Yeah," I say. "That's about it."

"That *is* it," Clive says. "And that's all you have to say."

"Okay, but . . ." My brain can't shut off fast enough to stop my mouth. "What if they ask me about other stuff?"

His gaze sharpens. "What other stuff?"

"I don't know, just . . . anything." I resist the urge to tug at my collar, even though I feel like I'm choking, and I knot my hands together in my lap instead. "About the Sutherlands, or—"

"Ah," Clive says. "I see where this is going."

My shoulders tense as I ask, "You do?"

"Liam, observations about Sutherland family dynamics are not critical to this investigation," he says. "For example, Griffin's behavior during lunch. I know you were at Parker's table, but the family has already given a detailed statement about Griffin's addiction. Which, as you may have heard, is being appropriately treated with the best possible care. There's no need to rehash that. You shouldn't be asked about it, and please don't offer."

"I wasn't going to," I say, stung that he'd think I would.

"You may get asked about Parker's state of mind during lunch. It's best to remain neutral here. Larissa says the conversation mainly centered around vacation spots?"

Sure, I think. *When she wasn't insulting Augustus's school or forcing Kat to show off the diamond ring she— Holy hell.* I slump down in my chair as it hits me that Kat was probably lying about that, too. Engagement ring, my ass. Jamie must've stolen it.

"Liam," Clive says sternly. "What's that look for?"

Goddamn it. Why can't I control my face? "Nothing," I say, straightening so quickly that the movement makes my chair swivel a few inches. I hastily scoot back so I'm facing Clive again and add, "It's just . . . there might have been some other things that came up during lunch—"

"None of which are pertinent to the investigation into Parker's death," Clive says smoothly. "So there's no need to mention them."

It hits me, then, that I don't have to be afraid of Clive. He doesn't care what I've been up to this weekend. All he cares about is keeping Parker's death "contained." Just like Ross said. And I might not have a better opportunity than now to figure out why.

"Why would the police ask me about Parker's state of mind during lunch?" I ask.

"It's a standard question," Clive says, but I don't miss the slight clenching of his jaw. "The simplest answer you can provide, probably, is 'I don't remember.' That's a phrase that works well in nearly all circumstances, especially for someone like you."

"Someone like me?" I echo.

"Young. Unknown. Recently traumatized by the tragic loss of your mother. Not particularly close to the Sutherland family." Clive ticks the list off on his fingers, then waves his hand as though he's just summarized and dismissed me all at once. "Nobody's going to be looking to you for any real insight. They just need to check a box."

Check a box. This guy has no clue what I've been through, and he doesn't care. Any "tragic loss" I've experienced is just a bullet point in his crisis communication plan. And maybe that's good—his attention's not on me, at least—but it's also insulting.

Still, I don't feel the same useless sort of anger I felt toward Luke before this weekend started. And I definitely don't feel numb. I feel . . . *interested.* And invested, because whatever happens next doesn't just affect me; it affects Kat and Augustus, too.

"I think . . ." I spin my chair in a semicircle, gazing out the window like I'm trying to remember something important. "I think Parker might've said something about . . . poker. I guess he plays a lot? If that's helpful."

Parker didn't mention that during lunch; Augustus did. But it's worth the lie to see Clive's lips press together so tightly that they practically disappear from his face. "It's not," he says. "In fact, that's exactly the kind of thing you shouldn't talk about. It'll only distract the officers from doing their job."

"Are you sure?" I press. "Because, I mean—*gambling.* I don't know much about it, but some people take it pretty seriously, right?"

"Parker rarely gambled, so—"

"Especially if you lose a lot of money," I continue, as if he hadn't spoken. There's something satisfying about pushing Clive's buttons; maybe because for once this weekend, I'm making something happen instead of desperately wondering why it did. "Which I think Parker might have. He made a joke about that at lunch." Clive's eyes widen into an alarmed stare, and I add, "Then again, maybe he wasn't joking."

"I'm quite sure that he was," Clive says.

"Should I mention it, though? Just in case."

"No. It's *not pertinent,*" Clive says, wiping his upper lip. "If you're asked anything about the lunchtime conversation beyond polite vacation chitchat, say 'I don't remember.'"

I never expected the meeting would go like this—that I'd just make stuff up until hyperefficient Clive Clayborne melted down in real time. I think Kat would be proud, which is weirdly gratifying. "Okay, yeah, I get that," I say. "It's just so confusing, not having any information about what happened. I don't understand why anyone would kill Parker Sutherland."

"Well, fortunately, you don't need to understand," Clive says, baring his teeth in what I would be hard-pressed to call a smile. "And neither do I," he continues. "We'll leave that to the police. Your job tomorrow is not to theorize or spread gossip.

Your job is to simply explain what you saw and heard in the immediate aftermath of the gunshot that killed Parker."

"Got it," I say. "So to be clear—I definitely shouldn't mention that people are saying there's something strange about, you know . . . the *way* he died."

Clive stiffens at his own words, and I wonder if I've pushed too far. Does he remember saying that in the safe house? I don't want to get Augustus in trouble. And even though it's satisfying to annoy Clive, I haven't learned anything truly useful here. I already knew that there's something about Parker's death that the Sutherlands don't want to come out. Clive's alarm at my gambling bait doesn't mean anything; he'd probably react the same way to any dirt I shared. It's his job, after all, to keep the Sutherlands squeaky-clean.

"Who said that?" Clive asks in a voice that's suddenly ice-cold.

Time to back all the way off. So I take his advice and say, "I don't remember."

CHAPTER THIRTY-FIVE

Kat

I've never had a pizza party quite like this one.

"Engaged?" I sputter, diving for the last piece of pizza from the two boxes Liam and Augustus brought to the cabin. They've only been here for fifteen minutes, but revelations from their time at the Sutherland compound keep piling up.

"Engaged," Augustus confirms. "And obviously, we have to let my aunt know who she's dealing with. But it's a little awkward explaining how we know they're engaged when they haven't told anyone."

"I really didn't think it would be this weekend," Liam sighs. "The timing is so unbelievably shitty. Annalise just lost her brother. She's not thinking straight!"

"I'll bet Luke was counting on that." That's what I try to say, anyway, but around the mouthful of pizza the words come out impossibly garbled. I close my eyes in bliss, savoring the warm, cheesy goodness. I almost feel human again; I've showered, changed out of Jamie's ruined dress, and now I'm fed. My mother is sleeping peacefully in the bedroom, and I'm encouraged by the fact that she didn't eat nearly as much granola today as she did yesterday. Her color is better, and I'm hoping she'll start feeling more like herself tomorrow.

"Well stated," Augustus says politely.

We bypassed the rickety dining table for dinner—there are only two chairs that aren't broken in the entire house—and are seated in a circle on the floor, pizza boxes between us.

"At least it doesn't sound as though he's trying to rush her into getting married tomorrow," Liam says, guzzling from a can of Sprite.

"Yet," I say darkly, wiping my hands on a napkin. "You're sure the necklace had a scratch on its clasp?"

"Positive," he says. "Just like you said."

"So here's what I think happened," I say. "Morgan took Jamie out of commission, stole the fake necklace, and swapped it herself. She probably planned on quietly fencing it and leaving Jamie high and dry. But then she heard about what happened to Parker and freaked out, so she's afraid to do anything except lie low."

"Wouldn't she act normal, though?" Liam asks doubtfully. "Return her mother's calls?"

"Maybe she'll explain herself at the Marlow tomorrow," I say.

"Do you really think she's going to meet you?" Liam asks. "Your text was kind of aggressive."

"She's used to it," I say, turning toward Augustus. "Did you give your family the description of the man in the woods?"

"Not yet," he says stiffly.

"Why not?" I ask.

Augustus hesitates, his eyes flicking toward Liam. Then he abruptly gets to his feet and says, "We brought some groceries, too. They're in the car. I'll get them."

I wait until the front door shuts behind him, then turn to Liam. "Am I missing something?" I ask.

Liam rubs the back of his neck. "I'm not sure if I should say," he says.

"Seriously?" I ask. "I tell you *everything.*" He rolls his eyes, and I add, "Eventually. Come on, the three of us are practically a team now. Aren't we?" He doesn't answer for so long that I feel a prickle of hurt. "Or is that only you and Augustus?"

"No, of course not. It's just . . ." Liam glances at the closed door, then seems to steel himself. "Look, you can't tell anyone, okay?" I cross my heart. "Augustus and I overheard his family talking in Ross's office. Parker accidentally killed Augustus's grandmother a few years ago. Boating accident while he was drunk."

I gape at him. "Why didn't you say something before?"

"We had, like, three other updates to give first," Liam says defensively. "And it's kind of a sensitive subject for Augustus."

"But *relevant,* don't you think?" I ask. "No wonder he didn't tell his family about me." My brain starts spinning a mile a minute, trying to absorb this new information. "It's interesting, isn't it? Killing the beloved matriarch . . . That's kind of a *motive.*"

"A motive for . . ." Liam blinks when he realizes what I'm implying. "For murdering Parker? The Sutherlands? Don't be ridiculous, Kat. That was an accident, and he's family."

"Families kill one another all the time."

"No, they don't," Liam says. "You really need to start running in different social circles."

"I'm trying," I remind him. "But *you* need to be less naïve."

"I'm not naïve. It just doesn't make sense," Liam says. "Even if the Sutherlands were hell-bent on revenge, why would they wait years and then strike in the middle of Ross's party? People with limitless resources could've gotten rid of their black-sheep son a lot more quietly."

"Maybe that's why. Because no one would ever suspect them."

Liam sighs. "You know you're exhausting sometimes, right?"

"Yes. But let's think this through. The Sutherlands couldn't have done it on their own," I say, tapping my chin with one finger. "That's not who I saw in the woods, and anyway, they were all about to eat birthday cake. All of them except for Griffin, and—*ohhh*. Wait." I seize hold of Liam's arm. "Griffin—he doesn't look like Parker and Augustus. He's not thin. He's *big*."

"Kat, come on," Liam says, sounding almost stern. "Griffin's in rehab."

"Allegedly," I say.

"Don't go there," Liam says.

"I just think—"

"We can call Chatham Shady Acres to check if you want," comes a voice from the doorway before I can say anything else. "Or maybe it's Shady Hill. I can never remember."

My cheeks burn as Augustus enters with two shopping bags that he places on the dining table. "Some of this should be refrigerated," he says before heading back outside.

"Is he . . . is he leaving?" I ask as Liam gets to his feet.

"I hope not," he says, and follows Augustus out the door.

Damn it. I'm supposed to be making nice with Augustus so he'll let me and Jamie leave, not . . . whatever this was. Should I go after them?

No, I should probably wait. At least five minutes, so Augustus can cool off. And Liam, too. I hadn't counted on him being quite so protective of Augustus, but maybe I should have.

I start counting, but I'm barely at sixty and already feeling antsy when the cuckoo clock starts clanging once again, making me jump. "You're right," I say, scrambling to my feet as the wooden figures spin around. "One minute is plenty."

Liam and Augustus are standing beside the car, heads close together, and they both look up as I approach. "Augustus!" I call out. "I shouldn't have said that about your dad. I was just thinking out loud." I stop a few feet away, hands on my hips. "I'm sorry that he's having a hard time. And I'm sorry about your grandmother. And I am still very sorry about Parker, if I didn't make that clear enough already."

"Anything else?" Augustus says.

I wait a few beats before saying, "I'm sorry you didn't bring three pizzas."

"Jesus, Kat," Liam groans, but Augustus gives me a weary grin.

"Never change, Chaos," he says. Then he runs a hand through his hair and adds, "I guess I can't blame you for thinking the worst, but you don't know my father. He *loved* Uncle Parker. Way more than Uncle Parker deserved. He'd never hurt him, not in a million years. He'd hurt himself first." He swallows hard and adds, "Like he's been doing for the past few years."

"I understand," I say. And I do. Griffin might fit the killer's mold physically, but now that I've had a few minutes to sit with the thought, I can't actually imagine that desperate, pleading man from lunch coldly disposing of his brother in the woods. Not to mention climbing into my window and trying to smother Jamie with a pillow.

Jury's still out on the rest of the Sutherlands, though.

"I guess you have leverage now, huh?" Augustus says.

I frown. "What do you mean?"

"On me," he says with a shrug. "I keep your secret, and you keep mine."

"That's not—" I gape at him, aghast, because even though I just accused his father of murder, it never occurred to me to *blackmail* him. "I wouldn't use your grandmother's death like that. I mean, yeah, of course I've been hoping to convince you to keep quiet about Jamie, but I wanted to do it by *helping* you."

"How, exactly, are you supposed to help me?"

I've been thinking about that ever since I texted Morgan. "Well, you want to know who killed Parker, right?" I say.

Augustus rolls his eyes. "It wasn't my family, Chaos. And it wasn't Barrett."

I'm not sure we can dismiss either of those possibilities yet, but that's not the point I'm trying to make. "Well, whoever it was was in the compound Saturday night," I say. "And so were hundreds of other people, most of whom were probably capturing the moment for social media." Augustus's face clears a little as I add, "I'm sure the police are looking through everyone's pictures, keeping an eye out for somebody who wasn't

supposed to be there, or who was acting strange or suspicious."
Which might include me, but . . . oh well. I'll cross that bridge
when I come to it. "But they didn't see the guy who killed
Parker," I finish.

"You didn't get a good look at him, though," Liam objects.
"And neither did we. He had a stocking on his head."

"I know, but . . . if I could see those pictures, I might recognize his shape. Or his hands." I throw up my own at Liam's
skeptical look. "I promise, it matters. I notice stuff like that."

"It's a good idea," Augustus says. "I'll ask Dan about
photos."

Liam clears his throat and says, "I have a theory, if anyone
wants to hear it."

He almost blushes as he says it. Apparently, Augustus finds
that as endearing as I do, because his face softens as he says,
"Go right ahead."

"Well, we know Parker was a big gambler, right? Maybe he
owed somebody money that he couldn't pay. I brought that up
to Clive—"

"You brought that up to Clive?" Augustus asks incredulously.
But not as though he's annoyed by Liam's theory like he was
with mine. More like he's impressed.

"I wanted to see how he'd react," Liam says. "He got pretty
freaked."

"I'm not surprised," Augustus says. "Uncle Parker's gambling is one of the many things about him that my family
wants to keep quiet."

"It does fit with what I heard in the woods," I say slowly.
"Parker asked, 'What the hell are you doing here?' Like maybe
it was somebody he knew but didn't expect. And after Parker

died, the man said, 'Serves you right, you goddamn idiot.' Plus, the killer got away when the compound was crawling with security. He knew what he was doing."

Before the boys can reply, a flash of light in the distance makes me squint. "What's that?" I ask. They both turn, and Augustus frowns.

"Headlights," he says.

"Headlights?" I repeat, the hairs rising up the back of my neck. "But this . . . this isn't even really a road. There's nowhere to go except this house, is there?"

"No," Augustus says. "There isn't."

"Is . . . Would your grandfather come here?"

But even before he shakes his head, I know that's not it. Every nerve in my body has sprung into high alert, warning me that these lights are bad news.

Someone's coming for us.

"We should go," Augustus says, pulling out his keys to unlock his car. The light keeps getting steadily closer, and the fact that it's so unhurried makes it even more menacing. Like whoever is driving knows that they can take their time. That we're sitting ducks.

"Go where?" I hiss. "There's no room on the road for two cars. And Jamie is still inside!"

Then, before either of them can answer, I sprint for the front door.

CHAPTER THIRTY-SIX

Kat

Think, Kat.

My heart is racing as I enter the cabin and spin in a semi-circle, looking for inspiration. I got the boys into this mess. How can I get all of us out?

"Are we sure this is even something bad?" Liam asks, appearing in the doorframe with Augustus behind him. "Maybe whoever's driving is just lost. How would anyone know where to find us?"

"If it's Parker's killer, he could've followed us from the staff quarters," I say, shutting the door behind them. I grab my phone off the side table, and then unplug Jamie's from its charger and pocket that, too.

"No. We would have noticed," Liam says. "Plus, why wouldn't he have gone after you while Augustus and I were gone? Why wait until hours later?"

I exhale in frustration. Now is not the time for Liam

Rooney's calm, reasoned approach to life. All of my instincts are screaming *Danger,* and I have to trust them. "Do you want to argue with me and assume the best, or get out of here before we have to deal with the worst?" I glance at the living room window. The headlights are coming closer every second. *Think, Kat.* "Augustus, I didn't see a back door. Is there any other way out of the house?"

"Basement," he says.

"Where does it lead to?"

"The backyard. But—"

"Can one of you carry Jamie?" I ask.

My eyes cut toward Liam, who looks as though he's swallowing another protest. "Yeah, I can," he says, disappearing into the bedroom.

"There's no lock on the basement door," Augustus says.

"That's fine. Just take us there, okay?" I say as Liam comes back into the living room, cradling Jamie against his chest.

"Kat . . . what . . . ," she murmurs groggily.

"Shh," I whisper. "It's okay." I can hear the car outside approaching now, tires crunching on the gravelly road, and the sound turns my blood to ice.

"This way," Augustus says.

He leads us past the kitchen, and then through a small door in the hallway that I'd assumed was some kind of pantry. "Down here," he says, reaching for a switch on the wall.

I grab his hand to stop him. "No lights," I hiss. "Close the door behind us."

"Right," Augustus says. "There's a handrail to your left."

I grab hold of it and begin my careful descent down a narrow wooden staircase. Liam comes after me, moving slowly with a still-mumbling Jamie in his arms. Then we plunge into darkness as Augustus shuts the basement door. The rail under my hand ends, and a second later, my foot hits a concrete floor. "I'm at the bottom," I whisper, cautiously moving forward. Before anyone can reply, bright headlights stream through a tiny window in front of me.

"He's here," Augustus murmurs.

I take advantage of the unexpected illumination to case the room. There are boxes stacked everywhere, a rusted push lawn mower, and a bunch of tools hanging on one wall. I peer more closely at those, and . . . yes. That will do. I pluck a hatchet from its bracket and check the sharpness of its blade. A tiny droplet of blood appears on my thumb. Perfect.

"Are you going to *hack up* whoever's out there?" Augustus whispers in disbelief.

"No," I say as the headlights snap off and we're plunged into darkness once more. "Where's the door?"

"This way," Augustus says, moving farther into the basement. I follow as silently as I can, although my heartbeat is so loud in my ears that it feels like a dead giveaway—a thudding and thumping that'll rise up through the floorboards like in "The Tell-Tale Heart." "There's a bulkhead that leads into the backyard," Augustus whispers.

My eyes are starting to adjust, and I can see the faint outline of a door that Augustus pauses beside.

"Now what?" he asks.

"When we're sure he's inside the house, we'll slip out here and make a run for your car," I say. "It's still unlocked, right? We'll get in as quietly as we can, and then we just . . . go."

"We just go," Liam repeats, panting from the strain of holding Jamie. "That's it?"

"That's it," I say as the front door opens with a loud, prolonged creak. I know it's not exactly a dazzling plan, but it's all I have.

Jamie stirs in Liam's arms, making the kind of small, confused noises that usually mean she's having a bad dream. "Why . . . ," she mutters thickly. "Where?"

"Is she going to . . . I don't know what to do," Liam says helplessly. "Should I put her down, or—"

"No," I snap as loudly as I dare. "She's okay. You're okay," I add in a more soothing tone, patting Jamie's arm. "Just rest." My nerves are stretched so tight that it feels like they're going to snap, and the last thing I need is my mother fully waking up while we're trying to outrun a killer.

"What's the hatchet for?" Augustus whispers. "Self-defense?"

I don't have time to explain the rest, or warn him that if this really is the guy we managed to chase out of Jamie's room earlier, he wouldn't come here without serious firepower that a hatchet can't match. In fact, I've been holding my breath waiting for the gunshots that I'd fire if I were him. But there's no sound above us except the heavy tread of footsteps.

I try to imagine what he's seeing. The living room we just vacated, littered with pizza boxes and soda cans. The galley kitchen off to one side. The bedroom down the hallway, piled high with suitcases and bags that we have to leave behind. The bathroom, littered with damp towels from my recent shower. We clearly can't have gone far, and we'll be lucky if it takes him five minutes to search the first floor.

"Now," I whisper.

Augustus opens the basement door. He leads us up a short staircase to a bulkhead that he pushes upward. It opens silently, and we step out into the backyard. We start creeping around the side of the house, Liam panting harder with every step. He's impossibly loud, making my skin crawl with anxiety, but I know there's no point in asking him to breathe more quietly. He's doing the best he can while carrying Jamie, who's twitching restlessly like she's trying to wake herself up from a nightmare.

Not yet, I think. *Trust me, reality is worse.*

A strange car comes into view—parked right next to Augustus's, like we're both guests at a very small house party. Augustus pulls his keys from his pocket, holding them tightly so they won't jingle, and heads for the driver's side. Liam moves toward the back seat, and I position myself by the passenger-side door. *Please,* I think, gazing at the tiny house that was our sanctuary until a few minutes ago. *Please let this work.*

A hulking figure passes in front of the living room window, silhouetted by the lamp we left burning, and I shudder. If we've given ourselves away, all he'd have to do is burst through the front door with the gun I'm sure he's holding. Four quick shots is all it would take.

Nope. Not thinking about that.

As soon as Augustus tugs on the handle of his door, I turn and take a mighty swing with the hatchet at the other car's front left tire. I drive the blade deep into the sidewall, then pull it to one side and let go. A whoosh of air erupts from the slashed tire as Liam flings open the back door of Augustus's car and stuffs Jamie inside. She murmurs in faint protest, but then curls into the soft leather seat like a runner collapsing into bed after a grueling marathon. Liam climbs in behind her, I dive into the front seat beside Augustus, and all of us slam our doors. The locks click, sealing us in.

We did it. I stare at the cabin's still-closed front door, my heart racing and my breath coming in jagged gasps. *But we made a lot of noise.*

And then, in what seems like slow motion, the front door starts to open.

"Go!" I shout.

"Buckle up," Augustus says grimly as the engine roars to life. The car jerks backward, then spins as Augustus executes a hasty three-point turn. We start flying down the narrow road, trees zipping past us so quickly that I'm instantly dizzy. If Augustus were to lose his grip on the steering wheel and crash into one, we'd be goners.

A loud crack makes me jump, followed by the horrifying screech of metal hitting metal. "Is he *shooting* at us?" Liam says in such an outraged tone that it would almost be funny if it weren't flat-out terrifying.

Augustus accelerates as I twist in my seat, half expecting to see someone running after us with superhuman speed. But all I can make out is a pinprick of light from the cabin and then, after Augustus makes a hairpin turn, nothing except a blur of trees. Another gunshot rings out, but it already sounds farther away, and there's no corresponding jolt to the car.

"Holy hell," Liam rasps. "Is everyone okay?"

"I'm fine," I say, surprised at how steady my voice is. "You?"

"I . . ." He lets out a shaky breath. "I will never, ever second-guess you about fleeing the scene again." He gazes down at Jamie and adds, "How is she still asleep?"

"She almost wasn't," I say. "But gluten poisoning is a bitch."

"That was quick thinking, Chaos," Augustus says. "Nice move with the tire. These woods aren't made for a high-speed chase."

"I'm just glad he didn't shoot yours out as soon as he parked next to you," I say. "That's what I would've done."

"You are officially my most interesting friend," Augustus says, and despite everything—that makes me smile. I know he's just reacting to stress with a joke, but it's still nice to hear him call me a friend.

"We make a good team," I say.

"We're not out of the woods yet," Augustus mutters. Just then, though, a streetlight appears in front of us, illuminating Bixby's main road. "Okay, never mind. We are *literally* out of the woods. So the question is—what now?"

CHAPTER THIRTY-SEVEN

Liam

We drive in silence for a few beats until I say the obvious. "Police?"

"No," Kat says instantly. "Please."

"Kat, come on," I say. "This has to be the guy who killed Parker. He has a gun, and he's *stalking* you. I don't know how he found us, but if he did it once, he can do it again."

"I know, but . . ." She twists to look at me, her expression pleading. "Can you give me just one night? Maybe Morgan will get back to me. Or Jamie will feel better, and we can—"

"What?" I say. "Go home? Do you really think that's safe?"

"Yes," she says stubbornly. "He doesn't know who we are."

"You're not thinking straight—"

"Because I'm *exhausted*," Kat says. For the first time all weekend, she sounds near tears. "I've barely slept in the past twenty-four hours."

"Me either," I say.

"At least you didn't spend last night in a closet!"

"Okay, listen," Augustus breaks in. "I'm not opposed to taking a beat here. Going to the police is complicated, and my family . . ." He clicks his tongue. "What if we head for the compound? Just for tonight? Get some rest, and we can figure things out in the morning?"

"The compound?" I say. "Do I need to remind you this guy was there last night?"

"No," Augustus says. "But a lot's changed since Uncle Parker died. Security's been massively stepped up. Key card access has been disabled, so everybody has to enter through the front gates, and they're guarding them like a military base."

When I don't respond, he sighs. "I know you don't know them well, but . . . my family didn't kill Uncle Parker, okay? And they definitely didn't just try to kill me. Or you, Kat. Even if they were capable of it, this wouldn't be their style. It's too messy."

"I agree," Kat says quickly. "A night at the compound sounds *great*."

I slump against my seat, thinking about my warm, soft bed in the guest cottage. And the armed guards patrolling the grounds.

I know I'm not thinking straight either, but I'm too tired to care.

"Okay," I say wearily. "One night."

Half an hour later, I'm back at the guest cottage. After Augustus and I got Kat and Jamie settled in one of Griffin's spare rooms, Augustus left to find someplace to hide his car. "Can't have it sitting in the driveway with that bullet hole," he said. "Get some rest."

"I will," I said.

I lay down on the bed, fully clothed, sure that I'd fall right asleep. But as soon as my eyes closed, all I could see was headlights. And all I could hear was gunshots. So I got up, and now I'm downstairs wandering through dark, empty rooms. Augustus is right; going to the police would be complicated. But we've already gotten away from Parker's killer twice—three times, if you count Kat's run through the woods. Our luck can't possibly hold for much longer. We need to know who this guy is, and in order to know that, we need to know why he killed Parker. But even after scrambling for twenty-four hours, we don't have a clue.

It's too stuffy in here; I need air. I slip outside, shutting the door silently behind me, and head for the backyard. There's a beautiful garden there, filled with flowering bushes, stone benches, and a quietly bubbling fountain. The stars are bright in the cloudless sky, crickets are chirping, and the air is fragrant with lilacs and roses. It's the kind of place where it's impossible to believe that bad things can happen, and our frantic dash from the cabin starts to feel more and more like a dream.

"The prodigal son returns," a voice says, and I barely manage to swallow a yelp.

Luke is standing beside the fountain, a half-filled glass in one hand. "Oh, hi," I mutter. "Didn't think anyone was here."

"Of course not," Luke says dryly. "Don't worry. I wasn't under the impression that you were seeking my company."

I stare at his shadowy form. Could there be a part of Luke—a very small, very deeply hidden part—that wishes he and I were closer? A part that genuinely cares for Annalise? He sketched her so beautifully. If he wasn't lying about being an artist, could there be other things he's not lying about?

He's the only parent I have left. Maybe I should give him a chance.

"Where's Annalise?" I ask.

"Sleeping," he replies. "She's had a very long day."

I don't think I'm wrong that there's actual tenderness in his voice. "You really care about her, don't you?" I say.

Luke huffs out a mirthless laugh. "Is that so hard to believe?"

"Kind of, yeah," I say.

He takes a sip of his drink, eyeing me over the rim of his glass. "I know you've been on my dating profile," he says. "You're not exactly subtle."

"And you're not exactly legal," I counter.

We lock eyes, until Luke looks away first. "God knows, I'm not perfect," he says. "I've done things I'm not proud of. But I love Annalise. This is the real deal, and I hope . . . I hope that you'll support it."

"Support it how?" I ask.

Luke's gaze slides back to mine. "You know how."

"Lie for you," I say dully. Of course.

I expect him to scowl or protest, but he just shakes his head. "Give me a chance to prove that I've changed," he says. "*She* changed me. And it would break her heart to think I'm not the man she's helped me become."

There are a million arguments against that, but I'm so taken aback by the sincerity in his tone that I don't say anything. Luke presses his advantage, adding, "Why don't you focus on yourself for now, Liam? You deserve some happiness, too."

"I'm happy," I grumble. Unhappily.

Luke snorts. "You haven't been happy since you moved to Maine. And, look, I get it—you've been through a shitty loss. I never did right by your mom, but that doesn't mean I don't know the kind of person she was. I can't fill those shoes; I guess I knew that so thoroughly that I didn't even try. But you get a second chance now, too."

This is almost a bonding moment, but . . . "I like Annalise too much to lie to her," I say, steeling myself for another argument.

"I'm not talking about Annalise," Luke says.

I frown. "Then who—"

"Augustus, you idiot," Luke says, sounding exasperated.

Hearing Augustus's name—here, now, out of Luke's mouth, after everything that happened today—jolts me so much that I take a step back. All I can think is *No*. I don't care how earnest Luke is suddenly being; he's not the right person to confide in.

"I don't know what you're talking about," I say stiffly.

"Oh, come on. You obviously have feelings for the kid."

"No, I don't," I say, even as an image from earlier today of Augustus carefully adjusting my tie flashes through my mind. *What did you want to ask about?* he'd asked, and I'd said, *Kat*. Luke is right; I'm an idiot. What I should have said was *You and me*.

"Give me a break—"

"You don't even know me," I say sharply.

I glare at Luke, waiting for him to challenge that—to tell me that of *course* he knows me. That we're father and son, more alike than either of us is willing to admit. But as soon as the words form in my brain, I know that's not a conversation I can stand to have right now. Before Luke has a chance to reply, I spit out, "If you did, you'd know that I have zero interest in Augustus Sutherland. He's a friend and nothing more."

"That's it, huh?"

"Yeah," I say tersely. "That's it."

"All right, then. I stand corrected," Luke says, swallowing the last of his drink. "I'm going to bed. We'll talk more tomorrow about this, yes? About *my* relationship," he adds before I can protest. "Not your apparent lack of one."

"Fine," I mutter, my shoulders slumping as a fresh wave of exhaustion hits me. I should have made an effort to sleep instead of coming to the garden, and I'd love to fix that mistake, but not if it means heading inside with Luke. "I'm gonna stay out here for a while."

"Good night," Luke says, brushing past me.

I grip the edge of the fountain and stare into its bubbling depths, wondering how long I have to stand here before I can go to my room. What if Luke pours himself another drink? Maybe I should cut my losses and slink past him up the stairs. I turn toward the house, still thinking through my options, when a rustling sound puts all my senses on alert. But before I can panic that Parker's killer has found us once again, Augustus steps out from behind a lilac bush.

I go limp with relief until I realize I have something new to panic about.

"H-how long have you been there?" I stammer.

"Ages," Augustus says, brushing a stray leaf from his sleeve. "I wanted to see how you're doing, but Luke was skulking around, so I decided to wait until he left. And then you came out."

Oh no. Oh no, oh no, oh no . . .

I bite the inside of my cheek. "So you heard—"

"Everything," Augustus says. The moonlight makes his eyes glow silver. "I don't buy a word your father says about my aunt, by the way, but I have to admit that he's a convincing liar."

I can't think of anything to say in return; it's hard to form words when my heart is ruthlessly pummeling my rib cage like an angry boxer. I didn't mean what I said to Luke about Augustus, but I can't figure out how to take it back.

The air between us feels thick, heavy with all the things we haven't said and probably won't ever say. The past few days have been a fever dream of fragile highs and shattering lows, and there's no space for simple truths. There's no space for something as basic as *I like you.*

I really, really like you.

Then Augustus adds, "Can't say the same for you, though."

This garden is running dangerously low on oxygen. "What?" I gulp.

His eyes burn into mine, making my pulse spike and my head go fuzzy. "Zero interest?" he asks, the ghost of a smile flitting across his lips. "You can't lie to save your life, Liam."

My heart is practically in my throat, but I manage to rasp out, "I never could."

I'm not sure which one of us moves first. But the next thing I know, his hand is cupping my cheek and mine is behind his neck, pulling him toward me as our lips meet. His are soft but insistent, tugging at mine like he's been thinking about this as much as I have. His arms slide around my waist, pulling me close, and warmth curls in my stomach. We fit together as though we've done this a hundred times. I sweep my thumb over his jaw, caressing the spot I was so desperate to touch yesterday. My mouth opens to his, our tongues meet, and the heady burn of desire floods my veins.

I can't believe I thought I knew what a kiss was before now. I had no idea. None.

When we finally break apart, my lips are tingling and my knees are weak. "Liam," Augustus murmurs, his forehead touching mine, but he doesn't say anything else. I don't speak either; I'm all out of words. All I want to do is kiss him again, but before I can, light footsteps sound on the path behind us. Seconds later, Kat steps into the garden.

"Oh," she says, blinking at Augustus and me as we turn. Neither of us move an inch away from one another as she adds, "Well, it's about time."

"I know you've had a hell of a day, Chaos," Augustus says, letting his hands drift down to my hips. "But could whatever you need seriously not wait?"

"I suppose it could've if I'd known about—this," Kat says, flapping her hand at us. "But I'm here now, so I may as well tell you . . ." She fumbles in her pocket for her phone and swipes at the screen. "I got a text from Morgan."

"Really?" I ask, feeling a prickle of interest despite Kat's horrible timing.

"Well, I *think* it's Morgan. It's not from her number, but it seems to be in response to the text I sent telling her to meet me at the Marlow tomorrow."

She holds out her phone. Augustus, with a long-suffering sigh, steps away from me and takes it, frowning at the screen. "This is all of it?" he asks, eyebrows raised.

Kat nods. "Yup."

"What does it say?" I ask, leaning over Augustus's shoulder as he reads the message out loud.

" 'I'll be there. Send Jamie.' "

And then, as we're all staring at Kat's screen, another text comes through from the same number.

You can trust me.

CHAPTER THIRTY-EIGHT

Kat

"It's a trap, Kat," Liam says.

"Morgan said I can trust her," I reply, holding up my phone.

Augustus snorts. "It's a little late to pretend you're that naïve," he says.

It's Monday morning, and we're in Griffin's kitchen with Augustus, eating cereal and arguing about what to do next. For me it seems clear, especially in the bright light of day: Keep Jamie here where she's safe, meet Morgan, and find out what she knows.

The boys, predictably, aren't entirely on board.

"Jamie wouldn't want you to do this," Liam says.

"Well, she can't go. She's still asleep."

"No one should go," Liam says, exasperated. "We said *one night.*"

"But that was before Morgan's text," I protest.

"You don't even know for sure that was Morgan," he says. "It's an unknown number!"

"Who else would it be?"

"I don't know, maybe *the guy who's trying to kill you?*"

Augustus, who'd been making more coffee during this exchange, comes back to the table and puts two steaming mugs in front of Liam and me. "Can I say something?" he asks.

"Sure," I say, dipping a spoon into the sugar bowl.

"I think—"

There's a rattle from somewhere behind us, so unexpected that I drop my spoon, sending sugar crystals scattering across the table. "Is that— Where did that come from?" Liam asks, twisting in his chair.

Augustus frowns. "Sounds like the back door."

My nerves prick as the rattle grows louder. "Are you expecting anyone?"

"No," he says.

All of us get to our feet. Liam and I follow Augustus past the pantry, where I see a door topped with high windows, covered with roller shades that are sheer enough to see through, and— Oh God.

A tall, hulking figure. *Not again.*

We all watch in horror as the doorknob twists but holds. "Should we leave?" Liam whispers, just as I turn and sprint back to the kitchen. I lunge for the butcher block on the counter, grab the biggest knife I can see, and race back to the hall.

The lock clicks. The door starts to slowly swing open, and every muscle in my body tenses as I raise the knife. Then a hand grabs me—Augustus, who firmly pushes me to one side before stepping forward. "Dad," he says.

Griffin Sutherland enters the kitchen, a set of keys dangling from one hand. "I . . . Jesus, what happened to your face?" he asks, his mouth dropping open as he takes in his son.

"Bar fight," Augustus says.

Griffin is just as big as the guy in the woods. But there's nothing frightening about his hunched shoulders and tired eyes. "I knew I shouldn't have left you . . . Well, not alone, apparently," he says, brow furrowing at the knife in my still-raised hand. "Hello."

I quickly lower the knife and say, "Hi, I'm . . . Augustus's friend. I was cutting bagels."

Griffin smiles wearily. "Bagels sound great."

"This is Kat," Augustus says. "And Liam."

"Liam. Luke's son?" Griffin says. Liam nods. "Good to meet you. And you, Kat. Are you a friend from school?"

I'm fully ready to lie at the first sign that Augustus wants me to, but his attention remains focused on his father. "Dad," he says. "What are you doing here? You're supposed to be on the Cape."

Griffin moves toward the kitchen, and we follow. "I'm supposed to be in rehab, you mean," Griffin says, lowering himself into a chair. "We might as well say it, right?"

I scan the counter until I spot a chrome bread box. When I open it, it's crammed full of every possible carbohydrate, including bagels. I pull them out and start slicing.

"Okay," Augustus says. "You're supposed to be in rehab. Why aren't you?"

He and Liam sit on either side of Griffin as I rummage

270

through the refrigerator for cream cheese. "I'll go back," Griffin says. "I know I need to. But I couldn't stay away with Parker gone, because . . . I know what they're like, Augustus. Your grandfather and the girls. They're in problem-solving mode and not paying any attention to you, are they?"

Augustus just snorts. I look around for a toaster but can't find one, and I don't want to interrupt, so I just put the un-toasted bagels on a plate and set them on the table with the cream cheese as Griffin continues, "Annalise might spare you a thought. But that's it."

"I'm fine," Augustus says. "I'm always fine on my own. Why are you really here?"

"Is it so hard to believe I'm looking out for you?" Griffin asks. He meets Augustus's gaze but can't hold it; after a few beats, his face crumples. His shoulders start to shake, and he lets out a choked sob. Liam and I exchange wide-eyed glances as Griffin swipes at his cheeks and says, "It's not like I ever managed to look out for Parker."

I sink into the chair beside Liam as Augustus says, "You tried."

Griffin buries his head in his hands, muffling his voice. "I didn't do nearly enough. There's so much you don't know," he says brokenly.

Augustus looks at Liam, who mouths, *Do you want us to leave?* I kick Liam under the table, hard, because I want to hear whatever comes next. Augustus shakes his head and says, "I know Uncle Parker was driving the boat when Gran died. Why didn't you ever tell me?"

Griffin raises his tearstained face. I've never seen a man look so defeated, and he doesn't seem to notice that Liam and

I are still there. "I'm sorry," he says heavily. "You deserved the truth. And it didn't do Parker any favors to hide it. The guilt ate him up, but he felt like he couldn't show it, and that made him . . . hard. Desperate. He did things he never would've done if the accident hadn't happened. I'm sure of that."

"Things," Augustus repeats. "Like what?"

The door rattles again, followed by a creak of hinges. Griffin swipes at his cheeks, frowning. "Who's there?" he calls. The creases in his forehead deepen when a silver-haired man in a dapper suit appears from around the corner. "Clive?" Griffin says. "What are you— Since when do you have a key?"

Oh God. *Clive*. It's Ross Sutherland's right-hand man, and I have nowhere to hide.

"I have a master," Clive says. His eyes land on me and narrow. "And who is this? A guest of yours, Augustus? You do realize you're supposed to register anyone who comes through the gates with security, don't you? Especially now."

"How do you know I didn't?" Augustus asks.

"Because they would have told me," Clive says, eyes still on me. "What's your name, young lady?"

I gulp, but before I can figure out how to respond, Griffin speaks up again. "Never mind that," he says sharply. "We have bigger problems, such as the fact that you essentially just broke into my house. What gives you the right?"

"I have a key—"

"What gives you the right?" Griffin repeats, his face reddening with anger.

"Griffin, you're not yourself," Clive says in a soothing voice. "The guards told me you'd returned, and I was worried. You're not ready to be here. You need to be at the Cape."

"I think I'm capable of deciding where I need to be," Griffin says. "Just because I'm an alcoholic doesn't mean I'm incompetent."

"Of course not," Clive says. "But your judgment occasionally lapses."

"Oh, does it?" Griffin stands, towering over Clive with his six-foot-plus height. "Do you think it lapsed on Saturday when I tried to get Parker out of here? I knew he was planning something! And I *told* you that."

"Griffin," Clive starts, "let's not—"

"Let's not what?" Griffin asks. "Be honest?" His face gets even redder as he moves closer to Clive, and for the first time since I've met him, he looks intimidating. "I told you Parker was gloating about all the money he'd have after the party. We both know Dad wasn't giving it to him, so where was it coming from? Nowhere good. I knew that, and I tried to warn you. But you didn't want to 'ruffle feathers.'"

Liam and I exchange round-eyed glances. *Gloating about all the money?* Was Liam right, and this was a gambling scheme gone wrong? But Parker said he'd have money after the party, which doesn't seem to fit. It's not like he went into the woods to play poker.

Then again, anything is possible.

Clive puts a hand on Griffin's arm. "Why don't we get your dad—"

"No!" Griffin says angrily. "I'm not *getting my dad*. He doesn't need to be consulted for every word I say and every decision I make."

"Preach," Augustus mutters.

"I could've saved Parker if you'd listened to me, Clive,"

Griffin continues. "I knew him better than anyone. He had flaws like we all do, and covering them up didn't help." He gazes around the room, as though he just remembered there's an audience, and makes a sweeping gesture with his arm. "So why don't we let the truth come out, huh? Why don't we tell my son, and his friends, and anybody who asks how Parker died? How he wasn't just walking through the woods on a whim while everyone else was having cake. He was—"

"Griffin," Clive says, the warning clear in his tone. "Don't start something you'll—"

"He was stealing his sister's necklace," Griffin finishes angrily. "There. I said it. And the world kept right on turning, didn't it?"

Wait. What?

"We don't know that Parker was stealing anything," Clive says, desperation edging into his voice. "He could've been simply borrowing it—"

"Jesus, Clive, can you stop spinning for five seconds? The rubies alone in that necklace are worth two million dollars. Parker wasn't *borrowing* anything."

Rubies? My brain is short-circuiting. I stare wildly at Liam and Augustus, seeing my shock and confusion mirrored in their eyes. "Um, Dad," Augustus says. "Just to be clear. Are you saying that Uncle Parker stole Aunt Annalise's ruby necklace?"

"It was in his pocket when he died," Griffin says heavily.

Annalise's ruby necklace.

In. His. *Pocket.*

But that means . . . Holy hell, what does it mean?

"It's horrible, of course it is," Griffin says. "Stealing from his own sister. But Dad never gave Parker a fair shot, and he's always spoiled Annalise. I suppose Parker thought—well, I don't know what he thought, to be honest. He didn't give me any details about what he was planning. I'm sure he was too ashamed."

Griffin's entire body sags, as though it's been drained of all the righteous anger that had been keeping him upright. "So that's the story, kids," he says wearily. "The Sutherlands aren't perfect. Parker wasn't perfect. He tried to rob his family, and he paid the ultimate price. Put that on the front page and let the world gossip. Who cares what people say? Turning my brother into some kind of posthumous paragon won't bring him back."

The world around me grows dark and then bright again. I'm too hot and too cold all at once. I don't know what to think, or feel, or believe.

What does it mean?

"This is . . . this is obviously highly confidential information that Griffin just shared," Clive says. "I must insist that everyone in this room exercise discretion—"

"Oh, for God's sake, Clive," Griffin sighs. "It's a little late for that. Come on, let's find Dad so I can fall on my sword. I truly don't care." He turns to Augustus and adds, "I'm sorry I wasn't honest with you before."

"No problem," Augustus says faintly.

Clive glares at all of us in turn. "Discretion!" he hisses, before his eyes settle on Liam. "As for your interview with the police—that will need to be rescheduled, obviously. Our messaging needs to integrate the latest data point."

It's almost admirable, this guy's commitment to his job.

Liam looks relieved as he says, "Fine by me."

Clive ushers Griffin out of the kitchen. Liam pokes my arm, then shows me the time on his phone. 8:40. "If we're going to meet Morgan, we should leave now," he says. That's how big of a bombshell Griffin just dropped—even Liam realizes it's worth throwing caution to the wind to chase a lead at this point.

"Yeah, okay," I say. "Augustus? Are you coming?"

"I, uh . . . No," he says numbly. "I think I'm just going to sit here for a minute."

Liam puts a hand on Augustus's shoulder. "Everything will be okay," he says, brushing a stray curl from Augustus's cheek.

Augustus exhales, leaning his head against Liam's hand. "What is *going on*?"

"We'll figure it out," Liam says. "Kat, I'll get Luke's car and meet you outside."

"All right," I say.

Liam squeezes Augustus's shoulder and exits the kitchen. Once he's gone, I take a long, bracing sip of coffee. "Augustus?" I say tentatively.

He rubs a hand down one side of his face. "Yeah?"

There's a lot I should say, but I don't have much time. "Would you mind keeping an eye on Jamie?" I ask.

"Sure, why not," he says wearily. "It's not like there's anything else going on."

"If it's too much—"

"It's fine," he says. "Go."

"Thank you," I say. "I just need to grab a couple of things from upstairs."

I head for the hallway but don't get far before Augustus's voice stops me. "Chaos," he says, "hold up."

I turn, and his eyes bore into mine before settling on Liam's empty chair. "Look out for him, okay?" he says. "He doesn't have your killer instinct."

CHAPTER THIRTY-NINE

Liam

"So," I say as Kat and I start the drive to Randall.

"So," she echoes.

I want to say something profound, or at least useful. Something that will help make sense of everything we just heard. But all that comes out is "That happened."

Kat rubs her eyes. "You know what it means, right?"

"No," I say helplessly.

I feel like I don't know anything anymore, and I already regret racing out of the compound and leaving Augustus behind. He must be reeling, and I'm doing . . . what?

Looking for answers, I guess. But why did I think I wanted more answers? Everything we've learned so far has been terrible.

"It's all connected," Kat says. "It wasn't bad luck, or a coincidence, that Parker was shot right when Annalise's necklace was supposed to be stolen. These aren't separate crimes."

"They're not?" I say blankly.

"Of course not. Think about it."

"I'm trying."

I force my sluggish brain back into the kitchen we just left. The way Griffin had shouted at Clive that they could have saved Parker. *I knew he was planning something! I told you Parker was gloating about all the money he'd have after the party. We both know Dad wasn't giving it to him, so where was it coming from? Nowhere good.*

"Are you saying Parker was part of the heist?" I ask.

"He must have been," Kat says. "I've been thinking. You know how this whole thing started because Morgan had been cultivating a Sutherland contact?"

I nod.

"She told everyone it was a 'disgruntled member of the Sutherland household staff,' but . . . what if it was *Parker*?"

"I mean . . . I guess it could be," I say doubtfully. "Parker was hard up. But why would he go through all that trouble? He could've grabbed his sister's necklace any time. He could've grabbed a dozen necklaces."

"Sure, but he wouldn't have a perfect replica to leave behind," Kat says. "There'd be an investigation. Maybe he didn't want to take a chance on getting caught."

"Maybe," I say. "But how does someone like Morgan manage to 'cultivate' someone like Parker Sutherland? Where would those two even connect?"

"This could be where your gambling theory comes into play," Kat says. "Underground poker games? Illegal casinos? Morgan knows people who run those kind of things."

Despite everything, it's a little bit gratifying that Kat hasn't tossed out my single contribution to solving this mystery. "If it's true that Parker was Morgan's contact," I say, "do you think Jamie knew about him? Or Gem?"

"No way," Kat says. "It all fits into the bigger picture of Morgan double-crossing everyone at Spotless. She lied about her contact—Gem would *freak* at the idea of a Sutherland being involved. She took Jamie out of commission, and she took the fake necklace. Then she gave it to Parker, because he could move freely around the party that night."

I fall silent as I try to absorb all of the new information flying at me. "I guess that makes a twisted kind of sense," I finally say. "Morgan recruits Parker. They agree to double-cross Gem, screw over Jamie, and split the money. But then—"

"Something went wrong," Kat says.

I snort. "That's kind of an understatement."

"I'm not talking about Parker getting shot," Kat says. "I can't even think about where that fits yet. I keep getting stuck on the fact that there aren't enough necklaces."

"Huh?" I say, blinking as trees flash past me. The GPS in Luke's car is sending me down winding back roads on the way to Randall, and we're the only car in sight. I'm fueled by anxiety and going a lot faster than I should. I tap the brakes and add, "What amount of necklaces, exactly, are you looking for?"

"Two," Kat says. "We know that the fake necklace is in Annalise's dressing room, because you saw the scratch on its clasp. Right?"

"Right," I say.

"How do you think it got there?"

I can't keep up with her. "Um . . ."

"Here's what I think," Kat says. "Parker died with the fake necklace in his pocket. Security probably found it, assumed it was the real thing, and gave it to Annalise. She tucked it away, then moved it into the guest cottage with the rest of her things."

"Okay," I say. "So?"

"So where's the real necklace?" Kat says. "If Parker died with the fake in his pocket, that means he didn't have a chance to make the swap. And if he didn't have a chance to make the swap, the real necklace should still have been in Annalise's room."

Finally, I'm starting to grasp where she's headed. "Two necklaces," I say.

"It would have been total confusion, right? Like, 'Where the hell did this exact replica come from?' But Griffin didn't say anything about that."

"Well, Griffin just bailed on rehab," I remind her. "He might not be up-to-date on all the latest twists and turns. Plus, he's kind of preoccupied with the fact that Parker *died*. How does that fit into your theory? Who's the guy from the woods, and why did he kill Parker?"

"I don't know," Kat sighs. "I can't explain it. We're missing something."

Sun streams through the windshield as the GPS directs me to turn left and we pass a WELCOME TO RANDALL sign. "We're missing a lot of somethings," I say.

CHAPTER FORTY

Kat

The main street of Randall on a Monday morning could be the movie set for a peaceful, bustling small town. Traffic is light and polite, pedestrians stop to chat with one another on the sidewalk, and shop owners flip hand-drawn OPEN signs as it gets closer to nine o'clock. Even my overwrought imagination can't picture us getting murdered outside Elsie's Tea Emporium.

"Maybe this isn't such a good idea after all," Liam says as he pulls into a parking spot across from the Marlow Hotel.

I knew Reckless Liam wouldn't last long, and I need to get moving before he disappears completely. "It'll be fine," I say, unclipping my seat belt. The motion makes both the phones in my pocket slide out onto the center console, and Liam reaches over to grab them.

"Why do you have two phones?" he asks, handing them to me.

"One is Jamie's," I say.

He blinks as I stuff them back into my pocket and zip it. "You took Jamie's phone?"

"Well, obviously," I say. But apparently, it's not obvious to him, because he still looks confused. "I don't want her waking up and making any rash calls."

"Rash calls?" Liam repeats. "To who?"

Gem. Morgan. The police. "Anyone," I say.

Liam sighs. "Kat, I understand why you're protective of your mother. I would be too, after what your father did," he says. "But she's an adult. Why do you keep treating her like a child?"

"I don't."

"You do. You've been making decisions for her all weekend. I realize she's been unconscious for most of it, but still. You could've left well enough alone *multiple* times."

"I'm just trying to help."

"How does cutting off her ability to communicate help?"

I press my fingertips against my aching temples. Ever since Parker died, all I've wanted is to get away safely with Jamie and keep her secret. I'm not sure this little side trip to Randall is going to accomplish either of these things, and yet—what else can I do? As soon as I stop moving and let Jamie catch up, the endgame becomes inevitable.

"Because I know exactly what she'll do once she realizes what's happened," I say. "She'll turn herself in."

"Would that really be so bad?" Liam asks.

I stare at him, open-mouthed, until his words sink in and my temper spikes. "To have my mother locked up in jail for God knows how many years?" I snap. "Yeah, Liam, that would be pretty fucking bad!"

"I know, I know. I'm sorry. All I mean is, even if Jamie had been able to swap the necklace and become an accountant like she wanted, the past . . . it's still there, you know? You'd always be looking over your shoulder, waiting for the other shoe to drop." He sighs. "That's how I feel living with Luke, anyway. Maybe I'm just projecting."

"You are," I say, but with a lot less venom. Liam is so calm and easygoing I sometimes forget he has his own problems. Big, painful, life-altering problems that he shoulders with a lot more grace than I ever could. It's not like he doesn't understand what it would be like for me to lose Jamie, when his own loss is so much worse. And maybe . . . just maybe . . . he has a point. But I can't think about that right now. "It's okay. We're both on edge."

"It's not too late to back out, you know."

I zip up my hoodie—or Jamie's hoodie, to be accurate. The Perry the Platypus one, which I pulled off her while she slept. Under better circumstances I would've washed it, but now I'm just grateful that it's vomit-free. My hair is in a bun like hers, and I'm wearing sunglasses. I don't want Morgan to take off if she spots me and realizes I came instead of Jamie. This way, maybe I can at least get close enough to talk.

"I don't want to back out," I say. "And don't worry. Morgan isn't stupid. This place is too public to try anything. Just make sure you stay in the car, okay? And keep the engine running. We might need to get out of here fast."

"Okay. Be careful."

"I'll text you updates. And . . . thanks." I get out of the car and pause with one hand on the doorframe. "You didn't have to do this. *Any* of this. One of these days, I'll make it up to you."

"Please don't," Liam says with a rueful smile.

I stick my tongue out at him before closing the door, then turn to face the street. There's a single car parked in the Marlow's circular driveway, which makes my heart beat faster, until the valet opens its door and helps an elderly man onto the pavement. Morgan is nowhere in sight; the only people near us are two young mothers with strollers, chatting. Still, my nerves spike, and I can't make myself wait an extra ten seconds for the crosswalk signal. I jaywalk across the street and make my way to the entrance of the hotel.

"Good morning, miss," the valet says as I head for the revolving door.

"Morning," I say, and push my way inside.

The lobby looks just like I remember it: well lit, filled with flowers, and small enough that I can tell right away that Morgan isn't there. I glance at the time on my phone; it's exactly nine o'clock. I look at the empty seating area, the door, the path to the elevators, and then inadvertently catch the eye of the young woman standing behind the counter.

"Hi there," she calls. "Can I help you?"

"Um, hi," I say, moving closer. "I'm supposed to meet my friend? She's about thirty, tall, with short hair and lots of tattoos . . . here." I run my hand up my arm, and the receptionist smiles politely.

"I haven't seen anyone like that," she says.

"She could be wearing long sleeves, though," I say, realizing that Morgan might not want to stand out as much as she usually does. "Or, um, a hat, or—"

The receptionist beckons me closer. I step forward uncertainly, and she puts one hand to the side of her mouth.

"I haven't seen anyone under the age of sixty besides you all morning," she says in a loud whisper.

"Oh, okay," I say, trying not to sound disappointed. For a second, I was convinced she was about to give me a secret message from Morgan. "I'll just wait, then."

I settle myself into a lobby armchair and watch the minutes tick by on my phone. Five minutes, then ten. Check-in texts start rolling in from Liam, and I give him the same answer each time: *Not here yet.*

After fifteen minutes, I start getting antsy that I'm in the wrong spot. "Is there another place somebody might wait?" I ask the receptionist. "Like a café or something?"

She nods. "There's the restaurant where we serve breakfast and dinner. It's past the elevators, through the double doors before the restrooms."

"I'll check it out," I say.

I pass a few guests along the way, but the receptionist was right: everybody here qualifies for a senior citizen discount. Including, once I arrive at the restaurant, all of the customers. I linger for a few minutes anyway, walking back and forth in case I missed some hidden corner where Morgan is lurking, but all I'm doing is getting in the way of the single harried server who's working the room.

"Miss," he says tersely. "Please take a seat."

I back out of the room instead, saying, "I'm not hungry after all."

Bathroom, maybe? I head for the same ladies' room I used the night after I slept here, wondering if there's any chance I'll run into Instagram Girl again. It seems like messaging Liam from her account happened a year ago, not a day ago, and thinking about it makes me feel strangely nostalgic. Life was much simpler back then.

But the restroom is empty. No Morgan anywhere.

My phone buzzes with another text from Liam. *What's going on?*

I look at the time on my phone again. 9:25. *I think I've been stood up,* I text back. *I'll wait five more minutes.*

I go back to the lobby, and the receptionist gives me an apologetic smile as soon as she spots me. "No sign of your friend," she says.

"Thanks," I say, feeling deflated. Did Morgan realize I wasn't Jamie before I even caught sight of her? Or was she never planning on coming at all? Was that text not even *from* Morgan? I stare at the clock on my screen until it hits 9:30, and then head for the exit. The receptionist looks up, her mouth twisting in sympathy.

"I guess I got the time wrong," I say, forcing a smile even though I want to shriek with frustration. Now what?

"Take care!" she chirps as I push through the revolving door.

On my way, I text to Liam as I pass the valet. When I reach the sidewalk, he waves from the car, and I lift my shoulders in a shrug.

And then, right before the crosswalk signal changes, something—no, *someone*—slams into me. A blur in a blue T-shirt knocks me to the ground, and a hot, sharp pain shoots through my right side as it slams into concrete. Before I have a chance to react, my phone is ripped from my hand.

What the hell? I sit up, dazed, as the blur takes off.

"Miss! Are you all right?" the valet calls, rushing toward me. "I'm so sorry! Nothing like that has ever happened here before. Did he take anything?"

"Yeah, he—" I scramble to my feet, clutching my aching hip, but the words die in my throat when I see Liam halfway across the street. *Look out for him,* Augustus had said. *He doesn't have your killer instinct.* And what is that instinct telling me now? There's no possible way this was a random attack.

"Liam, no!" I yell, making a shooing motion with both hands. "Go back! Stay in the car!" Then I turn and run like hell after the guy who grabbed my phone.

CHAPTER FORTY-ONE

Kat

Like I told Liam the day we re-met, I don't often participate in after-school sports, since I rarely stay in one place long enough to make joining a team worthwhile. But when I do, it's track. I've always been fast, and this year, I got faster.

I sprint past the hotel, the pain in my side forgotten, and instinctively turn into the first street I see. There's a blue dot in the distance, and I manage to find another level of speed as my entire world narrows to closing the distance between him and me. My arms and legs pump in smooth rhythm, and it feels unbelievably good to be doing something with a clear, simple, achievable goal. *Catch him.*

I dodge a few people walking dogs as he disappears down another street, and when I fly around the corner, he glances over his shoulder. When he catches sight of me, he zags behind a bunch of parked cars and vaults over the fence into a nearby park.

I can do that, too, I think, clearing the fence like it's a hurdle. He keeps looking over his shoulder, which slows his stride, and before he's made it halfway across the park I'm close enough to reach out a hand and yank hard on his T-shirt. He goes sprawling to the ground, my phone flying out of his hand, and I scoop it up.

"Who are you?" I pant, backing up a few steps.

I'm poised to take off again, but once I get a good look at him I realize he's too winded to get to his feet, let alone chase me. He's older than I thought, a thirtysomething guy with a bristly crew cut and cheeks that are bright red from exertion. He exhales deeply, then holds out a hand and says, "Give me the phone. Trust me, you don't want it."

"Trust me, I do," I say. "Who do you work for?"

He makes a move like he's about to reach into his pocket, and that does it; I'm not sticking around for a weapon. I spin on my heel and run back the way I came at full speed, my phone clutched in one sweaty hand. I don't stop, don't slow down even a little, until I'm back in the hotel parking lot. Then I pause, breathing heavily, and look around me. I'm completely alone; the guy in the blue T-shirt is nowhere in sight.

What just happened?

Trust me, you don't want it. What kind of thief says something like that? Why wouldn't I want my phone?

Except . . . did he think this was *Jamie's* phone? She's the one who was supposed to be here. Not me.

I text Liam a quick update—*I'm fine, got my phone. In the hotel parking lot. Be there soon*—then stuff it into my pocket to take out Jamie's. Why would Morgan, or anyone, want Jamie's phone? Is there something incriminating on here? Something that would seem innocuous to Jamie but dangerous to someone else?

I tap in her passcode—my birthday—and open her messages. Gem has checked in a bunch of times, and I scroll guiltily past those. I've been ignoring my own messages from Gem, who must be frantic after we didn't show up yesterday, because I can't figure out what to tell her. I'd been hoping Morgan would give me something to work with.

There's nothing unexpected in the next few messages; they're mostly from me and Morgan, interspersed occasionally with some from Jamie's friend Kelly, automated messages about a doctor's appointment, and a guy named Ted who really, really wants Jamie to meet him for coffee.

She should, honestly. She needs to get out more.

My phone buzzes in my pocket; Liam's getting impatient. I scroll down through more of Jamie's messages, and stop at one from somebody she's saved as Asshole. It reads *No means no. I'm not going to change my mind.*

Who sent that—Jamie, or Asshole? I open it to find it was Jamie, replying to a message that says *Please, Jamie, I'm begging you.* Above that, she's written simply written *No,* in response to a message that says *I don't understand. It's not like you want to be with me. You can't stand me. Just sign and we'll both be free.*

The skin on the back of my neck starts to prickle as I scroll higher, looking for the beginning of the conversation. There are dozens of gray and blue bubbles in the past month, all with the same general theme: Asshole wants Jamie to sign something, and she won't do it. But the messages are frustratingly short on details until I get to a long one from Asshole, dated two weeks before we left for Bixby.

I know I fucked up. I know you're mad and want to punish me. But I've met someone, and it's getting serious. I want to get married again, but I can't do that when I'm ALREADY MAR-RIED. It was a 48-hour mistake, for crying out loud. I want to move on. Don't you?

Oh my God. Oh my God oh my God oh my—

I have no memory of sitting, but I'm on the pavement all of a sudden, and Jamie's phone clatters to the ground beside me. White noise fills my brain. Asshole is Luke. Luke is Asshole. *Luke and Jamie are still married.* After all these years, she never actually divorced his pathetic ass. *On purpose.*

During the entire flat-tire fiasco on the road to Bixby, both Luke and Jamie were putting on a show for Liam and me. Acting as though they hadn't spoken in more than a decade, when they'd been texting up a storm for weeks before. I could tell that Jamie was wildly uncomfortable the entire time, but I'd chalked that up to the trauma of seeing her ex-husband again. Emphasis, I thought, on the *ex* part.

I've always known Jamie is a con artist. But I never imagined that she'd con me.

First Parker with the necklace, and now this. My head is throbbing, so I close my eyes and press a palm to my temple. It doesn't help, though, and it means that I don't notice someone approaching until they're almost on top of me.

"What are you doing?" Liam asks, startling me so much that I let out a strangled scream. "Jesus, Kat, are you okay? You stopped answering my texts!"

I gaze up at him, shading my eyes against the bright sun, and can't think of anything to say except, "You weren't sup-posed to leave the car."

"Yeah, well, you weren't supposed to chase a mugger. Plans change."

He crouches beside me and lightly touches my arm. I look down at his fingers, noting with almost clinical detachment that I can't feel them. That's how numb I am.

"What's wrong?" Liam says. "Why are you on the ground? Did that guy knock you over?"

"No," I say with a mirthless laugh. "I knocked *him* over. Then I realized he was probably after Jamie's phone, not mine, so I decided to take a look through it. And . . ."

I hold the phone out to Liam and say, "I think you should read this."

CHAPTER FORTY-TWO

Liam

I don't know how long Kat and I sit in that parking lot, poring through the Luke-Jamie texts. None of it makes sense; why Jamie lied to Kat for most of her life, why she wouldn't just give Luke that damned divorce, and why both of them pretended they hadn't spoken in years when the four of us ran into one another at the side of the road.

I know Luke is an accomplished liar. But why would he lie about *this*? Why wouldn't he take the opportunity to yell at Jamie again, just like he'd been doing over text?

There's only one answer I can think of, and it chills me to the bone.

Yelling wasn't working, so he found another way.

I hand Jamie's phone back to Kat and say, "You know what this means, right?"

"That Jamie is a lying liar," she says in a monotone. "Who lies. All the time."

"Well, yeah, but also . . ." I rub the back of my neck. "Luke has a reason for wanting her gone. And she's almost *been* gone. Twice."

Kat's mouth drops open. "But . . . that guy was after *me,*" she says.

"So we thought," I say. "And it made sense, because you were there when Parker died. But what if we're wrong? What if Jamie's been the target all along?"

"If Jamie's been . . ." Kat frowns, then shakes her head. "It couldn't have been Luke who attacked us. For one thing, he's the wrong body type. And for another, he's always with the Sutherlands."

"And he doesn't like to get his hands dirty," I say. "But there are ways around that, aren't there? If you have enough money. Or think you *will.*"

Kat's eyes go round. "Are you saying that Luke sent a *hit man* after Jamie?"

"Maybe."

"A hit man who also killed Parker?"

"It might not be the same guy after all. Or maybe he was supposed to go after Jamie at the party and got Parker instead. Or he was supposed to *kill* both of them, because with Parker dead, there'd be more inheritance to split once Luke marries Annalise." A note of triumph creeps into my voice, because I feel like I might finally be hitting my stride theory-wise. And then I remember that I'm talking about my father, and my stomach drops.

Kat blinks. "Who are you, and what did you do with Liam?"

"Is that really so much wilder than anything else that's happened since we got here?"

She exhales noisily. "No. It's just . . . Look, you know I'm no Luke fan. He's terrible. But I always thought he was terrible in a *different* way. A less murdery way. Do you really think he'd do something like that?"

Would he? All weekend, I've seen flashes of a different, better Luke, and I haven't been able to tell if they're real or part of his act. His charcoal sketch of Annalise, and his concern for her. The way he seemed to effortlessly charm Ross Sutherland. Even last night, when he tried to get me to admit that I had feelings for Augustus before I shut him down.

He was right, and his advice wasn't half bad. Did he say it because he cares? Or because it conveniently aligns with what he wants?

"You said it in the car, right?" I say. "Bad stuff happening all at once can't be a coincidence. Maybe Luke knew Jamie was going to be here all along." I should've considered that before now, probably—that if something shady is going on, *of course* Luke is involved—but before I knew he and Jamie are still married, I thought his sole focus was Annalise. I didn't think there were any obstacles to my father getting what he wanted, other than the possibility that his mask would slip before Annalise said "I do."

Plus, until a few minutes ago, it seemed clear that Jamie was attacked because she was mistaken for Kat by Parker's killer. But now . . .

My phone vibrates in my pocket, and I pull it out with a grimace. "This is probably him, because he has impeccably bad timing," I say. Sure enough, I look down to a text from Luke: *Where the fuck is my car?*

"Is it Luke?" Kat peers at my screen. "What does he have to say?"

"I might've forgotten to ask to borrow the car," I say.

"What are you going to tell him?"

"Nothing. Let him rant," I say.

Which he does, because messages start piling up fast and furious on my phone.

But no, these aren't from Luke. The barrage is from Augustus, and when I open them, I realize he didn't just text me now; he's been texting for a while. At least half an hour. Since I found Kat in the parking lot, probably.

"Augustus is checking in," I say. "A lot."

Kat bites her lip. "Is Jamie okay?" she asks. "Is Griffin?"

"Hold on. Let me read from the top," I say, scrolling. " 'Can't get in touch with Dad. Or Granddad. Or Aunt Annalise. Almost desperate enough to try Aunt Larissa, but not quite.' And then, about ten minutes later . . . 'Mom Chaos is awake. VERY confused. God, this is awkward. She's asking for her phone. Did we bring it with us? I can't remember.' "

I pause to look at Kat, but all she says is "Keep going."

I return to Augustus's texts. " 'She wants to know why she's here and where Kat is. What am I supposed to tell her? Why is this my job? WHY AREN'T YOU ANSWERING ME?' Oh no. He's using all caps."

I frown as I scroll through the next few messages. "He says . . . Oh crap. He yelled at my phone a few more times, and then he said he's coming to Randall."

"What? No," Kat says. "He needs to stay with Jamie!"

"He doesn't *need* to do anything," I say, irritated. "And can you let me finish? I still have, like, half a dozen messages to get through." I flick past the text I just read and add, "He dropped a pin, says we should meet him there."

I open it to find the address of an office building in Randall, not far from where we are now. " 'My grandfather owns it,' " I read. " 'It's empty. We can talk privately.' "

Kat frowns. "Why would we need to talk privately—"

"Do you really have to ask that?" I say. It's disorienting, having her in my ear and him on my screen. "Can I just read his last text, please?"

She makes a twirling motion with her hand. "Go right ahead."

" 'Jamie is coming with me. I've been catching her up.' "

"Oh God," Kat says, growing pale. "Catching her up on *what*?"

I pocket my phone and stand, holding out my hand to help her off the ground. "I guess we're about to find out."

CHAPTER FORTY-THREE

Kat

Ten minutes later, Liam and I are outside an unassuming brick office building, waiting for Augustus to let us in. "Let's focus on the positives," Liam says. "Jamie must be feeling better."

"Good point," I say. "And she's not dead."

"Neither are we," Liam says. "Or Augustus." We're quiet for a few beats, and then he adds, "That seems to be it for positives at the moment."

"One more," I say, nudging his shoulder with mine as a figure appears in the building's foyer. "You're still my stepbrother."

Augustus opens the door then, fixing me with a deeply aggrieved expression. "I can't believe you left me in the lurch like that," he says, stepping aside to let us in. "I had to tell your mother pretty much everything. It was the worst conversation of my entire life. Have *you* ever had to tell someone that a masked man tried to kill them? Twice? And that was only the tip of the iceberg. She's freaking the fuck out, by the way."

"I'm sorry," I say, trailing him to the elevator. "So she knows about the necklace going missing, and Morgan poisoning her, and, um, Parker—"

"Everything," Augustus says grimly.

Oh God. I feel terrible. I never should have put Augustus in a position where he'd have to explain his uncle's death to my mother. As usual, I didn't think things through enough. I thought Jamie would stay asleep longer, and that if she did wake up, she'd be so woozy that she'd be willing to wait for me to come back.

Plus, I didn't account for getting mugged.

"I hate to say this, but it's about to get worse," I tell him.

Alarm springs into Augustus's eyes, and he whips around to look behind us. "Why? Were you followed?" he asks.

"No, not that. It's just . . ." I pause as the elevator doors open, then step inside. The interior panel glows with buttons numbered from 1 to 10, and I move out of the way so Augustus can press whichever one he needs. "Once I got my phone back, I realized that guy probably took it because he thought it was Jamie's phone. Like Morgan sent him to get it or something. So I looked through Jamie's messages, trying to figure out what they might have wanted, and I learned that Jamie and Luke are still married."

Augustus freezes before his outstretched finger connects with the button for the tenth floor. "Excuse me?"

"I'll get that," Liam murmurs, pressing it for him.

"Yeah, they never got a divorce," I say. "But he really wants one now, and they've been texting about it for the past two weeks."

Augustus sags against the back of the elevator as it moves

upward. "So. Much. *Chaos*," he groans, squeezing his eyes shut. Then they fly open and he says, "So is Luke . . ."

"Involved somehow?" Liam finishes. "That's what we're trying to figure out."

"Fucking hell," Augustus mutters as the elevator comes to a stop.

As soon as the doors open, a voice rings out, "Katrina Quinn! Get over here and start talking, *right now.*"

I step into the hallway and take in my mother. She looks better than she has in a while—still pale and wan, but there's fire in her eyes. All of which is directed at me. I take a few seconds to savor her recovery before snapping, "I could say the same for you."

"I'm out of here," Augustus says, disappearing down the hallway. Liam looks after him regretfully but stays put. He needs to hear this, too.

Jamie's brows pull together in disbelief. "Are you kidding me?" she asks. "You've been . . . I don't even have the *words* for what you've been doing since I got sick. All I asked of you was to let Gem know the job was off. And instead you did—this."

She gestures wildly around the hallway. "Can you even begin to imagine how terrified I was when I woke up in a strange house and you weren't there? And then *Augustus Sutherland,* of all people, has to tell me where I am? And everything that's happened this weekend? Kat, how could you involve him in this? How could you involve Liam? How could you involve *yourself*?" Her eyes get shiny. "You could have died. All of you could have died, and—"

"I did it for *you*," I say hotly. "Every single thing I've done was for you. I tried to help you. I tried to protect you. I saved you. Twice! Because we're supposed to be a *team*. Except that's not really true, is it? You've been lying to me for practically my whole life."

Confusion chases away some of the anger on Jamie's face as I hold up her phone, my entire body pulsing with betrayal. "I saw the messages between you and Luke," I continue. "You're still married. You won't let him go! Were you ever going to tell me that?"

My mother's eyes go round with shock, or maybe horror. "Kat, I . . . Oh God. Okay. This isn't how I wanted you to find out."

"You didn't want me to find out at all," I say bitterly.

"Let me explain, okay?" Jamie says, her voice taking on a pleading tone. "I was desperate for a divorce back then. But all I had was Luke's phone number, not an address, and I couldn't get in touch with him to serve papers. You kept asking if we'd have to see him again, so I just told you that it was done. I thought it would be, soon enough, so why make you worry?"

She swallows hard, tucking a strand of hair behind her ear. "Then the months went on and Luke *still* wouldn't return my calls. I would have had to go in front of a judge, and I was working for Gem, so that felt . . . complicated." She drops her eyes to the floor. "I started thinking, does it even matter? I didn't want to get married again; I didn't even want to be in a *relationship* again. Maybe this stupid marriage could be some kind of barrier between me and my own worst instincts. I couldn't marry another loser if I was already married, right?"

"Right," I say tightly. I don't care how sad she looks right now; I'm not going to feel sorry for her. "Justify it however you want, but you could have told me. Maybe not when I was four, but during any one of the *twelve years* since then."

"I could have," Jamie admits. "But I didn't want to."

I let out an indignant snort, and she adds, "Kat, you were so proud of me for insisting on a divorce straightaway. You used to talk about it all the time. You'd mimic me, except you always spoke with so much more assurance than I ever could. It felt like the best thing I'd ever given you—the belief that you could and should walk away from someone who didn't treat you the way you deserved. I didn't want to undo that."

I am *not* going to feel sorry for her. "So you thought it was better to lie?" I snap. "All this time, I thought we were a team—"

"We're not supposed to be a *team*, Kat," Jamie interrupts. "I'm supposed to be the person who takes care of you and keeps you safe. I'm not great at it, I know. I've let Gem run our lives for too long, because she's so much more competent than I am. I know you respect her and look up to her, and I . . . I've made a mess of so many things. Ever since the day you were born." Her voice quavers. "I'm sorry I didn't tell you about Luke. I should have. But I wanted to be better than I am."

I'm not— Oh, fuck it. I guess I feel a little sorry for her, because my tone is less strident when I say, "So why didn't you just give him the divorce when he asked for it?"

Two bright spots of color appear in Jamie's cheeks. "That . . . doesn't reflect well on me, I'm afraid," she says, glancing at Liam like she only just remembered he was there. "When Luke got in touch, I was trying to figure out how I'd make the finances of my new job work. It's not nearly as lucrative as the old one." She bites her lip. "Anyway, I couldn't be bothered to respond. Why should I, after so many years? Let him wait. But he couldn't. He got more and more urgent, and it occurred to me that he wouldn't be like that unless he'd found someone exceptional. Someone life-changing."

"Someone rich?" I ask.

Jamie's mouth twists. "Basically. And I thought . . . Well, I thought there might be something in it for me."

I stare at her. "You wanted a *payoff*?"

She flushes deeper. "Is that so wrong?" I don't answer, and she sighs. "Okay, maybe it is. But I thought it was worth a shot. And I wasn't going to hold out forever. Just until the end of the summer. Trust me, I was getting sick of hearing from him."

"And then you ran into him at the side of the road," I say, and she shudders.

"I couldn't believe that. I thought maybe he was following me, and I panicked. I was sure he'd start yelling at me right then and there, but he clearly didn't want a confrontation any more than I did. And now I know why."

"Did you know he was dating Annalise Sutherland?" I ask.

"God, no," Jamie says with another shudder. "I never would have agreed to take on the job if I did. Talk about the world's worst coincidence."

"Was it, though?" Liam says. He's been quiet for so long that his voice rasps on the words and he has to clear his throat. "Does that really seem likely?"

Jamie frowns. "What do you mean?"

Liam's eyes cut toward me. "Well, Kat and I were talking about it before we got here, and we thought . . . Luke had a reason to want you out of the picture, didn't he?" he asks. "And now you've been attacked twice." Jamie goes pale again, and he says, "Come on, you must have at least considered it once you heard the whole story."

"I did," Jamie admits. "But Luke . . . he's a lot of things, but he's not actually *violent*. Is he?" She turns worried eyes on Liam.

"That's what *I* said," I put in. "Despicable, but not murdery."

"Normally, I'd agree," Liam says. "But he really, *really* wants to be married to Annalise. They're already engaged. She's basically everything he's ever hoped for in life, and I don't know what he'd do if he thought he couldn't have it."

"This is exhausting," Jamie moans. Somehow, I manage to refrain from reminding her that the rest of us didn't have the luxury of sleeping through most of it.

"Liam." Augustus suddenly reappears in the hallway, startling me. "Annalise is blowing up my phone. Something's up at the compound, and people are looking for us. You must've heard from Luke, right?"

"Many times," Liam says. "I did steal his car, after all."

"Borrowed," Augustus corrects. "Anyway, I need to leave. Are you coming, or . . ."

He looks wistful but not especially hopeful, and I push Liam's arm. "Go," I say. It's the least I can do for Augustus, after forcing him into the impossible role of having to explain the past few days to my mother. "We'll be all right. We have lots more talking to do."

"Are you sure?" Liam asks. I nod, and he says, "Okay. I can try to feel Luke out a little when I get there, see if he lets anything slip—"

"Or you could just take a break," I say. "Have some more breakfast. Or lunch. Brunch. Whatever meal is time-appropriate for this endless day."

"I don't like leaving you here by yourselves," Liam says doubtfully.

"We'll be fine," I insist. "Right, Jamie?"

"Absolutely," she says, giving Liam a reassuring smile before turning toward Augustus. "Augustus, I haven't thanked you properly for everything you've done for Kat. And for bringing me here to Randall. I'm so sorry for what you and your family have gone through. There's no excuse for what I came to Bixby to do, so I won't make one. I don't fully understand what went wrong over the weekend, but I need to take responsibility for it. And I will."

I don't like the implications of that, but I swallow my protest. Liam was right; I've been treating Jamie like a child. And the worst thing is, she knows it. She knows it so much that she's afraid to be honest with me.

"I'm glad you're okay," Augustus tells Jamie.

"I'll text you," I say to Liam.

"You better," he says.

"Come on," Jamie says, plucking at my sleeve as Augustus presses the elevator button. "Maybe there's some coffee hidden in the kitchen."

I let her lead me away, but we've barely gone around the corner before I pause. "Hang on one second," I say, and retrace my steps.

Augustus and Liam are still waiting in front of the elevator. Before they can ask me what I'm doing, I launch myself forward and throw my arms around Liam's neck, nearly knocking him off balance. I'm not much of a hugger, and this hug is so fierce that it could be mistaken for an attack. But after a moment of startled stillness, Liam hugs me back.

"Jamie loves you," he whispers. "Don't ever doubt it."

I don't respond except to tighten my hold on him. He lifts me off the ground, and for a few seconds we just cling to one another.

"I'm glad you're still my brother," I breathe into his ear.

"Me too, Kat," he says. "Me too."

CHAPTER FORTY-FOUR

Liam

Augustus drove his grandfather's old Range Rover to Randall, and I follow it back to Griffin's house. The plan is for him to park and then get into Luke's Buick with me so we can drive the short distance to the guest cottage and meet Annalise.

"Did Annalise give any hint of what's up?" I ask when Augustus climbs into the passenger seat.

"Not really," he says as I pull the car around. "And I was afraid to ask."

I brake to let a squirrel dart across the road. "This is all such a mess."

"It really is," Augustus says. "Maybe we should just keep going. Drive to California or something."

"Why California?"

"Because it's very far away," he says.

Briefly, I imagine having a different kind of life, where a cross-country summer trip with the guy I like would make perfect sense. Then I say, "I'm sorry I ignored your texts earlier. That bombshell about Luke and Jamie took over my brain for a while."

"I get that," Augustus says. "Now."

"I should've let you know we were fine." The guest cottage looms in front of us, and I pull into the driveway. Augustus and I both get out and close the doors. "You didn't have to come after us."

That came out wrong. What I meant to say was *Thanks for caring enough to worry.*

"Yeah, I know," Augustus says. "I should've realized Chaos would be doing her usual scrappy con-artist-in-training thing. You didn't need me."

I did. I do.

Even though we have much bigger problems, it's still frustrating that my tongue constantly ties itself into knots when I'm around Augustus. I don't want him to feel like he overreacted; I want him to know that I'd have done the same thing.

"I'm glad, though," I manage to say. "That you came."

"Of course I did," Augustus says, threading his fingers through mine. His nearness feels good—both heady and comforting at the same time.

Then the shouting reaches our ears.

"Parker isn't even in his grave!" screams a woman's voice.

"Oh, good," Augustus sighs, releasing my hand as he reaches out to press the doorbell. "Aunt Larissa is here. That always makes everything better."

The door buzzes, and Augustus pushes it open. When we step into the vestibule, Annalise's quieter tone becomes audible. "Larissa, please. Parker's gone. Griffin is struggling. Can't we at least *try* to be on the same side?"

"There's no side to this!" Larissa snaps. "I'm telling Dad."

"You're 'telling Dad'?" Annalise repeats in disbelief. "You're fifty years old. How are you still using that line?" Then she catches sight of Augustus and me, and offers a strained smile. "Oh, good, there you boys are. Listen, I just talked to Clive—"

"Let me guess," Augustus says. "Damage control?"

Annalise's lips purse. "Actually, no. There's been a break in the investigation."

"The investigation into . . ." Augustus exchanges glances with me. That could be any number of things from our perspective, but there's only one the Sutherlands care about. "Who killed Uncle Parker?"

Annalise nods. "There's a man in the background of a guest photo"—I can't help myself then; I poke Augustus, because once again *Kat was right*—"who's dressed to look like one of our security guards but isn't part of the team. Police are analyzing the image now."

"Analyzing the image?" I say. "What does that mean?"

"Checking it against their databases, I believe. To see if he's a known criminal. Even if he's not, though, they have other ways to identify him. It's possible this man was just a guest, but . . ." She takes a deep breath. "I know you think the family hasn't been doing anything about Parker's death, Augustus, but we have."

"Does Dad know?" Augustus asks.

"Griffin is resting. This morning wore him out. But we'll tell him as soon as possible. Try not to worry," Annalise says. "This is good news."

Augustus nods, looking dazed. "No, yeah. It's great."

"It's *fantastic*," I say fervently. And then it hits me—we're talking about identifying the guy I told Kat that Luke might've hired. She shut me down quick, but . . . "Does *my* dad know?" I ask. "Where is he?"

A crease appears on Annalise's forehead. "I'm not sure, actually."

"What?" I ask, startled. Luke's practically been surgically attached to Annalise since we got here. "He went somewhere and didn't tell you?"

Larissa, who's been uncharacteristically quiet, lets out a loud snort. Annalise eyes her nervously before saying, "When the photograph came in, Luke said he had some business to take care of, and he . . . left. I tried calling him, but then Larissa came by—"

"I didn't just *come by*," Larissa snaps. "I heard you call him your *fiancé*. Because apparently, the two of you think a family tragedy is the perfect time for a secret engagement." She gazes triumphantly between Augustus and me, waiting for expressions of shock that neither of us have the energy to fake. "Wait," she says, frowning. "Am I the last to know?"

I can't deal with Larissa right now. Parker's killer is about to be identified, and Luke *left*? The timing for my father to pull a disappearing act on the fiancée he's been working so hard to charm is . . . not good. "Did Luke say anything about where he was going?" I ask.

"He can't have gone far," Augustus says. "You have his car."

And then, as I pull out my phone to check the timing of Luke's last text, I remember.

A few weeks ago, while Annalise was having dinner with

310

us, Luke made a big production of installing one of those find-a-friend apps on his phone. *I'll worry less if I can always know where you are, Liam,* he said in his best Affable Dad tone. He activated it in front of Annalise and sent me an invitation. I never accepted it, but I'm pretty sure I can still see where he is. I open the app, and sure enough, there's a big blue dot that reads *Luke.* And it's close.

I enlarge the map. Even though the Sutherland compound isn't rendered in any kind of detail, it looks as though Luke is right on top of the gray dot that represents my phone.

"I might know where he is," I say. It's a lie, but at least I know he's nearby. "I can go look for him."

"Do you want me to come?" Augustus asks.

I do, but . . . "No, that's okay," I say. "I won't be long."

I think it's time, finally, that my father and I have a heart-to-heart.

CHAPTER FORTY-FIVE

Kat

"We need to talk about what happens next," Jamie says.

"After what? Lunch?" I say, polishing off the last of my Lean Cuisine. We didn't find any coffee in the kitchen, but we did unearth a couple of meals in the freezer.

That's obviously not what she means, but old habits die hard, and avoiding difficult conversations is probably the oldest habit I have. This office is comfortable, silent, and utterly peaceful. While we're here, it's easy to imagine that everything will turn out fine. That we can walk out into the summer sunshine, find our way back to the Sutherland staff quarters, pick up our car, and drive home.

Like the last few days never happened.

"Kat," Jamie says quietly. "I don't understand what's going on. I don't know if Parker Sutherland really was working with Morgan to double-cross Gem. I don't know what Luke knows, or what he might have done. And I don't know why we've been attacked *twice,* but I do know this—it's my job to make it stop. And there's no easy way out."

I get that, but for a few more minutes, I want to live in a world where there is.

"What would it be like," I ask, "if you'd been an accounting assistant my whole life?"

"Oh gosh," Jamie says with a weak laugh. "Who knows. We wouldn't have moved as much, that's for sure."

"Where would we live?"

"At the beach," she says promptly.

"Like you did when you were little?" I ask.

Jamie doesn't like to talk about her childhood—about the parents who struggled so much with their addictions that she mostly fended for herself. The only part she can ever bring her-self to talk about is how she used to be able to walk to a nearby beach. "Sort of," she says. "But somewhere in New England. Not the Southeast."

I don't have to ask her why. That's where Ashley and Kylie Burke came from, and that's where we left them. For good. "I hope we get to do that someday," Jamie continues. "But if things go badly for me, I need you to know that you'll be taken care of. My friend Marianne will be your guardian—"

"Guardian," I gulp. "I have a *guardian?*"

"Of course you do," Jamie says. "I'm a single parent. I have to be prepared."

"And it's Marianne?" I know the name; we lived in her spare room until Vegas.

Something flickers across Jamie's face then. It's gone too quickly for me to place it, but if I had to guess, I'd say *guilt.* "Yes, it's Marianne," she says. "I know you probably don't remember much about her, but she's a good friend and she'll look out for you. And she's a very steady, dependable kind of person." Her mouth twists as she adds, "Unlike me."

I hate this conversation. I have a hundred questions, like *Where does Marianne live now?* and *What if we don't get along?* But those are all about me, and I've never seen Jamie look so defeated. It feels like she's aged a decade in a few days; there's no way anyone who saw us side by side now would take us for twins. "I know you think you didn't do a good job raising me," I say. "But in my opinion, you did."

Jamie gives me a rueful smile. "I didn't mean to imply that I don't think you've turned out wonderfully," she says. "Because you have."

"Maybe take some credit, then," I say.

She reaches over to clasp my hand in both of hers, and we sit in silence for a few minutes. Then she squeezes my hand and says, "I need to use the restroom. After that, we can get into more of the details of what will happen if I'm not around for a while. Okay?"

"Okay," I say dully.

Jamie leaves the kitchen. As soon as she's gone, I get up too; there's no way I can sit still with my thoughts right now. I need to be moving. I throw away our empty Lean Cuisine trays, wash my hands, and head into the hallway. The space isn't particularly large; there's the elevator bank in the middle, and two wings with near-identical cubicle farms surrounded by window offices. The carpeting is beige, the walls are bare, and there's a constant low hum from the overhead lights.

My friend Marianne will be your guardian.

It's impossible. I've barely spent a single day away from

Jamie my entire life. How would I manage without her? How would she manage without me?

I need a distraction. I make my way through one of the cubicle mazes, mentally cataloguing everything I pass. Maybe there's something here that I could use as a weapon, just in case there's another attack. Because somehow, the idea of preparing for a theoretical worst is better than the reality Jamie started to outline.

There's not much furniture here, other than a large desk in one of the corner offices next to the back stairwell. I open all the drawers, pulling out a letter opener—useful—and a single key on a metal ring. Possibly also useful?

"Kat?" Jamie's voice floats from the other side of the building. "Where are you?"

"Just looking around," I call.

I head back toward the kitchen, keeping an eye out for any doors that the key might fit into. There's only one that's not already open, built into a wall that's also home to the fire alarm and an extinguisher. It looks like a supply closet, and when I fit the key into it, it turns easily. I push open the door and peer inside, seeing nothing except a single mop standing in one corner.

"At least I didn't have to pick the lock," I mutter to myself.

"What?"

Jamie comes up beside me, and I hastily step back. "Nothing."

She frowns. "Did you just say that you picked that lock?"

"No," I say truthfully, holding up the key ring. "I found the key."

Her gaze drops to my other hand. "And a letter opener. Why do you have that?"

"Just in case," I say.

"In case of *what?*"

I wait a beat before saying, "In case we get any letters."

She can't help but laugh a little, but she quickly rearranges her face into a sterner expression. "This is the entire problem. You're in attack mode, all the time! It's no way to live."

"Technically, I'm in defense mode," I say.

"I'm *serious,* Kat."

"I know," I say, dropping the letter opener onto a nearby ledge.

"Come back to the kitchen. Let's talk," Jamie says.

"Okay," I say, right as my phone buzzes in my pocket. I pull it out, and my screen is lit up with a text. "Let me just see what Augustus wants," I say.

"Oh God, that poor boy," Jamie says with a grimace. "I think I traumatized him."

"He, um . . . Oh," I say, eyes widening. "It's about Parker's death. Augustus says there was a break in the case because—ha!" I look up from my phone, triumphant. "I *told* him to check guest photos."

"What are you talking about?" Jamie asks.

"Apparently, there was some guy on the compound Saturday night who was dressed like a security guard but isn't one, so now they're looking into him." I say. "Ooh . . . and Augustus managed to get hold of the picture. Let's take a look."

At first, all I can see are the two people who were meant to be in the photo, chatting in the sculpture garden. But then I notice the gray-suited figure behind them, and my pulse picks up. I feel like I'd know those shoulders anywhere; they've been haunting my thoughts since Saturday night. I enlarge the photo, and . . .

And then a tidal wave of shock slams into me.

Dimly, I'm aware that my heart has started battering against my chest, but the rest of my body is numb. I can't process what I'm seeing. I don't *want* to process it. I shut my eyes, but there's no point; the image is seared into my eyelids.

That face.

No, no, no. It can't be. I'm seeing things. I'm stressed and exhausted, and bad memories have been chasing me all weekend.

"Kat?" Jamie's hand touches my arm. "What's the matter?"

I have to look again.

I crack an eye and enlarge the picture even more until all I can see is that one person. I'm not wrong. I'd know him anywhere, even though the last time I saw him was through a computer screen. Dead-eyed and slack-jawed, standing in front of a concrete wall and wearing an orange prison jumpsuit.

"How?" It sounds like my own voice is coming at me from the other end of a long tunnel. "How can it be him?"

"Who?" Jamie asks.

I feel my phone being pulled from my hand, and I let it go. "My father," I say.

CHAPTER FORTY-SIX

Liam

I can't think of a good plan for tracking down Luke within the Sutherland compound, so I wind up heading toward the area where I walked with Kat on Friday.

When it comes right down to it, I don't know much about my father. But he normally likes to be in the middle of the action. If he's avoiding that for some reason—and can't fully escape because I took his car—then he'll be on the outer limits.

Eventually, that's where I find him, near the ravine that Kat stopped me from walking into. He's awfully close to the edge, almost peering into the abyss, and my nerves spike as I approach. He's not . . . He wouldn't . . . Right?

"Luke!" I call.

He spins around, startled, and my heart jumps into my throat as I brace myself to see him stumble or, God forbid, fall. But he doesn't, and as I get closer to him, I realize he's farther away from the edge than I thought.

"What are you doing?" I ask, stopping to let my pulse settle.

"What does it look like I'm doing?" he asks, sounding annoyed. But not *only* annoyed; there's something else running beneath his tone. Fear, maybe? "Observing nature."

He looks rough. Unshaven, hair mussed, oxford shirt wrinkled like he grabbed it off the floor. "Annalise is worried," I say. "About you, and about the fact that people know the two of you are engaged."

Luke stiffens. "How did you . . . Who knows?"

"Well, me, obviously," I say. "Larissa. And Augustus."

"That's it?" he asks.

"That I know of."

He looks mildly relieved, and I can't tell if it's because he doesn't want Ross Sutherland to know, or someone else. "She said you've been gone for a while. That you had some business to take care of," I say.

"Yes. I did."

"Are you . . . I mean . . . Is it here?" I ask, gazing around us.

"I had to make a call," Luke says, straightening his collar. "Someplace quiet. And my options were limited, since you stole my car."

"Borrowed," I say.

His nostrils flare. "Where were you?"

"What was your call about?" I counter.

"It's no concern of yours," he says dismissively.

"I think it might be," I say.

His eyes narrow. For a few seconds, we just stare at one another, until he snorts out a laugh and says, "It's not."

He doesn't think I know anything. Why would he? It's not like he has any idea what I've been up to since we got here.

He's been more than happy to let me run around entirely un-supervised. We could keep dancing around like this, or I could just . . . ask.

"Was it about Parker's killer? They might have identified him, you know."

"I know," Luke says.

I can't read his expression. He has his game face on, and I need to shock him out of it. "Did you know that the same guy is after Jamie?" I ask.

There's no missing the flash of panic in his eyes, no matter how quickly and skillfully he hides it. "Jamie?" he says. "What are you talking about? Jamie is . . . She has nothing to do with any of this. She's gone home, probably. All the caterers did."

"No," I say. "She's here. I've been talking to her."

His throat works convulsively before he asks, "About what?"

Am I doing this? I guess I'm doing this. "Lots of things," I say. "Like the fact that you two never got divorced."

For a second, Luke is as still as one of the statues in Ross Sutherland's garden. Then he advances on me so quickly that I take an involuntary step back. He stops before he reaches me, though, puts his hands on his hips, and starts to laugh. It's one of the most unpleasant sounds I've ever heard—harsh and bitter—and I move even farther away.

"You're such a miserable little sneak," he says. "Always poking and prying at me. Why? What difference does it make to you? You've got a roof over your head, don't you? I let you come and go as you please. Try being grateful for once."

"You must have been furious," I say. "When Jamie said no." He doesn't reply, and I put a little more distance between us. "What did you decide to do about it?"

His jaw clenches. "What do you mean?"

"I mean, you wouldn't just let something like that go, right? Not when you were getting ready to propose to Annalise."

His face contorts into a snarl, like he's about to bite out another angry response. But then he abruptly asks, "Did you tell her?"

"Tell who?"

"Annalise. Did you tell her about Jamie?"

I hesitate, not sure if I should show my cards. But my face does it for me, because Luke's eyes crinkle in relief as he says, "No. You didn't."

He takes a step toward me, and I can't help it—I take one back. My foot catches on a rock, nearly causing me to stumble, and I glance over my shoulder. Then I freeze, because I had no idea that I'd let myself get this close to the ravine. My eyes cut toward Luke, and when his throat tightens I know he's just clocked the same thing.

The drop behind me is so sheer that it makes me dizzy. But looking at Luke is even worse. Jesus, would . . . Would my own father shove me off a cliff to shut me up?

He's not actually violent, Jamie said, but I'm not sure Luke would even consider this to be violence. One quick, clean push that'd look like an accident, and he'd never have to deal with me again. Never have to worry about me telling Annalise who he really is, and I think—no, I *know*, as his eyes take on a calculating gleam—that he'd like that.

My heart skitters. Everything around us goes still, except for the far-off call of a bird. Then Luke takes a careful step toward me.

I look down at his hands, curled into white-knuckled fists

at his sides. Luke's never hit me; never once touched me in anger. Or with any other emotion, as far as I can remember. I guess he must've held me while I was a baby at least occasionally, but when I got older he didn't pick me up and swing me around like my friends' dads did. Or take me by the hand—not even after he'd lost me in Vegas for hours. We don't hug, and I thought I didn't care. If he'd tried to put on a show for Annalise, I would've backed away in horror. But it'd be a viciously cruel twist if the first time my father reaches for me is the last thing I see.

And then, before I have a chance to speak, Luke is striding toward me with his hands outstretched. I freeze with shock and horror, unable to move. His eyes are glinting coldly, and his face looks like a mask. He's really going to—

His hands curl around my collar, and he yanks me forward, so that my face is only inches from his. "Give me my car keys, you useless little shit."

My knees go weak with relief. "You . . . you need to let me go first," I gulp.

He does, and I take the opportunity to scramble away from the ravine. I suck in deep breaths, glorying in the feeling of clean air rushing into my lungs. There are a lot more questions I should ask him, but I'm done for now. That felt like way too close of a call.

"How did you find me, anyway?" Luke snaps.

"That find-a-friend app," I say, reaching into my pocket for his keys.

"I should've deleted that," he grumbles. "Fucking stalker phone."

Then I freeze again, but for an entirely different reason.

Fucking stalker phone. He's right. Oh my God, he's right. *That's* what has been going on.

"Keys," Luke says tersely, holding out one hand. "Now."

"I can't," I say.

And then I take off.

CHAPTER FORTY-SEVEN

Kat

Somehow, I ended up on the floor. I'm not quite curled into the fetal position, but close. I'm sitting with my knees drawn to my chest, my arms wrapped tightly around them. "Am I wrong?" I ask as Jamie stares at my phone.

She looks exactly like I feel: flat-out terrified.

I'm not wrong.

A sound escapes me. It's a half gasp, half hysterical laugh, which dies in my throat when the last words my father ever spoke to me flash through my mind: *You think you're funny, don't you, little girl?*

I was never a person to him—just a possession. As soon as I started to develop a personality, he wanted to stomp it out of me. Like he tried to do with Jamie.

"He's supposed to be in prison," I say numbly. "Why isn't he in prison?"

Then a new thought strikes, sending a burst of anger through me that's almost welcome. Anger is much better than fear. I scramble to my feet and demand, "Why didn't you *tell* me?"

Jamie tears her eyes away from my screen, her mouth falling open. "What?"

"You must've known he was released! Why didn't you tell me? This is Luke all over again—"

"No!" Jamie says, so loudly and emphatically that I stop midsentence. "Those are two *very* different things. I would never keep something like this from you, Kat. Never. I didn't . . . They're supposed to inform me. I have an email address set up just for this, and there hasn't been a single *word*—" She stops herself and hands back my phone, then digs into her pocket and pulls out hers. "Let me double-check." She swipes angrily at her screen before adding, "There's nothing. No heads-up whatsoever. I should've been given *a lot* of advance notice."

"Did you delete it? Send it to spam?"

"I wouldn't be that careless. I *wouldn't*. I know better than anyone how vindictive that man is. Even though I thought I'd erased all traces of us, I'd have gone even further if I knew he was getting out." Still, I can tell she's checking other folders, stabbing at her phone until she groans in frustration. "Nothing."

"This obviously isn't a coincidence," I say, and Jamie lets out a mirthless laugh.

"God, no."

My mind is spinning, puzzle pieces shifting and then locking into place with a sickening snap. Like a coffin closing. When I look at Jamie, I know she's gotten there, too.

"Parker Sutherland was killed in the woods behind Annalise's house, with the fake necklace in his pocket," she says. Her voice is calm, though I can tell she's anything but. "That was supposed to be *me*. Cormac . . . somehow, he must have known I was coming. He was there to kill me, but Parker showed up instead."

I shiver and say, "So he kept trying."

"But how did he *know*?" she asks, desperation edging into her voice.

"Luke?" I say.

"I never told Luke about Cormac," she says. "Or anything about our previous names. Besides, Luke didn't know what I was supposed to be doing that weekend."

"He could've found out," I insist. "Or maybe Morgan told Cormac. She knocked you out of commission, after all, which means . . . Hold on," I say as a new thought hits me. "Wait. That gluten poisoning . . . It saved your life, didn't it?"

"Yeah," Jamie says, blinking. "I guess it did. Morgan must've known something was about to go down, but . . . why wouldn't she just *tell* me?"

My phone vibrates with a new message then. "Feel like I should check this," I mutter, reaching into my pocket. "There's a lot going on." Then I blink at the all-caps message from Liam.

GET OUT AND LEAVE JAMIE'S PHONE.

"Who is it?" Jamie asks.

"It's Liam, but . . ."

Another message quickly follows the first. *I think someone is tracking her phone. That's how they found her.*

My breath catches. Oh God, he's probably right. And if he is . . .

More texts from Liam pile up, one after the other:
Maybe Morgan sent someone to steal the phone.
To make you untrackable.

326

Maybe she's trying to help you.

She is. In a strange, inexplicable, deeply roundabout way—she is.

"Kat!" Jamie says sharply. "What's he saying?"

Get out, Liam writes. *I have Luke's car. I'll drop a pin when I'm close.*

"We have to go," I say.

And then, from just a couple of halls away, the elevator doors chime.

Jamie and I look at one another, and I can see my own fear mirrored in her eyes. "Is that Liam?" she whispers.

"No," I whisper back.

CHAPTER FORTY-EIGHT

Kat

For a split second, I hesitate. I should show Jamie my phone and tell her everything. She's the adult, she'll make a plan, and then—

And then time will run out.

In a series of quick motions, I yank my mother's phone out of her hand, shove her into the supply closet, and shut the door. "Don't make a sound," I say, in the loudest whisper that I dare to use. "If you do, we're dead."

I test the doorknob—it's locked again, thank God—before stuffing both of our phones into my pocket. Then I grab the letter opener from the ledge where I'd left it, and take off as silently as I can through the cubicle farm.

A hazy plan starts to take shape. If that was my father at the elevator—and let's face it, who else could it be?—he's probably been methodically going through every floor below this one looking for us. As soon as he sees the empty Lean

Cuisine boxes in the kitchen trash, he'll know that we're here. While he prowls through the labyrinth of corridors and offices, I can make my way outside and get Jamie's phone as far away from the building as possible. That way, when he doesn't find us and goes to check her signal, he'll think we've both left.

Except . . .

I hesitate as the faint thud of heavy footsteps reaches my ears. He'll try every single door. What if he takes the locked supply closet for exactly what it is—a hiding spot—and shoots his way in, instead of simply moving along?

I can't take that chance. I need a better plan.

My mind races as I pass an empty office. I pull Jamie's phone out of my pocket, turn silent mode off and the volume up, and place it on the middle of the floor. Then I creep back into the hallway with the letter opener in one hand, ears straining. I can't hear a thing, which I hope means that Cormac is searching the opposite end of the floor. I move as quietly as I can down the hallway until I reach the back stairwell.

I slip into the stairwell, holding the door open with one hand while taking out my phone with the other. Then I inhale a long, steadying breath before unlocking the screen and calling Jamie's number.

Her jangling ringtone is like an alarm in the silent office. I ease the door shut noiselessly behind me and race down the stairs while holding my phone to my ear, taking the steps two at a time as Jamie's ringtone grows fainter. I reach the fourth floor and don't dare go any farther, because I don't want to be out of breath when—

Someone picks up right as I ease through the fourth-floor

stairwell door and close it behind me. The voice in my ear is deep and as cold as ice. "What," it says.

There's no indication that he knows who he's talking to, even though he must. My name would have come up on Jamie's phone, and if he knew where to find her, that means both our covers are blown.

I force myself to take a normal breath. Then, even though my heart is pounding out of my chest, I put every ounce of focus I have into sounding calm when I say, "What's up, Dad?"

There's a beat of silence before he growls, "Fuck you."

"Right back at you."

"Stupid little bitch," he hisses.

"Not sure how I'm the stupid one when you're in an empty office building and we're pulling into the police station," I say.

"Your whore mother wouldn't dare," he says, but I can hear a sliver of something new behind his impotent fury. Fear, maybe? If I could manage to put aside the fact that this monster contributed half of my genes, I could almost enjoy this. My loser father is *terrible* at killing people, which must be frustrating for him. "They'll fry her," he adds.

"Better them than you," I say. "Nice try, though."

I expect another angry, incoherent response, yet there's nothing but silence, for so long that I almost speak again. Then a low chuckle reverberates in my ear, sending a shiver sliding up my spine. "Nice try yourself," he says. "But this office isn't empty."

I fight against a surge of panic, barely managing to keep my voice steady as I say, "Oh, but it is." *He's just messing with me,* I think. *Trying to scare me into giving something away.* But it won't work; I can bluff as well as he can. "We're long gone."

"You sure about that?"

"I think I'd know if we weren't."

"Then tell me," he says, with so much sly malice that I can practically see the ugly smile spreading across his face. "Whose footsteps did I just hear?"

My composure shatters in an instant. *Jamie.* How did she get out of the closet? *Why* did she get out of the closet, when I told her we'd die if she did? We were close, so unbelievably close, to getting away from him. All she had to do was trust me.

But then again, all *I* had to do was say my piece and hang up. Instead, I taunted a dangerous, desperate man. And I'm the one who trapped Jamie upstairs; if we'd taken off together, maybe we could've made it out of the building and someplace safe to wait for Liam. This is my fault. *My fault, my fault, my fault . . .*

I squeeze my eyes shut and shake my head to clear it. I have to pull myself together. I can't let him know for sure that Jamie is there.

"You didn't hear anything. It's wishful thinking," I say, but my voice is so weak, so pathetically wobbly, that he laughs again.

"Your mother stole twelve years of my life," he says. "I'm about to pay her back."

"She didn't steal anything. All she did was try to protect us from *you!*" I cry out, not caring anymore if he can hear me. "You're too late, anyway. The police are coming. They're practically there—"

It's a desperate lie, and he knows it.

"Bye for now, little girl." He almost croons the words, a sick lullaby that makes every inch of my skin crawl. "I'm going to kill your mother."

Before I can reply, the line goes dead.

For a second, I'm empty of everything except an all-consuming terror. I can't move. I can't think. I'm a useless lump on the floor, my father's words ringing in my ears.

Bye for now, little girl.

That horrible singsong voice.

I'm going to kill your mother.

Then silence. Gone before I had the chance to reply. And how could I, anyway? What could I say after something like that?

What could I possibly say?

Not if I kill you first.

The words are like a tiny flicker of fire, the barest reminder that warmth exists. Like a sluggish heartbeat in a chest that looks perfectly still. Or a lone synapse, the last one working, sending directions to a foggy brain: *Get up.*

Get up.

A jolt of adrenaline launches me to my feet, and another one sends me through the door. I shove my phone into my pocket and stand in the stairwell, breathing heavily. My father is six floors above me, about to kill my mother, and what am I going to do about that?

The first time something like this happened, I was four years old and locked in a closet. I've had nightmares about that day ever since, but I'm not that scared little girl anymore. Cormac Whittaker might be the first and worst sociopath my mother ever trusted, but he's proven time and time again over the past few days he's hardly invincible.

Plus, now I know how to fight back.

White-hot rage sweeps through me, chasing away every last

bit of fear. "Cormac!" I yell, my voice echoing through the stairwell as I pound my way up the stairs. Two at a time, just like I came down. I clutch the letter opener in my right hand, wishing it were as razor-sharp as my hatred. But it'll do. I'll make it do. "I'm here, you coward, and I'm coming for you!"

I'm faster than he is; I know I am. I've been outrunning him all weekend. I've outrun him my whole life. I'm on the seventh floor, the eighth floor, the ninth floor. The door to the tenth floor looms in front of me, and I slam my shoulder into it. I burst into the hallway, brandishing the letter opener like a knife, ready for whatever's waiting for me.

But no. I'm wrong. I'm not ready at all.

The sound of a gunshot rings out, impossibly loud. Somebody screams. It's not until I collapse to the ground, cheek scraping the rough carpet, that I realize it was me.

CHAPTER FORTY-NINE

Kat

I'm too late. He got to her first.

That's all I can think after my legs give out and send me tumbling to the floor, the letter opener flying out of my hand. The echo of the gunshot is already fading from my ears, replaced by the pounding of my heart. A heart that's still beating even though my mother's has stopped.

My mother. Jamie. Gone.

How can somebody so full of life, so full of purpose and determination and love, just be *gone*? Five minutes ago, two minutes ago, one minute ago, she was here. She was living and breathing and I was going to save her; we were going to get out of here and have a different kind of life. Different in a hundred ways, except for the one important thing that was always and would always be true: we'd be together.

My eyes well up and tears spill over, running down my scraped cheek. My chest feels cracked open, ragged and bleeding, emptying everything that ever mattered onto the carpet beneath me. Letting it sink into the floor and fade away. I always thought the term *broken heart* was an expression, but turns out it's real after all. This is how it feels. And how it sounds: choked, hopeless sobs mixing with the pulse still roaring in my ears.

And footsteps.

My breath hitches. *Cormac.*

Coming for me next. And even though part of me feels like I'm already dead, there's a deeper, primal part that screams at me to move.

I rise shakily to my knees and manage to crawl toward the letter opener, grasping the hilt. I let out another strangled sob when I feel how flimsy it is and realize how deluded I was to think it could ever have been enough to save my mother. But it's all I have, and I'm not going to die empty-handed. Or on my knees.

I flatten one palm against the wall and use it for support as I stand. The footsteps are closer now—right around the corner. I glance behind me; the door to the stairwell seems impossibly far away. I'll never reach it in time, and anyway, I don't want to run. I can't leave Jamie alone with him, even if it's too late to save her.

So when I see a shadow rounding the corner, I launch myself forward, aiming for a low tackle that will cut him off at the knees. Maybe the element of surprise will be enough for him to falter, to drop his gun, and give me the chance to stab whatever part of him I can reach.

I make contact, and both of us tumble to the ground. Too easily.

"Jesus! Kat!"

I realize, past the haze of adrenaline flooding my veins, that I just knocked down a much thinner, lighter person than my father. A woman's face swims into view, round eyes fixed on the letter opener hovering a few inches from her chest. "Could you . . . not?" she gasps.

"Morgan?" I scramble backward, shock radiating through me. "What are you . . ." Then I'm on my feet, the letter opener still in my hand, ears and eyes straining as I wait for a second, much deadlier figure to appear. "Where is he?"

"Cormac?" Morgan asks, pulling herself into a sitting position. Her movement is unhurried—unafraid—and that makes all of my anger come rushing back. She *should* be afraid. Even if they're working together, that doesn't change the fact that he's fundamentally a monster. Whatever he did to Jamie, he'll do to her, too. Eventually.

Once he's done with me.

But before I can lash out, Morgan says, "He's dead."

"What?" My eyes dart between Morgan and the empty hallway in front of us. "How?"

"I shot him," Morgan says.

"You . . ." I gape at her as something flickers in my chest—a tiny thread of hope circling the broken pieces, ready to stitch them together. I only heard *one* gunshot. "But he . . . I thought he shot Jamie . . ."

Morgan's brow furrows, every line of her face tense. "Oh God, I hope not. I haven't seen her. I just . . . I came looking for you, and the next thing I know *he* was barreling toward me, and I . . . shot him." She flexes her empty hands, and for the first time I notice the bulge at her waist. The gun she must have holstered when she heard me scream.

"But then . . . that means he heard *you*. Not Jamie."

"Huh?" Morgan asks.

I don't have time to explain the phone call with my father. The small stirring of hope blooms into light and warmth, and I take off down the hall without another word, fumbling in my pocket for the supply closet key. Past a red-stained heap on the floor that would horrify me if I could think about anything—anything at all—except opening that supply closet door. I'm crying again when I reach it, full-on sobbing and shaking as I drop the letter opener so I can fit the key into the lock. And then I'm stumbling into Jamie's arms, and she's *here*, she's really here, warm and solid and very much alive.

For a few seconds, we just cling to one another in such a fierce hug that we might as well be melded together. "He's dead," I whisper into her ear, and I can feel her nod.

Then she pulls away and takes my chin in her hand. She stares me directly in the eyes and says forcefully, "Don't you *ever* do something like that again. We talked about this. I protect *you*. Not the other way around. Got it?"

"Got it," I gulp, right before Jamie engulfs me in another hug.

When we finally pull apart, Morgan is standing a few feet away. She looks exhausted and uncertain, worry and guilt playing across her features.

"Morgan, what's going on?" I ask.

"I, um . . . I found you through Jamie's phone," she says.

Way to lead with the least important information, Morgan.

"Yeah, I figured," I say. "And my father was doing the same thing, wasn't he?"

Morgan doesn't respond, and Jamie narrows her eyes. "The only way Cormac could've done that is if you helped him," she says. "You manage all our technology! So you set me up, and then you . . . saved me? Make it make sense, Morgan."

Morgan swallows hard. "Look, Jamie, this is an impossible situation. Me being here is a massive betrayal—"

"Of me?" Jamie breaks in.

"No," Morgan says. "Of the plan."

"The plan to kill me," Jamie says flatly.

Morgan's lips press into a thin line. "I thought I could live with it, but it turns out I can't. Especially because a lot of this is my fault."

"A lot of *what*?" Jamie demands.

"I, um . . . well. There's no good way to say this," Morgan says.

Jamie's nostrils flare with thinly concealed impatience. "Then say it the bad way."

"My screwup on the last job was so much worse than I told you," Morgan says. "I left my phone behind in the mark's house like some goddamn newbie. Even though everything on there is encrypted, it still led the police to Spotless. They've been looking into us, hard. And it's not the kind of investigation you can just move out of state to get away from."

"Oh my God," Jamie breathes. "I had no idea. Why didn't Gem say anything?"

Morgan lifts her shoulders in the most hopeless shrug I've ever seen. "Come on," she says heavily. "You must know."

"I *don't*," Jamie says, her face as confused as her tone.

She must be in denial, because all of a sudden—in a moment of piercing clarity—I do. The understanding crashes into my body like an assault, and I have to lean against the wall for support. "Because *Gem* is the one doing this," I say. "She's setting Jamie up, isn't she?"

Jamie's jaw unhinges as Morgan turns to her and says, "Yeah. She had me put the diamond vine ring in your backpack, and there's a ton of stolen stuff hidden in the ceiling of your apartment back home. So that once the police checked you out, they'd immediately connect you to the Spotless investigation."

"Checked me out?" Jamie echoes.

"After this weekend, because . . ." Morgan takes a deep breath. "You know my Sutherland contact, the one who got your staff credentials?" Jamie nods mutely. "She got a key card for Cormac, too, so he could sneak into the compound through one of the unguarded gates."

Wait. *She?* Did Morgan have two Sutherland contacts? This woman she just mentioned, plus Parker?

"Cormac went to Annalise's house before you were supposed to," Morgan continues. "He climbed through the window and stole the real necklace."

Ohhh. So that's why Annalise didn't have two necklaces when the fake was given to her from Parker's pocket; the real one was already gone. But none of what Morgan is saying so far has anything to do with Parker. I want to ask about him, but before I can, Morgan adds, "Then Cormac cut the trellis. Right at the top, so that when it was your turn to climb, you'd fall from as high up as possible. After that, he slipped out the back door and waited in the woods. If you managed to survive the fall, he'd break your neck and finish the job."

Oh my God. *My God.* My hand flies to my throat as Jamie gasps. The necklace swap wasn't a heist. It was a murder. My mother was supposed to die—and if I'd succeeded in taking her place, I'd be gone. Killed either by the fall or my father.

I feel sick and dizzy, but Morgan keeps right on going as if she hadn't just knocked the world off its axis. "Ultimately, it was supposed to look as though you died at the tail end of a heist that *you* planned," she says. "The police would trace you back to Boston, find everything that we'd planted in your apartment, and *bam.* A neat end to the Spotless investigation. One bad apple gone, and the rest of the operation gets to keep going. Plus, icing on the cake—the police would've given Annalise Sutherland the fake necklace from your pocket, and Ma would've walked away with the real one. It's worth a lot more than she told you." Morgan's jaw twitches. "But I guess the fake was stolen by some rando named . . . Vicky?"

She looks at me questioningly. I'd forgotten all about Vicky—and since I haven't talked to Gem for a while, I never told her that Vicky didn't take the fake necklace after all. My ever-evolving theories seem ridiculous now, and all I can do is swallow wordlessly. Morgan seems to take it as confirmation, adding, "I've been getting messages about that from Ma all weekend, but I've been afraid to follow up."

"Jesus," Jamie says faintly. "This is all so . . . *vicious.*"

It's the most horrible thing I've ever heard. I can't make sense of it. And I can't make it fit into anything I know about what happened to Parker.

"Yeah," Morgan says. "But Ma said it was the only way to fix my mistake. So I went along with her. Until I couldn't." Her gaze drops to the ground. "I thought that if I took you out of commission in a way that seemed like bad luck, I could buy time. This plan took a ton of setup, and it wouldn't be easy to replicate. I was hoping that if it failed, Ma might have a change of heart and figure something else out."

Morgan gazes around the office hallway, like even she can't believe how we got here. "Obviously, that didn't happen," she says. "While Cormac was waiting in the woods, he ran into Parker Sutherland. I don't know why Parker wasn't having cake with the rest of them, but his timing couldn't have been worse."

"So you weren't . . ." I don't know how to ask this except by blurting it out. "You weren't working with Parker?"

"With *Parker*?" Morgan says, looking baffled by the question. "God, no. Why would he be involved? He ruined things even worse than I did. Cormac panicked and shot him, and, well—you know the rest. Ma didn't back off. She only got more desperate."

"So you didn't know—" I start, but then abruptly clamp my lips together. I was about to say *You didn't know that Parker Sutherland had the fake necklace in his pocket when he died?* But why should I? I'm trying to get information, not give it.

"Didn't know what?" Morgan asks.

"I meant to say . . . so Gem decided Jamie had to pay for *your* mistake?" I ask, putting a protective arm around my mother while glaring at Morgan. "Decided she had to *die*? That's completely unfair!"

I don't care if it's a childish response—not when this much hurt and anger is coursing through me. Why should Jamie have to suffer for what Morgan did? Morgan is Gem's daughter, sure, but Gem always treated Jamie like one, too. And even if Gem was looking for a patsy to go down as the Spotless ringleader, why would *killing* her be the answer? Jamie's word against everyone else wouldn't count for much, and Jamie would have known that. She would have accepted her fate and considered it the price of doing business with Gem for so many years.

"I know," Morgan says.

I practically stamp my foot as I pull a still-voiceless Jamie closer to me and say, "Jamie's been nothing but loyal! Why would Gem do this to her?"

Morgan levels her gaze at me and says, "Because of you."

Now it's my turn to go silent. I can't think of a single thing to say. I just stare at Morgan, so dumbfounded that when I see a shadow appear on the wall behind her, I don't react. When a hand reaches out, lightning-fast, and clocks Morgan on the head with something that's hard enough to send her toppling to the ground, I don't cry out. When Jamie falls to her knees beside Morgan and tries to stanch the blood pouring from her temple, my throat works convulsively but refuses to make a sound.

"Don't worry about her," a voice says. "She'll live."

My mouth is painfully dry, but I finally manage to push out a single syllable. "Gem," I say.

CHAPTER FIFTY

Kat

My heart ricochets in my chest as I stare at the woman standing in front of me. Gem's gray hair is loose around her shoulders, and she's dressed in her usual sensible, comfortable clothes. The only difference from the Gem I've grown up with is that she's wearing clear gloves on both hands, and holding a gun that's pointed directly at Jamie.

My mind doesn't want to process her as a threat. Gem has always represented safety to me, and there's a stubborn part of me that wants to be relieved that she's here. Wants to believe the nightmare is ending, instead of starting a new chapter. Even though I know there's no possible way that can be true.

"Get up, Jamie," Gem says calmly.

"There's so much blood," Jamie says, her eyes on Morgan.

"I told you, she'll be fine. I didn't hit her all that hard."

Morgan lets out a weak moan then, and Jamie rises reluctantly to her feet. She moves as far from me as possible in the narrow hallway, and Gem's gun carefully tracks her. "So all of this was you," Jamie says, wiping her bloodied hands against her leggings.

"Except for the part where Morgan went rogue," Gem says. She touches her ear, and for the first time, I notice that she's wearing a small Bluetooth device. I suppose my father had one, too, which would explain why Gem decided to show herself. She must have heard him go down and go silent.

"You needed a fall guy for your daughter's mistake," Jamie says. "I can understand that." Her tone is strangely calm, and I wonder if she's in shock. I might be; my entire body feels numb. "But you don't have to kill me, Gem. We can work something else out—"

"Morgan said it was because of *me.*" The words burst out of me unintended, and Jamie's face spasms with frustration. I realize, a fraction of a second too late, that she was trying to keep Gem's focus on her alone. Still, I can't help but add, "What did I do?"

Gem's steely expression softens a little, and my heart squeezes painfully. That's the Gem I thought I knew—the heart of gold under the gruff exterior. But I must have been wrong for all those years, because that Gem would never do *this.*

"Not a goddamn thing," she says. "But *you*"—she turns back toward Jamie, tone hardening again—"were going to take her away from me. After everything I've done for you, Jamie. I treated you like my own! Gave you a new job and a new life, made sure you had everything you and Kat ever needed. And still, you decided that the closest thing I'll ever have to a grand-child would never see me again."

"What?" Jamie and I say the word together, but our tones are completely different. Mine is *What on earth are you talking about?*

And Jamie's is *How did you know?*

My lips part in surprise as Gem snorts. "Come on, Jamie, you've seen my intelligence team in action," she says. "You really think they're not just as thorough on my staff? In this business, I can't leave anything to chance. If you work for me, I know everything about you. I keep tabs on everything you say and do, both inside and outside the office." Her jaw tightens as she adds, "In other words, there's no such thing as a private phone line."

"Oh my God," Jamie says, her eyes going wide. "You've been listening to . . ."

"Everything," Gem says grimly. "Every call you made to your friend Marianne for the past few months. I know you're using me to go straight, and I know that as soon as you have a legit résumé and some experience, you're heading back to Nevada."

I blink, stunned, as Gem adds, "Because you think I'm a 'bad influence' on Kat. You were even planning to change her guardian! That's *me,* Jamie. It's been me since she was four years old."

It has been? I never knew that. I didn't even know I *had* a guardian until Jamie told me after lunch that it was Marianne, and . . .

And she looked guilty when she said it.

"But now all of a sudden you're too good for me?" Gem says. "You think I'm no good for *her?*" Her eyes blaze as she jerks her head toward me. "I practically raised that kid! It's not like you could manage it. If it weren't for me, she'd still be wandering the streets of Las Vegas."

I twist my ice-cold hands together, grasping for words that refuse to come. Jamie planned to take me away from Gem? She didn't tell me that, and I'm pretty sure I know why. Because I would have protested, dug in my heels, and blown everything. I never could've predicted this side of Gem, but Jamie—Jamie, who's spent her entire adult life bouncing from one sociopath to the next—finally saw Gem for who she really is.

Gem bringing me along to a job at Bennington & Main must have been the last straw. What had Jamie said then? *This isn't a new discussion. It was just . . . accelerated.* I'd assumed she meant that it was a discussion between her and *Gem,* and I'm sure it was. But there was a side discussion happening with Marianne, too.

And Gem eavesdropped on every word of it.

"I . . ." Jamie's eyes dart every which way, like a trapped animal. "I was just trying to do what's best for Kat. I want her to have a different life than I had, and—"

"You didn't have to cut me out!" Gem practically screams the words.

"You're right," Jamie says. "That was a mistake, and I'm sorry."

Oh God. I know that tone of voice. It's buried deep inside my brain; the placating way Jamie would speak to avoid my father's wrath.

My father. I turn on Gem, anger pushing past heartbreak. "You brought Cormac into this," I say. "If you know so much about everything, then you know exactly who you were dealing with. He was a monster, and he would've killed *me,* too."

"You weren't supposed to be here," Gem reminds me. "Once I knew that you were, he was under strict orders not to hurt you."

I almost laugh. Does she honestly think she had that kind of control over someone like him? Apparently, because there it is again—that infuriating flash of humanity in her eyes. As though she believes that she genuinely cares about me.

"But why him?" I ask.

Gem shrugs. "He was a tool. Like I said, in this business I can't leave anything to chance. If you work for me, I know everything about you. I know your past well enough that I can predict your future. I keep tabs on anyone significant, *especially* if they're shady. Or flat-out criminal." Her eyes flick toward Jamie. "I've been tracking Luke and Cormac since I met you. I knew Luke had started pestering you for a divorce, and I knew Cormac was released last year."

"Last *year*?" Jamie says incredulously. "No one told me! I'm supposed to be notified. That was part of my arrangement with the prosecutor's office, and . . . Oh God." A look of re-signed horror spreads across her face. "You saw those emails first, didn't you?"

"I did," Gem says. "And I deleted them."

Jamie presses her palms to her cheeks. "But *why?*" she asks. "I hadn't even started making plans for Kat until—"

"I didn't think you needed to know," Gem says. "It would have been a distraction."

I can't help the choked sound that comes out of me at that.

A distraction? I guess I shouldn't be surprised at anything this new version of Gem does, but she keeps finding extra levels of betrayal. "It was clear that he had no idea where you were, or who you'd become," Gem continues. "If he'd figured it out, I'd have dealt with him."

"Instead, you recruited him," Jamie says bitterly.

"I needed him," Gem says with another shrug. "It's not easy finding a con who's willing to take a job on a billionaire's compound. But Cormac still had a lot of anger toward you, so he was more than willing to help. And willing to move on to Plan B after Parker Sutherland died, which was a lot messier than I would have liked."

Gem cocks her head and narrows her eyes at Jamie, like she's sizing her up for a movie role. "You on the run, getting taken down by one of your shady associates. A harder story to sell, but we could've made it work. But Cormac blew his first crack at you in the staff quarters, and we had a hell of a time figuring out where you went after that. Your phone said you were in the middle of the woods, and I had to come here myself to get the lay of the land."

What's your Plan B?

I've been repeating that to myself for days, and my clueless attempt to be like Gem makes me feel sick now. I feel as though the old Gem is dissolving in front of me, melting away to reveal this horrifying new version. A calculating monster who spies on everyone who comes near her, refers to human beings as *tools,* and mined the worst moments of my mother's life in order to kill her: my nightmare of a father and—

"Luke," I burst out. "Is he part of this, too?" If we ever get out of here, Liam is going to be desperate for that information.

"A small part," Gem says. "I needed detail on the ruby necklace so I could make a copy. I knew Luke was dating Annalise, and that he was trying to get a divorce from Jamie. I told him I'd take care of the problem if he could get me a mold of the necklace and some high-res photos. 'For my replica business,' I said. Not that he cared. All he heard was 'Take care of the problem.' He managed it, and passed everything along to Cormac."

"And did he know *how* you were going to take care of the problem?" I say.

Gem shrugs again. "He didn't ask."

"Did he know Jamie would be at the party?"

Gem's lips thin. "I didn't know *he* would be," she says. It was a small crack in her meticulously constructed plan, and it's clear that it annoys her. "Seemed a little early in the relationship for that. He could've been easily handled, though, if everything else hadn't fallen apart. But since it did . . ."

Her flinty eyes get even colder as she turns her attention to my mother. "Here's the bottom line, Jamie," she says. "I need an exit strategy."

CHAPTER FIFTY-ONE

Kat

Jamie swallows hard and asks, "Like what?"

Gem keeps her gun trained on Jamie as she leans over Morgan and grabs Morgan's gun from the holster at her waist. She quickly pulls out the clip and shoves it into her pocket. Then, to my astonishment, she pulls a ruby necklace—twinkling and sparkling beneath the office lighting—from her other pocket.

I'm having a hard time keeping track of what's real, but I'm pretty sure the necklace is. Morgan said Cormac took it from Annalise's house before he shot Parker. Gem didn't get everything she wanted this weekend, but she did get that.

"I was hoping I wouldn't have to sacrifice this, but I don't see an alternative," Gem says, tossing the necklace on the ground. "It's the only thing that'll tie everything up. Because here's what the police are going to put together, Jamie, with a little help from me—your poor clueless employer, who had no idea you were using Spotless as a front. Your toxic ex got out of prison, and fool that you are, you went right back to him. It's tragic, isn't it, how often people return to their abusers?"

"I would *never*—" Jamie says hotly.

"Shh. Don't you want to hear the rest of the story?" Gem asks. Her tone is infuriatingly smug; the confidence of a puppet master who's about to pull off a shocking finale. "You told me the two of you were headed to Maine for a romantic getaway. What you really did, though, was steal Annalise Sutherland's necklace. Unfortunately, Cormac killed Parker Sutherland during the job, and you had to hide out here. You argued—he has *such* a temper—and you shot him." She holds out Morgan's empty gun toward a shell-shocked Jamie. "Then you were so overcome with guilt that you killed yourself."

"No!" I shriek as Jamie's face gets even paler.

Gem's gun swings toward me, but she keeps her eyes on Jamie. "You're going to get your fingerprints all over Morgan's gun, and then you'll give it back," she says. "I'll reload it, put your hand around it, and pull the trigger. If you resist at any point, Kat dies."

Jamie licks her lips. "But you love Kat," she says. I can see in her eyes that she knows *love* is entirely the wrong word, but she's grasping at straws.

"I do," Gem says with that same gruff affection. There's no shame or regret in her bearing; she truly doesn't seem to understand that it's not normal to switch gears like this. I guess when people are "tools," all that matters is what they can do for you. "So do you. You want to keep her safe, don't you?"

"How do I know she'll be safe when I'm gone?" Jamie counters.

"I went to a lot of trouble to keep her," Gem says. "Do

you really think I'd give her up unless you leave me no other choice?" She turns toward me and adds, "I know this isn't what you want, Kat, but I also know that you're a practical girl. And, above all else, you're a survivor. This is what you have to do to survive."

Jesus. Does she honestly believe I'd stay with her—that I'd *cover* for her—after watching her kill my mother? Is she truly that delusional, or am I as good as dead, too?

Either way, I'm not going down without a fight. There's still a wild card here—a part of the puzzle Gem doesn't know and won't understand. Because nobody does, including me. But that doesn't mean I can't use it.

Gem likes being the smartest person in the room, and she *hates* surprises.

"You're right about one thing," I say. "I'm practical. And as a practical person, I have to tell you that you made a mistake bringing that here." I lift my chin toward the necklace on the ground. "It ruins your entire plan, but you wouldn't know that, because all you've done since you got here is talk, talk, talk. You haven't asked a single question."

"Kat," Jamie says in a low voice. "Don't."

Don't what? Antagonize her? Too late—Gem's nostrils are flaring, and spots of color appear in her cheeks. *Good.* She's always told me that staying calm is the key to a successful job, and right now, she's not calm. I need to keep pushing her buttons.

I tilt my head and say, "Do you want to know what question you should have asked?"

Gem snorts. "By all means, enlighten me."

Does my plan have too many necklaces?

Gem frowns. "What are you talking about?"

352

"Here's the thing," I say. "Vicky didn't take the fake necklace."

Her expression gets thunderous. "You lied to me?"

"No. I just didn't have the right information. But after spending more time with the Sutherlands, I do," I say. "The fake necklace is in Annalise's dressing room. Because the person who actually took it was Parker Sutherland, and he died with it in his pocket."

That did it; for the first time in my life, I've managed to shock Gem. Her mouth falls open, and just for a second, her gun hand slips.

That's all I'm going to get, so I take it.

I lunge for her, colliding with enough force to knock her backward. A gunshot explodes, and I have no clue where the bullet went. I don't feel any pain, but I'm not sure I would have even if a bullet had torn me clean in half. I don't dare take my focus away from Gem to check on Jamie. *Please be okay, Mom,* I think as I struggle to pin Gem to the ground, concentrating all my strength and energy on immobilizing the arm holding the gun. *I won't be able to forgive myself if you're not okay.*

Gem makes a furious guttural noise. She bucks and heaves beneath me, and the gun fires again. This time I know where the bullet landed, as the wall beside us cracks. Dust fills the air, plugging up my lungs and making me choke. I'm still pressing Gem's arm down with all my might when a hand appears in my line of vision, curled around the letter opener I found earlier. A familiar hand, one that's brushed hair away from my face a hundred times.

As Gem twists nearly hard enough to loosen my grip, Jamie stabs the opener, hard, into Gem's wrist. Blood spurts, Gem screams and flails, and her fingers go slack. Jamie's hand scoops up the gun and disappears from view.

"Take Morgan's clip from Gem's pocket, Kat." Jamie's voice is behind me, surprisingly steady. "And make sure she doesn't have anything else on her."

I do what she says and then scramble backward, off Gem, the clip clutched in one hand. Jamie is standing a few feet away, with Gem's gun pointed straight at Gem's heart, and Morgan's empty gun shoved into her waistband. The faint wail of sirens reaches my ears, and when Jamie stiffens, I know she's heard it, too.

"Do you think that's for us?" I ask. "Someone reported gunfire, maybe?"

"I hope so," Jamie says. "It'll save me a call."

Gem writhes in pain for another few seconds, then staggers to her knees, cradling her bleeding wrist. When she catches sight of Jamie, her features settle into a grim expression.

"Thought I'd hit you," she says bitterly.

There's a loud click as Jamie cocks the gun and says, "Sorry, no."

The sirens are much closer now, and my phone buzzes in my pocket. I slowly slip it out, keeping my eyes on Jamie and Gem until my screen is in front of me. I have a bunch of messages from Liam, who I never answered after he told me to get out, and the top one simply says: *I called the police. I didn't know what else to do.*

"Liam called the police," I tell Jamie.

"Smart boy," she says.

A hunted look appears in Gem's eyes. "We can still get out of this," she says, and it gives me a morbid sense of satisfaction that now *she's* the desperate one. "We can pin everything on Cormac. And Luke."

"She's trying to distract you," I tell Jamie. "Don't fall for it."

"I won't," Jamie says.

"You can't stay out of jail without my help. I'll bury you," Gem tells her, rising slowly to her feet with both hands in the air.

"Then we'll rot together," Jamie says. "Sit back down."

Gem just stares at her for a second, and then bolts for the stairwell behind us.

"Jamie, stop her!" I scream. But Jamie doesn't shoot, doesn't move at all, and force of habit propels me after Gem. She bursts through the stairwell door, and I catch it before it has a chance to close.

Then Jamie calls out, "Kat, stay here!" in such a commanding voice that I freeze in place, still holding the stairwell door open.

Gem pauses for a moment, turns, and looks me square in the eye. "Listen to your mother," she says before continuing up the stairs.

Up the stairs? I thought we were on the top floor.

Jamie comes up behind me then and tugs on my arm, pulling me out of the stairwell.

"Why did you just let her go?" I ask in frustration as the door closes. "You could've stopped her. Shot her in the leg, or something."

"She won't get far," Jamie says. "Listen to those sirens—we're surrounded. Besides, Morgan needs help. Call 911, okay? Let them know there's a woman with a head wound on the top floor."

"Second-to-the-top floor, you mean," I say, pulling out my phone.

Jamie's forehead knits. "What? No, I mean the top floor. We're on the tenth. The elevator doesn't go any higher."

"Okay, well, maybe the elevator doesn't, but Gem just went *up* the stairs."

Jamie's mouth purses, then drops open. "*Ohhh,*" she breathes. The next thing I know, she's running toward the stairwell. "Call 911, and stay with Morgan!" she yells before pushing through the door.

I desperately want to run after her, but there are too many other emergencies happening. So I do what Gem said, and for once—I listen to my mother.

CHAPTER FIFTY-TWO

Liam

It's chaos outside the office building in Randall. Cops everywhere, along with firefighters for some reason, and a ton of rubberneckers. Nobody will let me inside, even when I remind the police officers stationed at the front door that I'm the one who called them.

"No entry," one of them says.

"But my sister is inside!"

The word *sister* comes out automatically, and I hope it'll lend some urgency to my plea, but the officer barely blinks. "Behind the barricade, please," he says blandly.

I'm about to argue further when someone yells, "Jumper! We got a jumper!"

Everyone looks up.

All I can see is brick and glass, so I dart across the street, to where a smaller crowd has gathered. I crane my neck, and then I see it—a figure silhouetted against the clear blue sky near the

357

edge of the building, long hair whipping in the wind. My heart lodges in my throat; it doesn't look like Kat or Jamie, but I'm too far away to be sure. And even if it's not, the word *jumper* makes this a terrifying sight.

Why is that person there, and where is Kat? Why hasn't she answered my texts? Something terrible must have happened since Augustus and I left, and the thought makes my stomach roll with guilt. I *knew* it was a bad idea to leave Kat and Jamie, but I did it anyway.

I'm going to hate myself for eternity if Kat doesn't come out of this building safe and sound. Plus, even though we've been reacquainted for less than a week, I already don't know what I'd do without her trademark mix of total acceptance and comfort-zone pushing. Or the way she's always looking out for me, like nobody else has since my mother died.

It didn't fully register at the time, with so much else going on, but the first words Kat ever spoke to Luke were to defend me when he showed zero concern about the produce truck debacle: *Liam is fine. Nice of you to ask.* She could've frozen me out along with him, but she didn't. Instead, she turned us into a team. And we stayed that way, even when I didn't fully understand the game we were playing.

I understand it now. I know it's dangerous, and that we've made a lot of wrong moves. But I'm not going to be able to stand it if Kat gets knocked off the board. I've already lost my mom, my home, and most of my friends. For a while, I felt as though I'd lost myself, too.

I can't lose the sort-of sister who helped bring me back.

I pull my phone from my pocket to see if I missed a new

text from Kat. There's nothing, though; the last eight messages are all from me.

Still, I add one more: *Please let me know if you're okay.*

"She's moving!" someone calls urgently.

I shade my eyes and squint at the figure above. To me, she looks motionless, but also—higher. She's stepped onto a ledge, I realize—the absolute edge of the roof. A few feet away from me, someone starts shouting through a bullhorn, giving directions that I can't fully hear over the pounding of my heart in my ears. Everyone around me seems to be holding their breath.

And then, we all let out a collective gasp when the figure suddenly goes flying—*backward*. She disappears from view, as if yanked by an invisible hand, and we're left staring at an empty ledge.

"Where did she go?" a woman beside me asks.

"Maybe a guardian angel pulled her back," a man replies.

And then my phone buzzes with the update I've been waiting for:

We're okay.

CHAPTER FIFTY-THREE

Liam

"No one is more horrified by this than me," Luke says.

We're in the guest cottage with Annalise, hours after the disaster at the office building. I got the chance to talk with Kat briefly once she came outside, and learned a condensed version of the truth. That Jamie's boss, Gem, plotted to frame Jamie for theft, kill her before she could legally change Kat's guardianship, and then—in the sickest twist of an extremely twisted plan—have a clueless Kat live with the person who'd coldly planned her mother's death.

With the help of both Kat's father and mine.

Kat's father—her *father*, holy hell—was the guy who'd been after Jamie all weekend.

Just like I thought, she was being tracked through her phone. Cormac showed up at the office building first, and Kat had nearly lured him out when Morgan arrived. Morgan killed him and started to explain everything to Kat and Jamie, but

360

she never got the chance to finish once Gem showed up and knocked her out. Then Gem took off for the roof, and Jamie realized Gem would rather leap off the building than get taken into custody.

So Jamie, just in time, pulled her back.

Gem is under arrest, Morgan is in stable condition at the hospital, and Jamie is cooperating with the police. I was questioned, too, but before my interview had gotten very far, a sharply dressed woman entered the room and seated herself beside me.

"I'm Rachelle Chisholm from Powell and Boggs, here to represent Mr. Rooney," she said smoothly, settling a gleaming briefcase on the table while I gaped in confusion. She turned toward me and added, "Mr. Sutherland sent me."

"Ross?" I asked, stunned.

"Augustus," she replied.

After that, I didn't say a word without her approval. By the time I left the station, the cops had gone from glaring at me to thanking me for my help.

"Am I going to be *charged* with something?" I asked Rachelle as we headed for her car. Somehow, the possibility hadn't occurred to me until right then.

"I doubt it. You're a minor, and they have much bigger fish to fry," Rachelle said. "But we never like to leave this sort of thing to chance."

"What about Luke?" I asked. It hit me, finally, why Luke took off in a panic as soon as he saw the picture of Cormac—he must have recognized him as the guy he'd passed details of Annalise's necklace to. Luke was probably trying to reach Gem when I found him.

Rachelle's calm expression didn't change as she said, "No one in the Sutherland family has engaged representation for your father."

Now, police are waiting outside the guest cottage to escort Luke to the station for questioning, and he's in full damage-control mode as he talks to Annalise.

"Did I want to get out of an ill-conceived marriage?" Luke says, putting a hand over his heart. "Yes. More than anything. I'd tried reasoning with Jamie, but she was too bitter to let go. She has incredibly deep-seated emotional issues. But did I have any idea of what was really going on? Of course not! I had no clue Jamie was in danger. All I ever wanted, Annalise, was to be free and clear so that you and I could be together."

I know that part is true, thanks to Kat, and I guess it's something of a relief. Luke might be a liar and a thief, but at least he's not an accomplice to murder.

On purpose.

"I see," Annalise says evenly.

I give her a wary look. Is she going to be swayed, somehow, into thinking she can fix my father? There's no possible way that can end well for anyone, especially her.

But then she says, "And you thought the best way to accomplish that was giving a jewel thief everything they needed to copy my necklace?"

"I didn't know that was going to happen," Luke says.

"What did you *think* was going to happen?" Annalise asks, her voice rising into a near scream. I've never seen her angry before, and I don't think Luke has, either, because he takes a surprised step back. "Do you understand the enormity of what you did?" she says. "It's not even about the necklace. It's about the fact that if you hadn't helped set this plan in motion, Parker would still be alive. His blood is on your hands!"

She's right, but *how*, exactly? That's the part of this mystery that Morgan and Gem couldn't explain. If Parker wasn't working with Morgan, or anyone else at Spotless, how did he end up with the fake necklace? Did he even know what it was, or did he think it was real?

Ultimately, from Annalise's perspective, I guess it doesn't matter. Cormac was there as part of the heist-slash-murder, and Cormac's the one who killed Parker.

Luke pastes on a sorrowful expression. "Annalise, my love—" he starts.

"Don't call me that," Annalise says. Her voice and her eyes are both as cold as ice; as it turns out, Angry Annalise is kind of intimidating. "I've learned a lot about you these past few hours, and none of it is good. Augustus told me what you did to those poor women online. Not to mention how you failed to properly supervise two small children, including your *son*, after your quickie marriage in Las Vegas."

Annalise reaches into her pocket, pulls out the engagement ring Luke gave her, and holds it out. "We're through. All your things will be packed up and left for you outside. I don't ever want to speak to you again, unless we need to communicate about Liam."

Luke blinks in confusion. "Communicate about who?"

"Your son. Remember him?" Annalise says. She reaches forward and stuffs the ring into Luke's shirt pocket before putting an arm around my shoulder. "Somebody needs to look out for him while you're accounting for all your felonies. He can stay with me temporarily, until I'm able to make arrangements with his uncle."

I stare at her as Luke's jaw unhinges. There's probably not a single thing I could do to piss him off more—even though I hadn't planned it—than stepping into the place he'd been working so hard to carve out for himself. "He's *my* son," Luke says.

"Nice of you to notice," Annalise says dryly. "I'm such a fool. You weren't *giving him space* all this time. You just don't care."

"Of course I care," Luke says. But halfheartedly, like even he knows he can't pull that statement off.

"You'd better go," Annalise says. "The police are waiting."

Luke stares at her with burning eyes, like he's trying to channel all his cunning and charm into the kind of smoldering gaze that will make her change her mind. When he gets nothing but indifference in return, it's as though a lightbulb just flickered out. His face becomes a smooth mask, the only hint of emotion a curled lip as he says, "Well, I guess that's that. I'm sure you'll replace me soon enough, since you can't stand being alone, but don't fool yourself that the next guy won't care about your money. It's your best quality."

Annalise's cheeks turn a fiery red, and I let out a muted gasp of protest. Luke's eyes flick my way, and his sneer deepens. "Dial back the faux outrage, kid," he says. "You got what you wanted. You must be loving this."

I'm not; there's nothing I would have liked more than to have been proven wrong about Luke. To have those occasional glimpses of a better person be real. But they were just the means to an end, and now that the end has been yanked away, he can't be bothered to keep pretending. Luke is the same guy he's always been, and the only thing I'm happy about is the fact that he might finally have to answer for some of the things he's done.

"Get out!" Annalise shrieks.

Luke leaves without another word, the door closing behind him with a soft, anticlimactic click. It occurs to me that this might've been the last conversation that I'll have with my father for a very long time, and despite everything, the thought hits me with a pang. It's like I told Augustus in the car earlier—no matter how often Luke shows me that he doesn't care, I don't think I'll ever stop wishing that he did.

And maybe that's okay. Because it's the part of me that's the least like him.

I turn toward Annalise and say, "I'm really sorry about . . . that."

"Don't be. You're not responsible for him." Her face is still red, but she manages a smile as she lightly pats my arm and says, "Are you all right?"

"I will be," I say. Then I clear my throat and add, "It's really great of you to let me stay here, but I don't want to hold you to that. I've caused enough trouble—"

"You haven't caused any trouble at all," Annalise says.

That's debatable on multiple levels. "I should've told you about Luke."

She sighs. "Believe me, I understand all too well wanting to give family the benefit of the doubt," she says. "And I don't want you to do anything you're not comfortable with, but you're welcome to stay here until we can get something else sorted out. However long that may take. God knows, we have plenty of room."

I shift uneasily from one foot to the other, and she says, "You don't have to decide anything now. Maybe just rest up while I make some calls?"

I should. I'm exhausted, but . . . "Would it be okay if I went to Griffin's house?" I ask. I haven't talked to Augustus since everything imploded at the office building, except over text.

Annalise smiles. "Of course."

My thoughts are a messy tangle as I walk there. I don't know what's going to happen with Jamie now that Gem's operation has been blown wide open. Jamie looked like she was at peace with whatever comes next, from the little I saw of her at the police station, but maybe she's just in shock. Kat seemed resolute too, even though her entire future is up in the air. I'd barely gotten to speak to her alone, but when I did, I apologized for sending the police.

"It was the right thing to do," she said. "We were in way over our heads. Besides, Jamie was planning on turning herself in all along. She wants everything out in the open. I guess that's the only way forward for us." She sighed then, and added, "I'm trying to get better about listening to my mother."

I hope she'll get the chance to keep doing that.

When I press the doorbell, a loud buzzer rings to unlock it. I push the door open and call, "Augustus?"

His voice floats down from above. "Come on up," he says.

The last time I went up these stairs, I was carrying Jamie. When I pass the spare room where I left her, it's neatly made up, as though no one had ever been there. There's a bigger room across from it, and as soon as I peer through its doorway, I start to laugh.

"What?" Augustus asks, appearing in front of me. He's in another all-white ensemble, a glitzy gold watch dangling from one finger, and I don't think I've ever been happier to see anyone in my entire life.

I point to the space over his bed and say, "You really did it. You hung it up."

He turns to look at my Christmas sun painting. "I told you I would."

"But it's so ridiculous," I say, still smiling.

I'd nearly forgotten about that painting, and the hour I spent with Luke making it. If I let myself, I could tumble down a rabbit hole of regret for all of Luke's lost potential. But I want this to be a lighter moment; it's funny that Augustus kept it. And kind of touching.

"It's my favorite thing," Augustus says.

You're my favorite thing, I think. But all I say is "Nice watch. Are you going to wear it or just keep holding it?"

"Still deciding," Augustus says, dropping it into his palm. "Dad gave it to me. It belonged to Uncle Parker, and he thought I might like to have it. It's a Rolex, but probably fake or he would've sold it before now. Not that I care, but . . . I'm not sure I want to remember him with jewelry."

"Fair enough," I say.

Augustus's expression turns thoughtful as he says, "You know, I wonder now if Uncle Parker even planned to steal Aunt Annalise's necklace. Maybe that Vicky woman took the fake after all, and Uncle Parker saw her with it. Maybe he was going to put it back."

Somehow, I doubt that—especially since Griffin said Parker

was gloating about all the money he'd have after that weekend. But I'm not about to say that to Augustus. "Maybe," I say. "That would be nice."

"Yeah. And as we all know, Uncle Parker was *nice,*" Augustus says with a grimace. "I don't know. I'm tired of guessing." He places the watch carefully on the dresser, his shoulders slumping. "I'm tired of all this."

All this. Does that include me? I couldn't blame him. My father helped toss a grenade into his family, and I'm not sure how to recover from that.

"Uh-oh," Augustus says.

Instantly, I'm on guard. I whip around and stare into the hallway, shoulders tensed against a new threat. "What?" I ask.

"Take it easy," he says with a light laugh. "It's just your face. You looked exceptionally morose all of a sudden."

I don't know which is more embarrassing—that I'm even jumpier than I was after my little-kid Vegas trauma, or that my pining for a guy I met three days ago is so obvious. "I was just thinking about how you and I got to know each other in the middle of a giant mess," I say. "I don't know where we go from here."

"Me either," Augustus says. "But I have a suggestion."

"What?" I ask. Half-hopeful and half-worried, because unlike me, Augustus doesn't wear his heart on his sleeve. I have no idea what he's thinking; he could be getting ready to say anything from *Kiss me* to *Get out.*

He takes my hand, and I can't stop a smile from spreading across my face even before he says, "Dinner and a movie. Let's try being normal, for once."

CHAPTER FIFTY-FOUR

Kat

"I would've thought you'd have better aim, Chaos," Augustus says as the dart I throw sails past the dartboard and bounces off the wall.

"It's not like it's going to stick anyway," I grumble.

"That's the point of the game," Augustus says. "Drop Darts. I invented it."

Liam grins. "You could always buy new darts."

"What, and ruin the fun?" Augustus says.

I watch him take a turn, grateful for a moment of normalcy. I wasn't sure Augustus would ever want to speak to me again, but he must have realized that Liam and I are a package deal. Or else our trauma bond became a real bond, and he actually likes me. Either way, I got invited to the Sutherland compound this morning, a week after Parker died, and I didn't even have to duck when Liam drove through the front gates.

Liam tosses a dart, and cringes when it bounces off the

metal edge of the board. "Thought I had that one," he mutters before retrieving it.

"Not even close," Augustus says. "Your technique is all wrong. Here, let me show you."

I wander away from the dartboard and spin a globe that's sitting on the desk, because chances are, this lesson is going to involve kissing. That's how it's been going for these two lately, and I'm glad for them. It's nice to know, when the world feels so entirely upside down, that good things can still happen to good people.

Wherever this lands is where Mom and I will settle once this is all over, I tell myself, closing my eyes as the globe's movement begins to slow. My mother and I left the Randall office building with our arms wrapped around one another, and when I leaned my head against her shoulder and called her Mom, she let out such a pleased sound of surprise that my heart seized up. I should've been calling her that all along, and I would've, probably, if I hadn't treated Gem like a surrogate mother for most of my life. *No more,* I decided.

Less than a week later, it's hard to remember that I called Mom anything else.

It's not going to be an easy road for my mother. She's free for now, and investigators are letting her bring me home to Boston tomorrow while she continues to cooperate from Spotless headquarters. Pulling Gem off the roof's edge was probably the best thing Mom could have done for her future, even though that's not why she did it. All she wanted was to prevent another death. But with Gem alive, prosecutors have a bigger target than my mother. Still, I'm afraid that won't be enough to keep her out of prison.

I'm trying not to think too far ahead. Gem is still my guardian, although the change to Marianne is being accelerated. Marianne has been in touch, and she's pretty great. She said that I can stay with her anytime, but I don't want to move that far away.

"What are you doing, Kat?" Liam asks.

"Letting fate decide where I'm going to live next," I say as the globe comes to a stop beneath my fingertip.

"Oh yeah? Where'd you end up?" It sounds as though Liam is right beside me, but I'm not sure, since my eyes are still closed.

"I don't know," I say. "I'm afraid to look."

I feel someone gently lift my finger, and then Liam starts to laugh. "What?" I ask, finally opening my eyes.

"I mean, it's a little hard to tell with the scale, but . . . I'm pretty sure you're going to be living right here in Bixby," Liam says.

I huff out a reluctant laugh as I look down at the area that Liam is pointing to on the globe. He's right; I landed firmly in New England. I suppose I could take that as a sign that Mom won't be able to go anywhere, but I'd rather think it's because this region checks all the right boxes for putting down roots: those beaches that my mother loves, an almost brother nearby, and some actual friends.

I don't know what else to look for in a home. I haven't had a real one in years, or maybe ever. Certainly not for the first few years of my life, when I was named Kylie Burke and had to live with my toxic father, whose death I can't bring myself to regret even a little. Not the brief time in Nevada with Marianne, the soon-to-be guardian I barely remember. Not those forty-eight hours in Las Vegas that changed the entire trajectory of my life. And not in the decade-plus since, while I was constantly moving from place to place whenever Gem decided that Spotless needed a fresh start.

The only thing I've ever known about home, really, is that my mother is there.

Augustus comes up behind Liam and rests his chin on his shoulder. "Fantastic," Augustus says. "You can move right into the compound with the rest of the pseudo-orphans for the summer."

No thanks, I think. All this luxury isn't for me, and besides, I don't want to be another kid in Annalise Sutherland's collection. I can't help but notice that she basically claimed Liam once Luke was out of the picture, and even though I know it's well-meaning and temporary, it almost feels like he's another piece of jewelry.

I'm probably being overly sensitive, though. I can't stop thinking about what Gem said about me: *I went through a lot of trouble to keep her.* Like I was a prize, or a pet. I never wanted that for myself, and I don't want it for Liam, either, no matter how pretty a package it comes in. But at least his uncle Jack is coming back to the country soon and planning to settle in Portland, so Liam won't have to change schools again.

Maybe if the worst happens, Jack will adopt me, too.

"You know, everything might turn out okay," Liam says, sensing my darkening mood. "Jamie helped catch Gem, right? That has to count for something."

"Yeah, but the police had already started looking into Spotless," I say. "The lead detective was all 'Can't you give me anything new?'"

Liam snorts. "Luke isn't enough?"

"Apparently not," I sigh.

A door slams then, and all three of us grow rigid. I'm not sure when we'll stop waiting for a hulking figure to come crashing after us, even though Cormac is gone. A petulant voice calls out, "Annalise? Are you here?"

"She's not," Augustus calls back.

I hear the click of heels, and then Larissa Sutherland appears in the doorway, frowning. She's wearing a crisp white linen sheath and clutching a large folder. "We were supposed to go through wallpaper samples for the Gull Cove house," she says. "But she's not in her cottage. I thought she might've decided to join you and your . . . friends."

The last word drips with disdain as she glares at me, and I can't blame her. Even though Mom and I had no clue that Gem was planning a murder last weekend, the fact remains that Parker Sutherland essentially died in my mother's place. And we still don't know *why*. It's the one hole that remains—how did Parker get the fake necklace?—and it's driving me crazy that I can't figure out how to fill it.

"She didn't," Augustus says. "She must've forgotten you were supposed to meet, because she went to lunch."

Larissa frowns. "With who?"

"I don't know," Augustus says, shrugging. "Some guy."

"Are you kidding me?" Larissa asks. Augustus shrugs again, and she rolls her eyes. "She's back to dating? Already? She'd better have enough sense to vet the next one."

Liam flushes. "Most people aren't Luke—" he starts.

"Oh, please," Larissa snorts. "Don't be naïve. Money brings out the worst sharks in the dating pool, and wealthy women can't be too careful. Annalise usually does her due diligence, and I'm not sure why she gave your father a pass."

"Due diligence?" Augustus asks.

Larissa gives him a shrewd look. "I suppose you might as well know. In a few years, people will try to marry you for your money, too." She picks a piece of lint from her dress and says, "Annalise sics her PI team on anyone who asks her out, and they're *very* thorough. She has an entire file cabinet filled with dirt on half the so-called eligible bachelors on the East Coast. If she'd followed protocol with Luke, she would have saved us all a lot of trouble. Lesson learned the hard way, I suppose." She tucks her wallpaper samples under her arm and adds, "Tell her I'll be in my cottage when she bothers to remember I exist."

She leaves, and the three of us exchange confused glances. I'm the first to speak, Larissa's words ringing in my ears as I say, "That's weird. If Annalise checks out everyone she dates, why wouldn't she have done the same with Luke?"

"Maybe she thought she was really in love this time," Liam says.

"She always thinks she's in love," Augustus says.

Liam sucks in his cheeks. "The signs were all there with Luke," he says. "I mean, *I* found out he was catfishing women, and I wasn't even trying."

We get so quiet that you could hear a pin drop until Augustus finally says, "It's kind of a weird coincidence that she skipped Luke, of all people, and then . . . chaos happened." He turns troubled eyes toward me, like he's expecting my twisted brain to explain it away.

And, yeah, a wisp of an idea is slowly starting to take shape.

But he's not going to like it. "Maybe she didn't," I say. "Skip him."

"She couldn't have known what he was like and not dump him," Liam protests.

That should be true. And yet . . .

"You know what would be interesting to see?" I say.

"What?" Augustus asks.

"A file cabinet full of dirt on all the so-called eligible bachelors on the East Coast."

Augustus's eyebrows shoot up. "Are you suggesting . . ."

"Can you get into your aunt's house?" I ask.

"No," he says. "I don't have a key." He tugs on a strand of my hair, which I'm wearing loose around my shoulders today. "And you don't have a bobby pin."

"Do you have a credit card?" I ask.

CHAPTER FIFTY-FIVE

Kat

"You're alarmingly good at this," Augustus says when Annalise's front door pops open.

"Your grandfather should invest in better locks," I say, handing back his card as I step inside. "It's not like he can't afford it. Which way is the office?"

"Down the hall and to the right."

Annalise's office is a bright, airy space, with light wood furniture and pale-blue walls. Extravagant bouquets of flowers top every surface, filling the air with a sweet, fresh scent. There's only one file cabinet in sight, a four-drawer unit nestled beside a closed door.

"We shouldn't be here," Augustus says. He's hovering in the doorway, his expression conflicted. "What are we even looking for?"

"Dirt," I say, heading for the file cabinet. I don't know

what kind of dirt, exactly, but I know that people like Annalise Sutherland don't make exceptions. They don't have to.

I tug the bottom drawer first, and it gives way easily. I riffle through a few folders before saying, "This is all tax stuff." The second drawer from the bottom holds the same kind of financial-looking files. The third looks more interesting; I see tabs marked WILL and INSURANCE and TRAVEL, and my curiosity wouldn't mind checking those out. But that's not what we're here for, so I move to the top drawer.

I give the handle a tug and report, "It's locked."

"Can you open that with a credit card?" Liam asks.

"No, but . . ." I cross to Annalise's desk and dig through drawers until I find what I'm looking for. "These should do the trick," I say, holding up a couple of paper clips.

"Is there anything you *can't* pick a lock with?" Liam asks, a look of wonder on his face.

"Gem was good for something," I mutter, and get to work.

After a few minutes, I pull the drawer open with a small cry of triumph—only to have a hand reach over and slam it back shut. "This is nuts," Augustus says. "We can't break into my aunt's personal files. She has every right to investigate people or . . . not investigate them. It doesn't mean anything."

"But wouldn't it set your mind at ease," I counter, "if we look through here and there's nothing about Luke?"

Augustus curses under his breath and grumbles, "I . . . I kind of hate you sometimes, Chaos." But he removes his hand and lets me slide the drawer back open.

Annalise is organized; there's a last name on every file, and they're in alphabetical order. Augustus crowds in beside me, scanning each file in turn until he lets out a relieved sigh. "No Rooney," he says, pulling out a folder marked SHALCROSS. "I remember this guy. Turns out he had a wife and three kids in Australia." He flips through the folder and adds, "I always wondered how Aunt Annalise found out."

I push all the folders to the front of the drawer and sweep my hand across the back. "What are you doing?" Liam asks.

"If I were Annalise, and I happened to have a Luke Rooney file, I'd be extra-careful with it," I say, running my fingers along the edge of the wood. "Especially after last weekend."

"Oh, come on," Liam says, sounding exasperated. "The cabinet is locked, and no one was expecting *you*."

My fingers find a raised seam, and I dig my nails into it. I can feel a crack. Small at first, but when I pull, it grows wider. "I know," I say, tugging harder. "But—"

Pop! The crack gives way, and I hold up a piece of wood with a flourish. "Fake panel," I say, handing it to a startled Liam. Then I reach into the space the panel used to cover, and pull out a single manila folder.

The lettering on the tab, as neat as all the others, reads ROONEY.

"Fuck," Augustus says quietly.

I start looking through the folder, and— Oh God, it's worse than I thought. It's *all* there. Luke's history on First Comes Love. Pictures of the mold Luke created from Annalise's ruby necklace. Even a photo of what must be the actual handoff of the mold between Luke and Cormac, the camera capturing a small shopping bag being passed between them. And then—

"That's Spotless," I say, staring at a photograph of Gem's office. I flip through more pictures, until I reach one that makes me gasp. I hold up the familiar image wordlessly. I don't have to say anything; we've all spent enough time with that face.

It's my mother. Poor oblivious Mom, hauling a bag of groceries, with no idea that she'd just become a line item on a private investigator's report.

Augustus takes the folder from me. "Aunt Annalise knew," he says numbly, slowly flipping pages. "She knew everything, and she did . . . nothing."

I expect to feel something then—rage, probably—because Annalise could have stopped everything that happened last weekend. She could've put Gem in jail before my mother was ever in danger. But all I feel is blank, empty confusion. Like I'm a character in a play who's forgotten all of her lines, standing silently in front of an expectant audience.

A creaking door breaks the spell. I hear a woman's voice, humming, and the click of heels on hardwood. Closer and closer to where we are. "Annalise is home," I hiss, my eyes darting around the office. "We need to hide. Augustus, is that a closet?"

I don't wait for an answer. I push the file cabinet shut and open the door beside it, peering into a dark, windowless space that's much bigger than a closet. It looks more like a storage room, and it's nearly empty except for a few boxes stacked neatly to one side. "Come on," I whisper, grabbing Liam by the arm and pulling him into the space with me. "This'll do."

But Augustus doesn't move. Even as the footsteps grow closer, he keeps standing in the middle of the office, the folder dangling from one hand. I make frantic beckoning motions that he ignores, until finally, in desperation, I pull the door shut.

Everything goes dark. "Shit," Liam breathes, fidgeting beside me.

"Shh," I say in a barely audible whisper.

"Darling," Annalise calls out, surprise in her voice. "I thought you were . . ." Silence stretches for a few endless seconds until she asks, "What is that?"

"It's your file," Augustus says. "On Luke Rooney."

"How did you—" There's a light scuffling, as though Annalise is grabbing the folder from her nephew's hand. When she speaks again her voice is reproachful, but still warm and somewhat placating. "Augustus, please try to remember that my personal life is just that—*personal*," she says. "It doesn't concern you."

She's bluffing, I think. *She doesn't know how much he's seen.*

Augustus cuts straight to the chase, though. "You knew," he says. "You knew Gem was planning to steal your necklace, and you let her." His voice drops so low that I have to strain to hear him. "Why did you let her? Why didn't you break up with Luke? Why didn't you call the police and have all of them arrested? If you . . . God, Aunt Annalise, if you'd done any of those things, Uncle Parker would still be here!"

"And you want that?" Annalise asks, her voice rising in sudden anger. "You do realize that Parker loathed you, don't you? That he made life impossible for your father, and for me? That all he ever did was take from people, and hurt them, and *kill* them?"

My heart starts hammering and I instinctively reach for Liam, clutching his sleeve and then his hand. He squeezes, utterly silent.

"Gran was . . . That was an accident," Augustus says.

"An entirely avoidable one. Parker was *drunk*," Annalise says. "Mother begged him not take the boat out that night. He made her feel guilty, told her that everyone in our family always expects the worst of him. That she needed to prove she trusted him. And look where that got her—and us. This family has never been the same." A tremor enters her voice. "Remember the memorial service we had for Mother at the beginning of the summer?"

"The one where Uncle Parker forgot to order the flowers?" Augustus says.

"Yes. I was so upset that I cornered him afterward, and reminded him that he'd never even apologized for crashing the boat. Do you know what he said?" She doesn't wait for an answer. "He said, 'You need to learn to let things go.' Things! As though I was bringing up some childhood argument, and not our mother's death. All I could think was that Parker had become a cancer on this family, and if he couldn't be cured, he needed to be cut out."

Augustus doesn't respond right away, and it's so quiet that I can hear Liam breathe. When Augustus finally speaks, his voice is hoarse. "Aunt Annalise, what are you saying?" he asks. "Did you . . . Did you tell Cormac to shoot Uncle Parker?"

"Of course not," Annalise says, sounding genuinely horrified. "Do you really think I'd associate with someone like that? No. All I did was present Parker with a choice."

"A choice?" Augustus repeats. "About what?"

"About the heist," Annalise says. "I made sure Parker heard about it—those lowlifes he gambles with are useful for planting information—and then I waited to see what he'd do with it."

"What do you mean, 'what he'd do about it'?"

"I mean what I just said. Parker had a choice. He could have told me that someone was after my necklace, or he could have decided to beat them to it and make the swap himself. He chose the latter. I doubt he even thought twice about it."

Oh my God.

I knew, back in the dart room after Larissa left, that something wasn't right. That Annalise Sutherland must've known more than she'd let on about Luke, and had her own reasons for keeping quiet. But I never could have imagined that it was this bad. I release a low, shaky breath, and Liam squeezes my hand so tightly that it hurts.

"But making the swap meant . . . the person who stole your necklace was supposed to *die*," Augustus says. "The trellis was cut, and Uncle Parker—he didn't have a key to your house. He would've had to climb in, just like Jamie was supposed to. Did you know that?"

Annalise doesn't answer, and Augustus's voice grows ragged. "You did," he says. "You were counting on it, weren't you?"

"It was *Parker's choice*," Annalise says tightly. "Nothing would have happened to him if he'd done the right thing and told me about Gem's plan. I could have forgiven him for what happened to Mother, because I'd have known he was capable of change. It was a test, Augustus, and he failed miserably. No matter what, Parker always picked the worst possible path."

She'd said that at Ross's party, hadn't she? While I was hiding behind the horse sculpture, eavesdropping on Parker and Annalise, she'd said, *Why is it that every time you have a choice between being decent or being awful, you choose to be awful?* I had no idea at the time that she wasn't simply expressing frustration.

She was warning him. And then she told him goodbye.

"Parker's selfishness killed Mother," Annalise continues. "And I think it's somewhat fitting that it ultimately killed him, too."

Beside me, Liam inhales so sharply that I'm afraid Annalise must've heard. But then Augustus speaks up, his voice shaking with anger. "No, *you* killed him!" he says. "Have you lost your mind? How could you do something like that?"

"Honestly, Augustus, I thought you of all people would understand," she says. "Your poor father is a shell of his former self because of Parker. Maybe now he can heal."

"Dad loved Uncle Parker! He'd never want this."

"You're upset," Annalise says. "I understand." A note of steel creeps into her voice. "But here's what *you* need to understand, darling. As far as the rest of the world is concerned, none of this ever came to my attention."

I hear the faint rattle of paper against cardboard, and I picture Annalise brandishing the Rooney folder like a weapon. "It was a mistake to keep this," she says. "Once I take care of it, I expect you to do what our family has always done."

"Lie?" Augustus asks.

"Protect one another."

He scoffs. "Like you protected Uncle Parker?"

Annalise sighs. "You'll come around, once you see how much better your father is without Parker's toxic presence in his life. But until you do, let me remind you that your boyfriend and his little con artist stepsister did an awful lot of aiding and abetting last weekend. They've gotten out of this scot-free because I authorized Powell and Boggs to spare no expense on their defense. If I change my mind and decide to get tough, it won't matter that they're still teenagers. That's what juvenile detention facilities are for." Her voice softens as she adds, "I hope it won't come to that, of course. I know how much they mean to you."

Her heels click across the floor and then down the hallway, until they fade entirely. After a few moments of silence, Augustus says, "You may as well come out. She left—for Granddad's house, probably. It has a fireplace."

Liam rockets out of the closet and envelops Augustus in a tight hug. Augustus buries his head in Liam's shoulder as I hover behind them, my heart thumping erratically. I can barely believe what we just heard, and I have no idea what to do about it. Annalise is right; she could make life miserable for Liam and me, not to mention turning up the heat on my mother's case. Annalise hasn't pressed charges, but she could.

She could do a lot of things.

When Augustus lets go, Liam asks, "What do you want to do?"

"Do?" Augustus laughs shakily. "I can't *do* anything. You heard her. She'll send both of you to prison if I try, and who would even believe me? It sounds like the world's most insane conspiracy theory."

"We'll back you up," I say.

Augustus sighs. "Chaos, I say this with love, but you are *not* a reliable witness. And neither is Liam. It's not your fault," he adds with an apologetic look. "But when Luke Rooney is your dad . . ."

"I know," Liam says. "What if you didn't have to worry about that, though?"

"Huh?" Augustus asks.

"If you knew you'd be believed, would you want people to

know what Annalise did?" Liam says. "Would you want her to pay for what happened to Parker?"

Augustus's brow furrows. "Well, yeah, but—"

Liam pulls his phone out of his pocket and presses the screen. *"Darling,"* comes Annalise's voice, and I let out a startled gasp. *"I thought you were . . . What is that?"* Liam taps his screen again, and the voice stops, leaving the office utterly silent.

"I recorded her," he says.

"Oh my God," I breathe as Augustus's eyes go wide. "Liam Rooney! After all this time, you've finally figured out how to be sneaky."

"You taught me well," Liam says with a tired smile, before turning his attention back to Augustus. "Do you want to use this?"

"*Can* I use it?" Augustus asks. "Aren't there laws against that?"

"Not in Maine," I pipe up. "It's a one-party consent state." Both of the boys stare at me, and I shrug. "What? Don't you look up surveillance laws when you visit a new state?"

"No," Augustus and Liam say in bemused unison.

"Well, you should," I say.

Liam shakes his head before turning back to Augustus. "You probably need time to think about this," he says. "If we share the recording, it'll be the scandal to end all scandals, and—"

"Did you get everything?" Augustus breaks in. "The whole conversation?"

Liam swipes at his screen for a moment, then taps it again. *"I hope it won't come to that, of course,"* Annalise's voice says. *"I know how much they mean to you."*

"Yeah," Liam says. "I got everything."

Augustus's jaw hardens. "Then I don't need time to think about it. Come on. Let's get out of here, and give the police the surprise of their life."

He pulls Liam toward the door, and I scramble to follow them. A tiny flicker of something almost like hope kindles inside me as I remember what the lead detective of the Spotless investigation said to my mother: *Can't you give me anything new?*

He said it to Mom, but he might as well have said it to me. We're a team, after all.

Acknowledgments

I've always wanted to write a heist book but could never figure out how to make it work with the type of realistic contemporary thrillers I like to write. Once I got the idea for *Such Charming Liars* I felt as though I'd found a way forward, but it had such a complicated plot that it could easily have fallen apart without the support of the brilliant team that's helped me create eight books.

To my agents, Rosemary Stimola and Allison Remcheck, thank you for being amazing brainstorming partners (and amazingly patient—sorry for all the times I emailed you yet another draft and said "read this one instead") and for all your support of my career. I'm so grateful for the entire team at Stimola Literary Studio, including Alli Hellegers, Adriana Stimola, Erica Rand Silverman, Pete Ryan, and Nick Croce.

To my editor, Krista Marino—thank you not only for making this book shine, but for making me a much better writer overall. You'll never know how much worse my first drafts would be if I didn't have your voice in my head correcting mistakes before you see them. Thank you for your keen insight, your patience, and the way you champion every book.

I'm grateful to my publishers, Beverly Horowitz, Judith Haut, and Barbara Marcus, for all their support, and to the amazing team at Delacorte Press and Random House Children's Books, including Kathy Dunn, Lydia Gregovic, Dominique Cimina, John Adamo, Kate Keating, Elizabeth Ward, Jules Kelly, Kelly McGauley, Jenn Inzetta, Tricia Ryzner, Meredith Wagner, Megan Mitchell, Shannon Pender, Elena Meuse, Madison Furr, Adrienne Weintraub, Keri Horan, Katie Halata, Amanda Close, Becky Green, Enid Chaban, Kimberly Langus, Kerry Milliron, Colleen Fellingham, Elizabeth Johnson, Kenneth Crossland, Martha Rago, Tracy Heydweiller, Linda Palladino, and Denise DeGennaro.

Thank you to my wonderful international rights colleagues at Intercontinental Literary Agency, Thomas Schlueck Agency, and Rights People for finding homes around the world for *Such Charming Liars.* I'm grateful for the support of my international editors and publishers and feel fortunate to have met so many of you in person over the past few years.

To my readers: thank you for sticking with me through so many books, both series and standalones, and for loving my characters as much as I do. Thank you also to the amazing booksellers, librarians, teachers, and reviewers who are the heart of the book community, and to my YA colleagues for constantly inspiring me.

Thanks to my friends and family for always being there through all the ups and downs of publishing, including the nieces and nephews who make up my own personal young adult consulting group: Zachary, Shalyn, Aidan, Gabriela, Carolina, and Erik. Special thanks to Mom and Dad for giving me the kind of childhood where it was okay to dream and for reading every single handwritten book I shoved into your hands. And to my son, Jack: You were ten years old when my first book was published, and now, you're the age of my protagonists. I love you lots, and I'm so proud of the young man you've become.

About the Author

Karen M. McManus is a #1 *New York Times* and internationally bestselling author of young adult thrillers. Her books include the One of Us Is Lying series, which has been turned into a television show on Peacock, as well as the standalone novels *Two Can Keep a Secret, The Cousins, You'll Be the Death of Me, Nothing More to Tell,* and *Such Charming Liars.* Karen's critically acclaimed, award-winning work has been translated into more than forty languages.